£4

AMAL SINGH

THE GARDEN OF DELIGHTS

This is a **FLAME TREE PRESS** book

FLAME TREE PRESS
6 Melbray Mews, London, SW6 3NS, UK
flametreepress.com

US sales, distribution and warehouse:
Simon & Schuster
simonandschuster.biz

UK distribution and warehouse:
Hachette UK Distribution
hukdcustomerservice@hachette.co.uk

Thanks to the Flame Tree Press team.

The cover is created by Flame Tree Studio with thanks to Shutterstock.com.
Map illustrations © 2024 Kehkashan Khalid.
The font families used are Avenir and Bembo.

Flame Tree Press is an imprint of Flame Tree Publishing Ltd
flametreepublishing.com

A copy of the CIP data for this book is available from the British Library
and the Library of Congress.

PB ISBN: 978-1-78758-908-7
ebook ISBN: 978-1-78758-910-0

Printed and bound in Great Britain by Clays Ltd, Elcograf S.p.A.

AMAL SINGH

THE GARDEN OF DELIGHTS

FLAME TREE PRESS
London & New York

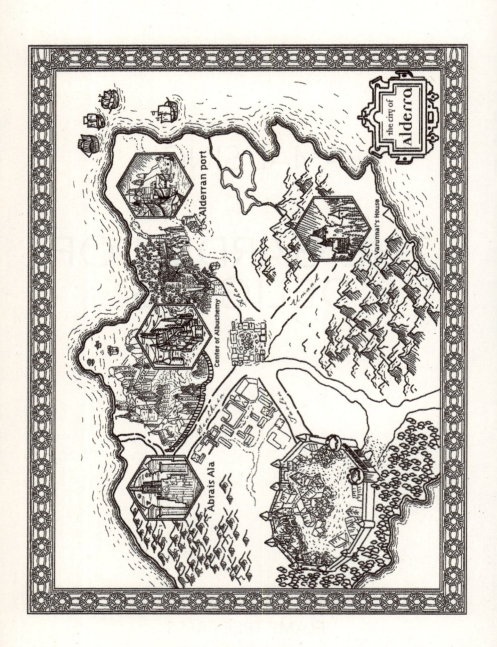

Temple of Eberam

Lake

The Garden of Delights

Marketplace

Mayor's Mansion

Docks

Sivurassa

For Mummy, Papa, and Vibhav

CHAPTER ONE

The Florral and the Champion

Before the Garden, there is a bog. Its murk is a place for Delights both wild and gentle. It is suffused with scents both earthy and alien, reminiscent of mossy oceanic depths and the cold heights of a mountain. The bog contains fist-sized islands of grass, and the grass contains thumb-sized dewdrops. The water of the bog is shallow, but it contains other depths.

In the bog, there blooms a Lotus. The Lotus is flanked by a Rose and a Tulip, flowers that have no place growing in a bog. But they are there, because their existence is magical, inevitable, necessary. The Tulip is rare, but it stands tall, like it knows its place in the world. The Lotus attracts few, because it holds the essence of time, and not many can mold time to their will. The Rose is another story. The Rose is power, the Rose is change, the Rose is sought by many.

And one of the many who seek the Rose enters the bog silently.

He has black hair and gray eyes. His skin is barkshade, glistening with sweat. His blood is coiled with a Delight that allows him to run faster. But the Rose will allow him to do so much more. He is known as a Florral, and he has just ended a war. Following him is an entity known as a Champion, intent on destroying his existence.

The Florral's naked feet disturb the murky calm of the bog, and plunge into its shallow depths. He can feel worms wriggling in between his toes, and the cold mulch beneath. But he is unperturbed, as his hands reach for the Rose and pluck it. He is anticipating something to happen, but it doesn't. The bog is quiet, and the jungle thrums with whispers of wilderness. His heartbeat quickens, then steadies. He lets out a breath, and pockets the Rose.

Each beat of his heart reminds him that he's still young. The world turns for the young, sings for the young, dances for the young, and it's the withering old who are trampled beneath. When he runs on a field where a silent war has been fought, he's assured that the next steps he takes won't be his last. That the hardness beneath his feet won't surge through his bones like lightning and crack his shins. That his heart won't just stop beating.

He leaves the bog, and the forest, and takes the winding road toward his destination. He walks for a long time, feet bare, but the smell of the forest lingers with him, like an afterthought. His feet fall on a barren, hard ground, but feel the texture of grass, like a memory that's hard to shrug off. His bones remember the time spent in the bog, foraging for the Rose, foraging for wild Delights, to keep him going.

He knows the Rose will change him, and so he keeps it tucked away. He's almost afraid of the Rose, of the power it contains. The other flowers in the bog were benign. But the Rose can shape the world.

Even though he's a Florral, the Rose is too much. But it's a time of excess, and he needs the flower. To stop the Champion who follows him.

It all started with the end of a war and the decline of a city that now smolders because of him. The smoke curling from the burnt bridges, the spires, the cracked domes, the haunted images of a dying city are fresh in his mind. A destruction wrought by his hand. But he doesn't blame himself. He blames the war. He blames the hate that preceded it. He blames the lull that now persists in the air, a lull that may not last long.

The hollow quietness after the war is deafening.

He smells the Rose, and is reminded of its power. His blood runs with the vestiges of the Rose, the original flower, the flower that made him into what he is today. The flower that started the war. Again, he mustn't blame the Rose. He must only blame the words that drove a people to hate the Rose. And the Lily. And the Tulip. And the Daisy, and all the others that bloomed from the hands of Eborsen.

He runs, without looking behind. He knows if he turns to look, he will stop. He knows if he stops, the battle is already lost. Because the one who follows him is a god who is short of mercies.

His feet carry him across a terrain of stone and moss, thorn and bramble and quicksand, until he reaches a rocky plain. As far as his eyes would allow him to see, there is a green nothingness interspersed with flecks of white and gold. A land from memory, baby-new. His throat feels like sand, skin like unvarnished leather. Lack of water in his body, lack of rest in his soul. If only he could cross the terrain, he would reach the edge of the Lake of Passage. Then he could spend the rest of his life in solitude, knowing he helped bring a modicum of peace between two species.

He remembers, he's still young, and there's life ahead of him.

But then, he hears a sound and his legs cease. His tired feet would have crumbled under him if not for his sheer will. He turns around and sees the Champion, the god, standing twenty feet from him. Cer eyes are jade, cer hair tied in a knot above cer head. Cer left hand is a blackened stump, thanks to him.

Cer right hand is holding a flower too. He's amused, surprised, and angry. Flowers are for Florrals like him, not Champions like cer.

The Champion waits. The air stills. Above, clouds separate, and a beam of sunlight pierces through, splashing on the ground between them. He waits for the pause between them to build. The Champion makes no move.

He speaks.

"You would let go of all your beliefs just to get at me? You could simply unroot this land and bind me with chains of dust and grime and stone. You could just sing me into submission. And yet, you hold a flower. The flower that goes against everything you stand for."

The Champion looks at the flower in cer hand, and a smile crosses cer face, a smile that tells him everything. Ce would descend to any depth, and shrug off every moral in cer bones.

"Desperate times," says the Champion. "Besides, I grow weary of my songs. They have limitations. And I want to end this war, once and for all."

"The war has ended," he says. "I finished your army. They are catatonic, looking up at the skies, their eyes glazed over by both remembrance and forgetfulness. Tell me, Tyi, did the Abhadis bow before you? Kiss your hands? Melt their gold so you could wear jewelry? Didn't the Champions take a vow to *not* interfere with this petty skirmish between the Abhadis and Inishtis?"

"We did, but then you came along."

"Ah, you use *we*, as if you are one of them. You have never been. Champions are not Abhadis or Inishtis. Champions are Champions. Don't lie now."

"I can say the same about Florrals."

Tyi breaks a petal off the flower ce is holding. A full leaf, in fact. Even from a distance, he can tell it's the rare eight-and-a-half-leafed Crocus. The half leaf carried a major concentration of the Delights the Crocus offers. He is doubtful if the Champion knows that fact. The slightly darker hued half leaf stays safe on the body of the flower as Tyi chews on the leaf ce has broken off.

The Florral wonders if he should use the Rose now. "What do you hope to achieve here, Tyi? The leaf you broke off won't help you."

"We'll see about that."

And then, Tyi's feet lift a few inches above the ground. Ce kicks against the grass and the momentum propels cer forward. Ce covers twenty feet in an eyeblink and the next second ce is standing inches away from him.

"Surrender," ce says, grabbing his throat. Cer breath is warm on his skin. "Surrender, or I can go back to being more persuasive."

The ground shivers around them. Flecks of mud flow and splatter over them. A deep rumble grows outward from under the ground, and soon, chains of stone erupt, grazing threateningly against his feet, like vipers ready to bite.

The Florral scoffs. He realizes he won't need the help of a flower. He won't even have to look at the Rose. He is enough, all by himself. He can end it all, here.

He reaches inside his own reserves as he holds the Champion's gaze, smiling all the time. Then, he enters cer mind.

The flower you ate requires patience and courage. Its Delights are manifold. It gives a lot but also takes in return. It gave you speed and flight, in a burst. But you were too quick. It will soon deplete your mental wherewithal. Your fortitude. Your wit. Your being. This is your fate now, Tyi. You will be a Champion no more. In fact, by following Abhadi orders, you have forfeited all rights to be a Champion.

He releases cer. Tyi's pupils go gray and cer tongue sticks out. Cer head lolls to the side, while cer body stands straight. Ce is without control, a scarecrow in a field. Unmoving, unthinking, unflinching.

"You...you...." Cer lips move, but the words are mere whispers.

"It will wear off, but by that time, I'll be long gone," says the man known across the Three Realms as Alvos Midranil, a Florral. "I'm taking the flower. I have better uses for it. For better people than you."

"I'll go...but they'll come...uhhh.... And soon, I'll come for you...."

Tyi's eyes flit right and left. The grayness in them remains. Alvos can tell the helplessness raging in cer bones. The curse of a flower snipped too quick. The curse of a loss of control. The curse of too sudden a change. It will all come rushing back to cer.

He slides the flower gently from cer hands and walks away. No one follows him.

Not yet.

CHAPTER TWO

The Caretaker and the Girl

The door to the Garden is made of stone older than memory. It has no discernible marks or runes or hinges. It is not held in place by any frame, oak or mahogany, teak or bamboo, granite or limestone. It doesn't have a knob or a handle and is bare, featureless, and cold. It is flanked on its two sides by flame vine, blood jasmine, and ivy. It does not declare in bold words what it hides behind it. Magical runes don't crawl across its surface ready to gleam at a word spoken. It's a plain old door, standing sentinel to the most wondrous of places, a place touched by the first wind, the Garden of Delights.

The Caretaker presses his palms gently on the surface of the door. A sliver appears immediately along its length and from its insides comes a sound of creaking, of levers turning, cracks groaning, of things *opening*. In the presence of the Caretaker, the door relents, shirking its stone obstinacy. It flies open, as if it was just another door, and reveals the Garden.

The Caretaker sighs, despite having done this process a thousand times before.

Before stepping inside the Garden, he looks at the girl accompanying him. Her skin is wheatish, and her eyes are mud-brown. Her hair is done in a pigtail, and she wears a blue dress, speckled with white snowflakes. She folds her palms respectfully, but her eyes command respect. She's curious, perhaps far too much. When she asks a question, she knows the answer to it already.

"Should we step inside?" she says.

"After you," says the Caretaker. His eyes are the color of the ocean floor, his skin jaggery. His hair is the color of ash and sawdust. When he speaks, he speaks with a calm certainty.

The girl enters the Garden, and the Caretaker follows, walking on the cold stone path, his naked feet tense with memory, his keen eyes affixed on the center of the Garden. Pebbles, red, white, green, and purple, adorn the short walkway paved on both sides by vines. The walkway leads to the first of the five Sectors of the Garden, a lush, expansive area replete with flowers like the Lily of Alderra, the famous Bacillus Rose, and the Six Leaf Clover of Nevarn. The other sectors are vast, and have other flowers of vaster importance.

"Is it like you had imagined?" asks the Caretaker.

The girl brushes an invisible gnat off her hair. She lets out a short gasp, as if she'd inhaled the First Sector of the Garden.

"It is prettier than I had imagined."

"Before we go farther, I need to see the letter signed by your father."

The girl is holding a crumpled piece of yellowed paper, which she unfurls and hands to the Caretaker. He takes it gently and holds it against the sunlight, his brown bony hands shaking as he does so. He looks old for his age, the Caretaker, and the shiver in his limbs doesn't help hide the fact. Satisfied with what he has read, the Caretaker folds the paper neatly and hands it back to the girl.

"This should work," he says with the gentlest of smiles. With that smile, the Caretaker de-ages, the creases on his face disappearing for a sliver of a moment. He takes the girl's hand and they walk toward the center of the garden, where, amid general green shrubbery, blooms the flower known as the Bacillus Rose.

"Bacille is the name of the town where its seeds were spotted first. It is of the family Bacillum Terminus. But of course these terms won't interest you in the slightest."

"Actually, they do," says the girl. She looks down upon the Rose. A medley of colors play elaborate visual tricks, the petals folding and unfolding upon themselves, interlinked, both in movement and in stasis. The Bacillus Rose is a million roses ensconced inside each other, with a million shades of red.

"I know this is the only flower I am allowed to see, because of the purpose of my visit. But I would love to come back and know more about the Garden."

"My apprenticeship position is full at present, but I would love to have you for a short term, whenever fate permits."

"That would be lovely," says the girl.

"Now for the purpose of your visit," says the Caretaker. He bends down and holds the stem of the Rose at a particular point from the root, carefully avoiding the thorns. He presses the stem slightly. The symphony of colors ceases and for a moment the flower is just another rose. Devoid of real magic, but still magical enough, because it's still a rose. The Caretaker takes out a small pair of scissors from his coat pocket and snips a petal, without disturbing the other petals in the process. He leaves the stem and the symphony resumes. The rose becomes the Rose again.

"Is it done?"

"This is just the first step," says the Caretaker with a smile. "Come with me."

The Caretaker turns around with a calm flourish and starts walking toward the entrance of the Garden. The girl stands, observing the Bacillus Rose as the severed petal grows back fully.

★   ★   ★

The Caretaker's laboratory is mostly bare. It does not boast of useless trinkets, ornate measurement units, flasks and utensils of all shapes and sizes. A working table rests at the center of the room, adorned by mortar and pestle, two beakers – one large, one small – one stove, one measuring cylinder, a pair of gloves, and twelve glass bottles labeled in symbols only known to the Caretaker's eyes.

Once he is near the table, the Caretaker's hands move swiftly. He grinds the Rose petal to pulp in the mortar. He then uncorks a bottle labeled with a symbol of a winged, upward arrow, and puts two drops of the solution it contains into the mortar. The solution then goes inside a beaker which he places atop the stove.

Next, comes the heat and the wait. The girl watches the process as if mentally taking notes.

"What is your name, child?"

"Iyena," says the girl. "Iyena Mastafar."

"Iyena is a beautiful name," says the Caretaker. "Mirror and turbulence. Calm and rage."

The girl smiles.

"I am assuming you're not from Sirvassa."

"I am from Alderra," says the girl. "My father has come here on some business and we're to stay for at least a year in this city. When I got enrolled into the town school, a classmate of mine told me about this place."

"Trehan, most probably?"

"Yes, he's the one," says Iyena. "What is your name, Mister Caretaker?"

Before the Caretaker can speak, a ringing sound echoes in the lab. He turns around and switches the stove off. He opens a table drawer and takes out a vial the size of his thumb. Then, he wears his gloves, and carefully upends the liquid concentrate inside the vial.

"Remember, Iyena. The Bacillus Rose gives its drinker a Priming Delight. I give it to all my new customers first, that's why it needs the most tending. It essentially prepares your body for whatever would come next. I'd say it senses the true nature of your being. You must drink this potion at noon, when the sun is high in the sky. Then, the next day, you come here again, and you'll truly know what Delight you want."

"What if I want to defeat monsters?" asks the girl confidently. Once again, her eyes blaze, and command respect. Her words don't trickle out of her, jittery. No, her words are like a waterfall, quick and assured.

A wisp of a thought crosses the Caretaker's mind, but he brushes the possibility off. He eyes the girl curiously.

When the girl returns, inevitably, she'll want a Delight she truly desires. She might want a stronger memory, and he'll mix a Dahlia with a Tulip. She might want telepathy, and he'll snip a Chrysanthemum. Or she might just want unending pockets, and he'll snip a Lily.

But she's not like the others. The Caretaker can tell. Citizens of Sirvassa arrive on his doorstep with either a dazed fervor, or a casual curiosity. In the case of the former, eagerness oozes out of them like honey. The latter are seasoned patrons, having tried multiple Delights. They want to glide, to sing, to dance. They want to look at the stars and know what they'll eat the next day. They want to inhale the scent of a wind, and know the direction to a place. Small everyday wonders. Small everyday Delights.

The Caretaker obliges.

Sometimes, they want the big things too. They want to lift a giant stone. They want to soar over rooftops. They want to pluck thoughts out of their enemies' minds.

The Caretaker warns, and then obliges, with conditions.

But the girl is different. He can tell that her mind swivels, a whirlpool raging inside her, even if she doesn't show it. He can tell her fingers itch to snatch the Rose and eat it whole. He can tell that the girl is a cage, and inside the cage, there's another girl.

"That's tricky, but it can be arranged too," says the Caretaker, like a teacher would tell a student about a difficult subject which needed to be learnt. The girl's face brightens.

The Caretaker can tell she will defeat a monster someday. And it will be easy for her.

"Iyena, remember this. A Delight is only as good as the person using it. Use it in the times of elation and glee, it will give you the most. Use it in times of sorrow, it will take a lot from you, while still giving desired results, but results you may not want at that time. Use it wisely."

"I will," says the girl.

As he watches the girl walk away, the Caretaker's heart clenches inside his chest. He has done this a million times before, and yet this happens every time. It all starts with the Bacillus Rose, the Flower of Eborsen, which makes the body familiar to the ingestion of Florrachemy, and makes the blood warm and receptive to a Delight.

It is also the flower that was used, long ago, to identify Florrals.

CHAPTER THREE

Iyena Mastafar

Three Days Ago...

Before meeting the Caretaker for the first time, and telling a lie that would change her life, Iyena Mastafar arrives on the shores of Sirvassa. Her feet fall on broken petals as she steps onto the pier. Snipped mustard-yellow leaves, among dead tendrils of seaweed. Red petals of some broken rose atop a wooden pillar jutting out of the murky waters. Flakes of a flower of impossible color lying with abandon on the creaking wooden floor.

Behind her, the *Remnant* blows its clarion, an earth-deep sound announcing its arrival. She looks back at the ship, then at the road ahead of her, connecting to the city she had only heard of. Sirvassa. Here, the skies are a clear blue, with inklings of white, and at the horizon, a vibrant purple, a color she hasn't witnessed yet in the skies of Alderra. Back at home, she saw only two shades, gray and brown, in the skies, on the road, and the buildings. So, yes, it wasn't a bad decision at all when she agreed to this voyage. She had to put in a permanent leave of absence at her school in Alderra. Sern Aradha's strict eyes turned into a vacuous stare when Iyena gave her the letter.

"Don't forget us in the city of dreams," she said. "Remember, your foundations prepared you for new learnings." Sern Aradha's words strengthened Iyena's resolve, more than anything her father had ever said. With a trembling hand, she touched the bony fingers of Sern Aradha – the best teacher she had known – and said farewell.

But the decision to come to Sirvassa had not been entirely hers. Like many other decisions in her life, this was a decision her father had made for her. And much like other times, Iyena's first impulse had been to refuse.

She was trying to make a stick man fly when her father told her they were moving.

It was a noisy morning in Alderra. The skies were clogged with smoke and the streets were clogged with people, an unremarkable day in the capital of the Three Realms. But what Iyena was about to do was remarkable. She was letting her breath guide her to memorizing the first lesson of Albuchemy Sernir Harrott had taught that day, her eyes closed, her mouth murmuring the first three laws of fire and metal and how they worked in conjunction.

A pungent whiff of chemicals picked at her nostrils, as she gave the stick man two commands, one to walk two steps, and the other to stop. The stick man — a five-inch aluminum wire mannequin — powered by Iyena's Albuchemy, had obeyed, but after one and a half steps, its metal body had slumped, skittered off the oak table, and fallen on the ground, making the sound of a bell.

Iyena picked it up and put it back on the table. Then, she reached into the dark recesses of her mind, and brought forth the first law of Albuchemy.

Each metal has a purpose. Heat drives that purpose.

Heat, metal, and words. Aluminum was a metal that was made for movement, so the stick man already was at an advantage. Iyena had heated it to the desired temperature. Even as she stared at her imperfect, slightly grotesque figure, which had no eyes and no mouth, the kiln burned behind her, showering flickering red embers around.

She had given the stick man her own desire. The shape of the words she spoke, the commands she gave. She had desired to change its state. From movement to motion. From mere motion, to flight.

But it hadn't obeyed her. Something in her cadence was wrong.

"Fly, you moron," said Iyena, banging her palm on the table. The stick man tumbled down and fell on the carpet, its metal knees wobbling, its arms flailing. The stick man cut a sorry, desolate figure, and Iyena almost felt for it. Someday, change itself would obey her. If not Albuchemy, then perhaps something else.

"Iyena."

She turned. Her father stood in the doorway, clutching his walking cane.

"Making it move, are we?"

"I am sorry, Father, I know I wasn't supposed to...yet.... But...."

"Your cadence was right, if you were wondering about that. But sometimes it's not always about the words and the cadence and the heat. Sometimes, it's about intent."

"But I intended it to fly," said Iyena stubbornly.

"No," said her father. "You intended it to *fly*. Like a bird would fly. Flight in itself is complicated and consists of various elements. Your intent and your words must account for that."

"Okay, then I will—"

Anaris brushed her words away with a quick, dismissive grunt. "You can leave it for now. We are going to Sirvassa."

"What?"

"The City of the Petal Rain. We are moving there."

"But Father, I have a test tomorrow. Sern Aradha—"

"I have already spoken to Sern Aradha. Your education is to be continued in Sirvassa next year."

Iyena remained silent for a while. The presence of her father always gave her icicles in her heart, and a drowning sensation.

"Is it about my behavior with Sern Renvir?"

"That was last year," said Anaris Mastafar.

"Is it about my refusal to learn about the Ways? Because I am—"

"It's because I have business in Sirvassa," said her father. "Everything isn't about you."

"But it affects me too, Father," said Iyena. "I have friends here."

"And you'll make friends there, too," said Anaris, in a grave tone. "Now go and say your goodbyes. We leave at dawn, the day after tomorrow."

Her father's words felt like pincers on her skin. She picked up the stick man, twisted it into a grotesque oddity, and threw it out the window in rage. Four stories below, somewhere on the street, it would have hit someone. But Iyena couldn't care less. She couldn't shout in front of her father, and so her rage took another form.

"Iyena, I understand your anger," said Anaris. "But we have to do this. You and I. Father and daughter. You'll not only be going to school, but you'll also be helping me be better at my job."

Iyena took a deep breath. She guided her breath, this time to calm her rage. A deep sense of guilt rankled her insides. She should have controlled her anger. She should have been better.

But Sern Aradha had said anger when gulped down became poison.

"I thought Alderra was final," said Iyena. "I thought we wouldn't have to change places for the purpose of your job again."

"This time, it's substantial, Iyena, I promise," said Anaris. "None other than Minister Yayati has chosen me for this task. There are things we have to accomplish in Sirvassa, Iyena. Imagine me as a general, and I choose you as my lieutenant."

"How exactly am I supposed to help you? What do I get in return?"

"Ever so transactional like your mother, aren't you?"

Iyena stared at her father's unreadable face. Her mother, who wasn't present for this conversation, would probably have thought otherwise. Her mother would have thought Iyena was too resolute, unbending, like her father. Her mother, who would have provided a counterpoint.

If only she were present.

In quiet moments, Iyena found herself making the shape of her mother's face with her fingers. Tracing her outline in the air, willing her to appear again. To step back inside the door she'd stepped out of, four years ago.

Anaris knelt in front of Iyena. Then, he took her hand in his. Iyena felt warmth radiate from her father's palms.

"Sirvassa is where your mother grew up," he said. "That's what you get in return, Iyena. That city is your blood."

Iyena considered her father's request. Apart from what her father was asking her to do, visiting Sirvassa also meant a chance to know her roots. And with that, probably, a chance to retrace her mother's steps. Her pattern of thoughts, the cadence of her breath, the shape of her words. With that, if Iyena could get that far, the true reason for her leaving.

She agreed.

It was the last request of her father that Iyena agreed to whole-heartedly.

★   ★   ★

"Iyena, there are many more things to admire when we get to the city proper."

Iyena's trance is broken like a knee jerk breaks a dream. She nods absently, but her eyes are still affixed to a fluttering petal stuck to the wood board of the pier in an obstinate manner. Like an impossibility. Then the wood groans under her feet as her father takes hurried steps toward the end of the pier. Iyena follows him.

"Tell me once again what you will say to the Din-Tevair?" her father asks. His words have taken on an impatient quality, something which Iyena hates. Impatience often leads to rage.

Iyena recites her introduction to her father. She has done it at least ten times on her voyage, in the nights when the *Remnant* bobbed against treacherous waves, and during the summer-calm of the day. Iyena knows that when it comes, she won't have to narrate the entirety of her life in Alderra, all the teachings of Sern Aradha in mathematics and history and Sernir Harrott in Basics of Albuchemy. Also, she is being admitted in a class higher than hers in Alderra. She knows her foundations are solid, and merely repeating them will not impress Din-Tevair in the slightest.

"You need to brush up your pronunciations, Iyena," says Anaris, his voice flat, his face stern. His face is pale, and his eyes are hazel. Dark gray hair, swept back, neatly, with care. A pointed, angular face, full of hard lines. He resembles Iyena only in his resolve, and the conviction of his words. "Maani-Ba will have to teach you, after all."

"I don't think the Din-Tevair would mind my pronunciation as long as I am confident," says Iyena. "As long as my knowledge is there."

"Confidence is key only for the beginning, yes, but rigor in language takes you a long way. There are moments in life where confidence alone won't help you."

And by then I will learn everything, Iyena says to herself.

As they step off the pier onto the slick Sirvassan road, a carriage pulled by a Rhisuan beast shudders to a stop in front of them. An animal that looks fashioned out of everything and nothing, multiple limbs and eyes, flabs of flesh enveloping the ground, pulling a carriage double its size and weight with ease.

Anaris moves toward the beast, caresses its hide, and whispers something near its ear. The beast grunts.

"Come, Iyena," Anaris says and hops inside the carriage.

★　★　★

Her new home stands at the corner of a busy street overlooking the Sirvassan Square. Here, the sky takes a light shade of mulberry, and the roads are slick with a hint of rain. She doesn't find any petals here, but the roofs of the buildings all around her are connected in a crisscross meshwork of gleaming ribbons, shining intermittently, giving the city a surreal quality. The ribbons gleam every now and then, pinpricks of light meeting at junctures and exploding into a colorful miasma. The city glows eternally even during the night.

Her father hauls their luggage toward the door, where Maani-Ba stands waiting for them, hands on her hips. She is a stout woman, with long, black-gray hair and pudgy fingers. Iyena remembers Maani-Ba only from the photos her mother had shown her, back when she was still together with her father. The edges of Maani-Ba's lips when she smiles, and a slight vein bulging out of her forehead, make Iyena remember her mother even more.

"Let me take that for you," she says, and a slight lilt in her words, half-Sirvassan, half-Rinisian, tells Iyena that she left Alderra long ago, and now the place only exists in the dim hazes of her memory.

"How are you, Maani-Ba?" Iyena asks, even though she has never spoken to the woman in her life.

"Sirvassa takes good care of me, Iyena. My, my, you have grown. One year and you will overshoot your father!"

"She is here for gaining knowledge, and helping me in the process, aren't you, Iyena?" Anaris says, cutting off Maani-Ba, who purses her mouth and takes the luggage from his hands.

"There will be ample time to do many things," says Maani-Ba, and walks inside, following Anaris. Iyena lingers at the doorstep, reluctant to go inside, not before completely taking in all the sights around her. The meshwork above her twinkles like starlight. Two lovers, hand in hand, jog and dance and hop their way across a stone pavement, singing songs. Many carriages pulled by beasts in varying shapes and sizes, some winged, some not, zoom past her with dizzying speeds. And a distinct smell rises in the air, the smell of beauty, the smell of so many flowers.

A boy, running away from something, his legs a blur, ceases his sprint suddenly. He has stopped to stare at Iyena. His eyes are green and bright and curious.

"You seem new," he says, as if he owns the world around him. Exuberance of kings.

"How can you tell?" asks Iyena.

"The way you stand," he says. "Unsure of the ground you stand on."

"Very philosophical. How must I stand, would you tell me?"

"I am joking," he says and winks at her. "See you later. Now, I have to run." And he dashes away. And soon, Iyena sees a couple of boys, with hair the color of sand and dust, running at breakneck speed, chasing the boy who spoke to her.

"Did he take a turn?" one boy stops and asks Iyena.

"I am not sure," says Iyena, "but I think he went there." She points directly opposite to the direction the other boy took, toward a different road. The bigger boys stare at empty air and running carriages, unsure of where to go, unable to make up their minds. A moment later, they decide to split up, each taking a different road to chase the boy down.

Before she can turn to go inside, she catches a glimpse of the young boy, hiding behind the shutter of a shop. Across the black road, their eyes meet. His lips move. If she could hear what he was saying, Iyena would mutter, "You're welcome." But she only gives him a silent nod. The boy nods and disappears.

She breathes in the midevening air of Sirvassa and steps inside her new house, a place she will call home for the next year.

★ ★ ★

The house is vast.

A cavernous space, with carpeted floors, and vibrant walls, her new home extends as far as her eyes can see. First, a grand room smelling of must and petrichor and fresh flowers – of course there will be flowers – then, two separate rooms, one of which her father has claimed as his study. Beyond the study is a semicircular chamber with patterned tiles. Maani-Ba said it was for guests to eat and talk and drink. A table is already set with a gleaming white tablecloth and silver cutlery. Iyena was born into relative opulence, but even this is too much by her standards.

She takes the staircase to her bedroom upstairs, a room walled and floored with timber. There's a bed with fresh white sheets, beside a window overlooking the road she left behind. She drops her luggage and goes straight to the window. From this height, she can almost touch the glimmery fishnet that connects the rooftops of the city. She makes a mental note to ask Maani-Ba about the actual use of the mesh, other than being an ornament, a crown to the city.

Iyena empties her luggage on her bed. Damp and slightly crumpled clothes fall out. A favorite dress of hers, color like henna, is folded in entirely the wrong sort of way. She remembers folding it correctly, but the incessant bobbing of her ship and the tumbling of luggage every seven or eight days must have messed it up. She smells the fabric – it reminds her of seaweed and dust and wetness. Wet, but not quite. Dry, but the wrong sort of dry. She picks up the dress and sets it aside. Then, her eyes fall on an object she had almost forgotten she had packed. Tucked between the folds of another dress is a picture of her mother in a frame. In the photo she looks just like Iyena, except with straight, long hair. She is wearing a lemon-colored dress. Beside her stand two other women. One, much younger than her mother, and one, older, wizened, with gray hair that falls on her shoulders in wisps.

"We'll get a good frame for that photo." Maani-Ba stands at the door, hands folded across her chest.

"Is that you on her right?" Iyena points to the younger woman in the photo. Maani-Ba comes over to look at the picture.

"We took this when we went to see *The Fall of Mystheria*. Gazemi Asthan was spectacular."

"Father never lets me watch that picturetale."

"He's doing what all fathers do," says Maani-Ba. "You do what all daughters do."

"What's that?"

"Listen to what he says, but choose what is best for you."

Iyena chews on Maani-Ba's words. For the past two years, Iyena has been doing just that. Trying, against all obstacles, to choose what is best for her. It is the right thing to do, in all situations. That is her natural thought process when it comes to doing anything. Iyena knows she must have gotten this quality from her mother. Her mother had done what was best for her, even if that meant leaving Iyena in the dark for a year and a half about her separation from her father. Even if that meant only seeing her daughter every other winter, when the winds in the

Sessma Pass, leading to Troika, are hard and cold and brutal, and the skies are gray without mercy.

"Who is the older woman in this picture?" Iyena thumbs the image, and the face smudges a bit, as if it is fresh ink on wet paper.

"She is a friend of your mother and me."

"Where is she now?"

"Somewhere we don't know and have never bothered to find out."

"Then, is she truly a friend?"

Maani-Ba stares at Iyena. Iyena holds her gaze, knowing that she has spoken out of turn.

"Leave brilliant questions like this for school, girl. Aren't you tired? I'll make soup for you while you freshen up."

The brushing-under-the-carpet manner of Maani-Ba's speaking definitely is curious. But Iyena knows better than to prod further, especially on her first day in the city. She nods at Maani-Ba, who ruffles Iyena's hair, then leaves. That manner reminds Iyena of her mother, a memory tucked away in the deep folds of her mind.

CHAPTER FOUR

The Caretaker

During the night hour when the air stills and the stars sleep, the Caretaker gets to work on the potion he has been trying to perfect for the last four years. Each fortnight, he unmixes and remixes the extracts from the Dark Hibiscus and Singing Daisy from the Fourth Sector of the Garden. Each fortnight his potions turn the color of ivory, the color of the night, the color of magic.

He once gave a concentrated extract of the Hibiscus to Jaywardna Illyasi, the Mayor of Sirvassa, who had placed a special request to the Caretaker, a request so urgent and so dark, yet so enchanting, that the Caretaker had to accept it. The mayor had contracted an illness from his travels. A blackness that began from his toe threatened to consume the entirety of his right leg, which was old and gnarly and replete with liver spots. The potion not only ceased the spread of the disease, but made the leg pink and prime and young, leaving the mayor happy but befuddled.

If the leg can be cured and made young, so can the entire body, maybe forever. And so, each night, the Caretaker works tirelessly, so he doesn't have to wear the blanket of age permanently. Each night he tries to cheat a curse. A curse placed upon him by a goddess, a curse so devious that it gives him a taste of youth when the sky is dark, but snatches it at the inkling of dawn. Each night, a ghost shakes loose from the body of the Caretaker, at the stroke of midnight, and he is his younger self again. A self he had forgotten in wars that time kept snug in its pockets, wars that made and unmade the world he lives in. Each night he does this charade, shrugging off age like a dusty blanket, and wearing another newer one.

But as soon as dawn comes, so does old age.

The concoction turns into a deep amber, and against the dark of the night sky, it looks like a gift from an ancient god, an elixir. The Caretaker's lips curl into a bright smile. It's the cusp of midnight, the purest of hours, and the Caretaker brings the potion to his lips.

The potion warms his throat as it courses down to his belly. If it were to truly work, he would see the effects in the morning. Morning will bring his youth back into permanence.

With swift and graceful motions he cleans his workbench, and arranges beakers and bottles and stoppers. He splashes some water on his face, his hair, and the nape of his neck before heading out of the laboratory.

The chill of the night air prickles at him. He locks the gates of his laboratory and moves toward the Garden compound for his nightly inspection. Each night like clockwork, he pays a last visit to all the sectors of the Garden, checking each petal, each blade of grass, each flower. Only this gives him a good night's sleep.

The stone door is ajar when he reaches the Garden. A fell-bird begins her lament in the distance. The Caretaker stops and listens carefully; mixed with the sound of the bird is the sound of a man sobbing. Two lamentations in one night, a dark omen if there ever was one.

The sound comes from deep in the Garden, and toward the Garden he takes his steps.

Moonlight splashes on the Bacillus Rose and on the Lily of the Alderra, but the other flowers in the First Sector lie shrouded in darkness. The Caretaker glides across the dew-wet grass. When he reaches the Second Sector the sobbing becomes louder, the grief it carries more profound. The voice is full of deep ache and longing. The Caretaker ignores the Tulip of the Seven, his pride, the brightest flower to behold in the Garden, the one which blooms in the night. Every fortnight, before retiring, the Caretaker tends to it, carefully measuring its shimmer, bottling the scents it throws. It becomes ready for extraction the next day.

He doesn't see it yet but the Tulip has been snipped crudely, before its time.

The Caretaker crosses the Second Sector and comes to the middle of the Garden. The Third Sector is a conspicuous space, a glorious pentagram of thornbushes and wild vines, shrubbery that would look out of place anywhere in Sirvassa, but which looks like it belongs to the Garden. Here bloom sixteen flowers of myriad, powerful scents, the chalices of myriad, powerful Delights. A small stone statue of the Half-Formed God stands in the center. A man sits hunched beneath the statue, ripping off grass-blades, chewing them, one by one. He cuts a curiously feline figure, murmuring, as if saying out loud incantations older than time itself.

The Caretaker presses his palms on the man's shoulders.

"How did you open the door to the Garden?"

The man looks up and meets the eyes of the Caretaker. He is gaunt, has full red lips, eyes blue and full of deep understanding. His hair is windswept and coarse. His cheeks sport a white stubble, like sugar icing on a brown surface.

"I copied your movements and remembered by heart the spots on the door," he says.

"Why are you here in the Third Sector?"

"I am sorry, Master," he says and his eyes dart toward the spot of his crime, toward the Tulip of the Seven and its grossly severed state. Its petals are smeared with smoky tendrils of a blackness. The Caretaker's gaze lingers at the flower, his pride, and he swallows his rage. His eyes are fierce yet his words are gentle.

"What did you gain from the flower, Trulio?"

"Nothing," says Trulio. "Nothing. I went on a useless adventure and lost everything. I hoped...I hoped the flower would give me back what I yearn for. But it gave me only shadows I can't touch, and music I can't listen to."

"If only you'd listened to me," says the Caretaker. "The flower will blossom again." Then, the Caretaker's eyes flit toward the passage that leads out of the Third Sector into the Fourth, and then to the Fifth – the forbidden sector, the sector where the Lotus blooms. Damp ground and a trail of footsteps, muddy, assured.

"Trulio, did you hazard a visit to the Fifth Sector?"

There's barely a whisper from Trulio. When he speaks, his voice comes out jagged.

"I am sorry for not believing in your words, Master."

"Answer what I asked, Trulio," the Caretaker says sternly, but gently.

"I...I did, Master, but couldn't go past the Fourth."

"What were you hoping to obtain, if I may ask? What Delight?"

"The wonders of the Tulip are well known, Master. I was hoping to get only a glimpse of...a glimpse of Shahina. By going into the Fifth Sector, I wished I could go back in time."

Trulio breaks down. He howls, burying his face in the Caretaker's robes. "I lost her, Master. I lost her forever to a demon I thought I could fight."

"Come, it's late. Let's go inside. You must be tired and you need a warm bed to sleep in."

The Caretaker offers Trulio his hand, and Trulio takes it, like handling a feather. As they make their way out of the Garden, the Caretaker's eyes fall on the Tulip. Two of its petals are smeared with a tar-like substance, two others broken. The once-glorious flower hangs silently like a scarecrow.

Darkness falls over the Caretaker's eyes, seeing his pride, his child, meet such a fate at the hands of utter ignorance. The flower will take careful tending over an extended period of time, the contracts it has enabled with the townsfolk to be canceled. The Caretaker thinks of all those advanced orders, all those hopeful visitors eager to inhale a charm, ingest a magic, to make someone happy, if only temporarily.

Trulio deserves a punishment for a crime he was foolish to commit. But before punishment he needs care and rest.

★　★　★

Morning comes without warning. The Caretaker slides out of his bed, and immediately regrets waking. His youthful cloak is there no more, and the weariness in his bones is back. He looks at his hands, the same spotty and aged things. The potion did not work, yet again.

Each morning he remembers his curse, each morning an endurance test.

"Trulio!"

The apprentice appears in his bedchamber, the light of the morning bringing his gaunt face into sharp relief. He looks even more haggard than he did the night before, but the spring in his step is inexplicable. Perhaps he is too keen to prove himself, yet again. Too keen to apologize. But a good apology never comes with a hurry. Great penance needs greater patience.

"Master," he says. "The morning is bright."

"That I can see," says the Caretaker. "Will you make me Potion of the Storm? My bones...they creak like the shoddy work of a bad carpenter."

"Yes, yes of course, Master, anything you need."

"You come back and then we will talk."

Trulio nods and walks away, retracing his steps religiously. The Caretaker struggles to get up, the shock of age all too real. Like the laboratory, his bedchamber houses the bare minimum. A bed, a table, a chair. A leather-bound journal. Ink and quill. The quill is dry, the ink bottle filled to the brim. It has been long since the Caretaker wrote in his journal. It has been long since he had something to write about. But perhaps the pages will have to be filled with Trulio's tale. For now, a vapid tale of useless adventure and inevitable heartbreak will have to do.

The window in his room overlooks the expanse of the city of Sirvassa. The sky is a stark blue, clear, devoid of clouds, and other pinpricks of the universe that make themselves known most mornings. Toward the south the Temple of Eborsen stands alone, shaped like a watchtower. A blue-and-gold flag attached to a pole on top of the temple flutters against the wind. The city lies sprawled, stone houses dormant with empty insides, better made cement constructions boasting of city folk, rich and poor alike. Turrets connected to each other with shimmering strings, lighterflies buzzing around them, making a double helical pattern, only visible in the evenings.

"Master."

Trulio's sharp voice pulls the Caretaker out of the enigma of Sirvassa. The apprentice stands near the door, holding a steaming cup for his master. Trulio has an uncanny chirp to his manner, far removed from the emotional shambles of last night.

"That was quick, Trulio, thanks," says the Caretaker, taking the cup from the apprentice's hands. "Sit, please."

The apprentice sits in the chair. The Caretaker sips the potion. The coldness in his bones abates as warmth courses through his body.

"That's the journal. That's the pen. I need you to write me an account of what you experienced in your journey. I also need you to immediately cancel all appointments pertaining to the Tulip."

Trulio looks at the Caretaker like the troublesome child who is expecting a slap but is given a gift in return. The Caretaker can sense his giddiness, but he knows that Trulio's penance will be long.

"Master, before I start, I need to ask you something," says Trulio. There's hesitation in his voice. Unmistakable. Cold. Like something is about to erupt from him.

"Ask away." The Caretaker sits back down on his bed.

"The Garden. Can't we build a bigger one in another city? Perhaps a bigger city than this one. Perhaps, Alderra?"

"And why would we do that, Trulio?"

"Better customers. Imagine the kind of Delights they would want. Sirvassa, the beautiful city that it is, its people lack imagination. Out there, we would get to experiment with the nature of the potions themselves!"

The Caretaker knows only too well the failure that comes with experimentation, and the inevitable heartbreak. But more than that, the Caretaker knows that expansion of the Garden would bring nothing but misery. Unsupervised, untested, the Delights would become Sorrows for the too-eager, molding the magic they enjoyed into something dark.

"And who will tend to that bigger garden? Another one like me?"

"We can train eager young minds. We can fill the world full of wonder. Believe me...I was there in Alderra. People *want* our Delights! They yearn for them, they are desperate for them!"

Trulio's eyes convey his elation more than his words ever could. His body thrums with excitement, like a daimler-fly about to burst after glimmering with its last light. But the Caretaker is unimpressed. His thin lips curve slightly upward in a semblance of a smile.

Then he lets out an uproarious laugh. He pats Trulio's shoulders. "Trulio, you certainly jest."

"But Master—"

"None of what you just said would happen. Not because I don't want it to, but because it's impossible."

"You're saying that, Master? You, the one who defeated—"

"Not another word, Trulio."

Trulio hangs his head. He turns around in the chair, quiet as a feather, and opens the journal. The Caretaker finishes his drink, and gets ready for a meeting with a friend, a meeting he's been avoiding for too long.

CHAPTER FIVE

Iyena Mastafar

On her first day of school, Iyena mistakenly calls her teacher Sernir. The moniker is given to a person who holds a much higher position of teaching authority, and in a city like Alderra, a Sernir could teach even the minister the error of his ways and he wouldn't bat an eyelid.

Fortunately, for Iyena, the teacher doesn't bat an eyelid either. He stares at her curiously, then laughs like a child. "I can't be a Sernir even if I tried to be," he says. "Here in Sirvassa, however, you can use the word Tevair."

Tevair. A word meant for a teacher, like Din-Tevair is meant for the principal. Tevair. Two syllables, much like Sernir. Iyena swirls the word in her mouth. It has a different ring than the other word. She can get used to it. She has to get used to this newness.

"Tevair Dines Granagh, I am Iyena Mastafar of Alderra, daughter of Kedhran Anaris Mastafar. I apologize for my previous misplaced use of the word."

"No need to apologize, Iyena," says Tevair Dines. "Fascinating to hear that your father is a Kedhran. Is he here on ministry business?"

Iyena presses the edge of her left palm with her thumb and index finger. Then, she lets her hands fall to her sides and chews her lips.

"It's okay to be nervous, Iyena. If you choose not to answer, that's your choice."

Tevair Dines leans against the wooden podium, where a splayed copy of an old text is kept. Its pages are bone-white, with a cover that looks like it's made of ivory. If one looked closely, they would find the book imbued with the wood, almost like it is a part of it, as if the wood itself had consented to be a part of the process. Back in Alderra, Sernir and Sern would teach from memory. Students were expected to memorize and internalize everything. That oral teaching process had been going on for millennia, and was expected to continue.

At times, Iyena would sit inside her room, back in Alderra, a room that overlooked a smoky sprawl of close-knit buildings, and observe as Sernir Ammana spoke in hushed, poetic intonations with her father. She could never tell what was being talked about, but it was clear that her father – and by extension, the Alderran government – was intimately involved in the school system.

Iyena considers Tevair Dines's question. She has never shown any inclination to know what her father does for a living. Yes, during her time in Alderra, visits from ministry officials were the norm rather than the exception. From what she could glean from snippets of conversations she had eavesdropped on (she liked to do that), she could tell her father was a very important man. Perhaps the third most important man in the Ministry of Alderra.

And the third most important man in the Alderran Ministry had asked her to be vigilant at a Sirvassan school. He'd shown regular interest in what she was learning in Alderra too. But to take daily notes on her education in Sirvassa was out of character, even for her strict father.

"We're here to enjoy the city," says Iyena, as her father had told her to say. "Mothers of Alderra tell their children tales of Sirvassa at night."

"Spoken like the daughter of a Kedhran," says Tevair Dines, smiling. Iyena moves toward the open, haphazard seating arrangement. Curved, wooden chairs fashioned with a free hand, tree stumps around which stones jut from the ground acting as chairs. More odd seats are splayed all around the open theater, one end of which overlooks a green expanse that has no end in sight, and the other end has Tevair Dines standing on the podium, canopied by a construction which resembles the outer shell of the deep-water-dwelling Elterbeast. It even has curves and ridges upon its exterior, which seem to move when one averts their gaze from it.

Tevair Dines goes to the podium and flips a page. He begins to speak, but then closes his mouth, distracted. He looks around the class, furrowing his brows. "Trehan isn't in yet?" he asks.

"He complained of a stomachache, Tevair." Iyena looks at the girl who answered Tevair Dines's question. She has a sheaf of parchment with her, stacked atop her lap, as she sits cross-legged on the grassy ground, leaning against a piece of wood. The girl locks eyes with Iyena and beckons to her. Iyena gingerly walks over to the girl and takes a seat next to her.

"Must be all the salousse he has been eating," says Tevair, which invites laughter from the class.

"Who is he talking about?" asks Iyena.

"Son of the Lockmaker. He has a tendency to be late to class."

In Alderra, a latecomer was sent back home, or worse, cursed by the Sernir to forget what they had learned the previous day. This encouraged order and discipline. But even as Tevair Dines begins his class, and lectures about the types of crops in summer in Sirvassa, their imports and exports through the sea, Iyena can sense that he is in no mood to dole out any punishment.

"Iyena Mastafar, you seem occupied," says the girl, without making eye contact with Iyena. "First day nerves?"

"It's not that," says Iyena. "Everything here is different. The way you talk, your names, your roads, your air. Even the way you sit."

"Wouldn't have it any other way."

"What's your name?"

"Sidhi Anterra," says the girl. "I'm from Jumen, a small town not far from Sirvassa. Just near the coast."

"I love the sea," says Iyena. There's a glow in her eyes when she speaks of the sea. Sidhi glances at her, and shrugs absently.

"I don't think much of it, having seen it all my life. It's the mountains I love more."

The absentee boy doesn't arrive until the class is over. Tevair Dines instructs the class politely to ask their parents and elders about the types of crops and the types of foods they had when they were young. The next class will thereby delve into historical context, and how food habits have changed in Sirvassa – and the realms – over the years. Iyena makes a mental note to ask both Maani-Ba and her father about Alderra's past.

When the classes are over, the sun is high in the sky, and the skies are a clear blue. Students trickle out of the silvery gates of the school huddled in groups ready for the other side of their day. Iyena steps out of the open classroom onto the grassy field. To her right is the gate that leads outside the school, and to her left the grass stretches farther beyond to a purply wilderness, shrouded by tall trees, beyond which the Llar mountain range peeks out like a white ghost, cloudlike. A flowery, fruity smell persists in the air, a smell Iyena hasn't quite gotten used to yet. As more and more students march toward the exit, Iyena tears her gaze away from the mountains.

"Iyena, there is no school after hours here."

The sun casts Sidhi's tall shadow on the ground. The shadow kisses Iyena's footsteps. Iyena hurries her steps and catches up to Sidhi, balancing a sheaf of papers in her hands.

"I was admiring the view," says Iyena. "Sidhi, will you help me with Tevair Amram's homework?"

"What's there to help? We have to talk to five different people throughout the day and know about their workday, that's all."

"That's the part I didn't quite understand. How is that 'homework'?"

"You don't have to submit everything tomorrow. Give it a week. See how Varsha and I present our work, and learn accordingly."

Outside, the students disperse, climbing atop carriages pulled by Rhisuan beasts. The carriages are tarped enclosures with windows and padded seats. Some tarps are colorful, some more neutral in hue, giving each carriage a distinct personality. The beasts are all the same – a dozen bulbous eyes on a thick hide. Students pat the animal gently, murmuring inside its ears their destinations.

"Come, that carriage is empty." Varsha points toward a carriage that is slightly smaller, and stands slightly askance compared to the others. The beast pulling it looks generally tired of the world.

Iyena follows Varsha. But before she can climb onto the carriage, the beast gives a loud grunt, like multiple stones clanking against each other at the bottom of a copper vessel. Then, more such sounds emerge, from all around her. All the beasts begin grunting, and their round, wet, bulbous eyes dart to the white heavens.

Above, the sky is covered. First, with the ever-alluring, ever-present meshwork that shines even during the day. But there's something else beyond those lines. Something higher up in the air, an inkblot spreading wider and wider. Air rushes through the gaps in the spiderwebs and hits Iyena, almost sweeping her off her feet. Others look similarly disoriented, clutching their papers and their bags tightly to their chests, huddled against each other in groups, lest an individual get blown away by the gale.

The black stain in the sky becomes bigger, develops wings and claws and a tail with a million spikes, and a sharp beak like a gleaming sun-sword. It descends like thunder. Iyena grabs Varsha's arm and ducks, shielding herself from the incoming onslaught of the flying monster.

The monster above lets out a death screech, a sound of razors on razors on a million stones. Its sound drowns out Iyena's own scream, which eventually vanishes someplace between her throat and her mouth. But out of the corner of her terrified eye, she sees no one budging. No one is as scared as she is. No one has ice in the pit of their stomach; no one has faces turned to ash. Their eyes are fixated on the monster above. The monster descends sharply, prepared to pierce through the meshwork.

But then, the web dazzles.

A sharp lightning runs through the spiderweb patterns, meeting at junctures, bursting into blue flames, and leaping up in the sky. Tendrils of electricity reach out of the mesh and grab the monster's neck, its wings, its barbed tail, coiling around its black behemoth of a body in a thousand shimmery circles. The monster is yanked downward, then thrown upward, flung all around, the electric coil digging deep into the beast's flesh, burning it, charring it. The monster gives out no dying scream as it flaps helplessly against the doom-coil around its body.

Slowly, its body begins to wither away in black and gray flakes that fall through the meshwork like snow. The coils retract and become one with the mesh, again. The sky is back to being clear and blue. The monster is gone in a white vapor. The Rhisuan beasts cease their grunting.

Iyena's breath comes in sharp gasps, and her skin feels clammy. All around her, students climb into their respective carriages like nothing had happened. Varsha, too, grips the edge of the carriage and heaves herself onto the first seat. Then, she holds out her left hand for Iyena.

"Watch your step," says Varsha. "There's a piece of nail jutting out."

"What in the Alderran depths was that?" Iyena breathes heavily, her words coming out in spurts.

"Oh, that. I'd completely forgotten today was the day. Climb, I'll tell you."

Iyena climbs into the carriage. It shudders, veers left, threatening to crumble completely, but then stops.

"Every newcomer in the city wonders what the *jalan* is for," says Varsha, pointing upward at the mesh. "Not everyone gets to experience it firsthand."

"Wait. Does that mean...the monster...like...does it arrive every...." Iyena stops, measuring her words, her breath still heavy.

"Every three months, yes. The city wasn't shrouded like this always. The jalan was constructed to stop the monster. They say it regenerates in a cave in the mountain, and that it can't be killed. It can only be stopped."

"Who made the meshwork?"

"The Caretaker."

There's a glint in Varsha's eyes when she mentions the Caretaker. The edges of her lips curve into a thin smile.

"Who is he? What does he do?"

"Everyone thinks he's a Florral, but I don't agree."

It's not Varsha who answers Iyena's question. The boy she saw a day ago stands near the carriage, one foot on the wooden ledge meant to climb, one on the ground. He is sandy-haired, and there is an air of unabashed bravado about him. His fingers curl and uncurl, manic, as if he is about to expunge a wild energy he is holding in his veins.

"School is over, Trehan," says Varsha. "Wait till you hear what Tevair Dines thinks of you."

"I'm sure he thinks very highly of me," says Trehan, his eyes still affixed on Iyena. "We meet again, new girl."

"My name is Iyena Mastafar."

Trehan crosses his fingers and makes the Sirvassan greeting gesture. Iyena does the same.

"Now, were we talking about the Caretaker? Because I am planning to visit the Garden of Delights today. I hope the Delight I get this time is more powerful than the last time."

"What's a Delight?" asks Iyena. Trehan's eyes sparkle.

"Wish I could show you, but it's better to experience it," he says. Iyena thinks the boy is being needlessly evasive. But then Varsha chimes in with an explanation.

"A Delight is a magic that the Caretaker gives us with his potions. All temporary. But all so wonderful. The last time he used the Delight in school, bothering Tevair Granagh endlessly. He came so close to being expelled."

"You're overreacting, it wasn't like that. I merely disappeared a pencil."

"It was his mother's pencil," says Varsha. "Iyena, you should have seen Tevair's face. He was close to tears."

"New city girl, Iyena Mastafar—" begins the boy.

"It's Ai-yena not Ee-yena," says Iyena. "Get your pronunciation of my name right."

"Sorry, Ai-yena." The boy gives a curt, apologetic bow with a devilish smile on his face. "Would you like to know more about the Garden of Delights?"

Iyena scratches her chin, considering the question. Then, after a moment of pondering, she nods.

CHAPTER SIX

The Caretaker

The walk from his cottage home to the laboratory is long and leisurely. The Caretaker ambles along the weather-beaten path, ignoring the moss that has grown on stones, the fallen leaves, the crushed ants and beetles on the road. He doesn't waste a glance on them.

He opens his laboratory and finds the remnants of last night's experiment, and then some. He remembers clearing everything, but after Trulio's arrival, he had to open up the place again, to prepare a sleeping potion for his apprentice, who had been raving like a lunatic deep in the night, singing hymns in praise of a lost love, hymns that took the melancholy quality of a dirge.

To put it simply, he had given up on the night after putting Trulio to sleep.

With haste, he clears the tubes and utensils and beakers from the tabletop, cleans the wood with a plain cloth, and pats it dry. Next, he arranges the cupboards neatly, placing the equipment in niches where they belong. There's a precision to his movements, and his hands move with as much surety as the rising of the sun. Even as he goes about his business, his eyes keep falling to the age spots on his forearm. He keeps covering them, not wanting to be reminded of his old age every passing moment.

When he's done, he takes a moment to admire his handiwork. Behind him, the open door creaks against its hinges, a rebellion of sorts. There's no list of guests the Caretaker has to entertain today. He takes a deep, musty breath, which reminds him of time spent in his childhood in mud-homes making dung cakes for fuel, and lying on stacks of hay basking in the sun. He shrugs off the memory quickly and reaches for a bottle of amber liquid inside the cupboard. A healing potion for his friend, Jaywardna Illyasi. After pocketing the bottle, he walks out of the laboratory into the balmy Sirvassan day.

★   ★   ★

The Caretaker crosses the narrow wooden bridge that runs over a stream to reach Mayor Jaywardna Illyasi's estate. The water of the stream is a clear blue, and the rush of the water against river-smooth stones fills the air. The banks of the small stream are adorned by lush green grass, overgrown in places, patchy in others, a smattering of pebbles, and torn, forgotten footwear by too-eager children, or too-passionate lovers.

The estate is a spacious ground that gives way to a massive four-storied bungalow. A wide road, which leads from where the bridge ends, is flanked on both sides by vibrant way-markers that glow upon the arrival of footsteps on the road. The road leads to an unremarkable iron gate. It has seen colonies of rust come and go, but has stood the test of time. It does its only job well enough. Since the beginning of Sirvassa's sovereignty, the mayor's bungalow has been untouched by forces of man and nature alike, quite miraculously. The Caretaker observes this simple fact, and finds it amusing. He has had no part to play in this, despite the title the Sirvassans have bestowed upon him.

Four guards stand near the gate, wearing sharp black-and-blue suits, the Sirvassan insignia of a crimson fell-bird singing on a branch sewn on their chests. When the Caretaker approaches, one guard salutes him dutifully and opens the door. The Caretaker nods at the guard.

"Mayor Illyasi is expecting you," the guard says.

"Thank you, Marramis," says the Caretaker. "I hope you enjoyed the Delight I gave you."

Marramis gives a gleeful smile. "My two children were enchanted with what I had to show them. I have promised them the same trick on their next birthday."

"I hope you use the Delight sparsely and wisely."

Saying this, the Caretaker takes the narrow, cobblestoned path toward the entrance of the bungalow. He ignores the fading murmurs of the other guards as they ask Marramis about his usage of the Delight. He will probably get more customers, one of these days. He will probably have to refuse them too.

When he reaches the bungalow's main door, he finds it's already open. He steps inside gingerly. The spacious marbled hall, the curving double staircase shaped like a giant with outstretched arms, the glittering chandelier, and the ever-entertaining Waystrewer, Mayor Illyasi's pet. As he enters, the Waystrewer trots toward him on its six furry paws, its wavy thin tentacles flailing in the air, its two eyes-which-aren't-eyes fixated on the Caretaker with love.

The Caretaker kneels down and embraces the Waystrewer. Its tentacles clasp his arm and his torso, and he is immediately filled with hope and warmth and glee, a sensation so positive that the Caretaker forgets, even if momentarily, the curse he is carrying.

"I keep saying he loves you more than me."

Mayor Jaywardna Illyasi stands near the staircase, eating an apple. He is wearing a morning robe, crimson and white. His gray-and-sawdust hair is neatly parted in the middle, and his black, penciled mustache is sharp as a razor. A tall man, who would be taller if he weren't so hunched all the time. But men handling governments take an invisible weight on their shoulders very quickly.

"If only I could take him with me," says the Caretaker wistfully. "He would chew apart my Garden."

"And become the most powerful beast in all three realms."

The Caretaker lets out a scoff. Jaywardna Illyasi smiles at his own jest. Both men embrace each other like friends who have met after a long time.

"So, still looking for another Florral, are you?"

The Caretaker gives Mayor Illyasi a look.

"C'mon, don't be like that. Only I know how desperate you are to find one."

"Florrals are a myth, and I don't chase after them."

The Caretaker knows his statement is a lie, but he doesn't care. Florrals, the Inishti magicians who don't need Delights from flowers to perform magic, chose a life of solitude after the Second Abhadi-Inishti War. He knows Florrals are still out there, and it's only a matter of time before one arrives in Sirvassa. If not, then the Caretaker will have to search for one himself.

"Didn't you say the last Florral was living in exile somewhere in Troika?"

The Caretaker gives a heavy sigh. The mayor, with an impish smile on his face, continues, "Anyway, wherever your search takes you, I wish you the best. Whatever you do, don't stop making people happy. They stay happy, I stay happy."

"How's the leg?" asks the Caretaker.

"All thanks to you, it's becoming better by the day."

"That's why I am here."

The Caretaker shows him the vial he has brought with him.

"You go right to business, don't you? Come inside, have a bite to eat. I have to tell you something."

The Caretaker follows Jaywardna Illyasi inside his study. The room is vast, opulent, filled floor to ceiling with books, and gives off a fruity smell, despite the absence of any ornamental flowers or perfume. A map of the Three Realms is on the wall opposite a large window that overlooks the bungalow grounds. The Waystrewer follows the men inside the study, and makes itself comfortable on the cushion of a swiveling chair.

Mayor Illyasi leans against a large table, and takes the last bite of his apple.

"The Sirvassan Kerron has been losing its value steadily. The petal-rain hasn't done us any favors this year."

"I'm not here to discuss politics," says the Caretaker.

"No, but this involves you too," says the mayor grimly. "The influx of tourists from all over the realm has been declining. Alderra has been breathing hard on my neck. That Abhadi-supremacist pest

Yayati keeps demanding answers to useless questions. You know what he asked me the last time he sent me a coppergram?"

"What?"

"He wanted me to *allow* petal-rain over Alderra too. Allow. That was the word he used."

The Caretaker bristles at this remark. "The petal-rain is Eborsen's gift," he says. "That much is known to anyone who has even a working knowledge of the Lore of the Three Realms and its history."

"You think I didn't tell him that?" Mayor Illyasi's nostrils flare up. The Waystrewer comes over to him and gently wraps its tentacles around his legs. It takes some time, but the mayor's temper dies down.

"Now he wants to come over to *pay his respects* to Eborsen. Thinking a god in slumber would grant wishes and boons just like that."

The Caretaker can't help but be amused by the mayor's remark. If gods could impart curses, they surely could give boons.

"Anyway, that's only part of his agenda. The truth is, I am now answerable to the Three Realms Registry and the Vaishwam Chair. They need a plan of action."

"You aren't answerable to anyone except yourself, Jaywardna," says the Caretaker. "When Sirvassa became a sovereign city-state for all Inishtis, that was a responsibility you took on yourself."

"That's the thing. With these mounting pressures on me all around, I don't think I am doing a good job of it anymore."

There is silence, which is only disturbed by the gentle purring of the Waystrewer.

"You are the Protector of Sirvassa," says the mayor in a barely audible whisper. "You saved the city once. Everyone loves you and likes being in your company."

The Caretaker doesn't like the tone of Jaywardna Illyasi's words. It almost always precedes an impossible request.

"What are you getting at?"

"You know what I'm getting at," says Illyasi. He sounds desperate, his eyes dark pools of misery. The Caretaker is keenly aware of his friend's upcoming plea. Something he has denied in the past. The Garden is one of the chief reasons anyone visits Sirvassa, along with its legendary petal-rain. Aside from carrying terrific healing properties, the collected petals are also lucrative exports from Sirvassa, acting like currency when the Kerron loses its value, keeping the city-state prosperous. So it would be logical to open up the Garden, too, for a larger business, something the Caretaker is against.

The Caretaker has never asked anyone for money. That is not what the Garden was for.

"Has my apprentice spoken to you? Because, curiously, he asked me something similar last evening. Let me tell you what I told him, so you don't ask me this question again in six months. I will *not* open another Garden. And certainly not in Alderra."

"Well, it was worth a try," says Illyasi, exhaling sharply. Then, he starts rubbing his thumb against the edge of the table, as if scratching away an inkblot. It's a nervous gesture, and the Caretaker catches it.

"There's something else," says the Caretaker.

The mayor looks up. "You don't miss much."

"Out with it."

Illyasi rubs his forehead with his palms, like he's making an effort even to consider speaking his next words. All of it's a show, and the Caretaker knows it.

"Will you become the Mayor of Sirvassa?"

The Caretaker stares at his friend. If Mayor Illyasi is hiding something, he is doing an excellent job of it. Jaywardna Illyasi isn't a man who thinks himself to be incompetent. He is a man of immense pride, and carries that pride on his shoulders. Yes, it would have pained him to utter those words. But the Caretaker has his own pain to consider first.

"I can't do that, Jaywardna," says the Caretaker. "I am not made for that chair."

The mayor sighs. "I'll be frank with you," he says. "With me in that chair, the non-expansion of the Garden can't be an official policy.

Alderra, Eborsen bless me, can rot in the piss of their Champions for all I care. But recently even the Vaishwam Chair has started nudging me in that direction."

The Vaishwam Chair, a council of three people who are neither Abhadi nor Inishti, neither Champion, nor Florral, but an entirely different race altogether. Their skin a mottled blue, and their minds a cold glacier, they were the ones responsible for the Restoration Pact after the First Abhadi-Inishti War. Their existence has always struck the Caretaker as odd and frankly, ironic. It took another species to intervene for two races to observe a truce, however temporary.

"Many in this city don't have confidence in me. You, on the other hand, are a man of your words. There hasn't been a truer, purer soul around. I just want to bow out in grace, before anything untoward happens that puts the future of Sirvassa in jeopardy. You can make decisions I can't make. I assure you, no one would bat an eyelid. Change of command comes with a change of policy."

"That's *not* how you do things, my friend," says the Caretaker. "I expected better of you."

Jaywardna Illyasi flinches at the biting words. His shoulders tense up, and his jaw hangs agape. The Caretaker knows how to handle Illyasi. He can be friendly when needed, and cruel when needed.

The Caretaker puts an arm around Mayor Jaywardna Illyasi's shoulders. Mayor Illyasi relaxes.

"Minister Yayati has plans for this city. I don't know what, something not good. Sirvassa has been a thorn in his side for decades. If he could get this city under his wing by any means, he would."

"Right," says the Caretaker. "So you want to abandon this city."

"No," says Jaywardna sharply. "I am thinking of the *city*, for the love of Eborsen. Whatever is best for it. And I know you are the best among us."

"You have been showering praises on me since I set foot here. That's very uncharacteristic of you."

"Listen carefully now. If my sources are true, Minister Yayati wants me to sign a conjoining treaty. Some of his dignitaries have started coming into the city even as we speak. I will have to entertain them, listen to them, and sign things. Eborsen bless me, I shudder to think of the sheer paperwork. I don't want to do that, but my hands are tied."

"Why? Does Yayati have something on you?"

"I wish it were that simple," says the mayor. "Look, if I declare you as my successor, I will be free. I have been in this chair for far too long, and Yayati knows all my tricks. But he doesn't know all of yours, if you know what I am saying. He won't even know how to deal with you. I am talking about the future of Sirvassa."

Mayor Illyasi massages his left leg vigorously. The Waystrewer snuggles up against his knees, wrapping its tentacles around the mayor's legs. The Caretaker watches this with amusement.

"Take your potion, Illyasi." The Caretaker places the vial of potion on the desk, and turns around to leave. "I will see you next time."

"Is that a dismissal, then? Won't you even entertain my request? For old times' sake?"

"Do what you were elected to do, Illyasi. That will be better for both your conscience and mine."

The Caretaker walks out, without waiting to catch the expression on Illyasi's face. If he had, he would have found the sadness and the helplessness of a craven man.

CHAPTER SEVEN

Iyena Mastafar

Trehan, the sandy-haired boy, doesn't tell Iyena about the Garden of Delights immediately. The next day in school is spent in rigorous learning of her syllabus. Iyena, adept in the Ways, a bookless manner of learning employed in Alderra, catches on quickly to all the reading she has to do. Ranging from the types of Albuchemy, to the Sirvassan lore, its fraught history, the many gods, to the trade of petals across shores, to the quiet origins of the Garden of Delights.

In the last class of the day, Tevair Sarathi tells them about the Healers and the preparations involved in gathering petals after rain, changing their composition, making them into potions that cure all diseases, even the incurable ones.

"Tevair Sarathi." Iyena raises her hand in class, much to the dismay of her classmates. "Do the Healers also cure the Wilt of the Morning?"

"That, and the Lungrot, and many, many others," says Tevair Sarathi.

"Hope it cures boredom, some day," whispers Trehan to his classmates. This invites uproarious laughter from the students, so much that even Tevair Sarathi can't help but chuckle to himself.

"Trehan, on a normal day, I would have given you an apt punishment for that remark. But we are only five minutes away from the end of day, so I'll just clap lightly."

Tevair Sarathi closes the book on his podium, and claps at Trehan.

Iyena, who was ready for another question, stares at the proceedings with a barely disguised awe. Something like this would never be tolerated by Sern Aradha, back in Alderra. Iyena closes her own books and sighs deeply, not joining in the shared laughter of her classmates. But she is forced to smile when Varsha gently pats her back, urging her to take it easy.

★   ★   ★

When the school finishes for the day, Iyena joins a group of students inside a carriage, opting to take a longer route to her home.

"This city is too bright and too full," says Trehan, his unruly hair sticking out at odd places, and with a perennial smirk across his face. He says it with the unabashed confidence of someone who has lived in all cities of the realm, yet calls none his true home. He utters all his sentences in a mock, non-conversational tone, like only he is in on a joke, a child of pride.

The school carriage shudders a bit, then continues its languid crawl across the Sirvassan road. A scorching, midafternoon sun beats down upon the Rhisuan beast, who, with its twenty-four eyes and thick tree-branch-like legs, finds the journey cumbersome.

"I have told Tevair Sarthi to employ the Evkel. They're much more reliable than this animal, and never forget an address." Trehan chews his fingernails as he passes judgment upon the poor beast, entirely forgetting his chain of thought. Iyena observes him keenly.

"I think you're wrong about the city," says Iyena.

"What?"

"You said the city is too bright. I think it has the right sort of brightness. Also, much less populated than Alderra."

"You're a big-city girl, Iyena," says Trehan. "Live in Sirvassa for a year and you'll know what I mean."

"I intend to," says Iyena. Trehan holds her gaze for a long time, then looks away. The sun falls angularly on his face. Iyena stares at him for a respectable amount of time, then tears her gaze away, suddenly self-conscious.

"Will you make something for us, Trehan?" a ponytailed girl with one front tooth missing asks. A faint whistle comes out of her mouth as she speaks.

"Make something...? As in...?"

"The Delight you got from the Garden, obviously. The animal isn't moving fast. Our homes are far away and we need entertainment. Now, show us!"

"I won't do it for free," says Trehan, leaning back on his seat. A balmy afternoon wind throws his already messy hair into disarray. "I only have a couple of vials left and I'm saving it for a special occasion."

"Oh come on," says the girl. "Don't be such a fikul."

Trehan raises his eyebrows. "What did you call me?"

"You heard me."

"What's a fikul?" asks Iyena.

"King Darshala had a Pillar named Fikulaus," says Ujita, a black-haired, bespectacled girl, tall for her age, but also much wiser. "Fikulaus was adept at making music but was known throughout the kingdom to be a miserly man. This behavior once cost the king dearly. Fikulaus was barred from that kingdom. But his name stuck."

"You're leaving out the juicier and much more important parts of the story, Ujita," said Trehan. "Iyena, I'll tell you the complete *and* the more truthful version some other time."

"You're still a fikul," says the girl.

Trehan glares at her. He grips the wooden railing of the carriage, veins bulging out of the back of his hand. The wood creaks and groans, spouting tear-shaped pods that grow into vines, wicker-like, solidifying around Trehan's hand like a glove. He shows it to the others, who gaze in awe at the makeshift gauntlet.

"It's of no practical use, but it's still something," says Trehan. Iyena's eyes go wide in mute wonder.

When the carriage drops the third to last student on their doorstep, Iyena asks Trehan the question she has been meaning to for the longest time.

"Will you take me to the Garden of Delights?"

Trehan throws his head back and laughs, his hair falling onto his shoulders. Then, scrunching his eyes, and heaving with more repressed laughter, he says, "It's not a place where you go for vacation, Iyena."

"Then remove that smirk off your face and tell me how to visit that place," says Iyena, as businesslike as possible.

★   ★   ★

Night envelops Sirvassa like an old lover. Iyena peeks through the gap in the curtains of her bedroom and finds a cat prowling the cemented sidewalk, keenly aware of its surroundings but oblivious to most other things. Moonlight splashes on a shattered cobblestone in front of a fruit vendor. Faint wind rustles the awnings of shuttered cloth shops. A playactor whistles a song, skipping steps, jumping and touching his feet, gliding magically through the air, leaving a shimmer in his wake, then landing gracefully on the road.

"The sun sets early in this city."

Iyena turns to see her father standing by her bedside. Anaris is holding a rolled-up parchment in his hands. An inkblot stain spreads outward from the tip of the index finger of his right hand. Yet again, he was working deep in the evening, and had perhaps hesitantly signed the parchment. Or not. He tries to hide the quiver in his finger by holding the paper too tight.

"It's not like most cities," says Iyena, sitting down on her bed.

"Enchanting, isn't it?" says Anaris. "Iyena, I've read this…peculiar request of yours." He waves the parchment. "I can't allow you to visit this Garden of Delights."

"But why, Father?"

"I wasn't expecting you to forget so soon what I have instructed you to do for me," he says softly. "You're at school to learn the Sirvassan System, and then tell me all about it. Nothing more, nothing less. You are not to diverge from the path I have set for you. Besides, your visit to this…this Garden. It could be dangerous. I have heard of that old man…what do these people call him?"

"The Caretaker."

"Yes, he seems like the wrong sort of person," says Anaris. "I have asked around. No one knows where he came from. No one even knows his real name."

"But everyone seems to like him so much."

"If everyone jumps into the Lake of Nevermore, you'll jump too?"

"I've heard the lake transports you to another world. I will jump," says Iyena confidently.

"My word is final, Iyena. You are better off concentrating on your studies." Anaris's voice is harsh, and his face looks tired. Iyena sinks back in her pillow, drawing her blanket over her chest. Anaris's expression softens. He sits beside Iyena. "This is a new city, child. I don't want you to get hurt, that's all. Make new friends in the school. Invite them here, if you want. Remember, as I told you, the more we learn about them, the better it is for us. But keep it limited to learning."

Iyena nods. Anaris kisses her on the cheek.

When her father leaves, Iyena begins hatching a plan in her head.

★   ★   ★

In the morning, Iyena doesn't wake up to the call of Maani-Ba as she usually does. Instead, she glances through a gap in her blanket as Maani-Ba dusts the corners of her room. Motes of dust swirl in the air, hanging in stasis, bright against the sunlight pouring into her room. Iyena emulates a cough and wheezes as she speaks.

"Maani-Ba, please close the door as you leave."

"Are you sick, child?"

"Yes, Maani-Ba," says Iyena, softly purring, adding the moniker deliberately. Maani-Ba gives Iyena a quizzical frown. Sitting down on her knees by Iyena's bed, she grabs the blanket and yanks it off.

Iyena closes her eyes immediately. Maani-Ba places the back of her palm on Iyena's forehead.

"No temperature," says Maani-Ba. "Shall I bring the draught of the Sasi, with added cardamom, as you like? Will soothe your cough."

"It's fine," says Iyena.

"No school today, then?"

Iyena shakes her head.

"Din-Tevair Granagh would require a letter of leave, signed by your father."

Iyena snatches a parchment off her bedside table and hands it to Maani-Ba.

★   ★   ★

Anaris's study is a museum; books ensconced in well-lit wall-niches, two tall oak cabinets that have never been opened, two spherical lamps like the sun and the moon hanging in the air, one bright and one dark, shining and dimming alternately, as the daylight progresses, a table full of yellowed paper stacked to the height of a small cat, pens of myriad inks, and a silver goblet of unfinished wine.

Iyena tiptoes inside the study deep in the afternoon when her father is off to work. She has never asked her father about the nature of his work, but she knows it has something to do with the government. It's evident from the multiple stamps, red and blue and gold, imprinted on the papers and the folders.

Her heart thumps as she reaches the table and finds the letter of leave, duly signed, supported by a stone weight. Her father won't come back till late in the night, but as her hand reaches for the pen with the red ink, her mind goes off wandering in the realm of impossibilities. Her father might waltz in right now and say, "Iyena, I got off early today. Let's go visit the Sirvassan Square.... Oh, what are you doing with that pen?" Iyena will have no answer to that question and she will spend the rest of her week in detention.

Her gaze is affixed on the gap between the curtains that shows her the view of the front door. No shadows, there. Maani-Ba is fast asleep upstairs.

She spreads another parchment on the table, the more important kind. She grabs the pen with the red ink, and with a careful, measured stroke, copies the signature in one flourish. She brings both papers to the light, comparing the signatures. Satisfied, she smiles, proud of her achievement.

She places the pen back, as it was. The stone weight goes back on top of the leave letter. As she gets up from her father's seat, her gaze falls inadvertently on the thing she avoids looking at whenever she comes inside her father's study. Her heart jumps at the sight of it, this time too, as it has done countless times before.

The six-feet-tall automaton with blue eyes. Ever watchful.

As Iyena leaves the study, she holds the gaze of the metal behemoth. She brings one finger to her lips, whispering to the automaton to keep a secret. The automaton doesn't reply.

★　　★　　★

Iyena's last class of a mostly uneventful school day is taught by a stout, bearded professor – Tevair Ahinya – under the shade of an Atharva tree whose branches hang like a canopy over the school grounds. Tevair Ahinya wears a faded yellow shirt stained with stew and coffee, and speaks in an ancient Agarban drawl, which Iyena finds enchanting, dreamlike, but the rest of the class finds boring. Sirvassan history is Iyena's favorite subject. None of the other students find it as interesting as she does.

"The way of this land is the way of the world," says Tevair Ahinya in a singsong manner, and a lullaby-like voice that carries through all the way to the back of the class, where Trehan and his friend snore like it's already midnight. Ahinya throws a chalk at Trehan. It bounces off his head and falls on the grass.

"What's the way of the land, Tevair?" asks Iyena.

"Iyena Mastafar, you would have known the answer had you not been absent yesterday," Ahinya chides, but then gives out a hearty laugh. Iyena gulps. Her cloth bag rests by her side, and she can almost feel the slight bulge of the vial the Caretaker gave her, a vial full of amber liquid. She couldn't make sense of the inexplicable urge to bring the full vial to school, even though the Caretaker had warned her not to go about displaying the Delight to everyone. Even a day later, the Garden of Delights is etched in her mind like a fresh painting. She can feel the pull of the gray stone door, coiled with vines and night jasmine. In moments of slumber, she walks through the five Sectors of the Garden. Her mind fills in miasmic details of the sectors she didn't see, and elevates the ones she did. In her waking moments, she can trace the outline of the Caretaker's hand on the door, and wants to place her own palm, and will the door to open. She waits for a moment of glee, so she can ingest the Delight of the Rose.

She waits to return to the Garden.

"They used to call Sirvassa the Land of Pulse and Promise," says Tevair Ahinya. "Grains we produced were exported throughout the realm and people flocked here from around the country to get jobs and make a living."

"What happened then?" asks Iyena.

"Sirvassa became a sovereign state."

"But that shouldn't have anything to do with exporting and giving people jobs."

"Now, now, those reasons are all steeped in politics, which is way beyond your learning grade, Iyena. Perhaps, in a couple of years you will learn why. We still, however, export our very costly petals. Outside, in the wider world, Sirvassa is known best for our petal-rain, those magical, healing flower snippets that adorn our streets."

"Tevair, please, the next two days are holidays. Can we please go home?" Trehan wakes up from his slumber and tries to make his point by yawning wide.

"Say, why don't I take everyone to the Tumbar Creek today? Give a proper history lesson."

"Wow, that sounds like so much fun," Trehan says in a mocking tone.

His black-haired friend chimes in. "The creek is out of bounds to us, Tevair," he says.

"Not when accompanied by a senior," says Tevair Ahinya.

"What's the creek?" Iyena whispers to Ujita, who is busy taking notes, her carefully covered notebook splayed open on her lap, words tumbling out of the margins.

"Nothing, it's the school's only idea of a field trip," says Ujita, not even glancing at Iyena. "I wish they would just once take us on a trek. I wouldn't even mind the Temple of Eborsen. Anything but the creek."

Iyena looks at Tevair Ahinya. He stands still but his body seems to be on the precipice of bursting with excitement, his hands poised to clap at any moment. The creek might just be his way out of an uncomfortable situation at home. Maybe an argument with his wife he wants to avoid at all costs. Maybe an awkward dinner with a relative. Iyena will never know.

"Come, students, we will learn and have fun, both!" Tevair Ahinya throws his hands in the air. Iyena gets off the ground, dusting away mud and grass that clings to her uniform. She looks around – no one seems to be in any hurry. The day continues to be uneventful.

But even the dullest of days find ways to turn around.

★   ★   ★

The Sirvassan main road tapers then runs west, where it meets the ruins of an old picturehouse – a brutalist construction that once housed old wonders and entertained Sirvassans. Past the picturehouse runs a trail canopied by tall conifers, littered with smooth pebbles, entrails of rodents, and forgotten leather shoes. The Rhisuan beast, despite its imposing appearance, cowers in front of the trail, which disappears deep into the woods. A faint rush of the creek follows the sound of a fell-bird singing. The school carriage thunders as the students climb down onto the moss-covered ground. The professor is the last to disembark. The Rhisuan beast makes a satisfied grunt, then deflates, kneeling down to rest. Iyena lets out a muffled shriek upon the sight of the bloated beast becoming wrinkly and paper-thin in a matter of seconds.

"It's an aged Rhisuan," says Ahinya, noticing Iyena's utter shock. "Normally, you won't even notice the transition."

"I wish I never have to see this sight again," says Ujita, flinging her backpack over her shoulders.

"I think it's magical," says Iyena, after the initial shock abates. It has only been a few days since Iyena arrived in Sirvassa, and she's already seen the kind of magic her mother sang to her about when she was merely a toddler. She remembers those songs and stories vividly and now Sirvassa, the city her father never cared much for, is giving her all these delights.

"Typical tourists," says Trehan.

"Come, now, the creek awaits us, students. I'll tell you the tale of the Carpenter's Golden Axe."

Tevair Ahinya starts walking toward the trail. The class follows him reluctantly. Iyena sees shrugging, hears exasperated sighs, and senses a general frustration as she walks, matching steps with the teacher. Perhaps all those feelings will come to her in due time – now she only feels elation and wonder. The world is both old and new, both alien and welcoming, and she wants to see all of it.

The trail soon disappears as forest cover thickens and the afternoon shade gives way to a general, enveloping darkness. The forest bed crunches beneath Iyena's feet. The rush of the creek becomes louder, and the singing of the fell-bird becomes more erratic.

Soon, sunlight filters through a gap in the trees, splashing on the wet, grassy earth. Ahinya hurries his steps, and so does Iyena. The others continue their sluggish crawl, as if they were wet sacks of grain being lugged forward by an excruciatingly slow vehicle.

Tevair Ahinya runs like a child toward an old, gnarly tree whose many branches hang limply over the creek's waters. "This is that tree, the tree you hear about in stories. The carpenter Mughba was cutting that branch when his axe fell in the water. He prayed to the goddess of the river and the goddess presented him with a silver axe. Mughba was an honest man, and so he refused it."

Trehan casually struts toward the tree, whistling. He glances at the branch Ahinya is pointing at, then jams his foot near the base of the tree. A part of the thin branch shivers, leaves flopping about with abandon, weaker twigs breaking off and falling into the waters below.

"...he refused to take the golden axe too. The goddess was impressed!" Tevair Ahinya claps his hands at his virtuoso narration of the story, ignoring Trehan completely. Iyena, however, watches the sight unfold like a dark dream as Trehan starts climbing the tree. Iyena's eyes follow Trehan's easy, athletic movements as he ascends, his lithe frame moving inexorably toward the golden fruits hanging from the upper branches of the tree.

"The sangba fruit is the sweetest this time of the year," says Ujita. "Trehan, bring a couple for us too."

"Come and get your own," Trehan yells from above. He yanks the fruit off the branch, shows it to his friends below, like a grand prize he has claimed, then takes a bite. Juice oozes out of the round fruit and smears his chin. He wipes the juice off and continues gorging on the fruit.

Then, his hands go limp and fall to his sides. His head lolls to his left, and white foam bubbles out of the corner of his mouth. His body convulses, then goes stiff. But the momentum carries and he plunges, until a second, lower branch breaks his inevitable fall. He remains still on the branch like a sari on a clothesline.

Iyena's cry remains in her throat, but the sound comes from her left. The girl who had asked Trehan to make the gauntlet is screaming. So are the other students, horror writ on their faces. Tevair Ahinya's stout frame is suddenly active as he tries to climb the tree, his old muscles striving to go into fourth gear.

In that moment, Iyena's hands inadvertently reach inside her bag. Her fingers caress the smooth surface of the vial. She knows she will have to go back to the Garden another time. The vial she has contains only a Priming Delight. It won't work on its own, at least that's what the Caretaker said.

Trehan's face goes pallid, and then gradually begins taking on the blue of the sky, almost transparent. He looks like a ghost from where Iyena is standing.

Something dark takes hold of Iyena as her hands move of their own volition. She takes out the vial and gulps its contents down.

"Help me!" Ahinya screams from above, as he crawls along the branch that holds Trehan. Trehan's black-haired friend, whose face has gone pale from fear, runs toward the tree, and stands below the branch, poised to catch his friend.

"No, idiot, you'll get crushed by his weight!"

And then Iyena sees Ujita and Kahina running toward the tree, holding a piece of fabric between them. They somehow managed to go to the carriage, yank the tarp off it, and bring it back in a matter of seconds. Iyena dashes toward them to help.

And soon all the students gather near the base of the tree as if pushed into a trance, holding the tarp taut and ready to catch a falling body. Ahinya pries Trehan's unconscious body off the branch. It falls heavily on the tarp, like a dead boulder, but manages not to tumble and fall on the hard ground, instead almost sinking slowly into the cloth, even as the students maintain their grip, their faces red from effort.

"He has to be taken to a Healer, fast!" screams Tevair Ahinya. "Trehan, can you hear me? Please respond!"

Trehan still doesn't move. His face is devoid of all color

But Iyena sees something else. She sees the blood rushing through Trehan's arteries and inside them, a blackness persisting, ever growing. The blackness, the poison, is in a race with the red of the blood and threatens to overcome it, blot it out completely.

And Iyena can reach it. The Delight cruising inside her tells her that much. Iyena knows this isn't supposed to happen, not until another visit to the Garden. But she can hear Trehan's heart thump, slowly, with thickening blood. She knows its true nature. She can hear the flow of the blackness. She knows its nature too.

She can touch it. And she can change it.

All she has to do is to change black to red. Make blood out of a poison. Give life to a thing carrying death. It is as simple as turning a page, as simple as breathing, walking, all those other things which come naturally to people.

She touches Trehan's cheek and does what she knows will work.

And the blackness abates. It dissolves, mixing with the red, deepens into crimson, like a rose. Color flushes back into Trehan's face, his neck, his arms. The group of students gives out a collective sigh. Iyena staggers back on the ground, her eyes fixed on Trehan's face, her heart full of terror and wonder.

CHAPTER EIGHT

The Caretaker

Once again, at night, the Caretaker painstakingly prepares the same potion. His bones ache, as if his entire marrow had been hollowed out. His muscles knot and twist, his eyes flare up, as he snips the Daisy and the Dahlia crudely, this time rebalancing their presence, a drop of the former, a gulp of the latter. He heats the potion and then immediately lets it cool down, in hopes of getting a better consistency. The potion bubbles, and takes the color of honey first, then the color of tar.

From a distance, it all looks like a mad charade of a man plagued by a curse. But the Caretaker doesn't want to observe himself from a distance. Because that would mean acceptance of his folly, acceptance of his fate. Before he succumbs entirely to his fate, he wants to exhaust all options.

The color of tar tells him he has come to the end of his charade. A heavy weariness dawns upon him. The Caretaker vows to never make the potion again. No concoction would bring his youth back. No potion would undo the curse.

To undo the curse of a goddess, he would have to talk to another god.

★   ★   ★

"The Night of the Unending Stars comes once every five hundred years," says the priestess, tilting her head to the right, as if making sure the Caretaker has thought this charade through. "You could be patient and see the words of Ina unfold into truth or lie. Then make judgments on the nature of prophecies."

The Caretaker doesn't respond immediately. Years of conversation with the Priestess of the Temple of Eborsen had taught him this simple fact — choose your words with patience. He lets the silence between them build, until it is broken by the priestess.

"I remember when you first came to the steps of this temple," she continues wistfully. It is out of character for her, and it heightens the Caretaker's instincts. He listens carefully. "Your shawl was ragged, your eyes were too distant. This temple takes the weakest and gives them hope. Your predicament was unusual. It's not every day an individual gets cursed by a powerful goddess."

"I have done good for myself, won't you agree?" the Caretaker says simply, without an ounce of pride. His voice is soft. The priestess smiles, but her expression quickly fades into stoicism. As if she is a creature of compulsion. As if the sanctum of the temple has stopped her from showing levity.

"The Half-Formed God doesn't grant wishes," she says. "You of all people should know that."

"I am not asking for a wish. I am asking for a boon. A curse can only be undone by a boon."

"I am aware. Tell me what have you done to deserve a boon?"

"They call me the Protector of Sirvassa," says the Caretaker. He doesn't like the shape of his words, the tenor of his speech. Desperation trickles down his lips like water from a leaky faucet. He takes a deep breath and straightens himself. "One would think protecting a holy city from an adamant beast that keeps returning would count for something."

"Pride has undone many men in the past. You aren't much different. Protecting this city…it was your duty as a citizen. Which makes me think. You haven't exactly *protected* anyone from anything. The beast still returns. Your magical meshwork only makes it angrier and it keeps coming back. Do you have it in you to really stop it? Do you have it in you to really change the nature of things? Do you even know why it keeps coming back?"

"You think I haven't tried? It's a regenerating beast, and it has to be kept at bay. I spent days near its cave, looking for ways to capture it and slay it. But it eluded me. That was when I constructed the jalan. So even if it keeps coming back, it won't harm any citizen."

The Caretaker says all those words simply to mask something he couldn't say: the true reason why the beast keeps returning. Saying it would be futile, and counterproductive. He knew this simple fact the day the beast first turned up, terrorizing the Sirvassans, sending them screaming inside their houses. The beast had in fact flown straight toward the Temple of Eborsen, ignoring the townspeople. The beast didn't want anything to do with the people. The beast wanted to desecrate Eborsen's resting place. It was an age-old myth, which, after Eborsen had taken his eternal sleep, had become lore, a living reality. Everyone speaks about gods like they existed in an age long gone. Early Sirvassans had seen their god go into his slumber, after defeating the beast.

Except, the Half-Formed God had left a job half-done. He had defeated the beast on the Llar Mountains, but failed to capture him inside a prison on its rocky slopes. It was his pride that had led him to believe that he had saved the world.

And now, the Caretaker was left to clean up a shoddy act of a boastful god.

He stays silent. The priestess plays with the bangles on her wrists, absently. Her gaze shifts to the blackness on the Caretaker's arm. Her expression softens.

"The curse has taken a toll on you."

The Caretaker hides his arm under his cloak. "This is my own doing, I am afraid. My efforts have not been very fruitful."

"I can see that," says the priestess in a motherly voice. "I can sense your desperation. And you are right. A curse by a goddess can only be undone by a boon from another, more powerful god. And who better than Eborsen the Great? But the time of his rising is not yet ripe. Pardon me for my cruel words. I am not discounting your achievements. Your reputation does precede you. But a boon is a boon, and you must prove yourself even worthier than you think you are. Or else, wait for the Night of the Unending Stars."

It's a dismissal. The Caretaker knows better than to prod further. Even if what she had said was actually true, and if, by some odd twist of fate, the Caretaker actually managed what seems like an impossible feat, the priestess wouldn't want to disturb the nigh-eternal sleep of Eborsen. That is her only job, and all these words were just meant to act as a balm.

"I'll come again, then," says the Caretaker. He measures his words, and they come out of him heavy with regret. The priestess places her palm on his head. On a normal day, this act of blessing would comfort him. Not today.

★   ★   ★

When he returns, he finds Trulio meditating near the gates of his laboratory. Three stones levitate in the air around Trulio, as he murmurs whispery nothings under his breath. The stones do a complex dance of themselves, following an unusual pattern where the smallest – also the lightest – stone rotates in a helical arc around the two heavier ones, while the second heaviest stone itself rotates, albeit slowly, around the heaviest. It looks oddly like the motion of planetary bodies, but it escapes the Caretaker how Trulio managed to attain a levitation as complex as this one. Perhaps a relic from his travels, or he grossly underestimated his own assistant.

Trulio opens one eye, and the stones fall down. He slowly gathers them and puts them inside a pouch tied on his belt. Then, he approaches the Caretaker and touches his feet.

"I'm impressed and curious," says the Caretaker. "Which flower allowed you to do something like this?"

"Actually, this is not from any flower. In my travels, I went as far as Jehervan, a place where old magic is still alive and thriving. An old woman taught me this."

"Had you mentioned about the sap extracted from an Azalea stem, mixed with a finely powdered Geranium, diluted with a cup of water, boiled and then immediately cooled down to the temperature of blood, I would have given you the full charge of the Garden right away, and considered retirement," says the Caretaker, placing his hand on Trulio's shoulder, and then patting him lightly. "But that day is far away."

"That's a very odd way of saying you are impressed, Master," says Trulio.

"I am. It takes a lot of mental fortitude to meditate and levitate, both at the same time. It also shows you learned something of note in your travels."

"Thank you, Master. I live for words of praise which you shower on me, if only so sparingly."

Trulio smirks as he says the words. His eyes twinkle, and his face shows no lines when he smiles. It's the smile of youth. The Caretaker is suddenly filled with an intense yearning of a similar youth. All his sleepless nights poring over failed potions, his heart and mind working in unison with one common goal, to set the clock back to where it was. He is suddenly flooded with the sum total of all those desires, the ecstasy that comes with it, the passion, the sorrow, and the heartbreak.

But the emotion is fleeting. And it vanishes like smoke in thin air. He looks at his withering hand. Perhaps Trulio notices the sudden change in his expression, and he presses his own palm gently upon the Caretaker's hand.

"Master, would you like me to prepare tea for you?"

The Caretaker nods.

★　　★　　★

The Caretaker stirs his spoon, uncharacteristically noisily, the metal making eerie, grating noises against the ceramic of the teacup.

"What is on your mind, Master?"

The truth is right there, at the cusp of the chasm between memory and voice. All the Caretaker has to do is snatch it, and present it in all its naked glory. *Your Master, your Gurun, is a young man, hardly five years older than you. Your Gurun has been lying to you.* "If you don't want to share, it's fine," Trulio begins. "But I'll do what I do best. Tell you a story to put your mind at ease."

"Write it down, I'll read it. You don't need to—"

"I insist."

The Caretaker knits his brows. Trulio looks at him almost apologetically. He has never interrupted the Caretaker, and this is a first. The Caretaker urges Trulio to continue with a slight wave of his hand.

"What I meant to say is…telling a story is always better than writing it down," Trulio says. "Eyes are deceptive receivers, and look for hidden clues while reading. They might betray you. Ears, on the other hand, take the story as it is, without judgment."

"Wiser words have never been spoken," says the Caretaker. "I am all ears."

Trulio clears his throat. Then, with a gentle pause and a theatrical flair of someone who has spent countless years of his life telling stories by a fire, he begins. "There was once a far-off planet named Morhan, in a galaxy called Undula-Four-One. The most prosperous of all planets, it was the center of industrial excellence, and manufactured vehicles that could travel space at the speed of thought. The secret fuel behind those vehicles was precious gemstones that were excavated from the poisonous mines overseen by an ant-god."

"Ant-god?"

"Ant-god. Black, vaporous even, multiple-limbed, taller than six buildings. An entire religion, named Shruism, worshipped the many alleged forms of the ant-god. Devotees would flock to the mines to have a look at the gems. When a religious sect called Sen-Shruis got wind of Morhan's secret, they declared an all-out war and captured the woman who led the Morhan government."

The Caretaker shifts uneasily. He has listened to stories like this before. But having similar words pour out of Trulio's mouth while his imagination lives perennially in a state of fantasy feels refreshing to him. Calming. He finishes his tea and sets it aside. Then, he folds his knees and hugs them, resting his chin atop his knees, and listens to the rest of the tale like a little child. Trulio continues, animatedly, moving his hands, raising his voice for effect when a moment requires it, slowing down his tenor to exacerbate drama. If Trulio weren't working under the Caretaker, he would be a thespian.

"...a warrior rose, a renegade war general who was shamed and put into an intergalactic prison. She made a deal with Morhan, in exchange for immunity, and went on to defeat the armies of Sen-Shruis. But it all came at a great cost. She lost everything she lived for, including her own sanity."

The Caretaker takes a deep breath. He leans back against the wall, straightening his legs. His joints ache, and his muscles scream.

"Thank you, Trulio, for this wonderful tale of adventure and heartbreak. Next time, perhaps, something lighter would do."

"As you wish, Master."

Trulio gathers the teacups and leaves. The Caretaker lies down, hoping for the ache in his bones to recede.

★   ★   ★

A half moon splashes sparse light on the floor of his room. In the distance, fell-birds sing their midnight lament. The temple bells clang twice and stop, while their metallic echoes provide a counterpoint to the hymn of the fell-birds. Somewhere, a Sirvassan citizen, lonely, with a cup of madira in his hands, goes up to the roof of his house, and weeps. All these sounds envelop the sound of his heartbeat ringing in his ears. Slow, arrhythmic beats of old age, giving way to a steadier, more youthful sound.

An hour past midnight, the Caretaker's conversion is complete. He looks at his hands, his feet, and feels an energy like he hasn't before. Knowing it will only last for three or four hours, he makes a decision. Sleep evades him today. He gets up and goes outside the premises of the Garden for a nighttime stroll for the first time in many years.

Outside, the Sirvassan road is slick, black, and clean. The air is crisp and cool and feels good on his young skin. He takes a deep breath, and his lungs feel fuller than ever before. A gust of wind whips his hair. He makes a tight fist, and limbers himself.

Then, he runs.

He runs past the lesser market area, then the first residential complex, small, close-knit two-story buildings that house multiple families. The road snakes ahead and forks into two other roads, one leading toward the main Sirvassan market square, and the other toward the larger residential complex. He takes the one to the square, allowing his feet to take control of his body. He hasn't run like this in a long time. His heart feels light.

At this time of the night, there's nary a person on the streets. Ordinary, hardworking Sirvassans go to bed at a respectable hour. One or two night lamps, though, are visible. Writers, poets, thinkers, or plain insomniacs.

Farther ahead, the wide road tapers off. He can see the shadow of the Llar Mountains to his left. He smells a faint, salty whiff of the sea to his right. He doesn't know how far his legs would carry him, or how far he should go before turning back. He crosses a narrow road flanked on both sides by box-upon-box apartments, lower income households hastily constructed during the last elections. Now they stand empty and house families of mold and rust.

The narrow road leads to an alley that opens near the docks. The smell is stronger here, mixed with offal and fish, wet rope and wood. He stops and lets the air hit him. The rush is its own Delight, which no flower, no potion could ever give him.

He feels a tug on his elbow. Like a post-run cramp, but stronger. Before he can fully realize it, he is yanked to his left, and a shadow is upon him. He kicks, and there's a howl, which is muffled immediately, as if his assaulter doesn't want his voice to be known. Strong arms grab his neck and push him farther into the darkness of the alley.

Then, there's a light upon him. The Caretaker sees the masked faces of his two attackers. One is tall, and built like a boulder. The other is relatively short, almost puny, but built similarly.

"Did he see you?" It's the voice of the one he kicked. It's a pained whisper, and the Caretaker recognizes it. The other person grunts in denial.

"Are you the Sirvassan police?"

"What are you doing here in the middle of the night?"

The Caretaker heaves, and then spits on the ground. "I was running."

"Running?"

"Yes. Getting some of that fresh night air in my lungs, that's all."

"What are early mornings for?"

"I am not a morning person," says the Caretaker. "I won't be a bother to you people, just let me go." He reaches inside himself for traces of any remaining Delights. Summoning could work in such a situation, but the place he is in doesn't have any weapon-like object that could be used. All other Delights he consumed in the past seven days have mixed with his blood and been rejected by his body long ago as waste. No, he will have to deal with this situation the old-fashioned way.

"What did he see?" Both voices now devolve into mere whispers. But the Caretaker can still hear them.

"Nothing. He's right, he was only running. We could actually let him go."

"I don't think so."

The Caretaker's eyes land on a heavy object resting by a wall. The light isn't enough to make out its shape. He squints to see clearly, but when nothing is visible, he uses a bit of his summoning to move the object closer to him. The air is filled with a dull groan of wood against wood, and a hard screech of metal. The Caretaker lets go and the object stops.

"What was that sound?"

"You go outside and check. I'll stand guard to him."

One man leaves, while the other fixes his gaze upon the Caretaker.

"Look, it's not like thievery doesn't happen in Sirvassa," says the Caretaker. "I know. I have been where you are."

"Really?"

"I was a thief once. I have given up that life."

The masked man comes near the Caretaker and places one of his legs upon his knees. Then, he presses upon it, hard, bringing the weight of his body. The breath is knocked out of the Caretaker's lungs as he winces in pain.

"There's one thing you must understand. We are not thieves; we are not criminals. We are what will bring this city some sort of justice."

"Are you the Corrilean Army? They have been trying to get their demands met the last two years. I know someone who knows the mayor. I can help you."

The man, for a split second, exposes his lips by removing his mask, but only to spit on the floor. "Mayor Jaywardna, that pest, that blot on the face of this land."

"So you *are* the Corrilean."

"Stop talking!" says the man, a hint of impatience in his voice.

His partner returns, grumbling to himself.

"What happened? Who was it?"

"Probably a rat," says the man who has returned, scratching his chin.

"Such a big rat?"

"I don't know, why don't you go and check it yourself?"

"Come here, we need to talk."

The two men retreat into the shadows, but the Caretaker can make out their sharp words and broken whispers. He steals a glance at the box he pulled toward himself. It's an odd-looking chest, not rectangular, but oval in shape. It contains no lock, no hinge, but rather a leaflike protrusion along its length. A lever?

Something to hold, and perhaps twist? For what purpose? To reveal what?

After a while, the whispers stop. A tense silence follows. The Caretaker realizes they have still not gagged or bound him. Which could mean two things – either they are plain incompetent thugs, or whatever they are doing is so much bigger in the large scheme of things, that one person knowing doesn't matter. He is inclined to put his money on the latter.

Voices, again. The Caretaker strains his ears to listen.

"What do we do about him?"

"Wipe his memory and dump him on the streets."

Coldness slithers through the Caretaker's skin. The two men come out of the shadows. The taller man reaches toward him. The Caretaker can make out the incantation he is muttering under his breath. The words are old Alderran, used by Abhadi priests. Shaky, broken images of a war from long ago plague his mind again. He was right. These aren't petty thugs.

He can feel the pull of his words, and under his skin, the levers of his mind start turning backward.

He thinks hard and fast. Had it not been for his curse, he would be a withered old man right now. The summoning wouldn't have worked as beautifully as it did. He almost smiles to himself even as bits and pieces of his memory, of the place he was in, of the night run, of the dockside, and of the two assaulters, threaten to vanish in a brain-haze. The man is going through the removal with surgical precision.

The Caretaker's mind rebels. It pushes back against the lie it is shown. The words grip his memory, shake it, but memory finds a way back. And in doing so, his mind does something else.

From deep and dark recesses, it retrieves another Delight. Droplets of a potion the Caretaker had taken to relieve himself of some pain. It had elements of the Lily of the Seven.

Levitation.

It takes every ounce of his being to retrieve and combine the two

Delights. First, he kicks at the feet of the taller attacker, interrupting his incantation, and pulls himself to his feet. Then, he clenches his fist, and the oval chest flies toward the man, hitting him on his shoulder. There's a sound of a sickening crunch, wood against bone, and then a pained scream, visceral.

The shorter man barely has time to react. "What are you?" he whispers.

The Caretaker pushes him aside and runs out from the shadows, into the rapidly darkening Sirvassan streets.

★   ★   ★

Morning brings a smoke-cloud of forgetfulness. The events of the night before are like words etched in sand, slowly losing their meaning to the sea. But his body remembers the effort and the fatigue, and fills the gaps that the mind can't. The spell that was cast on him was strong, but not strong enough.

He is sure of one thing. The men were planning something big. And before he forgets everything about last night, he will have to revisit last night. He doesn't want to, but for the sake and safety of Sirvassa, he will have to really make use of the ever-dormant Fifth Sector of the Garden.

He glances at his right hand. The blackness has returned, and with it, the meshwork of old age. Inside, he can feel his organs stiffening. He moves out of his room with laborious movements that ease slowly and steadily. For a span of two minutes, he feels out of his body, somehow both absent and present. The feeling passes as he reaches the doors of the Garden. There, he sees the sandy-haired boy chatting animatedly with Trulio, who has his palm on the stone door of the Garden. The boy looks at the Caretaker and smiles. Then he brings out a parchment from the pocket of his trousers and hands it to the Caretaker.

"Duly signed by my mother," he says. "Two months have elapsed since my last Delight. I am ready for another."

"We were just talking about the lovely weather," says Trulio. "Had a good night's sleep, Master?"

"Fitful," says the Caretaker. "But good enough for an old man." He pores over the permission letter signed by the boy's mother, the Lockmaker, especially the words *"...any age-appropriate Delight the boy wishes for..."* He folds the letter in two halves and gives it back to the boy.

"Your last Delight, boy, how was it?"

"I loved it. Made Tevair Amaram's pencil disappear at one place and had it reappear in the other. Then I impressed my...."

The Caretaker eyes the boy. The boy evades his sharp gaze and hangs his head. His ears go red. Digging his toes on the ground, he says slowly, "Just a bit of fun, that's all. Nothing major. I followed whatever you said."

"All Delights are for 'just a bit of fun'," says the Caretaker. "You can't go overboard, even if you wanted to. They are designed that way."

The boy looks up and his face cracks into a bright smile. The Caretaker looks at his apprentice. "Trulio, you were attempting to open the door," he says. "Please recreate the pattern so I can see."

Trulio does as he is asked. He taps on the cold stone twice, one with the index finger, then gently with the middle finger. Then, he presses firmly at the center, rotates his palm in a circular motion, and waits. The door doesn't respond. Trulio's face goes red with embarrassment. He steps aside. The Caretaker arches his eyebrows at his apprentice, then does the same motions as him, except his fingers are nimble, and gentler than Trulio's. The door slides open.

"It's all in the intent," says the Caretaker. "When you tried, you were more concerned with impressing me than opening the door. When you want the door to open, it opens." He observes the boy as he speaks the last sentence. His eyes alight with all kinds of wonder, even though he has seen the door and the Garden twice before.

They enter the Garden. The First Sector is pristine, with most of its charm spearheaded by the Bacillus Rose. The boy moves toward the flower, but the Caretaker makes a sound, and he stops in his tracks.

"Trulio, please help Trehan with a Delight that is new for him but also age-appropriate. Maybe the Second Sector will help you find something. I am trusting you with this, okay?"

"Thank you, Master," says Trulio. "I will not disappoint."

"I know you won't. I have some business in the Fifth Sector. When I am back, meet me at the laboratory."

"The Fifth Sector, Master? But that could—"

"For now, do what you are told. Help our customer. Don't keep him waiting."

Trulio gets the hint. "Come, boy, let's see what we can help you with. What do you want, levitation…. No, I think not. Something more original."

★ ★ ★

It's a long walk to the Fifth Sector, which is a smaller, and much more intimate, space. The air here is quiet, but every now and then there's a rustle. Surrounded by black granite walls and vines, the Fifth Sector consists of two small, circular ponds next to each other. Right at the center of each of the ponds is a Lotus flower, one pink, one white. The water surrounding the white Lotus is murky, with algae blooming around, white and black blobs of nothingness popping and bursting at irregular intervals. The water surrounding the pink Lotus is so clean the Caretaker can see his reflection, wrinkles and all. He stops to look at it, before tearing his gaze away and moving toward the white Lotus.

He takes a deep breath and carefully snips one, only one, petal off the Lotus. Another petal regrows to take the broken one's place. Then, without giving the matter any further thought, he eats the petal.

His senses are immediately flooded by images from the night before. He is plunged body first into a time-tsunami. Before he can react, he is facing his own self from the previous day, listening intently to Trulio's wild tale of another planet. His body is beside the pond, while his mind can see everything he has already experienced.

He looks at himself, transforming into the young man he was the night before. He watches himself tiptoe out of the Garden compound, stealing glances in the dark. He sees himself breathing in the night air and breaking into a run.

He follows himself to the inky blackness of the docks. He can almost smell the salt in the air. The alley looks dingier. The narrow lane that opened straight to the docks, where seawater would often rush in during high tide, is filled with decaying waste that no one has bothered cleaning up in days. He hadn't felt the stench the night before, but he can now feel his nostrils twinge a little bit.

He also sees something else. The strike of a match in the dark, illuminating a face. Scarred, twice, on one side, thin lips, short pudgy nose, gray eyes. His partner, tall, swollen lips – probably from a fight somewhere – and deep brown eyes. They are talking.

The water in the Lotus pond doesn't feel like water at all. Instead, it feels like murky nothingness. Much like the past itself. The Caretaker lowers himself into the pond gently. He feels no wetness. As his head goes beneath the surface of the water, he arrives near the docks, a safe distance away from the two men. The Caretaker feels the incessant pull of the time-pond, the ripples urging him to go back, to not infringe on the sanctity of the past so much that it's irrevocable. That the present and future become a nuisance.

He knows. He isn't here to change anything. He is here to observe.

"...swear on the rotten corpse of the Half-Formed God, I'm only in it because I want my son to study among the best. That's all. For me, it's just in and out."

"Noble intentions," says the other man, the one who lit the match, the one with the two scars. "Wouldn't have taken you for a family man."

"It's my face," says the tall one. "It's always been my face."

"Mine is worse."

The man with the scar grins, revealing stained and chipped teeth.

"You talk about being a family man," he continues. "Our boss, the one who wants us to do it, is a family man too. At least, that's what I've heard. He's high in the Alderran Ministry, probably the highest. Below the minister, that is."

"He has a daughter too."

"But have you wondered? Why the *Kkirinth*, of all ships? Isn't that Alderran? I mean, if you want to get at the Sirvassan—"

A commotion. A figure entering the alley. The Caretaker, in his prime. The two men, alert, extinguish the cigarettes, put on their masks, and follow the Caretaker to the end of the alley.

He sees himself getting ambushed. He sees himself getting pulled into the shadows. Even the present-him feels the tightness of the grip on his arm. A phantom grip from the past. It is the way of the pond. It makes him feel every nudge, hear every whisper, see every shadow.

He moves toward the area where the past-him got captured. He can hear muffled voices only now. Bewilderment. The two men speak in hushed tones about the fate of their plan, deciding whether to capture him or let him go.

"We could actually just let him go," says one of the men, the one who wanted a good future for his son. The second time around, his voice sounds earnest and kind. A part of that man truly believes that letting an eavesdropper go wouldn't harm their plans in any manner whatsoever. This is the kind of man who spoils plans. This is the kind of man who isn't sure of them in the first place. He is put into this position out of desperation.

The Caretaker moves closer into the shadows to get a glimpse of the surroundings. But suddenly, his body is pulled back in a rush, and his head feels light.

The Lotus pool. His time is up.

The Caretaker tries to grab a pole, but scrapes his leg against it, such is the momentum of the pool. Like a helpless leaf in a storm, his entire body trembles. His arm hits a load of empty wooden crates that come crashing down on the cobblestoned ground.

"Did you hear that?"

The Caretaker is thrust ceaselessly away from the shadowy alley, back into the small, murky Lotus puddle. He emerges out of the pond, from the dark openness of the past, into the bright, claustrophobic confines of his present, heaving and panting, remembering the face of the scarred man who had come out of the dark room to see if the crash was caused by a rat.

★   ★   ★

The sandy-haired boy has left by the time he comes out into the First Sector. Trulio is waiting for him, head tilted sideways, palms clasped together. He has an inscrutable expression on his face, but the Caretaker knows his apprentice too well. He knows the words that will come out of his mouth next. He was never one to mince words.

"How hypocritical of you, Master."

"Please, Trulio," says the Caretaker, as if preparing his statement. "We have far more important things to discuss."

"You forbade me to ever set foot in the Fifth Sector. You told me that it was out of bounds even for *you*."

"What Delight did you give to the boy?"

"Something something transformation something. But that's not the point. The point is that you *lied* to me."

The Caretaker grabs Trulio's arm and ushers him outside the Garden. The stone door closes as soon as the Caretaker steps outside.

"I have troubling news, Trulio. I want your help, and you need to trust me."

Trulio shrugs off the Caretaker's grip. He scowls, and his lips quiver, as if he is about to say something he will regret later on.

"Trust flew out of the window when you entered the Fifth Sector. There is something you are not telling me."

"Sometimes I can't tell if you are being serious or overdramatic," says the Caretaker. Trulio stares at him for a long time. The Caretaker has lied for Trulio's benefit a hundred times before, and he will continue to do so. You often lie to the people you are close to. To protect them from the truth. The Caretaker knows the truth of the Fifth Sector and it's something Trulio isn't mature enough to grasp. The pool is not for the faint-hearted.

"Okay, what is it I need to do?"

The Caretaker tells his apprentice about his ill-fated adventure in the night and his brush with the men at the docks.

"But Master, why would you go so far out of the city in the middle of the night? It's not good for your knees."

"I was feeling rather youthful during the night," says the Caretaker, telling the truth while telling nothing at all.

"These men you talk about...did they look like Sirvassan men? Or did they belong to a different state?"

"The lilt in their speech, their long, drawn-out syllables, sounded Sirvassan. At least one of them was born and brought up right here in the city."

"They could just be petty thieves, for all you know."

"Petty thieves don't aspire to a better life," says the Caretaker. "Petty thieves just aspire to more thievery."

"Fair point," says Trulio. "I'll visit the docks and try to find out what's going on."

"Thank you, Trulio."

Trulio leaves. The Caretaker stands on the cold, hard ground for a while, watching his apprentice go toward his lodging.

CHAPTER NINE

Iyena Mastafar

The late afternoon Sirvassan sky is pink and a mild chill persists in the air. Far beyond, the Alevian mountain range hangs like a white ghost against a clear sky.

The school carriage stops near Trehan's house. The Rhisuan beast pulling the carriage looks like a bloated raisin, cutting a tired figure. The skin around its eyes is gnarled and its belly blooms impossibly to sweep the ground as it moves. The beast groans, and tremors course through its body. Iyena puts a hand on the back of the beast, and it calms a bit.

Trehan steps out of the vehicle, still harried, still slightly pale, but very much alive.

"My child, what's happened to my child?" Trehan's mother rushes to the carriage, her hair in disarray.

"He ate a fruit yet to ripen," says Tevair Ahinya. "If it weren't for the quick thinking of his friend Iyena...." He stops, unable to complete the sentence. Trehan's mother reaches for Iyena's hand and takes it in hers.

"Thank you," she says. "Please, come inside. I have made some Enjing tea."

Before Iyena can respond, the air rankles with a sound of metal on metal, joined by a melancholy din, which rises until it reaches a crescendo. To Iyena's ears, it feels like a balloon bursting with glitter would feel to the eyes. The Rhisuan beast grunts and looks toward the sound. And soon, it shifts its entire frame toward the east, gripped in a trance by the sound.

"The afternoon prayers have begun," says Tevair Ahinya. "I live nearby, and my wife will be waiting, so the tea will have to wait for some other time. Iyena, why don't you socialize a bit? When the prayers are done, the beast will be here. Take it to your house. Once you reach there, tap it twice on the front knees and say the word *ehvass* in its ear. It will go straight to school."

Iyena nods.

★ ★ ★

Iyena sips the Enjing tea quietly, savoring its spicy-sweet taste, a hint of nutmeg and cloves, and herbs she can't place. Her father has never let her taste any beverage except milk and the occasional honey-lemonade, which he takes when he has a headache. Her body pains after the misadventure at the creek, and the tea relaxes her.

The room she is in reminds her of her grandmother's place back in Alderra, except this one has more things in it. A wall adorned entirely with locks: big, iron locks fit for a jail cell, hanging by nails, small thumb-sized locks that shine like pebbles, round brass locks for treasure chests, copper locks for homes. There's an oblong silver lock, with wings sprouting out of either side, and a golden lock with the face of a beast.

She can't see any keys.

Trehan's mother sits on the sofa in front of her, stirring her tea with an aluminum spoon.

"Trehan has mentioned you," she says. "The first day, he wouldn't stop talking about you."

"Really?" Iyena wasn't expecting such a revelation. Trehan seemed so detached in school. She could count on her fingers how many words he has spoken to her the entire time she has been in Sirvassa.

"Were you born in Alderra?"

"I was actually born in a small town called Imisu. It is by the Mahwa Sea. Since my father's work takes him from place to place...

we never lived in one city for long. But my longest stay was in Alderra, the capital city. Six years, because it's essentially my father's place of business."

"We have been in Sirvassa our whole lives."

Iyena takes a sip of her tea and finds herself unable to make any further conversation. She's much more interested in finding out what happened to her at the creek. The Caretaker had told her about the Priming Delight, how it wouldn't have any effect on her until she went a second time...and yet.... If she can find a way to visit the Garden once again, she'll know the answer to her questions.

"What do you think of the Garden?"

Trehan's mother stops stirring her tea and furrows her brow. Then, her expression softens, hiding her first, natural instinct.

"It's been here longer than we've been here," she says.

"Have you ever..." begins Iyena, then stops, not knowing how to complete the sentence.

"No, I believe that a person should spend their days using the abilities they were born with. The gifts God Eborsen has given to us are more than enough and we shouldn't taint our bodies further."

"It was due to the Garden that your son's life was saved today," says Iyena, shrugging. "The tea is excellent."

"Thank you," says Trehan's mother. "You like the locks on the wall? I noticed you were admiring them."

"Yes, they're beautiful."

"A part of my occupation. Sirvassans know me as the Lockmaker. Some of them open by keys, yet some are stubborn." .

"What do you mean?"

"Some don't require any kind of key to open them. They open and close of their own volition."

"Yours must be a demanding job."

"It comes with its benefits," says the woman. "Iyena, I am in your debt and I can't think of ways to thank you." Her voice is saccharine-sweet and silk-smooth.

"Please think nothing of it." Iyena's impatience grows. Outside, the temple bells have stopped ringing. The Rhisuan beast will be shifting its weight from one log-like limb to the other, anticipating the end of day so it can rest properly. Iyena's father will have reached home, and Maani-Ba must be worried sick by now. But most importantly, Iyena needs space of her own to think.

"A new city can be difficult at first. Settling in, making friends, adapting to the culture…. Consider me your friend, Iyena. And come to me if you need any kind of help. And I do mean *any kind*," she says, stressing the last two words.

"I will remember your words, thank you," says Iyena.

"Too bad Trehan isn't awake to give his thanks to you," says the woman. "But I will make sure he knows you were here." She stands and takes the tea from Iyena's hands. Iyena gets up and straightens her uniform. Her gaze falls again on the wall full of locks. A question tumbles out of her mouth, tinged with the curiosity of a child.

"Is there a key that would open any lock?"

"Yes, there exists one such key," says Trehan's mother.

"Hypothetically, would that key be able to open the locks that you spoke about earlier?"

Trehan's mother leans closer to Iyena and narrows her gaze. "It all depends on what the lock is hiding."

★   ★   ★

A wisp of gray smoke comes out of Anaris's pipe and curls upward, fading away in the chill evening air. His feet tap the pavement, his eyes glued to the awning of the shop in front of him. He chews the insides of his mouth, tobacco bitterness suffused with the un-taste of skin. He doesn't make small conversation with Sirvassan strangers. He waits.

Even before the carriage reaches the doorstep, Iyena can see this scene unfolding. The impatient yet elegant way of her father, waiting. She has made him wait countless times before, and has been at the receiving end of the quiet rage that comes after.

When the carriage stops near Iyena's house, Anaris takes a cursory glance at the Rhisuan beast, then turns around and enters the house. Iyena disembarks, whispers in the beast's ear the words the professor had told her to, and pats it twice. The beast grunts, then hobbles along the busy Sirvassan road.

Iyena follows her father inside.

The house smells of tobacco smoke and rose incense, the latter meant to ward off the former. Iyena walks along the hallway, straight to her room, without as much as glancing toward her father's study. Out of the corner of her eye, she sees Anaris leaning against the heavy oak table, probably gazing at the automaton. Ignoring the sight, she keeps walking.

"Iyena."

She ceases in her tracks. Turning around, expecting the full ire of her father to fall on her, she peeks inside Anaris's study.

"Yes, Father."

"Please come inside."

The study feels familiar yet alien. As if the walls themselves are bloated with her secret, but something else has given it away. The hanging moon lamp fills the room with a suffused glow even as the light from the sun lamp withers away, mimicking the outside sky.

"I have some people from work coming over tomorrow in the morning. They'll stay for both lunch and dinner."

"Okay, Father."

"These are important dignitaries from Alderra. We have some very important business to attend to."

Iyena nods along.

"I expect you to be at your best self when they're here."

"I…." She hesitates, but gathers herself. "I will be at school most of the time. So you won't have any problems."

"About that, yes." Anaris chews on his words, allowing the deliberate pause to linger in the air. "I advise you to take an indefinite leave from school. I need your help."

"Indefinite leave? I don't understand, Father."

"Despite my misgivings, I sent you to that school in hopes that you'd gain knowledge, and in turn, bring me that knowledge, so I could arrange for a better future for *both* of us. But now I have decided that your sharpness and wit will be best utilized in my various projects. I am assuming forging signatures is only *one* of your many talents."

Iyena trembles. She can taste metal on her tongue and a dizzying sensation grips her. She steadies herself soon and looks at her father's face, which does not show even a modicum of emotion.

"You will tell me all about this Garden you visited despite my clear instructions otherwise."

His words are ice, but Iyena still holds her own. "Father, the Garden is beautiful and harmless."

"I am sure it is beautiful," says Anaris. "I have heard rumors that its Caretaker, who doesn't go by any other name, which is suspicious in itself, is one of the Inishti."

Iyena has heard of the Inishti, a powerful tribe of magicians in the past who were banished from Alderra to roam forever in the wilderness, landless, homeless. In all those stories the Inishti are shown as a villainous, power-hungry, barbaric race of people, with black tongues and blacker souls.

Anaris comes and sits on the floor, taking Iyena's shoulders in a firm, fatherly grip.

"You know Abhadi don't mingle with Inishti," he says. Iyena has heard the same version of her father's sentence multiple times before, extolling the virtues of the Abhadi race. Abhadi won't touch the food prepared by a Wangian. Abhadi won't enter the home of a Songri. Abhadi and Alderran are one and the same, almost like kin. An Abhadi never remains in debt. Abhadi and Inishti haven't always seen eye to eye, but are two extreme sides of the same coin.

"Hold your head high as a proud Abhadi, my girl," Anaris says and walks back to his desk. "Even Gorn agrees."

Iyena's eyes dart toward the automaton. He stands lifeless but watchful as always. Iyena feels sure that when Gorn walks the world will end.

★　　★　　★

In bed, Iyena's fidgety mind goes to far-off places. It rests on the steps of the Temple of Eborsen, where she finds herself gazing at the half-invisible god's statue, a shimmering construction of a handsome, androgynous body cut in half, the other half to be imagined by true devotees. It is said true faith in God Eborsen means imagining the other half to be anything and nothing, but most devotees fill it with their own selfish image, or that of a beast, thus defeating the purpose of faith.

Her mind shifts to the summit of the Alevian Mountain from where the entire expanse of Sirvassa and the sea beyond is visible. Her mind goes to the small seaside town of Vedina where she disembarked from her ship and took a vehicle to Sirvassa.

Her mind goes to the entrance of the Garden. The smooth door of stone. The way the Caretaker's gnarled old hands touched it. The way the door flew open by inaudible command. The Bacillus Rose and its thousand petals. The power it held. The power that is roaring inside her. The power to change the nature of things. She turned poison to blood today.

Her gaze turns toward the unfinished glass of milk on her bedside table. Surely the nature of milk can be changed into something else? Surely its whiteness can turn into a clear, colorless liquid.

She tries. The milk swirls inside the glass and then its color fades. The glass of milk is a glass of water now.

But she can do so much more. What can the glass become? Can it become a brass container?

She tries again, but the glass turns to sand, the water inside it splashing onto the table and the floor below. Iyena sinks in her bed, a sudden fatigue overtaking her. The day bears down on her, heavy as a stone sinking to the bottom of a river.

CHAPTER TEN

The Caretaker

After his brief tryst with the nature of time, the Caretaker finally steps out of the Garden campus. In the peak of the afternoon, his old bones creak like a wooden door on its hinges. The last time he walked on the narrow street that leads to the Ablehdar road – famous for its tinkers, bangle sellers, view-per-meinar picturegroup hoarders – he was bargaining with a caravan owner for the cost of a journey he never made. Four months ago, the skies were mostly cloudy, the roads damp and smelling of petrichor, and shopkeepers eager to stop all trade before midafternoon. Now, the world feels younger, at the cusp of being reborn.

Where the stony path turns to the left, there's a green ribbon tied to a five-foot-tall metal pole. To the casual, untrained eye this would seem like one of the many recurring oddities across Sirvassa. But the totem exists for a reason – the placement of the ribbon means the stone path to the Garden campus is invisible to casual passersby. A customer has to tie the knot in the ribbon and only then the path reveals itself.

The Caretaker bends down and inspects the ribbon. It's frayed now, and its ability to replenish itself after a number of knots has been reached is now dwindled. There's only one knot for the day. The Caretaker glances around, removes the ribbon, and pockets it.

Leaving the Ablehdar road behind, the Caretaker enters the market proper. Awnings flutter in the air, held together by straight, majestically carved wooden poles, like so many masts of ships, bright yellow, radiant purple, midnight black. He hears screams, well-intentioned but passionate cries, customer to trader, trader to customer, the air echoing with a medley of bargaining. It's pear season, and the Enurtha variety of the fruit, smoky sweet when completely ripe, elegantly bitter when not, is flying off carts and boxes and carefully curated glass cabinets in shops meant for only the rich to enter. The ones who sell only from carts rely on this bargaining medley to keep up with demand and also make profits. The shopkeepers have one price and one price only.

But the Caretaker is not here to buy fruits. His eyes are fixed on a quaint shop tucked snugly between two large stores of vegetables and furniture. The crowd this time is maddening, barely room to breathe, skin touching skin, spit flowing from mouths and landing like raindrops on things to eat and things to make a household neat. The Caretaker struggles through rows of people, wishing for a Waylander charm upon the people who buzz like flies.

He arrives near the shop. Its small wooden door stands unassuming, wearing one small golden doorknob, round, shaped like the feather of the Ihear songbird. The door has no markings, no nameplate, no signpost to announce what is sold behind it. The Caretaker grazes his index finger along the sharp edge of the feather, careful not to cut himself. He waits for three heartbeats. One feather becomes two, side by side, like small wings. Then they flutter, and the door clicks open.

A damp and narrow hallway greets the Caretaker. A sickly sweet smell of apples and a whiff of must. The Caretaker moves wraithlike, his footsteps barely registering on the floor. The hallway opens to an expansive foyer, white-and-gold walls, drapes looking like waterfalls on windows with a view of an alley. The foyer leads to two rooms, one open, one closed. The Caretaker walks toward the room that is open.

The room is filled with brown earthen pots, different-sized, rows and rows of them. At the back, they're stacked atop each other in the shape of a tower that tapers at the top. The pots aren't labeled. The Caretaker squirms at the sight of them – if he were running this place, he would label them. Order is necessary in such things. Order brings about discipline. And in discipline there is magic.

A harsh clap sings through the walls. Then another, then another. The Caretaker walks toward the source of the sound. As he walks, his gaze falls on the pots, most of whose contents he is intimately familiar with.

"What did the Chimera tell King Virkhutsk before they fought?"

The question comes from the end of the hall, the voice warm, comforting, and welcoming. A voice he has answered many times.

"To stop complaining and wear the mask of iron."

"Over the mask of copper?"

"People wear many masks," says the Caretaker. "Even kings like Virkhutsk."

From the darkness at the end of the room a shape materializes. A woman, short, thickset, her hair tied in a bun above her head, wearing a bright orange robe, open, underneath which a white sari is visible.

"Yavani, you have been avoiding me."

"I have been busy," says Yavani.

"All good in the Seedvault?"

Yavani hesitates, then looks away. "Take a look at this." She points toward a pot about waist high, kept a few feet toward their right. She reaches toward it, and grabs a handful of the material it is filled with.

"The seeds of the Carunthian," says the Caretaker immediately. "It will flower into a beautiful Lily."

"You know the powers that would give?"

"Advanced telepathy, I am aware. Near complete absorption of a different being, so two people can reside inside a singular host."

"Its parasitic properties are well-documented."

"I know," says the Caretaker.

"Then you would realize how perilous it is to get ahold of these seeds."

The Caretaker breathes deeply the musty air. Then he coughs, and the cough rattles his ribcage. A thunder roars inside him, and each bone, each nerve aches in rebellion. When the storm subsides, he speaks, with power.

"Trulio, my apprentice...he ruined the Tulip of the Seven. Almost completely. I can tend to it with my own methods. But it would be better if I plant it anew."

Yavani places her hand on her heart. "Tulip of the Seven, heavens. What was he doing?"

"He is back from his travels. I am assuming he is nursing matters of the heart."

"And...what did he think the Tulip would do?"

"Bring back his love from the dead," says the Caretaker, putting into simple words his apprentice's grief. When it comes out of his mouth, it all seems foolish. Even the actions of a smart man such as Trulio become undone by grief.

Yavani walks over to a stout pot toward her left. The Caretaker stands still, letting her do the work. The Seedmaster chooses the seeds carefully, examining the ones that would ripen best into the glorious flower. When she's done, she comes back with a handful of shimmering, pea-shaped seeds and gives them to the Caretaker.

"Thank you," he says. He lingers for a moment longer. On any other day, he would turn around and walk away as swiftly as he entered. But today, there's hesitation in him. The old man, almost ready to crumble, steadies himself. He closes his eyes, as if making up his mind.

"What's the matter?" asks Yavani.

"There's something else."

The Caretaker pulls the sleeve of his robe and shows the Seedmaster his right arm. Where there once was thin brown skin, bulging with green veins and sinew, old but active still, there now is just bone, black bone, skin shriveled to a husk, like parchment wrapped around a stick.

Yavani's throaty gasp echoes through the Seedvault. When the shock abates, her lips purse themselves. "You are as much of a fool as your apprentice."

"Thank you for the kind words," says the Caretaker.

"Were you mixing the Hibiscus with—"

"T...he Daisy, yes. Needless to say, it didn't turn out the way I was expecting it to."

"Will you give up this charade of yours? It is of no use!"

The Caretaker brings his gnarled black finger to her lips. "Even the Seedvault has ears," he says.

When the Seedmaster speaks next, it's a whisper, only perfectly audible to two people.

"What do you want me to do?"

"I am here to ask you if you can invent some seeds for me."

Yavani opens her mouth to say something, but no words come. The Caretaker winces as an invisible ache grips him again, somewhere deep inside his body.

"That's either very old magic, which has been forgotten, or very new, which hasn't been invented yet."

"It can be done," says the Caretaker. "You know, Yavani. Every night, I spend four hours with bones and muscles and skin not my own, but it feels so good. I feel alive and young. But more than that, I feel eager."

"That curse is but yours to carry," says Yavani. "And curses don't get lifted by magic. Curses get lifted by boons."

"I am not here for sermons, Yavani. Sermons I get from the priestess aplenty. I know you can do it. I am here to know the price I have to pay."

Yavani sighs, rubbing the back of her left hand with her right. Her eyes don't meet the Caretaker's directly. Because if they meet, the Caretaker will know that the task is possible, even if monumentally difficult.

"Come with me," says Yavani. "I have to show you something."

Yavani turns on her heels. The Caretaker darts a glance at the overflowing seed pot to his right, licks his dry lips, and follows Yavani.

⋆　⋆　⋆

Yavani the Seedmaster's study is bathed in opulence. A hanging garden with jewels instead of vines and flowers is at the center of a vast, domed room. Sculptures made out of stone, charmed to both speak and move, if only a little bit, line the smooth ceramic walls. A staircase leads to an upper level, where the walls have crevices filled with leather-bound journals and books, tended by fell-birds. In a corner sits a high-backed chair, facing a large wooden table strewn with more books and an empty register.

As they walk, a statue greets the Caretaker. It is bone-white, and pink-speckled, with a man's head and a bird's body. "A morning in Sirvassa is the magic of routine," says the statue, its feathers trying to unfurl under the labor of magic.

"And the magic of routine is divine," says the Caretaker, an apt reply to an ancient saying.

"*The Seven Children of Hyenasa.*"

"A story as old as time itself," says the Caretaker. "I wasn't aware of your extracurricular activities, Yavani."

"You are ever so businesslike. Take seed, grow flowers, make customers happy."

"There's a routine in that," says the Caretaker. "I haven't sought anything more."

"Except for the thing you're here for. Because you must also think there's more to the world than your routine."

"Incisive words," says the Caretaker, his voice reduced to a pained whisper now. "But also wrong. Tell me, how permanent is this Delight? I never gave you a potion for this."

"Oh, this Delight is more potent than any of your diluted potions could ever achieve." The Seedmaster looks fondly at the statue that spoke, like a parent looks at a child. The Caretaker stands there, his mouth agape. He eyes Yavani curiously. Is she strong enough to eat an entire flower and channel its Delight safely?

"You have ventured into dangerous territory with that. You must still have traces of the Delight left," says the Caretaker. "Show me."

"We mustn't get ahead of ourselves. There is a bigger problem I'm dealing with."

The statue bids the Caretaker farewell. Yavani leads him inside a smaller room, which smells strongly of apple, a profound variation of the smell he experienced when he walked inside the Seedvault. In sharp contrast to the grandiose nature of the study, this smaller room is quaint and is awash in nothingness. As they enter, the doors close behind them with a dull click.

Then, the room dilates.

★   ★   ★

The walls collapse upon themselves, melting on the grassy ground like a candle. The grass spreads outward, far and beyond, rising and falling like a wave, an expansive meadow that becomes the sky in the distance. Mammoth trees hang in the air, suspended by an invisible thread, their spindly roots clawing at nothingness like so many spiders. Upward, the branches of the trees carry fruits of impossible colors, and on those branches, slithering, reptilelike, creatures of a forgotten time.

One of those creatures, four-limbed, crawls down the nearest tree, its apelike face contorted in a grimace, clutching a fruit. Its long reptilian tail grazes the bark of the tree making sounds of sandpaper on metal, sword against skull.

The Caretaker takes in this grotesque sight with an impassiveness of someone who knows all things, who has experienced horrors far worse. The creature chews and chews upon the fruit, and then spits seeds on the grass. Yavani bends down and picks the seeds up, showing them to the Caretaker.

"Why are we here, Yavani?"

"Look at the seeds carefully," says the Seedmaster.

The Caretaker takes out a small magnifying glass from inside his coat. The seeds look nothing out of the ordinary, golden, in their prime, ready for harvest. Ready for a good flower to bloom.

"I think they'll make for a beautiful Delight," says the Caretaker.

"Press them," says Yavani.

The Caretaker does so. He instantly receives a sharp jolt on his finger, and a pain courses from the tip to his shoulder. The seed splits into two and a thin brown ovule erupts, eager to live a dark life.

"What.... Is this a problem, Yavani?"

"All the new seeds turn up like this. I have spent the last two weeks destroying them, not collecting them."

"Is that why you have not been responding to my coppergrams? You should have told me this earlier," says the Caretaker.

"Look, at first I didn't even know what was happening. It began slowly, and then suddenly, like a cloudburst. Most of the rot has occurred in the last couple of days. I don't know how many trees are infected, but I suspect there are many." Yavani sighs heavily. "I would need a lot of assistants to collect the rotten ones and I am not sure where the rot comes from."

"This doesn't bode well for us, Yavani."

"You were asking for an invention. I am worried about sustenance. I am not even sure who, or what, brought this rot. I was careful, I was so careful."

The Caretaker looks at the ovule. There's something unnatural and grotesque about the sight, brown and black, a thing of its own. The rot doesn't look like it came gradually.

He looks at his own hand, blackened by a potion gone wrong. Could the rot be behind all this? His mind wanders into the past: all the Delights he has given to eager Sirvassans in the last few months. Things could go terribly wrong, if the rot isn't stopped from spreading.

"I am sorry," says Yavani, pressing the shoulder of the Caretaker.

"Don't be. It's not your fault. This is something else."

"What will you do now?" the Seedmaster says, fixing the Caretaker with a mournful stare.

"I will have to track down whoever has ingested the Delights since the last Bloom. If you can't be sure about the timing of the rot, I can't be sure of what seeds I planted in the Garden."

The Caretaker lets out a heavy sigh. Then, his thoughts plagued with the possibility of closing down the Garden, he rushes out of the Seedvault into the jangling streets.

CHAPTER ELEVEN

Survan's Feet

Survan enters his house, flailing his hands wide, a silly grin plastered on his face. His mother mops the floor while his father sits on a wooden stool, trying to insert a thread through the eye of a small needle.

"Careful, Survan, the floor is wet," exclaims his mother. Survan skids, balances himself, but the grin doesn't leave his face. He sits on a chair, swinging his legs like an excited child, even though he is well into his teens.

"What is the matter with you today?" asks his father, while not removing his razor-sharp gaze from the eye of the needle. He smacks his lips, as the thread fails to go through for what is probably the fifth time. Survan's mother rinses the mop inside a bucket as she looks at him, askance.

"Should I show you? I'll show you."

Survan brings out a small, thumb-sized vial from his pocket and shows it to his parents. The vial contains a bright green liquid, thin at the top, viscous at the bottom. Survan shakes it once, and the viscosity of the liquid becomes consistent. He pulls open the cork, the vial opens with a sharp hiss, and white smoke oozes out of the opening. Then, the smoke dissipates and the liquid becomes as clear as water. Survan's mother stares, while his father's gaze is fixed on the needle.

"Father, look," says Survan. It takes a couple of more pleading attempts from the teenager before his father can be bothered to glance at him.

"If your Delight can somehow magically sew my torn trousers," he begins, "then you have my attention."

"Can you be encouraging for once, Marvan?" says Survan's mother. Her gaze is accusatory, piercing.

Marvan shrugs unapologetically. "Survan, c'mon, show us your Delight."

Survan takes a gulp of the liquid and corks the vial back. Then, he stands up and waits for his Delight to kick in.

"What am I looking at?" says Marvan.

Survan waits patiently, remembering what the Caretaker told him. Wait, wait, till a hundred and twenty wingbeats of a fell-bird pass. He waits, he waits, putting a finger over his lips, silently telling his parents to be patient.

And then it happens. His feet lift off the ground. His mother claps her hands in glee. His father stares at him blankly.

"I am flying, I am flying."

Survan's heart flutters in elation. He had once dreamed of flying. This is better than that. In his dreams, he was soaring above Sirvassan rooftops. But, eventually, dreams shattered and he found himself back in his bed. Here, even though his feet are mere inches from the ground, he savors every moment of it.

★   ★   ★

Later that night, as he lies awake in his bed, he wonders if he will ever dream of flying again.

His mother comes to his bedside holding a warm glass of milk. His walls thunder with the snores of his father in the next room. His mother sets the milk on his bedside table.

"Tomorrow, I'll glide to the school," says Survan, as he takes a big gulp of the milk.

"Now, now, don't get ahead of yourself. Not on the roads."

"But I won't be on the road, Ama," he says. There's a glint in his eyes. A glint of opportunity, a glint of magic.

His mother ruffles his hair as he finishes his milk.

"Ask Father to turn. He snores when he sleeps on his back."

"Aren't you talking like a Healer?"

"Just something Tevair Amaram told us in school," he says.

"May Eborsen send you dreams of Ina," says his mother and kisses him on the cheek.

"May Ina send you dreams of Eborsen," says Survan. His mother takes the glass and leaves. Survan lies awake a long time, thinking of all the ways to accelerate while being inches from the ground.

He doesn't dream of flying.

The next morning, as he puts his feet on the ground, he feels something different. A strange flatness of texture, a failure of grip. When he stands up, he stumbles. His knees buckle, and he falls.

He gathers himself and shakes his head. As he hoists himself up, gripping the bedside table, his eyes fall on his legs.

His toes are gone.

CHAPTER TWELVE

The Caretaker

The Healer Sanctum is shaped like a lotus. The outer periphery is marked by walls carved in the shape of petals colored peach and blush, embracing the inner petals like a cupped palm open upward in prayer. Deep inside the arrangement, the Sanctum stands, an almond finger pointing at the sky, a carpel, a smooth stone, a deep, unforgiving shade of rouge.

A walkway extends outward from the outer periphery, adorned with fake petals, for the real ones are inside, safe in the hands of the Healers. The Caretaker walks along the resplendent path, his gait troubled, his eyes fixed resolutely on the entrance. On a usual day, the Healer Sanctum is a quiet building. No murmurs, no hasty conversations waft out of the Sanctum. For the most part, the Healers do their healing silently. For the most part, Healing is a quiet business.

But today is not usual. The Caretaker hears sharp, horrific sounds of pain and misery, quite uncharacteristic of the place. Uncharacteristic of the city of Sirvassa. Furtively, he enters the Sanctum.

The sight is not pleasant. The dull mahogany walls of the Sanctum provide a stark counterpoint to the horrors inside. A man sits on a long wooden bench, his eyes hollowed out. The Caretaker recognizes him – he'd wanted a Delight to see beyond walls. A woman is clutching her throat, her sobs throttled, as her face takes on odd colors, yellow and green and purple. The Caretaker remembers her – she'd wanted a peculiar Delight to woo the person she loves with an enchanting song.

Two Healers with troubled expressions on their faces stand in the foyer. They each hold a ceramic bowl. A dull, purple sheen hovers above the bowls, as the Healers try to blow it away rhythmically.

"This will not work, Dhriti," says the Caretaker. One of the Healers glances at him, and stops what she's doing.

"You," she says. "Is this...." She points a trembling finger at the ruined faces of the Sirvassan citizens. "Is this because of you?"

"I sincerely hope not, but some events have transpired in the past few days, and I must eliminate my Delights as a possibility."

"I knew something like this was bound to happen," says the other Healer.

"Your treatise on the Garden is well documented, Arsin," says the Caretaker. "But this is not the time to bring up the past. The lot of petals you have right now will not help you heal them."

Arsin the Healer looks at the Caretaker with an incredulous expression. Then, he sighs. Dhriti takes the bowl from Arsin's hand and places it atop a wooden bench.

"That's the thing, isn't it?" says Arsin. "The last lot of petals is close to finishing. We've taken all their essence and distributed them among Sirvassans, and it happened a lot faster this time. We can't just be waiting around for the rains."

"Who else is affected?" says the Caretaker.

"Including these two, fifteen. Some petals from the last rain had anti-inflammatory properties, so we were able to eliminate a couple of really bad symptoms. Still, it's not a lot. This is the first time we are seeing something like this. Entire limbs...gone."

There's horror on Dhriti's face. She's young, but the effort of describing the ailments seems to age her. Arsin's face doesn't seem to betray what he's feeling, but the Caretaker can tell the whirlpool of conflicting emotions plaguing his mind.

The Caretaker presses Dhriti's shoulder reassuringly. Then, he moves toward the man without eyes. He kneels down beside him and takes his frail palms in his.

"Carson, I am the Caretaker."

The man shivers and groans. With a raspy breath, he says, "You....
I trusted you. You said nothing would happen to me. I saw things...
and then, I didn't. What has happened to me?"

"Did you consume the Delight exactly as I'd told you to?"

"Yes, yes, oh Eborsen, yes, I did as you'd told me."

The man is in pain; that much is evident. The Caretaker exhales
sharply. Then, pressing the man's palms firmly, he closes his eyes. He
reaches out for the vestiges of a powerful Delight inside him, one that
allows him to carve out thoughts, one that allows him to supplant lies,
and alter truths. He reaches inside the man's mind and unfurls it. He'd
consumed the Delight of the Carnation and the Orchid. But he sees
the rot that caused the blindness, not in stasis, having done its job.

The Caretaker can't heal his blindness. But he can take the pain
away. He can make the man believe, and make him see things. That
much mercy he can impart, for now, until he can find a way to cure
the rot in the vault and in the Garden. It brings him anguish, this
helplessness, but he can't do much.

And so, inside Carson's mind, the Caretaker plants a joy. The
next moment, Carson smiles.

"What...what did you do?" asks Dhriti the Healer.

"A half measure," says the Caretaker. He moves toward the
woman. He does the same to her. This half measure is a necessary
evil. For a full measure to come, these people will have to wait.

When the woman smiles, and color returns to her face, she tries
to speak. She still can't, but is unperturbed by it. Instead, she croaks
out a guttural voice of gratitude.

The Caretaker gets up and faces the Healers.

"Keep giving them the anti-inflammatory potions," he says. "I
have the records of the others who have consumed the Delights. I
will return with antidotes in a couple of days."

"You mean you can bring his eyes back? Eborsen's endless skin,
can you do that?"

"If a Delight caused his eyes to vanish, a Delight can bring them
back. It's just a matter of time."

The Caretaker is surprised by the flat confidence in his own voice. The tenor, the rhythm of his words. Even he can't believe what he's saying, because for the first time in his life, he's not sure. For the first time in a long while, the Caretaker feels an utter loss of control. And he doesn't like to lose control.

He remembers at least twenty other citizens who have consumed the Delights in the past few weeks. He will have to visit them, first, before they can visit the Sanctum crying their throats out. He will have to wrestle back control.

The next few days, with Trulio in tow, the Caretaker scours the edges of the city for men and women who had arrived on his doorstep, wanting Delights. Some don't show any peculiarities, going about their days unaware of the calamitous happenings in the city. Some have begun to show trickles of the rot, their veins black and varicose, the Delights inside them converted into Sorrows. The Caretaker gives them half measures, like he gave Carson. And then he gives them a promise, even if it sounds hollow. They accept his promise with joy, and resume their lives.

"Trulio, any updates on the activities on the docks?" the Caretaker asks on the way to the Lockmaker's house.

"None so far, Master, but I'm making progress," says Trulio. "You will have something in a couple days' time."

If Sirvassa doesn't die by then. The Caretaker's shocked at the brutality, the cruelty of his own thoughts. But it's soon accompanied by a sudden whiff of hope, too, however faint. He latches on to these temporary whiffs. They keep him going.

When they reach the Lockmaker's house, she's already on the doorstep, tending to a small orchard near her patio. She notices them first, before they can get a word in, and smiles at them.

"Not as vibrant as your Garden," she says. The Caretaker's mind is immediately brought at ease. A whiff of promise.

"Still enchanting," says the Caretaker. "How are you? How is Trehan?"

"Never been better. Do tell, what brings you here to the edge of Sirvassa?"

The Caretaker tells her. Her eyes narrow in curiosity, then wrinkles of anguish form on her face. She looks alarmed, but also comforted, an odd mixture.

"All I can tell you is that both of us are healthy. Although he *was* a hair's breadth close to a disaster recently, my boy."

"What happened?" asks the Caretaker.

"School trip. He ate a poisoned fruit. Luckily, he was saved."

"Oh, were there Healers around?"

"No," says the Lockmaker. "In fact, curiously enough, a girl saved my boy. Iyena Mastafar."

The Caretaker remembers the name. The girl who'd taken the Rose, but hadn't returned for her true Delight. The girl who wanted to fight monsters.

"How did she save him, care to elaborate? If you know?"

"That's the thing, even she sounded unsure," says the woman.

A dark thought grips the Caretaker. He tries to shrug it away, but it's so potent that it coils itself around his mind in a cold, sharp embrace. He takes a deep breath. When he exhales, the breath lingers uncomfortably along with the silence between the three figures. The Caretaker nods at the Lockmaker affectionately.

"Why don't you stay for tea?" says the Lockmaker.

"Perhaps next time," says the Caretaker, and bids her goodbye. He starts walking at a nimble pace, as his apprentice walks behind him furtively. "Come Trulio, we have some work to do."

CHAPTER THIRTEEN

A Melancholy Bargain –
A Journal of Travel, Trauma, and Teachings

Master has a curious way of doling out punishments. I still remember that hazy, autumn day when I had stolen a vial of blue liquid from the laboratory and enjoyed its Delight. My vision had grown red, and I could see everything in the dark. My eyes had become so sharp that I could see darkness itself. Now, I can describe what darkness looks like – it's a cumulative weight of everything light touches and leaves. Poetic, isn't it?

But that day, I couldn't see Master come out of the shadows and grab me by my arm. His grip was strong for an old man, and his sharp, bony fingers dug into my feeble arms – I was much too young at that time, and wasn't as muscular as I am now. Master gave me quite an earful, a detailed lecture on how stealing was a vice, and how I must pay. I was ready for whatever punishment the Master would give me.

And all he told me was to plant a flower in the Garden.

I guess he wanted to discipline me by teaching me the tenets of discipline itself. By teaching me how hard it is to make a small vial of Absynthia. By teaching me about the care and warmth required to grow a flower whose petals, in turn, would give a thimbleful of Delight.

Florrachemy is odd. It requires so much patience and hard work, and gives so little in return. I find it absurd that my Gurun would continue running this Garden to give people a taste of these Delights.

But I am getting ahead of myself. I am required to write down a full account of my travels. That is my punishment. I wonder when these punishments will start to actually look like punishments.

I must begin at the beginning.

In the beginning, there was nothing. Not even nothing, and the universe merely existed as a pre-thought, a musing of someone who carved everything out of non-nothingness. There was no concept of existence, because existence itself was undefined, and its contours were hazy at best.

But I digress. I must not delve that far back. So, I must begin again.

In the beginning, Eborsen, the Half-Formed God, created the rivers, the mountains, and everything that sustains life.

No, that is still too far back. Beginnings of this universe are overrated. Eborsen himself rests deep inside the earth he created, unconcerned with his creation. And so, I must begin where my part in this story begins.

I had come to the Caretaker's doorstep a scared child, shivering, drenched in rain, dirty water dripping from my hair, pooling on the ground where I stood. My own reflection in that small pond was ghastly. My face was smeared with dirt, and my arms were scratched bloody. I had no memory of where I had come from. I just knew hunger. I just wanted a roof over my head.

The Caretaker was kind enough to let me in. He gave me shelter and warmth and food. I knew that people can't be kind for no reason. That was what life had taught me. But this old man was actually kind. Still, I wanted to repay him. So, I went under his tutelage. He taught me everything about the Garden, about Florrachemy, how magical seeds sprout into flowers, and how those flowers give Delights. And most of all, how he wanted everyone in Sirvassa to have a taste of those Delights. He wanted everyone to know about the unlimited possibility the world held.

It's a noble endeavor. But it gets tiring. Master stubbornly refuses to take any Kerron from the population and he refuses to expand the Garden. I'm sure he must have his reasons for that, and so I don't bother him with unnecessary questions.

In the first couple of years under his wing, I never saw Master practice Florrachemy himself. I was convinced that he was just an old man, doing his best. I was convinced that the tall tales of powerful Florrals – magicians who used Delights to perform unthinkable feats like moving mountains, magicians who didn't need a flower potion every time they needed to perform magic – were just tales. Stories told to children on a stormy night.

Then, one day, it happened. And I have been in awe of him since.

I was in the Sirvassan market, buying vegetables, and haggling for the price of a pumpkin. Master likes a hearty spiced-pumpkin mash with fried flatbread every now and then. Over the years, I had become somewhat of a Master myself, in preparing his favorite meal, in taking care of the Caretaker.

As the shopkeeper brought his asking price down, his eyes went to the skies, and swelled in terror. I followed his gaze, and saw a giant winged beast soaring in the skies. The beast kept circling, not swooping down, not flapping its wings. Its blackness left vapor behind its gargantuan body. Its bright beak, sharp, its tail, studded with spikes. If it came down upon the city, it would wreak havoc with one great swoop of that tail.

"Oh Eborsen, what is that thing?" said the man, trembling with fear. Horror gripped me, too, and made my insides cold. I was unable to move. The crowd around me erupted in shock, shouting for mercy. Pandemonium in the market.

And then mercy came in the form of an old man, wearing a plain white kurta, sporting faded brown slippers. His skin was patchy brown, with age spots all across his hands. The Caretaker looked older than time itself, but as he looked at the skies, his eyes – oh Eborsen, those eyes – held a raging fire I had only seen in younger men who went to battle riding the backs of beasts far bigger than them.

In front of me, Master ate a flower. I knew enough about Florrachemy to know that the act of eating an entire flower could prove to be fatal. But Master was special. Perhaps the blood inside him could flow with an unassuming calm even with the rage of the unbridled Delight coiled around it.

He kicked off the ground and flew into the sky. I saw him grab the beak of the monster and drag it across the empty sky, as black smoke trailed behind it. Both wrestled in the air, man and beast, and the Caretaker flew with the beast until it was no longer visible in the skies.

Master came back, late in the night, bone-weary, with bloodied scratches all over his body. Blood oozed out of him in rivulets, and his eyes looked haunted, like he had gazed deep into the abyss of time itself.

"Trulio, help me," he said and fell into my arms. I dragged his unconscious body to his chambers. Then I made a potion for his health and well-being, by practicing the same discipline he had taught me once. He later told me that much of his strength waned not because of the monster, but because of what he did next. He painstakingly constructed a shield around the city of Sirvassa from a complex concoction of Delights. A snip of a Lily, a bit of a Daisy, some Rose. The magic was all in the permutations and combinations of those flowers. I learned it from him in theory, but to execute it is still beyond me.

Only Florrals could do something like that. But Master rejects this notion. He keeps saying *anyone* could perform such feats, if only they put their minds to it. He isn't special. The Florrals aren't special.

★　★　★

I asked Master for permission to travel around the world, and he gave it without flinching. I asked him who would help him in his daily chores, and he evaded the question with kind eyes and gentle words.

"There's not much tending that's needed to be done anyway," he said, looking toward the Garden, and perhaps hiding the anguish that had crept onto his face.

"One word, Master, and I won't go," I said.

"I won't rob you of a chance to have different experiences, Trulio. The Garden will always be here. I'll always be here."

With these words, he stepped away. I wondered if he didn't want to face me. In the twenty-odd years of my existence, I'd spent fifteen with Master. He was my ever-guardian, my guiding light, the anchor to my ship. And I was leaving him. What did that say about me?

I decided if I entertained those thoughts too much, I'd go mad. And so, I evaded these thorny questions my mind threw at me, and gathered my belongings.

But before I stepped out of the Garden, Master came to me and handed me three vials.

"Use these Delights sparingly, and only when you need them desperately. Remember this, Trulio. Delights are not shortcuts to avoid what the world throws at you. They are meant to elevate what you already have."

He told me what each thumb-sized vial held. With his words, my confidence grew. And the Delights I held in my hands felt warm, comforting. They both tugged at me, and pushed me in the direction I wanted to go.

"Until I see you again, Master. May Eborsen shower his petals on you," I said, and left the Garden at the crack of dawn. Later, I climbed aboard the first ship to leave the shores of Sirvassa. My destination – Khorin, the city of salt and spice and everything nice.

CHAPTER FOURTEEN

Iyena Mastafar

Although her father told her to stay alert and indoors, Iyena doesn't get as much as a whisper from him as the day wanes into the night. Her room feels like a prison cell even though the evening view is splendid, with vibrant-winged fell-birds gliding through the air as they sing, leaving a shimmery trail behind them. Their light makes a counterpoint to the light of the strings over the city, the meshwork, connecting turrets and pillars and poles. She's seen the Sirvassan streets go from being dormant in the morning to thrumming with activity in the evening.

She hears roaring laughter from below. It sounds like one of the important guests her father is hosting. They'd arrived early in the morning. A stout old man with a walking stick had entered first. Her father had touched his feet, and was constantly shadowing him as they walked inside his study. Accompanying the stout man was a thin, tall, mustached person – who seemed to be his secretary of sorts, lesser in importance, summarily ignored by her father. She'd seen Maani-Ba scurrying about, carrying trays full of food and drinks, overworked to her bones. Iyena had even offered help, but Maani-Ba had refused. Now she sits gazing cluelessly out her window, yearning to be a part of the world outside.

A procession on the streets below. A red stage, moving on wheels, half shrouded by a canopy. A couple, kissing and dancing, on the stage. Around the stage, more people gather, throwing multicolored petals on the newly betrothed.

"The Way and the Fall."

Iyena turns and sees Maani-Ba standing near the window. She's arrived silent as a whisper. Her eyes, too, are affixed on the wedding procession below, as if lost in deep pools of memory.

"What does that mean?"

"It's a marriage custom, unique to Sirvassa. This procession leads to the Room of Opposites. Both the bride and the groom enter the room, one at a time. No one knows what happens inside the room, except the couple. If both of them come out, with a half-snipped green petal resting on their shoulders, their marriage is deemed to be a success."

"And if not?"

Maani-Ba doesn't answer. Iyena knows better than to prod further. She tears her gaze away from her and fixes it on the road, where the celebrations begin to fade as they turn a corner.

Iyena notices a recognizable shadow across the road. Sandy hair, uncertain gait. It is Trehan, but he isn't walking purposefully. Perhaps he has business to attend to further in the city. He had mentioned something about there being an antique shop this side of the city. She wants to scream a greeting at him, but with Maani-Ba at her side, she controls the urge.

But then Trehan stops, wheels around, and starts walking *toward* her building. He is carrying what looks like a tumbler in his hands. But why here, why now?

"Who is that boy?" asks Maani-Ba, just the question Iyena is trying to avoid. Father shouldn't come to know, at least not today, not after yesterday's lecture.

"It's someone I know from school."

Trehan looks jittery. But then he composes himself. He looks up and his eyes go bright upon seeing Iyena through the window. A smear of red flushes Iyena's cheeks. She slides her window open and leans out.

"Trehan, what are you doing here?"

"I came to say th-thanks," he stutters. Through peripheral vision, Iyena can see a sliver of a smile crack on Maani-Ba's face. Her fingers tap on the windowsill, as if waiting for Iyena to make a movement, or say something. A heavy pause lingers in the air.

"What are you waiting for, child? He has come to thank you, after all!"

Iyena's eyes dart toward the door.

"He is busy and will probably remain busy for at least a couple of hours," says Maani-Ba. "I've seen you climb a mountain, I'm sure the drainage pipe won't be an issue for you."

Iyena kisses Maani-Ba on the cheek. Then, she clambers over the windowsill, gripping the edge of the window tightly. The pipe to her left is bolted to the outer wall at six evenly spaced intervals through a thin metallic frame, which juts out enough to support her feet. Maani-Ba leans over the ledge, ready to hold her in case she slips. Iyena lets go of the ledge and finds footing on the nearest metal frame, holding the pipe. The first rule of climbing is taking baby steps. Iyena slides an inch, and the metal of the pipe scrapes her pants. She winces, but keeps sliding downward. She finds another footing.

"You can jump," says Trehan. Iyena slowly turns her head to gauge the height. It's not much, but enough that a wrong fall could badly twist her ankle. Then she'd be spending the rest of her stay in Sirvassa actually bedridden. All this because she helped a boy. All this because she saved a life.

It probably would be worth it. Iyena takes a leap of faith. Above, a gasp escapes Maani-Ba's lips.

Iyena lands safely, beside Trehan.

"You could have invited me in," says Trehan.

"If you take me to the salousse shop, I'll tell you why I didn't."

Trehan's face looks weak, still, but breaks into a sheepish grin. He gives Iyena the thing he is carrying – a ceramic vase, inlaid with shard-sized stones, looking sharp, but smooth to the touch.

"This is beautiful, thanks," says Iyena, taking the vase, yet thinking of a suitable place to hide it inside her room, shielded from her father's eyes.

"Why didn't you come to school today?"

They both turn a corner and the street opens to a wider area. The road is swarming with townsfolk wearing colorful dresses fit for a wedding, yet this is a normal evening for an average Sirvassan. Flanked on both sides with sweetshops and eateries, the road throbs with activity. The wedding procession is a vibrant haze in the distance, and drunken shouts of men and women can still be heard.

"I've been told not to," says Iyena.

"But you want to, right?"

"Of course."

"Salousse is this way," says Trehan after a pause. After much push and shove and polite excuses to edge ahead of the evening crowd too busy eating to talk much, they both arrive near a small shop tucked away in a corner. A woman with a long nose and a white paste on her forehead sits inside a hut on wheels, thick green spittle on her chin. Through a small window she hands out square brown pockets of a papery material, filled with rice and nuts, smeared with a thick brown liquid. The crowd eats the entire pocket in one go, and as they chew and swallow, their own lips and chin get stained with a greenish spittle.

"Famous, famous shop, you won't get a better salousse anywhere in the realm!" the woman yells.

"Two for us, please," says Iyena before Trehan can open his mouth. The woman's hands move like clockwork, and soon she thrusts a couple of salousse pockets in Iyena's hands.

"I think children shouldn't consume salousse." A tall man wearing a hat voices his opinion, holding seven pockets of the edible in his hands. Iyena gapes at him, even as she hands one salousse pocket to Trehan.

"You first eat your own salousse, before commenting on what others eat," the shopkeeper replies, her voice tinged with snark. "Children get a sweeter, nonintoxicating version. You think I'm that irresponsible?" The man opens his mouth to speak but then decides against it, his face contorting in a confused frown.

"Six meinar," says the shopkeeper.

Trehan hands her the complete change in coins. "Let's go to a quieter place. This is too crowded. I know the best spot."

★　　★　　★

Iyena has only heard whispers about the abandoned water tank. Constructed four hundred years ago, back when Sirvassa was still ruled by a king, it now stands on a well-maintained spot lush with greenery. A leisure spot for most Sirvassans, the water tank invites fell-birds to chirp and rest and make their nests, and other wild animals to ascend its heights. The stairs coil around one central stone pillar and reach the main water loft fifty feet above the ground. A narrow walkway is constructed around the main loft, where two people can walk abreast.

Iyena places her hand on the stone wall and feels a faint murmur from inside the tank. Ghosts of water cling to the inside wall and continue a quiet mayhem. She turns and sees the sprawl of Sirvassa fifty feet below. The temple, the mountain, the creek to her right, where she rescued Trehan. And the Garden of Delights tucked somewhere in the middle of the city, invisible to non-curious eyes. She grips the railing firmly and breathes the cool air of the evening.

"There is only one city like this in the entire realm," says Iyena. "Troika. It is in the south, a valley snuggled between three mountains."

"I have never been outside Sirvassa. My mother would never allow me to leave the city."

"I miss my mother," says Iyena, looking into the distance.

"I am sorry."

"She's not dead," says Iyena, a light frown on her face. "Why would you assume that?"

"Sorry, again, for that careless assumption. Where is she?"

"In Troika. She and my father separated five years ago. I wanted to travel the world, like my father. But in every city we go to, he tries to keep me from exploring too much."

"Is he trying to protect you?"

"If that's the case then he has a very strange way of showing it."

Iyena lets go of the railing and absently scratches at the vase Trehan gave her. A sudden image of her father gets etched in her mind, hard to shake off. He's looking at her with his hawklike eyes, as she tries to make a stick man fly. She can't be sure if he's disappointed, or angry, or both. She can't be sure if she even cares.

"How did you save my life yesterday?"

"The Garden," she says. "The Caretaker gave me two vials of a Delight."

"I made the vase for you, using up the last gulp of the vial I had."

Iyena looks at the vase, then looks at Trehan.

"You use the Delight every time you have to perform... a magic?"

"Yes, that's how the Caretaker says it works. Enough for everyone to enjoy a little magic, but not so much that it becomes an obsession."

Then, without giving it a moment's thought, Iyena changes the vase into a teacup, then changes it back. The tips of her fingers go cold, as if dipped in ice, then flush with heat, as if molten wax was poured on them. Trehan's eyes flash with surprise.

"I turned the poison in your body into blood," she says.

Trehan gives Iyena a blank stare.

"Perhaps I took a strong dose," she says. "Or perhaps I can do this all the time."

"Do you realize the possibilities of this? All over Sirvassa, people enjoy a little bit of the Garden every week and then they never go back. They might, if it's a necessity, but it's never an urge. You, on the other hand, can do it whenever you want."

"What does that make me?"

"You're still Iyena," says Trehan. "It's getting dark, and I know you don't want to get an earful from your father."

"Trehan, I want this to be a regular thing," says Iyena. She doesn't believe, truly, in the words that come out of her mouth. But today she feels both giddy and calm and warm, and she wants to hold on to that feeling for as long as she can.

"You mean climbing this tank or us?"

"You know which one I am talking about."

Trehan grins. They both climb down.

★   ★   ★

Climbing the pipe back to her room proves to be effortless for Iyena. When she grips the ledge of her window, all she can hear is silence from her room. The window is slightly ajar, just the way she had left it. She slides through her window noiselessly and enters her bedroom.

But before she can climb into her bed, she hears a creak, and her legs become stone. She turns to see her father standing at the door, his left hand clutching his cane, the fingers of his other hand twitching.

"Evening, Father," says Iyena, hoping the paleness in her face doesn't betray her.

"Iyena, it's dinnertime. I was calling you, but perhaps you were busy sleeping."

"I'll be downstairs shortly, Father," says Iyena.

"And shut that window," says Anaris. "It's cold outside."

"Yes, Father." Iyena nods vigorously. If her father knows about her evening exploits then he is obviously not showing it. Perhaps because of the important guests present in his study, he can't afford to look distracted. Perhaps, she will see that other side of him tomorrow.

She slides the window shut. Then she puts on the dress she always wears when there are guests in their home. She's weary, but she has to see this through. She wears her best smile and walks out of her room.

★   ★   ★

The dining room is empty, but the table has been set to perfection. Roasted eggplant, clarified butter floating over a red gravy in which potato and capsicum chunks bathe. Fragrant rice over which saffron strings are sprinkled, like streaks of morning sunlight over a white sky. Iyena's stomach rumbles and knots. She mustn't touch the food before the others have sat down. But the others aren't here yet, despite her father's earlier insistence to make it to dinner on time.

She looks at the rice fondly before detaching her gaze. There's a noise coming from her father's study. The sound sieves through porous walls between the study and the dining room. She constructs a map of the study in her mind – she is standing ten feet away from the cabinet that has never been opened. Iyena tiptoes toward the wall and presses her ear against it. At first the noise seems like the stout man is angry at her father. But then comes a laugh, manic, completely lacking in mirth. Perhaps her father has made a joke. Which is unlikely because she has never seen her father display any sort of humor in front of anyone.

The laughter peters out into conversation. Iyena tries to follow the trail of words but they slide off the walls, barely reaching her. But the wall itself gives way to an air vent overlaid with crisscross wires. Waning light from the study splinters through it and splashes on the dining room floor. Iyena peers through the vent, trying to get a clear view.

The stout man, whom her father holds in the highest esteem, stands near the desk, his right hand gripping the edge, his left on her father's shoulder, like a friend. To their side stands the other, lanky man.

"I would like to see the expression on Mayor Illyasi's face once he comes face-to-face with this, Anaris," says the stout man. "You have done me proud."

The lanky man shifts. A huge golden shadow falls across the room. The automaton *opens*, its sides unlatching to reveal a mold, from which steps out a tall being, taller than the men in the room.

"Turain-One, Minister Yayati is pleased. Say thank you," says Anaris.

A voice, deep and resonant, sharp and horrifying. The being, the automaton named Turain-One, speaks his first words. Iyena isn't sure it is a 'he'. But she can feel her stomach coil inside, python-like. Questions raze her brain like a wildfire.

"Turain-Two will be ready soon," says her father. "And it can fly."

"This is spectacular. Now I know I didn't send you here for nothing. Believe me, the higher-ups in Alderra were skeptical."

"Come, Maani-Ba must have set dinner. A delicious feast awaits you."

Iyena detaches herself from the wall and rushes to the side of the table. Her heart thumps wildly, and she feels a pinprick of fear on her neck, her stomach a cold knot. She licks her dry lips and flattens the creases on her dress. The dining room echoes with the drumming of footsteps.

First comes the stout man, followed by the lanky man, and then, limping across the carpet, clutching his cane tightly, comes Anaris Mastafar.

"Minister Yayati, Secretary Anuv.... Meet my daughter, Iyena Mastafar," says her father. Iyena greets the two men with the standard Alderran greeting, fingers interlaced together and stretched out. The minister and the secretary stop in their tracks, consider the greeting for a minute, and then do the same. Then the minister smiles and takes a seat. The secretary follows, taking the seat to the minister's right. Anaris takes the host seat.

"I hope the mayor has been apprised of the dinner dress code, Anuv," says Minister Yayati as he slurps on the gravy. Secretary Anuv shifts in his chair, and then nods.

Iyena quietly sits down in the chair to the right of the secretary, who looks the least imposing of the three men in the room. She wishes Maani-Ba was there in the room with her. She wishes she didn't have to be present until the dinner is over. But most of all she wishes she hadn't heard or seen the conversation inside her father's study. The evening with Trehan is all but a distant haze in her mind.

"I suppose if you're here, Minister Yayati, it would please you to visit the Temple of Eborsen," says Anaris.

"Ah, glad you brought that up," says Minister Yayati. "I would want to give my offerings to the Half-Formed God. Assuming, of course, no Inishti desecrates the place of worship here. By the breath of Inies, the lengths I have to go to in Alderra to make sure it doesn't happen."

"I will ask Mayor Illyasi to make arrangements," says Anaris. "Iyena, you must also accompany us."

Iyena nods and chews her food in silence.

CHAPTER FIFTEEN

Iyena Mastafar

The Temple of Eborsen stands at the edge of the city, bridging the gap between a road that ends in white stones and the rocky fold of the Llar Mountains beyond. The natural white stone outcropping ascends gradually until it blends with the steps of the temple, an architectural oddity that looks like it was shaped by the earth and wind and water rather than hands and sweat. Like it grew out of the ground like a tree.

The main temple compound is mostly white, streaked with black and gray smears, natural lesions in stone. More steps lead to a frustum dwelling supported by four pillars, atop which is mounted the flag of Eborsen, which flutters even in the absence of wind. A string of bells hangs on the north face of the dwelling, connected to a ringing mechanism that has, without fail, operated twice a day for the last two hundred years.

Iyena reaches the top of the stairs first. Behind her, the three men take the steps laboriously, the amount of time taken to reach the top directly proportionate to their age. Iyena faces the statue of Eborsen himself, the Half-Formed God, left side human, the other side the vastness of the universe, sitting cross-legged over a marble stone. His three right hands clutch a hammer, a rolled-up parchment, and a multi-petaled rose. His bone-white eye, even closed, sees all of the universe.

Secretary Anuv, the kind, lanky man, arrives at Iyena's right. "You come here often?" he asks.

"This is my first time," says Iyena. "I haven't seen much of Sirvassa."

"You should see more. It's a beautiful place."

A clang of a bell interrupts their conversation. Iyena looks up to see a sari-clad priestess with a white paste on her forehead walking toward them. Her hair is the color of midnight, tied in a neat bun, her eyes keen and sharp, her skin radiant.

"I wasn't expecting devotees at the Hour of the Futures," she says. "But you might as well."

"I am Secretary Anuv. Alderra Ministry's Department of Miscellany." Secretary Anuv offers the Alderran greeting, to which the priestess responds with a greeting of her own, a light tap on the secretary's palm with her index finger. Secretary Anuv stares at his hands for a moment, as if struck by lightning, then smiles at the priestess.

"Who are your friends?" she asks. They are soon joined by Iyena's father and Minister Yayati. Secretary Anuv introduces the two men with an air of presumed authority, which doesn't seem to impress the priestess. Iyena senses Anuv's body stiffening up. Inside the temple, there is no rank, she has heard. Your worldly greetings, posts, cues, gestures, are best left outside. Inside the temple, before Eborsen, all are equal. All are nothing and everything.

"We're here to give offerings to Eborsen the Great," says Minister Yayati.

"Eborsen doesn't take offerings," says the priestess in a tone that is flat but conversational. The words aren't intended to mock, rather educate. "Perhaps in a different land, a different custom is followed. But remember, this is the original temple, the resting place Eborsen fashioned out of nothing."

"That I have heard, yes." Minister Yayati purses his lips, as his eyes dart toward Anaris.

"The minister would want to make an offering out of kindness and devotion," says Anaris.

"The minister might want to provide food and shelter to the homeless. That is the only true offering Eborsen would consider."

"Pardon me, priestess, I wasn't aware of the customs followed here," says the minister.

"It's the Hour of the Futures," says the priestess after a brief pause. "Each week a devotee is chosen at random and is offered a glimpse into their future."

"I had heard of this practice, yes," says Minister Yayati. "Frankly, I wouldn't mind a peek into upcoming events. We're here, after all, for a mighty important affair."

"You ignored my use of the word *random*," says the priestess. Her gaze shifts to Iyena, who is a mute spectator. Iyena's pulse quickens as the priestess locks eyes with her. A prickling sensation grips her from neck to toes, and her insides feel plunged into ice. The other half of the Half-Formed God pulsates, forming a shape out of nothing.

"It wasn't my intention," says the minister. Iyena is pulled out of her trance. The minister stands erect, confident, but in his manner there's a shred of arrogance too, which the priestess had caught. But Iyena doesn't concern herself with the ways of her elders. She is much too interested in the phrase the priestess uttered. The Hour of the Futures.

She takes a deep breath and gathers her resolve.

"How does it work?" says Iyena, inviting a look of scorn from her father. "If you show upcoming events to a devotee, what do they do with the information?"

"It's up to them," says the priestess. "They can't change what is to come."

"Then why show them at all?"

"Iyena, you must not question the ways of the temple," Anaris interjects.

Iyena looks at her father, and takes a step back.

"It's healthy to question," says the priestess. "She's a child, she is curious, and she must know." The priestess moves closer to Iyena, kneels down, and takes her palm. Iyena traces the feeble lines of age on the priestess's arm, but her skin is smooth to the touch.

"We show them so they can be more cognizant of their actions," says the priestess. Iyena has seen the same gaze before. The same, kind, all-knowing eyes. The eyes of the Caretaker.

"But they will do the same actions, still," says Iyena.

"Except, perhaps, with greater impetus, or reduced vigor. It's of course, entirely up to the devotee if they want to have a glimpse or not," says the priestess, and turns around. She lays a hand on the base of the statue. As she does so, the statue of Eborsen starts spinning. First slowly, as if being gently rotated by invisible hands, the languorous movement of a windmill, then vigorously, like a hurricane. The blacks and whites of the statue merge into a terrific smear of gray, a single spire jutting from the ground. A redness grows from the depths of the rotating statue and takes a form.

A Rose.

The flower shoots out of the spinning miasma and falls in front of Iyena's feet. A Rose with a million small petals, delicate, the edges thin as a hundredth of a hair's breadth, gleaming redder inside.

"Eborsen has chosen you, child," says the priestess.

Iyena gazes at the Rose in awe. In the Garden, the Caretaker had used the same Rose, snipped a petal of it, and made a potion. A potion that is rushing in her blood right now. A potion that had allowed her to change the nature of things.

"It is the Bacillus Rose, isn't it?" says Iyena.

"You know about it?"

"The flower of a million petals. I have read about it," she says. She senses her father's eyes drilling holes in the back of her head.

"What else do you know about it, child?"

"Just that," says Iyena.

The priestess nods affectionately at her. Iyena wants to say more, but decides against it. She instead caresses the petals of the flower she has only seen once before.

"You may choose to decline," says the priestess, her voice firm, yet delicate. "Eborsen won't think less or more of you."

"I'll do it," says Iyena, tearing her gaze away from the Rose.

"You are wise beyond your years, child. Follow me."

Iyena takes a reluctant step toward the priestess when Anaris speaks. His voice is laced with the barest hint of anger, but there's also a reluctance in his speaking. As if the answer he'd receive would break things.

"What will a child see, priestess?" he says. "Iyena spends most of her days inside. Another trip to the market, perhaps? A good dessert that Maani-Ba will prepare tomorrow? She already knows what her days will look like for the coming week."

"I don't understand the point you're trying to make here," says the priestess.

"Perhaps more important people should get to see what the future holds."

The priestess gives a curt smile to Anaris, as her eyes shift to the minister. "No," she says simply. "In the eyes of Eborsen, no one is less or more important."

"It's fine, Anaris. Maybe your daughter will see something that concerns all of us. No point questioning the will of a god."

Iyena can't think of a suitable reply to the minister. She instead looks at the priestess for direction. But this is not a moment to fight battles. This is a moment to keep quiet and observe. If last night was any indication, the purpose of the minister in Sirvassa is malicious. But despite the power raging inside her blood, she has no part to play, no sway, no offerings.

Iyena's skin prickles with opportunity, and tenses with anticipation. She takes a reluctant step toward the priestess, not looking back at the three men. But then, something else boils inside her, a sudden raw urge, simmering to the surface. Her face flushes. She clenches her fists and turns to face the minister.

"Maybe I'll just see the sky changing colors. The clouds shifting, the sun shining upon a good, just city, Minister. I am but a child, after all, and nothing I see will concern you."

Saying this, Iyena faces the priestess. The edges of her lips curve into a smile and she offers her hand. Iyena doesn't look at her father, the minister, or Secretary Anuv, for that matter. She savors her small victory in that moment and takes the priestess's gentle hand.

CHAPTER SIXTEEN

Iyena Mastafar

Iyena feels the cold, clammy arms of dread reaching toward her when she stands in front of the chamber. She has no reason to feel scared, yet her stomach feels hollow. The door to the chamber is black as soot, but unassuming. Iyena can't tell the material it's made of just from touching. It has markings all over it, old scripts, illegible to her, but perhaps second language to the priestess.

"Remember, Iyena, you can still say no. The Hour of the Futures will begin as soon as we enter."

Iyena tries hard to remember the events that led to this moment. All cloud, all vapors, the details come to her in trickles. She followed the priestess up a flight of narrow, spiraling stairs, white as bone. Throughout the short journey toward the chamber – which is a floor above the main temple – the priestess remained quiet. Iyena kept her steps in check, not too loud, not too quiet, making just the perfect amount of sound, keeping the sanctity of the temple. They crossed paths with another priest, dressed in similar dull orange tones as the priestess, but a green cloth tied around his head. The priestess hadn't mentioned but perhaps he was of a lower order. The priest had a stoic expression on his face. He was carrying a basket full of white dahlias. A smell similar to what she had encountered inside the Caretaker's laboratory wafted from the basket.

She remembers the scent. The scent of promise. The scent of brightness.

"I want to do this," says Iyena. The priestess touches the runes on the door and they glow bright as she mutters a chant under her breath. One by one, the markings glow, as if molten gold has been poured all over them through a sieve. The door dilates, revealing a spacious room, a deep crimson in color. The priestess enters and Iyena follows.

The room is a Rose.

The walls fold upon themselves a million times over, moving to the eye, but static in actuality. They flutter like a rose in the wind. Where the wall touches the floor, there are more folds, one atop the other. Sometimes, the floor is in front of the wall. Other times, the wall overtakes the floor, moving, quivering, like a rose.

In the center of the room a blackness hovers, unshapely.

"The hour begins," says the priestess, and steps out of the room. The door closes, leaving Iyena alone. She smells must, dry leaves, and an earthy fruit. She sees red walls. The blackness in the center of the room takes the form of a spindle, vapory entrails branching off like sharp, dark threads. Like thorns. A thread detaches itself from the center and flies toward the wall. With an inky splash, the red wall becomes smeared with grayish black splotches. The blots grow outward from the center and through them, a light comes. Slowly, the light engulfs the room. Iyena shields her eyes.

But then the brightness abates. The wall in front of her is no wall, but a dark forest.

Iyena steps forward and finds herself deep in the forest, leaving the room and its red walls behind. Dead leaves crunch under her feet, coldness sieving through the soles of her shoes. The fruity smell lingers as she moves forward. The trees in the forest aren't like the ones she has seen anywhere before. They are gray not brown and their roots clutch the ground in a brutal handshake. Their branches seem liquid, shimmering with starlight, and they bear no leaves, no fruits. The sight of the trees makes Iyena forget her recent past. In her mind, she was always here.

Ahead, she sees a shimmer, like a mirage on the green, leafy ground. She breathes and her lungs are filled with the scent of wood and seaweed. She finds herself at the edge of a lake so vast it might be an ocean. But she knows, in her mind, it's a lake. A lake that has always existed since the beginning of time.

At the edge of the lake, a figure sits hunched. Shrouded completely in a brown, leathery robe, he is drinking water from the lake. Ripples form near the edge where overgrown grass the color of deep henna dips in the water, spreading outward like so many tentacles. The water looks undrinkable, and yet the figure quenches his thirst as if he would die if he got up.

An inexorable force pulls Iyena to the lake and she is overcome with a sudden urge to drink the water. But she resists. This is the Hour of the Futures and none of it is real.

None of this has happened, she remembers.

Yet, she crouches beside the figure and dips her hand in the lake.

"It's cursed," says the man sitting by her side. "Don't drink the water."

The man has a wounded face. A scar runs from the edge of his lips to his ears, and his eyes are bloodshot. His skin has a spiderwebbed pattern on it. His hands quiver like a leaf in a storm.

"What is your curse?" Iyena asks and drinks the water from the lake. She knows whatever has happened hasn't yet happened. The water is cool and sweet but she knows it isn't water she is drinking.

"What have you done?" says the figure and retreats into shadows that didn't exist a moment ago. At the center of the lake, a disturbance. Water ripples and separates, revealing a gaping chasm, dark and deep. Tendrils made of fish skin, bones, and vine crawl out of the depths and entwine, forming a face. Its eyes pools of blue where dead oysters roam, its mouth a meshwork of broken lobster shells. Iyena staggers back, horrified, yet no scream comes from her mouth.

None of it is real, she knows, but it might still come to pass.

"It's a mere child this time," says the goddess. "You didn't warn her."

"I did," says the man from the shadows, not revealing himself.

"Then it's her curse to bear too," says the goddess.

Iyena feels her anklebone struggling to maintain its integrity. It shudders inside her skin, yearning to wrench free. Then her entire lower half gets pulled inexorably toward the sea goddess, whose mouth full of clams and seashells now yawns, revealing a hideous maw. Iyena screams as the slimy, watery jaw comes down on her.

Darkness.

Then redness again. The scent of fruit, the scent of honey. She is inside the room again. Her heart hammers in her chest. The hour isn't over yet. She can tell. The spindle moves, and another dark sliver detaches, throwing itself on the red wall. She is pulled toward the petal wall yet again, for a future that hasn't happened yet.

This time she finds herself surrounded by giant statues, their hands and legs made of stone, their faces entirely wrought out of flowers. A vast rolling field, full of grass green and red and blue, kissing the sky in the distance. One statue bends down and offers a giant hand, a hand bigger than the *Remnant*, the ship she came to Sirvassa on. There is no smell of seaweed and salt this time. She smells freshly cut grass, wet cement, and over-brewed tea. This future looks like an impossibility to Iyena. There's no land that boasts of giants such as these, at least not moving, talking ones.

Iyena climbs atop the hand of the giant. Its other hand carries a giant saucer filled with steaming, brown tea, white fumes wafting and going over the giant's head, becoming a cloud of tea vapor. The giant moves and the green field drops below Iyena swiftly.

"Where are you taking me?"

"Wherever queens go."

Another lie, another impossibility. Iyena knows the realm doesn't have kings or queens anymore. Then, was it just a phrase, casually uttered by a giant who doesn't know better?

As the giant moves, the lush green expanse reveals itself. It dips and rises, dips and rises, until it meets a blue-purple sea, whose waters are calm. Ships the shape of flying birds with golden fluttering masts are visible in the distance. Iyena holds on to the giant's fingers, finding purchase in the cracks on his stone skin like ledges of a balcony.

"Don't hold on too tightly," says the giant. "I will soon have to let you go."

The edge of the sea approaches fast as the giant picks up speed. No ships are docked near the beach where the ground ends. The sand is shiny, and from a height, it seems as if broken diamonds are littered all across the beach.

"Iyena Mastafar, glad to be of service," says the giant. And all around them, more giants gather, their towering frames blotting out the sun altogether. The sea churns in the distance and the masts of the ships flutter vigorously. The sky turns orange and pink, the color of candy. Wind rips through Iyena as the giant throws her across the ocean. The sea goes beneath her dizzyingly fast as she soars over the ships, the water, the fishes. But she is unafraid because it is just a vision.

She almost comes close to the sun when darkness swallows her again.

She is back inside the chamber. The room has stopped spinning, the walls are a pale red and not the bloody crimson of an hour ago, and the black spindle at the center of the floor is no more. The priestess stands near the entrance, gazing at Iyena impassively. The Hour of the Futures is over.

★　★　★

"What does it all mean?" Iyena asks the priestess as they walk down the corridor toward the stairs. The sky here is a clean blue, unmarred by clouds or smoke or vibrant colors as the vision had shown her. Iyena feels disoriented, as the edges of her eyes blur away. She blinks repeatedly to force herself to be in the constant present, but the image of the lake goddess and the impossible giants refuses to go.

"It means nothing if you don't put your mind to it," says the priestess. "It could mean something if you think hard enough."

"That's not a clear answer," says Iyena.

"I admire your curiosity, child, but that's all you're getting for now," says the priestess.

They climb down the stairs and cross the same priest they did an hour before. The priest has the same stoicism about him. He is carrying the same basket of dahlias and the same scent greets Iyena. Mesmerized, she almost stops in her tracks and looks at the priest as he disappears behind a stone pillar. After a moment of flowery disorientation, she gathers her senses, and follows the priestess out of the shadow of the temple compound, into the brightness outside.

The three men are still standing there, waiting. Iyena looks at the minister. She can almost hear her father's words before they come out of his mouth. She will again be told to remain in her bedroom and not venture outside. She will be told to not meddle in affairs beyond her years. She doesn't need the Hour of the Futures to know that. She just knows.

But when she approaches her father, he smiles at her. It's a genuine, warm smile, a smile she had seen years before in Alderra.

"How was your experience inside, Iyena?" he asks.

"Very ordinary," says Iyena.

"Sometimes the most ordinary things are the most important," says the minister.

"Come, you must be tired," says Anaris, holding out his hand. His voice drips with empathy, and is laced with a saccharine sweetness. This behavior is utterly alien to Iyena. If it's an alternate future Iyena has suddenly been thrown in, perhaps by the sheer force of that giant's throw, then it isn't readily apparent. But she must still be cautious, and walk on eggshells around her father.

Reluctantly, she takes her father's hand.

CHAPTER SEVENTEEN

The Caretaker

The tea shop thrums with the boorish, uncouth activity of an inn. The Caretaker, sitting on a low chair, beckons the owner, a sad-looking man in his fifties with an unwashed face and gray hair plastered to his forehead with dried sweat. The man acknowledges, scrambling to clear plates and saucers, as an eager Sirvassan crowd floods the premises of the tea shop. Among the crowd are cloth and fruit merchants who have finished the trades of the day, indulging in idle gossip about incoming raw materials from far-off lands, women who run their own businesses of tailoring and picturetales, talking about new kinds of stories to tell, and teenagers after a busy day of school.

The tea shop itself is suffused with the warm aroma of cinnamon and nutmeg, of enjing root and parmouth stem, of herbs both native and exotic. The sounds inside the shop are shouts of men and women, and groans of wood against wood, as old customers leave the chairs they had occupied, and newer ones take their place. The cool, cement walls of the shop boast intricate murals of old storytellers sitting around a stone slab with quills in one hand and a cup of tea in another. Ammana's tea shop is not the only one in Sirvassa, but it's the busiest.

Today, the Caretaker chose it for the silence it offers, but instead receives only mayhem. Murmurs of the Delights of his Garden ruining the bodies of Sirvassans had reached the shop. The Caretaker hears faint calls for closing down the Garden. Even fainter are the calls to have him arrested. Yet, not many notice him, as he gestures at Ammana, the owner, yet again, who acknowledges him with a pained, helpless expression. On the counter, where the Caretaker sits, Kerron coins clank and impatient fingers drum against a large mahogany table.

"One pot of Enjing," says the Caretaker, loudly this time. Ammana places a tray of three steaming cups. The cups disappear within seconds, as more impatient hands arrive on the counter, hands turning into aggressive fists, ready to be violent if tea isn't served on time.

Despite the mayhem, the Caretaker decides to stay. The crowd dissipates and becomes more manageable as the hour passes. The discussion shifts to political matters, instead of the Garden. The Caretaker sips his Enjing silently. Ever since the meeting with Yavani, he has stopped the charade of perfecting his potion. He has found five more flowers in the Garden with the ever-growing rot, consuming, blackening, turning fully bloomed flowers into tar. To add to that, Mayor Illyasi has been sending him coppergrams filled with musings, and various gifts to buy his approval.

"You pray to Eborsen, you might as well pray to smoke."

The Caretaker turns. A man pounds his fist angrily on a table as his teapots threaten to fall off to the cold, marble floor. A woman sits opposite him, ignoring his tea-addled tirade.

"The God of Soil, Healing, and Prosperity, my stinking foot!" the man says. "I've been praying to him since my father lost his business ten years ago. I have not seen a single Kerron of that prosperity that was promised to me!"

The woman scoffs. "Only praying never helped anyone," she says.

"Don't you say that! Useless people are sitting on a hoard of Kerron *and* those cursed petals that fall from the sky. Where *are* the shares of those healing petals that were promised to us Sirvassans? Or is everything exported?"

The man snorts into his tea. Droplets of brown liquid splash on the clean table and onto the floor.

"Oye, I'll make you wipe that," yells Ammana at the man.

"Yeah, yeah," says the man, yelling back. "The way things are for me, I might have to wipe to make a living!"

Then, the man's gaze falls on the Caretaker, who had been listening to his tirade with interest and mild amusement. The man's brows twist into a knot. He snarls at the Caretaker.

"You!"

The man is loud. Much of the crowd in the tea shop turns their attention toward the Caretaker, recognizing him, murmuring among themselves about his presence. The man gets up from his chair and walks toward the Caretaker, pulsating with anger.

"My son came to you for your Delights," he says. Then, without warning, he grabs the collar of the Caretaker, pushing him toward the counter. "You gave him one of your stupid flower liquids. And now he has lost the ability to walk!"

"Then you should bring him to me immediately, instead of raving in this tea shop like a madman."

The man is stunned for a brief moment. The Caretaker racks his brains. The only people who visited the Garden in the past two months were the sandy-haired boy, that new girl who had just arrived in Sirvassa, and an eager brown-eyed boy who wanted to glide.

"Survan, is it? Please bring him to me. I am healing the others, I will heal him too."

The Caretaker measures his words, trying not to sound too confident. Because if the boy was affected because of the rot in the flowers, then healing him completely will be out of the question.

"I don't want your help!" says the man. Then he turns around and declares to the crowd, "This old man...proclaims himself to be the Protector! He doesn't do any protecting nowadays. All he does is dole out poisons! All your Delights are poisons!!"

The Caretaker grabs the man's wrist and gently pries his fingers apart. The man struggles and clenches his hand into a fist. Then, he lets his repressed rage take the shape of violence, pouring all his desperation into his fist, and punches the Caretaker on his jaw.

Two men immediately appear by his side, and drag him away, apologizing profusely to the Caretaker. The woman who was sitting with the man looks at the proceedings with acute disinterest.

"Many people will say many things around here," she says to the Caretaker. "Don't believe in any of it."

The Caretaker caresses his jaw, and feels the inside of his cheek with his tongue. The taste is metallic and he feels a painful lump growing. Ammana, the owner of the tea shop, slides across a bag of ice. The Caretaker gives him a nod of thanks. After applying ice to his wound, the Caretaker asks for more tea, the healing, herbal kind.

When the tea arrives, he takes his time to finish it. The next hour passes without any event.

★   ★   ★

When the Caretaker reaches the main compound near the Garden, he sees Trulio standing warrior-like with a quiver full of arrows and a longbow. The bowstring is tense, stretched back to Trulio's ear, his thumb and index finger holding the arrow with a grace not befitting him at all. Yet, the apprentice looks at peace as he prepares to take a shot. A silver coin tied to a thin string, hanging from a wooden ledge above the laboratory, becomes his target.

The Caretaker watches this with amusement.

Trulio releases the arrow and it speeds toward the coin in a blur. Time ceases to exist in that moment, trapped in a stasis, as the Caretaker watches the journey of the arrow. His own fingers move of their own accord, aching to hold an arrow. But the memory of a war fought long ago vanishes as soon as it arrives.

The arrow misses its mark entirely, hitting the wooden door of the laboratory with a sharp twang.

"Who taught you to hold the longbow like this, Trulio?"

The apprentice gets distracted, then disenchanted from the process entirely. His face falls upon seeing the arrow jutting out from the door. Then, it falls further when he sees the Caretaker's face. He runs toward his Master.

"What happened, Master? Oh, Eborsen, who did this?"

"It's nothing," says the Caretaker, swatting Trulio's concern away like a fly. "How many hours have you spent practicing *this*?"

"No, don't deflect. I must know! Eborsen's knees, this looks like someone hit you."

Trulio's face is a mask of concern. Both empathy and rage ooze out of him like honey from a beehive, and the way he speaks it becomes difficult to tell one apart from the other.

"It was a minor skirmish at Ammana's."

The Caretaker narrates the event to Trulio, who listens with rapt attention, shoulders tensed, one hand gripping the bow too tight. When the Caretaker is done, Trulio eases his manner, and says simply, "It looks like I will have to wipe that man off the map of Sirvassa."

"You will do no such thing, Trulio," says the Caretaker as he takes the bow and quiver from his apprentice. "Also, where are your manners? Touching my things without my permission."

Trulio is taken aback at the Caretaker's retort. He steps away respectfully, bowing a little. "Sorry, Master. I wanted to clear my head. I had been writing nonstop, as you had said."

The Caretaker wriggles his shoulders and shakes his arms. The longbow feels familiar in his hands, like the warm handshake of an old friend. The wood, even after all these years, feels new, thrumming with adventure. He looks at the wooden door. Trulio's arrow juts out. The coin hangs silently, unmoving. The Caretaker grazes the surface of the bow with his left hand, the aged black, rotten hand. He takes out an arrow and nocks it on the bow. Then, with the grace of an eagle ready to pounce on its prey, he takes aim.

The bow trembles but he holds it tight. The Caretaker is old, but his eyes are sharp, his breathing shallow, but consistent. Those are only two things needed for a good shot.

He releases the arrow. A twang echoes through the air. Twenty paces ahead, the coin lies wedged inside the wooden door, the arrow stabbed through its metallic surface. Trulio lets out a sharp gasp, as the Caretaker hands him the longbow.

"I would like to read what you have written, Trulio, but later," he says, caressing his jaw, moving his tongue inside, feeling the bruise again. "In the meantime, I want you to prepare me a good, hot meal." The Caretaker hands the bow and the quiver to Trulio. "Something which you're truly good at."

"As you say, Master."

★　★　★

The Caretaker sits on his bed, eating soup Trulio has prepared. The apprentice sits cross-legged on the floor, scribbling on his notebook lessons that the Caretaker imparts to him.

"Master, I understood the law of squares, but not of roots."

The Caretaker licks the spoon, as he watches Trulio struggle to make a chart of numbers against their square roots.

"How many roses do you get when you arrange three roses three times?"

"Nine roses, Master."

"Three is the number that when multiplied by itself gives us nine. So the square root of nine becomes three."

"But then what about ten? There's no number I could arrange an equal amount of times to arrive at ten."

The Caretaker sighs, not having the energy to go into explanations of decimals.

"Master, did you read my travelogue? I have given it a most memorable title."

"And what would that be?"

"'A Melancholy Bargain.'"

"That is a lovely title, Trulio. I am assuming the contents are as lovely, if not more." The Caretaker lies, and he lies well, not making any expressions, lest Trulio catch a whiff. The apprentice smiles at him.

"I'm sure my travelogue will set your mind at ease, Master."

"Now, Trulio, you must know that Mayor Illyasi has been at my neck for the last couple of months. I haven't slept as much as a wink since I found the rot that has been plaguing the Garden, and the Seedmaster's orchard. If you truly want to set my mind at ease, please tell me, what have you found out about the Corrilean and those men at the docks?"

"I made some headway with my investigation," Trulio says. "I went to the edge of the city. My disguise was that of a beggar."

"And?"

Trulio takes a deep breath.

"Immediately after you told me, I went to the docks covering myself in grime and dust, looking like I belong to the Beggars' Union or something."

"There's a Beggars' Union?"

"They have an entire franchise going on," says Trulio, grinning. "Spanning from the Sirvassan shores, to the plains of Alhassa. It's a network, but not that useful for our purposes. Anyway, I mingled with the members of the union, picking up idle chatter. You were right. Ever since the Alderrans, especially Minister Yayati's contingent, have arrived, things have not quite been the same around the city. The security around the docks, the men who work under Mayor Illyasi...I keep forgetting what they're called."

"The Sirvassan Red Guard," the Caretaker says. "What about them?"

"They were abruptly let go. On the orders of Illyasi himself. That's what the union told me. They don't know what's happening, but I dug deeper into this situation. When the Sirvassan Red Guard was let go, a sudden activity erupted among the common folk who live near the docks. A group of men, wearing colored kurtas, carrying pamphlets, were seen. They were distributing those pamphlets to people, singing and chanting in loud voices."

"Have we seen those men in the main city? Or is the activity limited to the docks?"

"Currently, only the docks. But something tells me they'll soon arrive in the main city."

"And what is that?"

Trulio cracks his knuckles, as if getting ready for something. Then he reaches inside his shirt and brings out a piece of paper, garishly pink, lettered in an ancient language, with a not-too-gratifying imagery of the old gods. Trulio hands the paper to the Caretaker, who frowns upon looking at it.

"I couldn't read what's written," says Trulio. "But those men *and* women clearly are part of something bigger."

"This is a recruitment pamphlet," says the Caretaker. "*Let go of the ways that chain you, and join us in a reckoning.* That's what is written in an ancient tongue. The old Abhadis used this language. Many have forgotten this language, but some still remember it. They want to bring it back."

"Why? We speak in the common language spoken by the Three Realms."

"Ask yourself, Trulio. Why does anyone want to bring back the past? It's not just language that they want to bring back, at least going by what's written here," says the Caretaker. "It's an entire way of life."

"But why would the Sirvassans care?"

"You are underestimating the power of compelling words garbed in propaganda."

"But to what end?"

The Caretaker kneads his forehead with his thumb. The creases on his face become even more profound, aging him ten years in an instant. Shadows of a violent past encroach upon him, once again. Hate has always been a powerful motivator, and if the Abhadis were good at anything, it was constructing an entire machinery of hate. This time, their intentions are the same but the methodology is subtle, different.

But in the Three Realms, Abhadis, Inishtis, and other races live peacefully, after an uneasy truce was obtained and the Common Code was introduced. The Caretaker knows. He fought in the war. He saw the ashes of his people get swallowed by the earth. He was the cause of the truce and paid for it with his youth. It was the relentlessness of the curse that forced him to look for another Florral. One who could take *his* place in the Garden and continue his work, and perhaps, in the process, alleviate decades of his suffering.

Why shouldn't an ordinary woman get a taste of a Delight that would give joy to her *and* ease her life, even momentarily? Why shouldn't a child who wondered what it was like to fly be allowed to fly? If an animal can't look up to gaze at the stars in the night sky, why won't you pick it up and show it what beauty the world has in store? It was what Eborsen intended, after all, but couldn't give to the people he spawned. The God of Soil and Prosperity, whose raw power surges through the earth, and made possible all the Delights. Delights are his way of bestowing kindness upon his people.

Indeed, the first Inishtis were all Florrals. But their powers also diminished with subsequent progeny, after intermingling with other cultures of the Three Realms. And after the war between the Abhadis and Inishtis, Florrals from around the Three Realms went into self-imposed exile, vowing never to become a part of any political alliance, nor to become weapons to be used by the self-proclaimed stakeholders of their race.

Who knows if they are tending their own Gardens in their secluded corners?

The intent of the Abhadis is exclusion. It is a thorn in their side that Inishtis are even being allowed to get a taste of Delights that no Abhadi ever could get from their Champions, who can move earth and mountains, stop air and water. The Champions who are the living embodiment of exclusion, the current living gods among mortals, keeping their raw power with them, never sharing.

The Caretaker sighs, and leans back on the wall, his eyes gazing at a black crack on the ceiling, threatening to spread outward and consume the plaster on the wall. Another rot to take care of. Another world threatening to crumble.

"I found something else, Master," says Trulio, breaking the silence. "The men you described to me. They were also apparently leading a group, unloading and reloading raw material from a Hansa ship. Fruits, vegetables, spices, and clothing."

"Did you find something else, more incriminating?"

"Among the items they were found to be unloading, I smelled a peculiar smell. Abradhan salt, spiked metal pellets, and Marissian honey."

The Caretaker exhales sharply. Trulio chews his lower lip, waiting for the Caretaker to instruct him further.

"The Marissian honey is an excellent binding agent. The Abradhan salt is not the normal salt you sprinkle. You sense what I am getting at, Trulio? A mixture of these three could be devastating," says the Caretaker. "Any updates on Iyena Mastafar?"

"None so far, Master," says Trulio. "But I'm sure she's healthy. For all we know, it could all just be timing. She took the Rose before the rot."

"You have done good work," the Caretaker says, after a pause.

The Caretaker wrings his hands, and casts a mournful glance at the floor, his mind racing. Trulio doesn't miss this, and immediately places his palm upon the Caretaker's palm.

"As you please, Master," he says in a reassuring tone. The Caretaker smiles and pats Trulio's cheek lightly. Trulio gathers the plates and bowls and gets up from the floor with the flourish of a theater artist who has given a good performance.

The Caretaker lies down, weary from the day's work, still anxious from the information Trulio has given him. Before long, he's carried away to sleep, forgetting entirely his night charade.

Outside the window, night blinks, and the stars glide away.

CHAPTER EIGHTEEN

The Caretaker

In the Caretaker's laboratory, behind a wooden cupboard full of beakers and vials of half-consumed, half-made, failed experiments, there's an oddly patterned marble wall, different from the other walls in the laboratory. Individual slabs sit uncomfortably against each other, in a haphazard manner, like pieces of a jigsaw puzzle arranged last minute. A pipe runs along the length of the wall, twists and turns, until it disappears beneath the Caretaker's workbench.

In the last ten years, the Caretaker has never bothered to look behind the cupboard at the wall, to slide it ten inches to the side from its usual position, never saw fit to tap a certain slab of marble a certain number of times, never mustered the energy to twist a spigot at a particular angle. Those combinations of movements are safe inside his mind, like a diadem kept safe by a mother beneath folds and folds of fabric. An opportunity never presented itself.

Until now.

The Caretaker wrings his hands as he looks at the space beside the cupboard. Trulio stands, shifting his weight from one leg to another, frowning, his sleeves folded up to his elbows.

"What are we looking at? What are we supposed to do, Master?" Trulio rubs his hands like an impatient child.

"This," says the Caretaker, pointing to the cupboard. "Slide it ten inches to the left, and no farther."

"Do I get a ruler?"

"No," says the Caretaker. "Use your best judgment."

Trulio shrugs. He grabs the side of the cupboard and starts pulling it toward himself. The wood creaks and groans against the marble floor, like an old beast waking from a centuries-deep slumber. Trulio's muscles bulge, the veins on his arms popping outward, the blood raging through them almost visible. The Caretaker's eyes are on the ground, at a particular spot. The cupboard leaves brown marks against the marble, an ugly arc, like a corpse being slid, leaving blood behind in its wake.

"Stop," says the Caretaker.

Trulio heaves and pants, wiping sweat off his brow with even sweatier arms.

"I thought I was near. You have keen eyes and an acute sense of measurement, Master."

The Caretaker ignores Trulio's praise and looks for a specific niche in the wall. He finds it: a marble piece, sliding over two other pieces, leaving a cleft. The Caretaker presses the rogue piece of marble back into place, and then twists the spigot at an angle of forty-five degrees. The three marble pieces are suddenly pushed back farther in the wall and disappear into darkness, revealing a misshapen hole. The Caretaker pulls the spigot *toward* himself, without turning it. When he does this, a creaking sound emanates from deep inside the wall. Like wheels moving on cement.

The Caretaker waits. The sound becomes louder and louder, until, out through the gap, comes a rectangular box, containing eight vials of multicolored liquids. Trulio holds the back of his hand against his gaping mouth, biting into it.

"Master," he whispers. "What are those?"

"I call them Florral-Makers," says the Caretaker.

★   ★   ★

Trulio brings a yellow vial against the sunlight, and looks at it in utter awe.

"Sensing that an opportunity like today might present itself," says the Caretaker, "I had prepared some aggressive potions. The eight vials you see are concocted with different concentrations of four chief flowers. The Red Daisy of Alderra, the Blue Crocus of Noronna—"

"But Noronna is a cold wasteland," Trulio interjects.

"Some flowers are terribly obstinate, finding ways to grow even in the harshest of conditions. They also give the most potent of Delights. Anyway, the other two flowers are the Ameranian Lily, and of course, the Bacillus Rose."

"Are these Delights any different from the ones we already give to the masses?"

"As I said, they are *aggressive*. The one you hold in your hands would allow you to both summon objects toward yourself and throw them away with breathtaking speeds. This one...." The Caretaker points to a blue vial. "This one would give you stamina *and* increase the impact of your attack."

"Master, what exactly are we planning?"

"To stop whatever the men at the docks are planning. Now, since my old age doesn't permit me to use much of the aggressive Delights, I would choose a simple one." Saying this, the Caretaker picks up a vial with a clear liquid.

"What does it do?" Trulio looks at the vial with a haunted expression on his face.

"You'll see," says the Caretaker, smiling at his apprentice.

"But, Master.... You are a Florral. Why do you even need to ingest all these Delights?"

"Even Florrals have their limits," says the Caretaker. "Mine is my age. If my body doesn't permit it, there's only so much aggression I can show. But remember, even the weakest Florral is stronger than twenty-five men combined."

"I wish I were a Florral," says Trulio, his lips curling downward.

"I'm making you one, temporarily," says the Caretaker. "You prepare your disguise. We go to the docks at night."

Trulio hesitates. "Master, is it prudent to go to such lengths? Should we not immediately inform Mayor Illyasi about these happenings? Shouldn't we directly confront him?"

"If he is involved in this in any way, approaching him directly would be counterproductive. Something is brewing in this city under his nose. Many people *are* displeased with how he governs and I won't be surprised if this is the work of a group of factions. The Corrilean are famously hateful of him. Add to that the arrival of the Alderrans and you have a conspiracy at your hands. And we still don't know what *exactly* that group of men is planning to do."

Trulio tenses like a stretched bowstring.

The Caretaker observes him.

"Do you feel scared?"

"I don't want violence," says Trulio. "Have seen far too much of it in my lifetime."

"Your lifetime is half of mine, and you haven't seen half as much as I have."

"Are you discounting my experiences, Master?" Trulio tilts his head slightly to the right.

"I wouldn't dare," says the Caretaker. "I am merely saying that sometimes, you have to look inward to know the right thing. And you know we always do the right thing. Or at least, strive toward it."

"I will be by your side, Master, following orders," says Trulio slowly.

Much of the earlier confidence returns in Trulio's voice. The Caretaker presses his shoulders firmly, putting a comforting weight upon them.

"It will be fine. We'll do it together."

Trulio nods, his lips pressed tight, the edges of his mouth puckered. The Caretaker takes the vial from his hands and puts it back inside the rectangular box.

"Sirvassan sky, ever so bright. Brighter be its shine, evermore, evermore."

The Caretaker turns to his left. A young, gray-haired man wearing a pink tunic and tapered black trousers stands near the door of the laboratory. His hair has flecks of glitter on it, and falls to his knees. His eyes have kohl, and his lips are ever so slightly smeared with red. To his right stands another man, with a starkly similar appearance, albeit with close-cropped hair, and a different tunic.

"Sorry, we are not functional today," says the Caretaker.

"Oh, it's terrible," says the other man, the short-haired one. "We are the Garbansa twins. We were looking for a quick fix."

The Caretaker looks at Trulio, who merely shrugs.

★　　★　　★

The Garbansa twins say each word with a musical cadence, so even the birds and the mountains can hear them and echo back. The Caretaker listens to their demands outside the Garden compound, nodding at appropriate intervals. While the twins talk animatedly, with hand gestures, the Caretaker listens impassively, hiding his right arm behind a thick sleeve, despite the warmth in the air.

"We hear there are flowers here that can permanently alter your voice," says the one who introduced himself as Ani Garbansa, the one with long hair falling to his knees. "I have long wanted a baritone."

"And I want a high-pitched voice that can shatter even the strongest of vases," says Ira Garbansa. He is an inch shorter than Ani and sports a thin white mustache.

"We have to put on a performance so enchanting that people forget who they are," adds Ani.

"We want to create art."

The Caretaker glances at Trulio. "I'm sorry, yet again, profusely. We are no longer taking requests as the Garden needs tending. Like most Gardens."

"But we have heard you keep backup supplies," says Ani in a singsong voice. "Please, don't deny us travelers. We have arrived from afar and we are willing to pay!"

"Your voice is so calming, Mister Caretaker," says Ira, playing with the sleeves of his tunic. "A voice like yours would please an audience of thousands."

"A voice like mine," the Caretaker scoffs. "You are better off without it."

"I want to see the Garden," says the younger twin, who was brought into this world a minute late.

"Now, now, Ani, manners, please. The Caretaker has important things to do." The older one grins at the Caretaker, as if expecting a reward in return. "Maybe some other time. We will have to use our natural voices to please the elite gentry at the party."

"The mayor and the minister will be so disappointed," says Ani, looking down on the ground. Then, they wheel around in a swagger, ready to leave.

The Caretaker's ears prickle. His eyes dart toward Trulio, who looks similarly alert.

"What party?" says the Caretaker. Ani Garbansa stops, turns only his head, and narrows his gaze. Then, he begins again, in a vivacious manner.

"Oh, we've been commissioned to perform a song at the upcoming dinner at Mayor Jaywardna Illyasi's bungalow. State officials from around the Three Realms are arriving. We wanted to prepare something special. And Sirvassan citizens speak highly of you."

"Although some of them had bad things to say, I am willing to err on the side of awesomeness," says Ira Garbansa.

"When is the party, if I may ask?"

"How soon can a potion be made, Mister Caretaker?" says Ani Garbansa, sensing the eagerness in the Caretaker's voice.

"Two potions, to be precise. I can be ready with them in under a fortnight."

The younger twin claps his hands.

"Lovely," says Ani Garbansa. "The party is actually in a month. It's a dinner, plus some song and dance to please the ministry higher-ups, as is the case with most of these affairs. We just like to be prepared in advance. What do you take in payment?"

"I gnaw at people's souls in return," says the Caretaker, without missing a beat. If the twins can be saccharine and nerve-grating, then the Caretaker can also be playfully cruel. The color vanishes from the twins' faces, all their singsong chatter gulped by the words of the Caretaker. The Caretaker's eyes are affixed on Ani Garbansa, who tried to be coy with him. Even though he can't see Trulio's expression, he knows his apprentice is enjoying this turn of the conversation thoroughly, probably even holding back a laugh. Ani Garbansa wrings his hands, while Ira Garbansa stands rooted to one spot, rather uncomfortably, shifting the entire weight of his body on one hip.

Then the Caretaker laughs, patting Ani Garbansa's shoulder. "It is a joke. People say all sorts of things about me and my work, depending where you come from."

"So..." Ira Garbansa hesitates, as if trying to put words to his jumbled thoughts. His twin looks ashen, apparently still not recovered from the Caretaker's jibe.

"We're talking about my payment."

"Yes, yes.... You take Alderran Kerron? Or is there a secret Sirvassan currency we don't know about?" asks Ira finally.

"Sirvassan Kerron it is. Five hundred now, as advance. Five hundred upon delivery of the items."

Ira Garbansa glances at his brother, who leans over to him to murmur something in his ear. The Caretaker doesn't like petty bargains, but the twins don't look like hagglers. They had already tried their hand by not immediately divulging the date of the party.

"It's a deal," says Ira Garbansa after a moment's thought. The Caretaker shakes his hand.

When they leave, Trulio scoffs.

"They both won't live long, Master," says the apprentice, eyeing the two figures as they walk away.

"Quite the judge of character you are, Trulio." The Caretaker turns and faces his apprentice. "Did you not realize that I asked them for money?"

"I noticed that. I thought it was high time, anyway."

"I didn't quite like their tone, so I thought I might as well make up for the waste of my time. But are you thinking what I am thinking?"

"It's obvious, isn't it? We have found our major event! A month from now, the men at the docks might plan to attack the party at the mayor's residence," Trulio almost hisses. "It actually makes perfect sense. Someone wants to unseat the mayor once and for all. And Minister Yayati is behind it."

CHAPTER NINETEEN

The Caretaker

For two weeks the Caretaker teaches Trulio the theory behind the potions and the Delights they offer. For two weeks, the Caretaker makes him believe that he, too, could be like a Florral when push came to shove, and he would be good at it. For two weeks, whenever he looks at Trulio, deep in study, he sees a man twenty-five years of age, hardened muscles but not overly muscular, a quick temper, but a keen eye for detail, a great learner, and overall an apprentice he can count on.

The Caretaker knows that Trulio is not an actual, true-born Florral. He knows if he were to give him a concentrated potion of Bacillus Rose, he would display extraordinary abilities, true to his nature, but they would fizzle out in a day. But the shape the world is in right now, he would be hard pressed to find a true-born Florral. If he were to give the reins of the Garden to someone, perhaps Trulio is indeed his best chance.

Trulio continues his disguise for another week. Not enough to mingle too much in the Beggars' Union, but enough to glean more information. When the two weeks end, Trulio arrives confidently at the porch of the Caretaker's hut, and announces that he is ready.

"I have some good news and some bad news, Master."

"Tell me the bad news first," says the Caretaker.

"We might have to rush into things, sooner than we wanted to. Their plan is under way to create some sort of an explosive. Something they will attempt to assemble tonight."

The Caretaker mumbles something incoherent under his breath. Trulio walks slowly toward him and sits on the cold, hard ground, crossing his legs, like an apprentice eager to be taught.

"What's the good news, then?" asks the Caretaker.

"The good news is that I feel much more confident about my abilities, Master." Trulio gives a slight smirk. The Caretaker shakes his head in dismay, and then bursts out laughing.

"It's no laughing matter, Master. In any war, a lack of confidence is a greater foe than a lack of weapons."

"Where do you learn all these phrases?"

"I come up with them on the spot," says Trulio. "I have many talents."

The Caretaker grins at Trulio. "We move at night, an hour after the last bell of the temple."

*　　*　　*

Night comes without preamble. The Caretaker looks at the Sirvassan expanse from his window, the sky suffused with amber streaks, the wind carrying a whiff of the last petal-rain, scents of earth and honey and possibilities. The Hour of the Futures comes and goes, too, and the Caretaker remains deathly still, playing the events of the prior few months in his mind like a picturetale.

First, the mayor asks the Caretaker to take his seat, despite knowing full well that the Caretaker hasn't ever harbored any intentions to hold office. Then, a generally quiet faction, the Corrillean, which only ever resurfaces during the times of Sirvassan elections, suddenly becomes very active. The Corrillean are just side players, trolls who make the most sound but amount to nothing in the larger scheme of things. Why would they aspire to unseat the mayor by attacking his bungalow? With the higher-ups of the ministry present? Who do they even have to replace him? It is clear that anarchy isn't something they want, because they are family men, with children to feed. A stable, functioning governing body at the center would be for their benefit.

And then, there is the matter of the rot.

"Master, I'm ready."

Trulio hardly looks recognizable. He has ruffled his hair, and caked his skin with mud. He is wearing rags, with holes that look like they were chewed by rodents. His feet, too, look impressively unwashed, with grime on his toenails.

"I don't have any money to spare," says the Caretaker. "Begone, you wretched fool!"

Trulio bows in a flourish.

"It's astonishing how much natural substances can accomplish. This is no Delight, Master."

"I am impressed," says the Caretaker. "Let's go."

"Where's your disguise, Master?"

The Caretaker hoped it wouldn't come to this, for him to actually reveal who he truly was. He had wanted to tell Trulio the truth long ago, but never gathered enough courage to do so. But what does he have to lose if only one other person knows about him, aside from the Seedmaster? Trulio can be trusted.

The Caretaker takes a deep breath. The hour of midnight comes, and the bells of the Eborsen temple toll relentlessly, a haunting, dirgelike quality to them. As soon as the bells stop tolling, the gray in the Caretaker's hair recedes, leaving jet-black hair. The wrinkles in his skin disappear, revealing the dark and smooth skin of a much younger man. His joints realign, his muscles redevelop. The curse completes its ghastly, temporary effect.

Trulio staggers, his knees buckling under him. He balances himself, and stops himself from letting out a loud gasp.

"Master..." he whispers. "Who are you?"

"I am Alvos Midranil," says the Caretaker. "And I am the last Florral."

The words feel heavy, and yet a weight is lifted off his chest as he finally admits the lie he has been living all these years. In uttering those words, he almost feels young again. He feels like the Alvos Midranil who'd defeated a Champion. A surge of relief courses through him, and a surge of power too.

"I don't understand," says Trulio, furrowing his brow. There's a mixture of confusion and rage on his face. The Caretaker can tell his apprentice feels betrayed. "You...you are the one who.... All those years ago...the stories...."

"I feel like I owe you an answer, Trulio," says the Caretaker.

★   ★   ★

I am Alvos Midranil. I am the last Florral. I stopped a war once. An army wept to the skies, tearless, because of me. I defeated a Champion. I brought a god to cer knees. Now, I can hardly defeat a fly, and I have only myself to blame for that.

I fled for sanctuary after stopping the war. I wanted safe harbor. The races were at peace. Instead, I got a curse. A curse I've spent most of my life fighting. A curse I still want to undo.

After defeating Tyi, and emptying my body of the last vestiges of a Delight, I was bone-weary and thirsty. After a long walk, I finally reached the Lake of Passage. It was deep, with sweet and clear water, a water of old myths and tales, a water that would replenish me and provide me with a way to the other side, to the shores of a continent that was my home.

I knelt on the shore and dipped my hands in. Gathering a gulpful, I brought the cool water to my lips. But the water disappeared in a quick flash, leaving my hands empty. I tried again, but caught nothing. The water was all there, shimmering, clear as day. The bottom reflected stones, seaweed, and pearls. In the distance, the sun kissed the silver-lined edge of the lake, the farthest shore that met the land of Mitran. The middle of the lake was as quiet and melancholy as dreamsong. It was all real.

Yet, my hands caught only air.

I tried to scoop it up again, but this time the water grew agitated. Ripples extended from the tips of my fingers like roiling ocean waves, and went to the silent center, disturbing the pristine quietness that was there a moment ago. My chest felt hollow. I had done something terribly wrong.

The center of the lake sank. Like stretched fabric when a heavy stone is dropped on it, pulling it inexorably downward. The edges began to slope to the center, the waters receding, falling, falling, making no noise until what remained was a gap, a memory of water. And from the center rose a lithe, white figure, draped in all the water that was pulled. Silvery. Godlike.

She was Ina, the Goddess of Passage.

"What thirst brought you to the shore, stranger, that you couldn't wait to pray to me?"

"Apologies, my humble apologies, my deity. It's a true thirst I carry, having fought a terrible battle," I said. "I am bone-tired, and I ask only for two big gulps and a passage to Mitran."

"You come to me at a time of my resting and you come with blood on your hands. You look wise, and yet you desecrate me like this?"

"If I tell you I fought for good, would you grant me passage?"

"Your battles interest me the least," said the goddess. I knew this. If I had arrived a week later, it would have been time. Had I arrived earlier, I would have caught the goddess before slumber, perhaps even bargained with her. I had heard she listened to reason. But today of all days, it was my folly. Under my breath, I cursed the Abhadis and their endless hatred, their stonelike, unmoving ways, their wars for lands and money and water and air, their temples of jade and ebony, their gods of sand and memory and light.

"There is no other way to Mitran, my home, the land of my people. I am being chased by forces who will go to every length to desecrate this land, just to capture me."

And even as I said this half-lie, my senses heightened. The shape of my words was given form. A sound, a snap, a crackle of twig, a rustle of leaves. Drumbeats. Hard tap against grassy ground. A march of madness. Behind me, the rest of the Abhadi army in the distance, the ones remaining, the ones not finished by me, led by a madman general.

"You hold darkness in you too. What they have done, you have done. They have blood on them, as do you. You are no saint."

Then the goddess took my name, because she knew all things.

"That is not right," I said. "Even now, they are marching toward me. I was thirsty, and tried to drink some water. If that's desecration, it's

nothing compared to what they will do once they find out the location of the lake."

"That sounds oddly like you are threatening a goddess," said Ina. "That never ends well for anyone."

I crumbled, a heaviness descending upon me. Kneeling on the rocky shore of the lake, I took a pebble in my hands. Turning it over and over in my calloused palm, I muttered under my breath a prayer and a song. It was the only way I was sure the goddess would relent, even a little bit. Removed from worldly desires, gods and goddesses still liked to be worshipped and a song in the old Inishti tongue in praise of the Goddess of Passage was the least I could do.

It was no trick. I do not believe in tricks, but carefully thought-out plans that come from a place of truth. It was my only choice. Other than dying at the hands of a bloodthirsty army. Other than dying, still young, because of a folly I didn't intend to commit. I could have – if I truly wanted to – taken the half petal of the Crocus in my pocket. It would have given me flight, and I would have effortlessly glided over the lake. The Delight would have been potent enough to carry me toward the shores of Mitran without the need of waking the goddess.

But that would have been true desecration. Going against the will of the nature of things. I didn't have it in me to change the nature of things.

I finished the song. Quietness fell upon the lake like a whisper. The water around the goddess shimmered against the sun. Beneath her, a chasm to the black depths of the lake. Legends said that at the bottom of the lake was the body of the woman shrouded by a blanket of pearls. The magic in the pearls kept the body from rotting, and that the woman was the true Goddess of Passage. But the blanket itself was incomplete. Of the ten thousand pearls it was supposed to be made of, the actual shroud contained nine thousand nine hundred and ninety-nine. The old songs said once the last pearl was sewn into the blanket, the goddess would take her true form and rise out of her watery grave. Till then, whoever took the shape of the goddess was merely an afterthought, a magical concoction from the wisps of Ina's soul, tucked somewhere inside the water.

After the silence, she spoke. "I haven't heard that song in ages."

"*Did it please you, Goddess Ina?*"

"*It did.*"

Another crackle of twigs. Harsher.

"*They seem to have arrived. Please, grant me passage, if not water to quench my thirst.*"

And before any other words were exchanged, the rest of the Abhadi army arrived. Bewitched fell-birds with a wingspan of ten feet, ordered to claw out eyes and deafen enemies with a piercing shriek. Minmassan beasts who could carry a contingent on their backs and run for leagues without tiring, their forklike, ebony tusks glinting with poison, ready to rip to shreds anyone that came in their way. And men, on foot, on the beasts, tired, adamant, angry, sweat glistening on their brows, their skin, their eyes aflame, following the orders of a mad general.

I sat helplessly on the shores. At the center of the lake, where the goddess stood a moment before, there was just water. The lake was as placid as it was before.

The general barked, "He must have drowned."

"*Or, he must have crossed,*" *said a man holding a bow and arrow, as his beast hunkered down on the stony ground.*

"*No, there wasn't enough time. Tyi told us he came this way, remember? Bless cer soul.*"

I looked at the back of my palm and my skin and my own reflection in the lake. A once-young face had been transformed into the face of an old man, creases and all. I couldn't even recognize myself.

"*You...old man! Did you see a Florral cross the lake by any chance?*"

The general had spoken to me. And it was time to play along. I understood. In cursing me, she had also saved me.

"*I can barely see you,*" *I said. "I came to drink some water, that's all."*

The general looked unconvinced for a moment, as if he had seen my true face. But then he turned around and barked more orders at his men. And just like that, the army retreated. The lake was silent again.

"*I would have drowned them, had they tried to cross.*"

Goddess Ina was back, and this time her form was more corporeal. She stood at the edge of the lake, where I knelt.

"Alvos of Inshasa, for your act of besmirching my waters, I have cursed you with old age. You will spend the rest of your years under an old, thin skin, hollow bones, weak muscles. Only for a few hours each night, you will have a taste of youth, yet each dawn will bring back old age. But your heart is also kind, and so, many years from now, when your penance is complete, you will have a chance to undo the curse. Look for the Night of the Unending Stars and you will know. Look for the one with two souls in one body, one young, one old, with a heart as kind as you."

With those words, she vanished, leaving me alone on the shores of the lake. But much later, where the stones and the pebbles met the clear water, there appeared a gap on the ground. The gap widened, the stones shattered, re-mended, and molded themselves into stairs, descending two stories below, as the waters parted. The passage to Mitran.

I gathered whatever reserves of energy I had, and took the stairs.

★   ★   ★

Both the men move stealthily among the narrow streets of Sirvassa, avoiding the main road, first restricting themselves to the crannies between shops and moving through abandoned mills and a picturetale theater. At this hour, they hardly see any patrolmen. The Sirvassan Blue Guard, responsible for nightly excursions, mostly keep themselves busy with madira and juicy, tender pieces of chicken.

When they leave the residential expanse behind, the Caretaker and Trulio start walking along the periphery of a vast drainage compound that runs at the borders of the city. A revolting stench persists in the air, rotting fish, swaths of algae, torn and forgotten clothes and shoes, leftover fruits and vegetables, all decaying merrily together. The drainage compound will open up to the sea, vomiting its dark abscess into the vast beyond.

"Trulio, did you always take this route?"

"Yes," says Trulio. "The smell is unpleasant, I know."

"I am holding my breath."

"Well, you are young, you can do that." Trulio bristles, and his jibe comes across harsher than necessary.

"You sound chirpy."

Trulio doesn't say anything. They leave the periphery, jumping off onto a narrow stretch of wet road. Faint murmurs and the nighttime hush of the docks persist in the air. In the distance, dark figures, some languid, some active. A fresh, salty smell, a welcome break from the stench of a moment ago.

A lamppost flickers into life, brightly illuminating the road, then goes back to a dull banana-yellow. The figures beneath the lamppost are only half-visible. They're not startled by the sudden light. They almost seem to revel in it. They seem to want it, and do their misdeeds in the open. Trulio grabs the Caretaker's arm and pulls him to the side, away from the light, deeper into the shadows between two closed butcher shops. Here, a smell of offal persists, and it makes the Caretaker briefly nauseous.

Matches are lit, cigarettes are smoked. Laughter ensues. From a distance, it almost looks like a general midnight chatter between dock workers who had a hard day in the sun. But soon, more and more figures begin to gather near the first Hansa ship, docked twenty feet from the end of the drainage compound. A ship that hasn't been used in ages, its prow rusted to oblivion, mold eating and thriving in its interior, making new families of mold. A ship so much in decay and disuse that it wouldn't garner a glance in a scrapyard.

But, surprisingly, a group of men haul a ladder and rest it between the edge of the prow and a cement landing, a sort of a sidewalk between the edge of the pier and the dockside road. Then, they begin their climb.

"What do you think they're doing?" asks the Caretaker.

"This is the ship where they've been storing and making their explosives."

"Are you telling me this place has had no supervision since..."

"...since two months, yes."

The Caretaker exhales sharply. Something doesn't fit, doesn't add up. Who is ordering these men? Even if one were to entertain the possibility of Minister Yayati being behind all this, why would he order the men to blow up Illyasi's bungalow in his presence?

"Master, you should have told me before," says Trulio, after a long silence.

"What would you have done with the information?"

"I don't know," says Trulio. "But it would have felt better to know that you trust me with your secrets."

"I didn't want the entire world to know that the Florral who stopped the war between Abhadis and Inishtis is living as an old man in Sirvassa. I didn't want to get anyone's hopes too high. I didn't want people to look at me like I'm a god. And when it comes to trust, believe me, Trulio, I trust you with my life. Does that make you feel better?"

He can't make out Trulio's expression in the darkness, but he must have grinned dramatically.

"Okay," Trulio begins, as if immediately shrugging off the touching moment the two of them shared. "Let's do this. I don't know how much they have inside that ship but I am assuming it's a fair amount. Counting the men, I see at least seven men on the road. Include the couple who went on board, a total of nine men."

"There must be at least six men as backup."

"Fifteen. Let's be generous, and let's say we are facing twenty men. That's a pittance for you, isn't it, Master?"

"Let's not get ahead of ourselves," says the Caretaker. Then he brings out the vials from inside his cloak. Eight vials in total. He hands four to Trulio and keeps the rest for himself.

"Drink the first two now, for speed and endurance *and* summoning and throwing. Combine that with the martial arts you learned in your travels, I think we can take them. Even if they know how to fight. But they don't look like they are built for brawls."

"Where do you come in?"

"I have chosen two very interesting Delights," says the Caretaker. "You'll see."

Trulio opens the vials and downs the potions in two quick gulps. The Caretaker does the same with his vials. Then they step out of the shadows into the light, and begin their silent walk toward the men.

"Greetings, friends," Trulio declares. "Do any of you fine gentlemen possess a match? The night is cold, and my lungs are in deep need of tobacco smoke."

Suddenly rattled by the appearance of two men, the dockworkers exchange befuddled glances with each other. Their manner suggests that they were caught in a shameful act, guilt clearly written on their faces. Their hands go to their waists, fingers itching to grab hold of something. The movement is not quick and graceful, but enough to threaten. That's when the Caretaker notices — all of them are wearing a leather belt around their waist, and from the belts hang sheaths. Uncomfortably long.

"Who are you? Who gave you permission to enter the docks at this hour?" The man who asks the question is short and bulky, and is wearing a tight sweater. His accomplice, right behind him, is too tall and too broad, stooping low like the lamppost behind him. There's a shuffle of feet, and five other men join the two, men of all shapes and sizes.

"We could ask you the same question," says the Caretaker, getting right into it. "I don't see any Red Guard around here, or you guys wouldn't be doing whatever you are doing."

"Stop this charade, and we can finish this in peace and without any bloodshed," says Trulio. "Tell us who you are working for and what is inside that ship?"

More hurried glances and more nervous tics. An uncomfortable pause swells between them. Then, suddenly, a flash of silver and a sound of metal against metal. More flashes, and the seven men become seven swordsmen. Their blades curve slightly, the sharp edges gleaming against the dull light of the lamppost. The handles are wooden and long.

But the Caretaker knows an amateur grip when he sees it. These aren't real swordsmen. They are merely carriers of lethal weapons, with no knowledge of killing.

And Trulio senses it too. Because the next moment, the sword is snatched from the hands of the short man, and flies toward Trulio, who grabs it by the handle like an expert.

"It was easy, Master," he says. "The potion is doing its job."

Before the Caretaker can react, three men charge toward them, brandishing their swords like a child would a stick. Trulio swings his hand in a wide arc and throws his sword at the men like a knife. The blade slices through the air, rotating like a fan, and cuts through the jugular veins of the two front men. Their blood makes a crescent moon arc in the air. The one remaining man staggers, his feet sliding against the blood on the ground. Behind him, more men gather, at least ten more, waving the same swords. Three more men slide down from the prow of the ship, landing with soft thuds on the pavement. They carry heavy chains, with blades at the end of them.

"Trulio, you wanted to see what I brought with me," says the Caretaker.

"I have been waiting with bated breath, Master," says Trulio.

The Caretaker reaches inside himself for an oddity, a madness. The crowd in front of them keeps increasing, as more and more men join the ones already there. The Caretaker flexes his fingers, bringing out the Delight he wanted, and then he lets go.

The men stop moving.

Their eyes still flit nervously, but their bodies don't do the bidding of their minds. They are like a swarm of bees suddenly glued to a vat of honey, unmoving. A picture from the past.

"All yours, Trulio," says the Caretaker. Trulio grins at his Master. Then he dashes toward the crowd like a battering ram.

He moves in a daze, and his legs are a blur. But the next moment he is holding a chain and a sword both, tearing through the men. He swings the chain, throws it deftly, and it loops around the necks of two men with a visceral clink, dragging their weight on the ground. With the men tied at the end of the chain, Trulio lugs at it, pulling, moving his own feet in circles, allowing the weight and the momentum to make an arc around the road. The Caretaker stands agape at what Trulio is trying to do, and can only marvel at the brutality on display. Impossibly joined at the end of the chain, the men are mere dead weights, as Trulio rotates, swings the chain with the might of the potion surging through him like a thunder, and throws the men, like a sportsman would throw a hammer.

Such is Trulio's strength that the two men fly in a neat arc and land with a thunderous splash in the sea.

"Are you impressed yet, Master?" Trulio bows again, as the remaining men stagger away from him.

But then, an impossibility.

From the prow of the ship appears another man, but he doesn't slide down the ladder, but instead glides. His eyes are black without pupils, and his skin is mottled gray. Fear grips at the heart of the Caretaker. He knows cursed Florrachemy when he sees it. He is looking at a Stigmar.

Stigmars are outcasts, but infamous users of Florrachemy, the rotten, irresponsible curse-childs, who take potions and boil them to attain a concentrated form of the Delights. But the blackness that remains at the end of a potion boil isn't a Delight anymore. Once consumed, it eats at the root of a Stigmar's being, giving them bursts of abilities, chaotic, cursory, but taking their senses and their self with it.

When the Stigmar speaks, he speaks in throttled whispers. It sounds like he is spitting air. But soon words, too, come out of his mouth.

"Go. Hide. I'll handle."

Four sharp words, but also a warning. The crowd, still reeling from the sensory assault of the Caretaker, and Trulio's violence, slowly begins to recede, dragging away their fallen comrades. Some race toward the sea, shouting, in search of the men who were unceremoniously dumped there by Trulio.

Then the Stigmar races toward Trulio. Trulio is ready for him, and fights back. But the Stigmar is overpowering, just by his very nature. Chaos unfurls around his movements, as he kicks and punches at Trulio mercilessly. The Caretaker tries to do to the Stigmar what he did to the crowd, but he senses his Delight waning. From the depths of his senses, he brings out another.

With one swift motion of his hands, he takes the chains lying on the ground and coils them around the Stigmar's body. The Stigmar resists but the Caretaker keeps pressing, increasing pressure relentlessly. His black eyes bulge outward, and so do his gray veins. He shrieks soundlessly, like a death sound of a crow. But the Stigmar is very much alive.

Trulio gets up and immediately summons a sword. But before he can swing it in a final death arc, the Caretaker grabs his arm. Something inside the Caretaker shifts. His bones grind, his muscles twist, his young heart becomes its old arrhythmic self.

"Master..." Trulio whispers. The sword falls from his hands and clatters on the ground. The spell breaks as the Caretaker crumbles on the dark cement road, the curse returning like a slap from a god, all the Florrachemy draining out of him. The Caretaker struggles to breathe, his chest heaving. He turns his head to look at the Stigmar.

The Stigmar breaks the chains.

Only one word stumbles out of the Caretaker's mouth.

"Trulio...."

The Stigmar comes fast. But this time, Trulio is ready. He doesn't need to summon a sword. As he sees the wretched thing run toward him, he turns in a blur and punches him hard in the guts. The wind is knocked out so hard from the Stigmar's lungs that it hits like a slap. But the Stigmar himself scatters across the road like a stone skidding on water. His cursed frame hits the edge of a pier and shatters the wood into shards.

The Caretaker closes his eyes. The last thing he remembers is Trulio cradling his body.

★　　★　　★

He wakes up in warmth. The coarse comfort of his own blanket around his body. The suffused heat of a fire crackling in the hearth. A simmering pot of Enjing tea, which he can smell. He opens his eyes. The window of his room, overlooking Sirvassa, flickers into his vision.

It's still dark outside. The night sky shimmers with stars, and the ever-pulsating glint of the jalan over the Sirvassan rooftops. There's soreness in his joints, and his muscles feel stretched and compressed, both at the same time. It's like every other night, but worse, because of the little adventure, made worse by the Florrachemy sluicing inside him.

"Master."

Trulio's voice is gentle and soothing. A hand grabs his shoulders firmly. The Caretaker struggles to get up. His room comes into full focus. Everything is the same, except for a dark shape huddled in the corner of the room, tied to a wooden chair with chains. The Caretaker blinks, and blinks again.

It's the Stigmar. He is gagged and bound and is struggling. His eyes look like the eyes of a man so far into the madness he had wrought upon himself that it's hard to come back.

"Master, it was hard to bring the both of you back here, but somehow I did it."

"Perhaps you write it into your journal, the entire process— Aah!"

The Caretaker winces as something creaks near his hip.

"Master, you fell upon a loose chain link. It was heavy. I am making a kadhan potion to soothe your pains. It will also bring about good sleep."

The Caretaker sits against the wall, straightening his legs. He brings his blanket closer to his chest, eyeing the Stigmar.

"Did he speak?"

"I have not tried my methods yet," says Trulio.

The Stigmar bares his teeth against the gagging cloth. It looks like he is trying to laugh. A slow crackle comes out of his throat, mixed with a gurgling sound. He sputters and coughs, but then laughs again.

"Oh, the poor man is trying to speak," says Trulio. He opens his gag a bit. The Stigmar bares his teeth, revealing black stains and blacker gums. There's a scar running across his cheek. The Caretaker remembers the scar. It's the same man he saw all those weeks ago, in the alley.

The Stigmar laughs. Then he laughs some more.

Trulio smacks him across his face. The impact is so fierce that a sharp snapping sound echoes across the room. The Stigmar's neck creaks at an awkward angle, then comes back to where it was. His lips bleed, and he grins manically.

"What is this creature, Master?"

"He has too much of a Delight running through him," says the Caretaker.

"What did he do?"

The Caretaker tries to piece together the Stigmar's condition. The existence of Stigmars every now and then was the reason he did not open the Garden to the outside world. Even rule-following, innocent Sirvassans would sometimes sway down a dark path, reading false facts in an odd book or two. Many years ago, a well-read clothing merchant had come to the Garden asking for a Delight that would allow him to sew faster. It was a fair ask, spawning out of a professional necessity. The Caretaker had obliged. But the merchant had gone ahead and boiled the potion, inhaling the fumes, instead of ingesting the liquid. The man had then become a machine, such was the speed granted to him by the Delight. But soon, the Delight had become a curse. He began to see tears and rips everywhere, using his needle to sew back cracks in walls. Slowly, the Delight began to consume him. He would have danced in the arms of madness, had it not been for the timely intervention of the Caretaker.

"He smoked it like a drug, and now the drug is giving it back to him. The Delight has to be emptied before he can be sane again."

"What should I do, Master?"

The Caretaker racks his brains. There's no Delight from the Garden that would work as an antidote because of the rot. It might just exacerbate the Stigmar's condition, making him into a zombie. A more herbal concoction would have to do the trick here. He scratches a spot under his ear, thinking. Then it strikes him.

"The garden...not *our* Garden, but the one behind my laboratory. The smaller one. It has a quinine plant. Crush it into the Enjing tea you are making and mix in some curcumin. Make him drink it slowly. He will vomit out his insides, and hopefully, with them, also the truth."

Trulio moves swiftly. While he is gone, the Stigmar stares at the Caretaker with hate-filled eyes, spitting bloody saliva on the floor. The Stigmar wants him to initiate conversation, but the Caretaker restrains himself. He is the perfect example of the desecration of Eborsen's gift, and the Caretaker wouldn't entertain something like that. He has his own curse to handle.

"I...saw...you..." the Stigmar begins. "Young. Flor... Florral.... I...thought...you...didn't...exist."

"I am here," says the Caretaker. "Existing just fine."

"You...will...be...finished..." says the Stigmar. "Your kind... the Garden. Finished."

Trulio comes back with the quinine flower and a packet filled with curcumin powder. First, he pours some tea for the Caretaker in a bowl, then he upends the herbs into the remaining liquid in the pot. The room is filled with a sharp herby, but bitter, smell. When the smell is gone, and the liquid is reduced much further, Trulio pours it into a ceramic cup.

"Drink it, you monster," says Trulio, bringing the cup to the Stigmar's lips. The man hesitates and struggles. "I will force it down your throat by placing a knife inside your mouth, across your cheeks. You don't want that, trust me."

The Stigmar hesitates some more, but Trulio grabs his windpipe, digging his nails into his skin, and the man screams. Trulio pours the warm liquid down his throat. The Stigmar sputters and gurgles.

"Stop struggling or you'll choke on it," Trulio barks. The Stigmar, shockingly, does as he is told, the specter of a death by choking falling before his eyes like a dark curtain. Trulio starts rubbing the Stigmar's back. The Caretaker is surprised at Trulio's utter brutality and then his gentleness, a counterpoint.

Within seconds, a deep green liquid hurls out of the Stigmar's mouth, mixed with some red. He wheezes and heaves, and vomits some more. The clean cement floor of the room is soon smeared with undigested food and bile and foul-smelling herbs.

"Good boy," says Trulio. "Thanks, Master."

Color comes back into the Stigmar's face. His eyes are no longer black. They are a deep hazel. His lips are still a pale gray, but a shade of pink can be seen at the edges, life returning to them slowly but surely. His breathing is shallow but certain.

"Tell us, now," says the Caretaker.

"Tell you what?"

"Why are you planning the attack on the mayor's bungalow? What do you plan to achieve?"

The man glares at the Caretaker. Then he falls into raucous laughter. He is no longer a Stigmar, but the derision and the hatred are still present in him.

"Mayor's bungalow? Why would we attack the mayor's bungalow? You lot are fools, really. Being a Florral doesn't give you a brain, does it?"

Trulio slaps him hard. Blood gushes out of the man's lips.

"Attacking the bungalow of that useless mayor won't achieve anything. We are here to cripple Sirvassa, the city. And we start with—"

The man vomits again. This time, a black liquid gushes out of his mouth, mixing with the already muddy vomit on the floor. He starts heaving and breathing heavily. His face contorts into a mask of pain.

"What did you give me?" he screams.

"Tell us, and I'll make the pain go away," says Trulio.

"Trulio, did you mix anything else?" says the Caretaker.

"I wanted to hurt him because he hurt you," says Trulio. "I mixed some poppy seeds."

The Caretaker shakes his head. He gets to his feet.

More blackness hurls out of the man. He screams like a flying beast whose limbs are being torn apart, wing and feather and bone.

"Please stop it, oh god, please stop it!!!" he yells.

"Trulio, you shouldn't have," the Caretaker whispers. The man shudders and gasps. Trulio grabs him by his shoulders to stop him from shaking. He then barks into the man's ears, "Tell us and we will stop!"

"*The docks!*" he yells. "*The ships!*"

Trulio's jaw hits the floor at the answer. He lets go of the man, and stares at the Caretaker. Then, with an ear-splitting shriek, the man goes silent, passing out from the pain.

CHAPTER TWENTY

The Caretaker

It has all happened too fast.

The Caretaker doesn't sleep too well, just after capturing the Stigmar. He twists and turns, the actions of the night having rattled him to the bones. The next morning, he decides to visit Mayor Illyasi and tell him all about the impending attack, to prepare him, and if possible, to guide him.

But when he reaches the bungalow, a peculiar sight awaits him. The mayor is surrounded by several Waystrewers, as he addresses a group of six people. Snippets of conversation waft toward him as he approaches the main gate, which is wide open today for some reason.

"…with all due respect, Mayor Illyasi, we want some sort of regulation in place. It's for the benefit of the city." A short man is speaking in slow, clipped notes, as if not confident of the request he is making. And truly, his request is dismissed, sidelined, as another woman speaks up authoritatively.

"Mayor Illyasi, our agency is struggling, to be frank. Two of my engineers have left and moved away from the city. How am I supposed to keep my operations running? Are you introducing any reforms, or not?"

The mayor looks at the woman, then at the man, and then beyond them, and his gaze falls directly on the Caretaker.

"Ah…." He claps his hands, then he looks at the short man and urges him to look behind. "I think you can get your answers from my dear friend here."

The group turns around to face the Caretaker. The man who had asked the first question immediately frowns.

"You. You are still running the Garden? Even after what happened to that tailor's son? I have heard of more such mishaps with men, women, and children. I was just telling the mayor that perhaps there should be stricter regulatory measures—"

"I have stopped inviting people to the Garden," says the Caretaker firmly.

"Well, you got your answer," says the woman. "Mayor, can we have a meeting about it tomorrow?"

"You will have your reforms soon, I promise. And all you people. Don't worry. Big things are planned for Sirvassa."

Mayor Illyasi looks like a haunted man as he says the words, as if he is under the spell of something sinister. Three Waystrewers are around him now, wrapping their joyous tentacles around his legs. The mayor erupts into a silly grin, unbecoming of a person of his stature.

The crowd dissipates. The Caretaker walks toward Mayor Illyasi.

"Do you have any idea what is happening in your city?"

"I have," says the mayor. His silly expression fades into something more serious. "But it's just too much."

"You look like you haven't slept in weeks."

"That's what this office does to you," says the mayor. "Sorry for suggesting that *you* could take over. Sorry for even asking you. Sorry for all those desperate coppergrams I sent. But things are seriously looking up. Minister Yayati is currently sitting with his advisors and jotting out a plan of action. Frankly, it's not as bad as I thought. He just wants a share of the Inigee river water, that's all! Imagine that! So far, he hasn't mentioned petal export even once. Most of his day goes into seeing the sights of Sirvassa. He visited the Temple of Eborsen too. Wanted to experience the Hour of the Futures, but was denied by the priestess. Had some unsavory words to say about her."

Illyasi rattles like he wants to get a load off his chest. The Caretaker tilts his head to the side and observes his long-time friend. Age lines mar his face like creeks in a barren desert. The hollows beneath his eyes have become pools of tar. Skin tags jut out near his neck, with brown-black streaks of folds running beneath. All signs of a man who hasn't been keeping well. A man desperate, fallen to despair and illness, but unwilling to let go of whatever pride he is holding on to. But the Caretaker knows there's a truth the mayor wants to tell, but can't quite bring himself to.

The Caretaker sighs, dropping his shoulders. "I came here to tell you something and you need to listen to me," he says. He tells the mayor everything. From his fateful late-night visit to the docks, to the planning with Trulio, to the night skirmish, to the captured Stigmar. Everything. Mayor Illyasi listens to him like an eager child, nodding at appropriate intervals, expressing shock at others. But when the Caretaker is finished, the mayor laughs.

"I have to admit, that's quite an imaginative story," he says. "And Minister Yayati was right. He told me that one day someone would come up with something like this. I am surprised that person is *you*."

"You don't believe me."

"An attack. On the docks." The mayor scoffs. "Pffh. You know for how long that would stop exports and imports? Months!"

"That's why you need to do something about it! I saw a Stigmar, for the love of Eborsen! I have him captured!" Desperation trickles out of the Caretaker's mouth, but his words don't have any effect on the mayor.

"I removed the Red Guard from the docks. You know why? Because they desperately needed a leave of absence. You don't think I have eyes and ears of my own? You think I don't follow what's going on in my own city? I have spies bringing me news from all corners of Sirvassa, and believe me I haven't heard anything."

"Jaywardna, please," says the Caretaker.

But the mayor shakes his head dismissively.

"I truly don't have time for fairy tales," he says, with his hands on the Caretaker's shoulders. He keeps a straight face as he speaks, but his tone is patronizing. "That is your department, my friend. Have you found one of your Florrals yet? I say keep them for the history books. Please tend to the Garden and bring it back in business, and see you don't kill any children while you are at it."

That sentence does it. The Caretaker removes the mayor's hands from his shoulders and lets them fall.

"Goodbye, Illyasi," says the Caretaker curtly. "Don't say later I didn't warn you."

"Till we meet again," says the mayor. "Actually, we are, quite soon. You must have received an invitation. This time it's not coppergrammed. It's a proper seal."

"What invitation?"

"A dinner at my bungalow. In honor of Minister Yayati. The cream of Sirvassa is coming, and many more from Alhassa, too. You should come. Mingle with everyone else. Maybe you'll even get a date, who knows? It will be better for you, actually, rather than remaining in isolation."

"How kind of you."

Contempt drips out of the Caretaker's mouth, tinging his words like bad paint on a wall. He takes a mournful look at the Waystrewers, then turns around and leaves, without bothering to greet the eager security guard, who has only ever said nice things to him. Even as the Caretaker walks past the stream, a plan begins to form in his mind. It would require careful use of the best Delights, and some responsible planning, mostly on Trulio's part, who would have to be disciplined away from taking rash decisions.

But by the time he reaches the Garden, it is already too late.

CHAPTER TWENTY-ONE

Iyena Mastafar

A thump, thump, thump on the door wakes Iyena the next morning. Flashes of the evening before jump out of the darkness of her memory and in front of her eyes. The two visions, the charm of the priestess, and her father's subsequent kindness. After they returned home, the rest of the evening was uneventful. Maani-Ba prepared a lentil soup and flatbread, which Iyena ate to her heart's content. The lentil soup was warm and spicy, and reminded her of Alderra. Times when her mother used to make the same soup for her, with added coriander sprigs on the top, her favorite bit. Iyena used to scoop it up with steaming rice.

She climbs out of her bed, belching, stomach acids reaching upward to her throat. Perhaps too much spice in the meal last night. Still groggy, she opens her door, and finds Maani-Ba standing, bearing a tray of milk and fruits.

"You're late," she says. "The carriage will be here any moment." Maani-Ba enters and places the tray on the mantelpiece, just to the right of a framed photo of Iyena's mother. The tray hits the frame, and it teeters at the edge of the mantelpiece, threatening to fall. Iyena grabs it and steadies it just in time. This wakes her up.

"I don't understand," she says, rubbing her eyes with one hand, and placing back the frame with the other. "The school carriage?"

"Yes," says Maani-Ba. "I've ironed your dress too."

"What about Father?"

"He's the one who asked Din-Tevair that your studies be resumed. The Din-Tevair, of course, was more than happy to say yes. You *had* stirred up quite the nest after you saved Trehan's life, after all."

Iyena pinches herself and looks around. She touches the mantelpiece, and the photo of her mother. She breathes in the air to be sure all of it isn't a lie. The air feels cool, crisp, the air of Sirvassa, filled with the wood smell of her own room. There is no persistent smell of roses. It is all familiar, all real.

"Is everything all right, Iyena?" Maani-Ba's voice is tinged with the deepest, most honest concern. This is an honesty Iyena knows and can tell. It comes from the heart. It is true.

"Everything is fine," says Iyena. "I just didn't expect Father to...." She finds herself unable to voice what she feels and looks at Maani-Ba in expectation.

"I didn't either," says Maani-Ba. "But here we are."

★   ★   ★

Iyena sits on the last seat as her classmates start trickling in. Her eyes are affixed on the revolving door, eager to catch a glimpse of the sandy-haired boy. Her feet are jittery, and pinpricks run through her body. In front of her a notebook lies open, with random scribbles she had made earlier, absent-mindedly. A wavy line meeting a circle, a rectangle jutting out of a pyramid. There is no rhyme or reason to those designs but they are there, a part of her mind written on the page.

"Looks like you had a nice holiday."

Iyena's gaze shifts from the revolving door to Ujita. Her slick, oiled hair is tied in a neat ponytail and she carries a stack of parchments. Her eyes look extra round and bulbous through the convex glasses she is wearing.

"It wasn't..." starts Iyena, but then immediately purses her lips. Perhaps it is better to pretend that she was on an extended vacation than to tell everyone the bitter truth.

"Well, whatever it was, you came at the right time," Ujita says, and hands her a parchment. Iyena gazes at the yellowed, crinkly paper, which holds the insignia of the school. The other papers in the girl's hands are of various textures, but all of them seem to say the same thing. Iyena's eyes go wide as she reads the contents.

"What is all this?" she asks.

"The syllabus is changing," says Ujita. "I don't know why."

"It's not changing entirely, though," says Iyena, pointing at the paper. "Appendix A clearly states that there are amendments to be made to the existing curriculum."

"Wait till you hear the amendments," says Ujita. "Apparently the Llar Mountains were not made naturally but created by some great engineer from Alderra long, long ago."

"But how could a mountain be created?"

Before the girl can answer her question, Trehan bursts through the revolving doors. His sandy hair falls on his shoulders and his eyes look dreamier than usual. Despite the dire news thrust on her a moment ago, the moment feels light, suddenly. Sunlight filtering through a dark cloud.

He walks casually over to Iyena and smiles a hearty smile. "Welcome back," he says. "I'm assuming Ujita has already filled you in."

"She has," says Iyena.

"Prepare to be dazzled," says Trehan. "Unlearn everything, and relearn everything."

"The school curriculum changes often, but not to this degree," Ujita chimes in. There is a barest hint of tremor in her voice. As if her brain would not be able to take the weight of extra, contradictory knowledge. As if she would collapse if she had to learn new things.

"I think we'll be fine," says Trehan. "Din-Tevair has promised that this won't affect our broader understanding of our world. In fact, it will only enrich it. Like salt in a previously unseasoned dish."

"You are talking nonsense," says Ujita.

"His words, not mine."

"Did he mention any reason behind these changes?"

Trehan shakes his head. He takes the seat to the left of Iyena. His gaze falls on her notebook.

"So, you're an artist too!"

"These are just stupid scribbles," says Iyena and tries to take the notebook away from Trehan.

"No, no, no," he says, as he grabs the notebook. "I think you're onto something here." He smirks. Iyena curses Trehan under her breath. His behavior is brash, odd, and very random, a far cry from the uncertain, nervous energy he displayed a week ago.

"Give the diary back or I'll do what I don't want to do," says Iyena. Trehan stares at her and within a second the smirk is wiped off his face.

"Turn my blood to jelly?" he whispers as he hands the diary back.

"Tar," says Iyena, and gives Trehan a dark smile. There's a shuffle of feet near the revolving door. A few other students enter the classroom, followed by Tevair Talavi, a shadow of a man, with gaunt cheekbones, and a large head. Two fell-birds follow in his wake, leaving shimmering patterns in the air. The birds perch on his shoulders as he stands in front of the classroom, his tall thin figure casting a long, spindly shadow across the room. When he speaks, he speaks with precision.

"I am Tevair Talavi, replacing your earlier Professor of Sirvassan History," he says. The fell-birds coo. The students, though unsurprised by this development, speak in hushed tones. Ujita raises her hand.

"What happened to Tevair Ahinya?"

"He is on indefinite leave," says Talavi, with the barest hint of remorse in his voice. "But fear not. I'm here to expand your understanding of Sirvassa and the world in general."

The fell-birds take flight, leaving another rainbow shimmering in the air. Talavi clears his throat.

"What was your last lesson?"

"We were learning about the spices grown in Sirvassa by the indigenous community, the Inishti," says Iyena. Talavi scoffs, and scratches his nose in response. A hush falls over the classroom, like a dark spell. The fell-birds come back, chittering, and perch on Talavi's shoulders.

"Unlearn, relearn," says Talavi. "The so-called spices were actually brought in by benevolent travelers from lands afar, the Abhadis."

Ujita raises her hand again. Talavi arches his eyebrows and points at her with a crooked finger. Ujita stands and clears her throat. "That's impossible," she says. "My grandmother is a direct descendant of the original Gaghwals, the Inishti people who grew the spices."

"And was your grandmother actually present those thousands of years ago to see if the spices were grown or brought in?"

"With due respect, Professor, were you actually present to witness the same?"

The fell-birds flutter about aggressively and the rainbow shimmer turns a deep, dark violet. Talavi's lips curve into a thin smile, which creates gashes in his gaunt skin. On a more pleasing face those would be cute dimples.

"Please leave," says Talavi coldly. Ujita does as she is told, and walks out of the classroom. A cold pit forms inside Iyena's stomach as she takes it all in.

★　★　★

As late afternoon approaches, the Sirvassan sky turns a hue of turmeric. The air is crisp and almost sweet. Outside the school, a group of people wearing jade uniforms and wicker baskets on their heads roam around holding brooms. The brooms aren't ordinary; their bristles are soft and meant to pick up not dust but something else.

The students shuffle out of the school in batches. Iyena walks toward the carriage with Trehan in tow. The Rhisuan beast grunts at the closest broom handler, who is looking at the sky, waiting for something.

"Ah, it's time for petal fall," says Trehan, his face beaming. Iyena places her bag on the seat of the carriage and looks around. Everyone is looking at the sky as if expecting rain to fall. But the sky is clear, devoid of clouds.

A soft brush on Iyena's arm. It's a yellow snipping of a flower. Half a petal. She brushes it off. But then another appears, a deeper hue of yellow, bordering on orange. She looks up. The sky is filled with a smattering of such petals, the color of honey, lemon, mustard, and dandelion. They fall all around, and the collectors in jade uniforms begin a dance of their own. Skipping, jumping, sliding, their feet nimble, their eyes assured, they collect the petals in their baskets. The ones they don't collect, they let fall and sweep off.

"It signifies a change of season," says Trehan. Iyena looks at the dance in awe.

"I've never seen anything like this in my life," she says, picking up a petal the color of lime. She smells it. It has a warm, earthy smell, not flowerlike, but something deeper.

"That's because it doesn't happen anywhere else in the world." It's Ujita who joins them, carrying a bundle of papers. "Observe the dance. It is so synchronized that one person collects petals of one color and one color only."

It is true. The collectors' feet tap in unison, and their bodies twirl around. If someone were to watch them from above, they'd see a pattern in their dance too.

"This happens only in Sirvassa," says Ujita, looking at the dancers fondly. "These petals have healing qualities, far beyond the medicinal capabilities of any state in the Three Realms. No one can change it. No one can tell me, or convince me otherwise. This is what I've grown up seeing with my own eyes."

Ujita's voice is laced with anger, and it radiates outward. Iyena feels it submerge under her skin as well. The red-hot rage that comes when your own history is denied to you. She hasn't known it personally, but as the bright, summer-yellow flower snips fall from an invisible source in the sky, landing on her school dress, she can feel it too. The beauty of the place and its glory. The delight and the rage. Everything.

★　　★　　★

Maani-Ba's face doesn't betray any emotion the next morning when Iyena tells her about the change in the syllabus. She goes through the motions: wiping the oak of the dining room table clean, arranging chairs, cleaning mantelpieces, arranging steaming-hot dishes properly in their dedicated containers, even as Iyena tells her about her odd day. Her eyebrow twitches when Iyena tells her about the fall of the petals, but then she goes back to being stoic about the entire affair.

"Iyena, child, these things happen everywhere," she says, after she is done with her chores. Iyena sits down at the edge of her bed, grabbing the sheets. "You must learn to accept these changes. Widen your worldview."

"But my friends don't agree with the changes," says Iyena, and her voice almost trembles. Even she is surprised at the sudden empathy, the sudden rage she feels at the newest developments. "It is their lived history."

Maani-Ba opens her mouth to say something, but then closes it. Her aged, bony fingers curl against Iyena's soft, young ones.

"Do you wish you could change things?" asks Maani-Ba after a long pause. Iyena looks in her eyes. The whites have some yellow streaks in them, but her pupils are alert, keen, wise. Does she know?

Iyena doesn't answer her question. Their silence is punctured by a knock on the door. Anaris Mastafar stands leaning against the frame of the door, his hands folded, a thin smile on his face.

"Breakfast is prepared," says Maani-Ba, standing in a rush, straightening the creases in her dress.

"I had it, Maani-Ba," says Anaris in a soft, kind voice. "Iyena, dear, have you had your breakfast?"

"Not yet, Father," says Iyena.

"Maani-Ba has prepared a very nice oatmeal bread," he says. "Go, have it with some cheese and butter. There's also tea and juice and biscuits."

"I'm not that hungry, Father," says Iyena, shifting on her bed. Maani-Ba excuses herself out of the father-daughter conversation. Iyena wishes she hadn't, her eyes glued to the place where she was standing a moment ago.

"You will need your energy for where I am going to take you," says Anaris. "And you will like it, I promise that." Anaris doesn't look imposing anymore. He kneels on the floor, just beside Iyena, taking her upturned palm in his hand, and scrawling empty letters on it with his index finger. Memories of six years ago waft back like a gale. A windswept porch in Alderra. Iyena sits cross-legged, watching swanships course across a purple sky, as her mother holds her hand, scribbling nonsense.

"What shape am I making?" she asks.

"A cloud," Iyena answers.

Her mother closes her palm, one finger at a time. "Now you're holding that cloud."

Iyena smiles, then points at the swanship. "Will I ever get to travel in that?"

"When you're old enough."

The rest of the memory is a dim haze.

"What am I making, Iyena?" asks Anaris. Iyena tries to focus, but his fingers are rough.

"A ship?" she tries. Anaris closes her palm, softly pushing back each finger.

"Now you're holding that ship," says Anaris. "The *Valdorna* docks today. I remember when we arrived on the shores of Sirvassa you expressed a desire to spend a day at the docks, so fascinated you were by the busy nature of the place. Since there's no school today, and I am off duty, how would you like to spend some hours with your father?"

Iyena remembers the docks. Her father mentioned only the busy nature of the place, but that is far from the truth. There were all those scents, salt, seaweed, timber, and broth. Women crouching on stone outcroppings with wicker baskets full of scaly fish, men carrying boxes full of spices and fruits and dropping them on small ferries. Hulls of ships changing colors when it was time for them to leave the shore.

"I would love to do that," says Iyena. She would much rather have spent the day with Trehan, but he had said his mother had prepared chores for him. She would much rather have spent the day finding the true nature of her powers, and if she could change more things as she wished. Perhaps change the nature of the water she drank, or the food she ate, make salty to spice and sweet. But she doesn't want to displease her father, especially since his request is nice and reasonable.

"Have something to eat, first," says Anaris. "I will wrap some work. We will go in the afternoon." As he gets up, his gaze falls on her mother's photo. For a brief moment, there's just silence. It looks to Iyena like her father might grab the photo and fling it out of the window in rage. But the grip of his fingers on his cane tightens, and his lips quiver, as if he is about to say something. A shadow falls across his face. But then, it passes. Anaris lets out a breath and walks out of the room.

★　　★　　★

The Amaran beast, a faster hybrid of the Rhisuan, and an infinitely more pleasant animal in general, pulls the carriage across the petal-ridden, yellowed main road of Sirvassa. Iyena watches the shops, the blocky houses, and more petal collectors race past dizzyingly fast. Cool, late afternoon wind whips at her. Behind her, Anaris sits, whistling an old tune, a song popular in Alderra, sung at the onset of winter.

"When the first Abhadi came into these lands, they brought with them texts they had written during their travels across the great white desert," says Anaris. "The text was their code and they stuck to it."

"What was in their texts?" asks Iyena, still looking out of the carriage as the city speeds by.

"Many things," says Anaris. "Ways of living, eating, conducting professionally, usage of magic, codes for men, codes for women, everything."

"Have you read those texts?"

Anaris scoffs, then lets out a hearty laugh. "Those are ancient, Iyena. None among us has access to the true original. Which is why Sern and Sernir teach those learnings orally. The Ways, as you are no doubt aware of."

"Is it important to follow those texts?"

"For many, it's their way of living. Only a few consider it just a book." Anaris shifts closer to Iyena, and places his hand on her shoulder. "And the needs of the many outweigh the needs of the few."

Anaris says it earnestly. Iyena knows her father means it from his heart, but something about those words troubles her. She finds herself not agreeing, but keeps quiet. At that moment, the Amaran beast jerks to a stop. The carriage lurches forward then steadies. Iyena hears a ripping sound as she tries to get up. She turns around; the edge of her dress has caught on a nail, and a lone piece of fabric, curiously, almost neatly, triangular in shape, is stuck to it.

"It's fine," says Anaris, noticing the torn edge. "We'll get you another one."

Iyena ignores his statement and climbs out of the carriage. The smell of salt hits her, and a warm-cold air prickles her skin. Next, immediately, comes the scent of jasmine, then fish, then an odd bombardment of wood mixed with moss and batter-crusted emanga frying in oil. The ground beneath her feet is wet, and the sea stretches out so far it disappears into a white haze in the distance, not even meeting the sky. Hansa ships are docked near brightly colored piers, surrounded by quivering, gleaming hunterflies, their lights dim in the afternoon, but promising to be brighter as the day gets dimmer.

Iyena almost looks behind her, making sure there are no giants around. Because the sea she saw back in the temple is the same sea roiling in front of her, the same sea she crossed all the way to come to Sirvassa.

"Is something troubling you, Iyena?" asks Anaris. Iyena is jolted back to the present.

"Nothing, Father," she says, flicking away a strand of hair from her face, which the wind keeps bringing back. "Why are we here?"

"It pains me to say it, but I lied," says Anaris. "Actually, I had to oversee a shipping of food items all the way from Alderra."

"But why?"

"Minister Yayati prefers his food to be a certain way. There's a big dinner event coming up at Mayor Illyasi's bungalow. Can't trust his Inishti—" he stops, breathes deep, then continues, "his *staff* to prepare a proper dish."

"No, I asked why did you have to lie to me?"

"You might not have agreed," says Anaris. "I know you don't hold a good opinion of me, dear, and I understand I have been an absent, strict father. This seemed like a way I could spend time with you."

"We could have spent time together at home," she says.

"Don't you like the docks?"

"Not today," she says. "It's too windy, and the air is too salty."

"Well, then, we won't be here too long, dear. You see that ship?" Anaris points toward a mammoth vessel, about thrice as big as the ones docked by its side. Its name – *Kkirinth* – is scribbled in cursive across the exterior of its wooden hull in an ancient Alderran script.

"We're just going to climb that, overlook, inspect as the men and women unload the food and the spices. Once we're happy, we will bid them goodbye and be on our way."

"That sounds fine," says Iyena, looking at the ship. A gust of wind brings the stubborn strand of hair back in her face.

★　　★　　★

The ship bobbles up and down, and Iyena struggles to find balance. The wood creaks and groans under her feet, a sound of an ancient elephant waking from slumber. From a distance, the ship looked pristine, majestic. But it's actually an old, broken beast, its once-sturdy wood rotting away to slime under water, its deep insides hollowed out by persistent termites.

A brass railing runs across the edge of the hull. Iyena's father grips it with one hand and his cane with another, a wince on his face as he barks orders at the men unloading crates and boxes.

"Show me that," he says, as two muscular men carry a large, mud-brown box with illegible engravings on it, and nails jutting out from every corner. The men stop, glance at Anaris, kneel slowly, and place the heavy box slowly on the deck. The insides of the box rattle softly. It doesn't sound like glass, but it does sound fragile.

"Why did I pay Rivian a fortune when the shipping is done in boxes like these?" says Anaris, tapping the edge of the box with his boot.

"We don't know about that," says one of the men, almost grinning, his teeth tobacco-red. "We just carry."

"Open it," Anaris says. The two men give each other curious glances, then shrug. Anaris narrows his gaze at the men and taps his foot with impatience.. "What is the problem?"

"We said we're just the carriers. We carry."

"Do you know who I am?"

The man lets out a thin stream of bright red spittle, which joins a puddle of water and grime on the ship's deck. "No," he says, chewing the last remains of his tobacco. "But you sound like you give orders."

Anaris reaches inside his trousers and brings out a thick wad of Sirvassan currency. He counts notes as the grin on the tobacco-chewing man's face grows wider. His assistance stares at the notes stoically.

"There'll be no need for that."

Anaris looks up. Iyena shifts her gaze from the box to her right. A woman, her face angular, gaunt, her eyes like a hawk, in sharp Alderran attire — loose-fitting shirt and trousers and a thick belt, a leather pouch on her waist — approaches them.

"My sister's price is always right," she says. "These boxes came from warehouses *you* manage, Anaris Mastafar. Perhaps you should talk to your people in Alderra."

Anaris gives a curt smile to the woman. "Pleased to meet you, Rivian," he says. "I'd greet you in Alderran formal, but then I'd fall." As her father says these words Iyena hears another grumble from the depths of the ship. More joints aching, more things breaking inside.

"Is that a snide way of suggesting my ship's not in order?"

"Take whatever you want from my words," says Anaris. "Rivian, this is my daughter, Iyena. Iyena, meet the captain of the *Kkirinth*."

Iyena gives the proper Alderran greeting to the woman, who responds likewise. A smile flickers on Rivian's face, and then vanishes. Then, she shifts her gaze toward the two carrier men.

"What are you waiting for, Jasan? Open the damn box," she barks. Jasan wipes his red spittle-smeared chin and gestures to his friend. Their faces wince with effort as they try to heave the stubborn lid off the box. Soon, Jasan's forehead starts showing beads of sweat, trickling down his cheek, falling on his trousers. The box makes a lot of scraping and groaning noises, and each second feels closer to the second it might relent, but it never does. Jasan gives a final grunt, and throws his hands in the air.

"Anyone else who wants to try their luck is most welcome," he says, panting. Before anyone can say anything, Iyena approaches the box. She kneels on the wet deck and examines its edges, where the lid meets the rest of the crate. She touches its surface and feels a surge inside her. The nature of the box. Time and moisture and heat have married two surfaces together. The lid is the box and the box is the lid. They have become one unit.

She knows she can change the nature of things. Make this one unit break into two. But she doesn't want to do it in front of everyone, especially her father. She rejects the urge and gets up.

"What were you doing, Iyena?" asks Anaris.

"Nothing," she says.

"Just pry the lid apart with the other side of a hammer, you dimwit," says Rivian to Jasan. Iyena knows it might not be possible to do even that. But she chooses to remain quiet. Jasan gestures to his friend, who hasn't said a word till now, to go inside the cabin. A war without words ensues between them, where neither of them is willing to relent to go inside the cabin. Rivian watches this, tapping her feet on the boards.

"Just unload this, you incompetent *bresna*," says Anaris.

"What did you call us?" Jasan glares at Anaris. "Can you repeat that last word?"

"*Bresna*. Ones with no brains nor hands nor legs. Or do you need me to elaborate in your language? There are more colorful words."

Jasan charges toward Anaris, shaking his fists, grunting like a beast. Anaris clutches his cane tightly, as if preparing to use it as a weapon if need be. Before anything can happen, however, Rivian comes between the two men, holding out her hands to stop Jasan.

"Anaris, there's no need for that kind of language," she says. "Jasan, you want to get paid or not?"

Anaris staggers back and glues his frame to the railing of the ship, his face a mask of revulsion. Jasan spits again.

"You called him a dimwit," says Anaris. "What's the difference?"

"It's my ship and those are my men. I can call them whatever I want. And who do you think you are, trying to start a fight with my men while your daughter is on board? Doesn't make you that good of a negotiator."

"I am not a negotiator. I'm an ambassador."

"Both are the same to me," says Rivian. She turns her head and speaks to the men in a different tongue. They nod aggressively, then heave the box backward together, until they reach a slanted plank that connects the pier to the railing of the ship. Iyena watches the box slide along the wooden plank, along with many more such boxes, and reach the pier in a soft tumble, where more workers pick them up and shift them onto Rhisuan-pulled carriages.

"You might not be aware but Minister Yayati is in Sirvassa at this moment," says Anaris, his voice now showing barely a shadow of the previous aggression. "It's best for you to—"

At this, the ship groans a little more severely than before. From its depths comes a loud creaking. Rivian's eyes twitch, darting from him to Iyena in a blur. Anaris clutches the railing tightly, as the ship wobbles to the left. Iyena is thrown toward the bulkhead, even as Rivian dashes to save her from hitting the hard wood. But then, the ship trembles and a loud blast from the depths drowns out every sound.

Iyena's ears ring with an incessant sound as the wooden deck gives way beneath her. She's in the air, her hands flailing, and the cold, mossy water comes up dizzyingly fast to envelop her. When the icy water hits her, the edges of her vision register a movement....

Then, black.

CHAPTER TWENTY-TWO

A Melancholy Bargain –
A Journal of Travel, Trauma, and Teachings

Before coming into the Caretaker's tutelage, I knew nothing about the ways of the world. But now I have traveled far and wide, walking on the frigid slopes of Noronna, getting stranded on the Isles of Meshwa with nothing on my person other than a twig, which I used to etch in the sands a poem, hoping a creature soaring in the sky would notice it, swimming off the island to find the ship that took me, finally, to the salty, moss-covered shores of Alderra. In Alderra, I first met a Champion who could sway an ocean with his voice.

I heard them chanting cer name. Varunnai.

The Alderra port is so busy that it pains the eyes to even look at it. With over three hundred ships ready to take harbor and a hundred more to leave its shores, the port thrums with a manic activity that's hard to describe. I have heard tales of memory-mixing on these shores; those taking refuge in Alderra, carrying pain and loss and heartbreak in their hearts, are taken to an underground chamber which smells of vinegar and salt and rotten cabbage. They are kept there for a span of fourteen days, after which the refugees breathe the Alderran air, born anew, their past pains forgotten, their entire being now belonging only to Alderra.

But there have been reports, too, of those memories coming back to haunt refugees, in bits and pieces. They are then dealt with separately.

I was no refugee. I was merely a traveler with a guise that was closer to a beggar. When I arrived at the Alderran port there was a storm warning. A massive wave was rushing inland, threatening to destroy everything in its wake. That was when I met Varunnai, the Champion. Ce stood calmly at the prow of a ship, gazing into the distance, waiting for the wave.

Ce stood, casting an envelope of quiet around cem. Screams of a potent, eager crowd waiting for their deaths. Bargaining yells of merchants, selling their wares in haste. Weeping of men and children. Silence of women. Everything snuffed out by a greater silence.

The wave, six times higher than the highest tower in the Three Realms, surged toward the shore inexorably. That's when the Champion Varunnai began a sound. It wasn't singing, and neither was it humming. It was something else. A breath, rather, mixed with clicks, and a bone-haunting rasp, that formed cer language. It was a frequency I would never want to hear again. But again, I wouldn't want to be crushed to pulp by a planet-killing wave. Yes, I talk in hyperboles, but that moment was hyperbole in itself.

As the Champion 'sang', the wave kept dying down in halves, and when it finally reached the shores, it eased down completely, hardly more vigorous than a usual high tide. The people gasped and murmured, despite knowing that the Champion had done it countless times before, and would continue to do it until cer dying breaths. If ce died, ever.

Needless to say, I was enchanted by the Champion. In Sirvassa, the Caretaker's raw power, fueled by Florrachemy, often left me dismayed. And here, far beyond the insulated Sirvassan borders, existed another kind of power. A purer, more visceral kind. Was this why Alderrans had a stronghold over the realm? Was this some sinister secret?

Was I pining to be under the tutelage of another master? I must say I was. It wouldn't be a betrayal, but surely felt like one. But the Champions were famous for their dislike of humanity. They spent their time gardening, and talking to animals, both big and small. They came only in the time of need, a need that they already sensed well in advance. Master kept a disarming quiet about him when I asked about his past. His eyes would search for precious nothings when prodded. Perhaps my answers lay elsewhere. In Alderra, the bustling metropolis of the Three Realms.

As the Champion stepped onto the pier and started walking deeper inside the city, a throng of people followed cer reverentially.

Soon, I too became a part of the crowd.

★　　★　　★

I didn't see the Champion for the next few days. Keeping my disguise as a beggar, I asked around for Varunnai. In response, I either got cold stares or tales of awe. In the eyes of Alderrans, Varunnai was a cruel god, yet merciful, who presented cerself selflessly, but only when ce was truly needed.

My first two mornings in the capital were rich, but uneventful. I spent cold nights beneath the city's low-hanging buttresses and beige and gray awnings, sometimes moving like a ghost through the night, sleeping an hour in front of a shop, making friends with a dog, or leaning against a pillar that supported an administrative building, eventually being chased away by a baton-bearing guard. I ate leftovers outside sweetshops and restaurants, sometimes given to me kindly by shopkeepers. At other times, especially during the night, I became a scavenger, picking up scraps, collating a meal from bits and pieces, a morsel of bread here, a piece of meat there. I didn't enjoy this experience even a little bit, having spent much of my life cushioned in Sirvassa. But it was still a necessary experience.

On the third day, events of my travel took a turn, when I asked a fruit seller a harmless question.

"Is Varunnai the Caretaker of Alderra?"

The fruit seller was arranging apples next to grapefruits, and counting the lot he had to sell for the day. Much of his cart was disorderly, and there was no rhyme or reason to the arrangements. I would have preferred if he placed all citrus fruits together, and all tropical fruits separately, but his cart was a haphazard mixture. But then, he had curious streaks of worry on his forehead. He was intent on ignoring my presence, and so I had to press for an answer. So, I picked up an apple from his cart, and took a bite. Ah, Alderran fruits are sickly sweet, and this is the only thing about the city that's better than Sirvassa. The juice trickled down my chin, as the fruit seller glared at me and swatted at my hands.

"Go away, you fool. What do you want?"

"I merely asked you a question," I said. "I'll pay you for the apple."

"You look like you can't even pay for the air you breathe," he said derisively. Those words felt out of character coming from him. His response didn't anger me, but instead spawned in me a firm conviction to help him.

"I don't have any currency, but what I have are skills."

The man gave me a defeated glance. I knew instantly that it was tough for him to keep his business flourishing.

"How much do you have to sell today?" I said. He let out a raspy breath. Then, he looked around, as if asking for permission to talk to me further. Not getting any, he told me all about his cart.

"It's the worst season for all of us fruit sellers. Vegetable carts don't fare any better. The ministry has increased taxes for everyone. Farmers can't sell what they reap without being robbed of their hard-earned sweat. Citizens can't buy because everything costs at least thirty per cent more. And guess where the extra Alderran meinar goes?"

"The ministry's pockets," I said. He nodded.

"You were asking about the Champion, right? Well, I look at that Champion who glides among us and I feel only disgust."

His words dripped with barely disguised contempt. I heard a commotion, and looked behind my shoulder. Crowds swelled near the Alderran market square, looking up at the sky. A steamship soared toward the west, spewing vile smoke that covered much of the blue sky. Its structure was queer. Half of it a bird, the other half a ballooned oddity, suffused with a warm, saffron glow.

"They gather as if they haven't seen a Hansa chariot before," said the fruit seller.

"I figure *that* is where the extra Alderran currency goes," I offered. "A ship like that would require so much raw material."

"All those ships...in the skies, on the sea, are just empty promises...to show others what Alderra is capable of. Meanwhile, we rot here. You asked me about the Champion.... Ce does nothing. Ce could do so much. With a breath and a half, Ce could undo all our miseries, yet ce remains detached. Varunnai, Theravan, Innoran, Tyi...all Champions are the same. People call them gods, but what kind of gods are they?"

I understood the man's plight.

"Allow me to help you," I said next. His eyes glazed over, as if a sheen of disbelief had come over them.

"How will you help?"

"You are a businessman, you do understand supply and demand, right?"

He gave me a befuddled gaze. He did understand the basic tenets, of course, but couldn't exploit them to his advantage. The way he spoke of his plight gave me a much needed insight into the man's character.

"What will you do?"

I told him. And later, deep in the afternoon, I brought out the first Delight Master had given me, and drank it whole.

It took the better part of my life to understand that Delights aren't just ordinary magics. Concocted carefully, with precision, a Delight can take on a quality and make life easier for anyone. If it were up to me to define them, I'd say that Delights are not magic, they are life simplified.

For example, the one I drank allowed me to convince anyone to follow what I say, no questions asked, for a limited amount of time. Master knew that although I was street-smart, I could also tend to get into tricky situations because of my tongue, and my oft-gullible nature. And so, he'd mixed Jasmine with Chrysanthemum and made a potion for me.

But I used that Delight not for myself, but to help the fruit seller in need. I emptied out the apples from his cart, put them into a bag, and went into the streets screaming and munching on the fruit.

"What a magical fruit, what a magical fruit!" I yelled. "Ah, it reminds me of home and heaven, and the embrace of a lover."

On an ordinary day, my actions would have had the result I had desired, but it would have taken me a fair amount of time. But with the Delight sluicing through me, my words pulled local Alderrans like ants to honey. They wanted to know what I was talking about. They wanted a taste of the fruit. They wanted to know where it came from.

And I told them to flock to the cart of the fruit seller. And I helped him clear out his cart. And then I helped him build his business, each day, until the Delight went out of my body.

By the time I was rid of the effects of the Delight, the fruit seller had customers he never knew he could have.

★   ★   ★

After the fifth day, the fruit seller told me his name. After a week, he invited me inside his home. His wife prepared a meal of potatoes and lentils and meat, simmering in a gravy of spicy tomatoes and coconuts. Two weeks earlier, a meal like that wouldn't have been possible for him. But as I broke some roti and dipped it in the spicy, savory, and slightly tangy gravy, I realized I had made it all possible for him. Inviting me was his wordless way of thanking me, because he couldn't find the appropriate words.

His house was like most Alderran dwellings. Low roof, brick walls, painted beige, and a musty smell pervading the air. I wrinkled my nostrils as I ate the food, and he noticed it.

"I'm sorry, it's all the smoke," he said. "Everyone here lives like this, everyone but the ministry."

"I can understand," I said, wishing I had a Delight to make the air cleaner. I made a mental note to speak to Master about it. But looking around, I could see many things that could be improved, many things which people in Sirvassa almost took for granted. Higher ceiling, better walls, better air, of course, and an overall cheery disposition.

"You never told me where you're from," he said. I chewed my food, evading the question. Would he feel a pang of jealousy if I told him I was from Sirvassa, a place so ripe with Delights, a place of promise? Or would he smirk with indifference? But then, I realized it wouldn't matter. I considered myself not to be from Sirvassa, or Alderra, or all those towns and cities littered across the Three Realms. I am of the Three Realms, and that is my identity.

"Sirvassa," I said, and immediately his eyes peeled in surprise. Then, he subdued his reaction, immediately, and his face took on a somber quality.

"The Garden of Delights," he said slowly. "It's there, right?"

"You know about it?"

"Everyone has heard tales," he said. "We thought the place was a myth."

"I can assure you it's not," I said. The room went very quiet after that. The fruit seller finished his food, and went inside the kitchen. I kept eating, enjoying the spice, and the mush of the potatoes inside my mouth. I bit into a stray bit of chili, and blew some air out of my mouth. My eyes went watery, very soon, but I kept on eating, not knowing when I'd again get to have a meal as delicious as this.

The fruit seller came out of the kitchen carrying a cold sherbet made of lemon, mint, and watermelon. We enjoyed the cool drink, together, as friends, and didn't speak of Delights, or business, or ruin, or elation, or sadness, for a long while. We stayed still, sipping, and let the cool rush of the moment envelop us. I saw him, his wife, his one son, sitting on the ground, as a family, a unit, seeing both distress and success together, and felt hollow inside. I did not have what they had, would probably never. Yet, I don't desire for more. They did, that much is evident. And there were more like them, small families, large families, some living in close quarters, some in sprawling mansions, always wanting something more out of their lives.

Alderra wanted more, and no one was giving it to them, because no one cared enough. This fact spawned in me a desire to meet the Champion again, to know why ce was so aloof, why ce had decided not to care, when ce could do so much. I wanted to be with the family of the fruit seller and give them balms through my reassuring words, but I also wanted to see more of this city that held so much pull over the Three Realms, and yet didn't have enough.

After finishing the drink, I stood and bowed deep in front of the fruit seller, thanking him for his generosity. Then I stepped out of his house into the smoky shambles of the city, again, directionless. Before I turned the corner, the fruit seller called out to me.

"Will you be back, sometime in the coming weeks?"

"Perhaps," I said. "I wish you luck in your business, friend."

"I wish you luck in your travels. May Eborsen shower his petals on you."

A Sirvassan goodbye, from the mouth of an Alderran. A thing of oddity. I smiled at him, and responded with a similar phrase. Then I took the winding road toward the center of the city.

*　　*　　*

In the week before I saw the Champion for the second time, I took employment as a cleaner in a small sweetshop. The owner was a thin, measly man, with a scruffy beard, and a protruding belly, which was a stark counterpoint to his otherwise spindly appearance. He ran the shop like he would run a smithy, full of grunts and iron and sweat. There was no passion to him, and it reflected in the taste of the sweets. Yes, his sweets were of a cardboard variety, and I've had water that tasted sweeter. The sweetshop owner complained a lot, screamed a lot, and even stole from his own sweet supply. When he sold his sweets, he acted like he was doing a favor to his customers. When he didn't, he mostly grumbled, looking up at the skies or chewing his dirty fingernails. I kept quiet because he gave me money, and money gave me food and kept me alive for another week. I was tasked with opening and shuttering the shop, and mixing chickpea flour with sugar and fat, which I did diligently and honestly.

On the seventh day of my employment, as I was putting the padlock on the shutter of his shop, I felt a cold slap of wind on my face. I looked up, and saw the Champion descend from the skies, onto a busy market square. As usual, a crowd gathered around cer like flies around meat, and buzzed along with cer. I wiped my grimy hands on my trousers and walked toward the crowd.

The Champion was on errands; I saw that much. Buying vegetables and fruits. Even gods had to maintain a diet, perhaps. As ce completed cer business, I followed cer down the busy market road, as the crowd around cer grew ever thin. The market road led to a vast open area that brought into view the sprawl of the city. I hadn't been to this part of Alderra, and what I saw took my breath away. A tall wooden arch, patterned with words from languages both forgotten and new, stood guarding the interior of the city. Another throng of citizens carrying flags that bore the religious symbol of the Abhadis, a blade surrounded by a circle with wings, swarmed out of the arch, singing loud songs. The Champion, unbothered, entered the arch, and I followed in cer wake.

A network of cables ran through the city, upon which hung carriages taking the population from one place to another. The cables stopped at regular intervals on various stations, as the citizenry disembarked. There were no bewitched beasts visible anywhere. The carriages moved on their own; some even flew with wings.

The Champion walked toward a vast square where roads met from the four chief corners of Alderra – Umaad, Senthrin, Tavlin, and Ahad. Senthrin leads to Abrais-Ala, a twelve-spired fortress that looks like an otherworldly pipe organ, gold and silver, and like a living musical instrument gives off a melody every two hours. Except the melody is not recreational. It's purely official. It's the building that houses the ministry and its twelve departments.

The Champion, however, didn't have anything to do with Senthrin, or even Tavlin for that matter, a road that leads to a vulgarly opulent town, where the richest of the rich of the realm bask in their wealth. Ce didn't even take a left to Ahad, the road that leads to the industrial center of the city, its heart, with its schools and healing centers, filled with Sern and Sernir (odd names for people who teach, I would say, names with no emotional resonance to them; Tevair, the Sirvassan-Inishti word, sounds far superior to the ears, if I am being brutally honest) and their ways of teaching and healing, filled with the Center of Albuchemy, which I would later learn in my centers, is the technological equivalent of Florrachemy.

Ce instead looked fondly toward Umaad, but rejected it. Ce then ascended the stairs leading to a vast bowl-shaped construction in the center of the square, the copper half-sun which glinted with an ethereal light washing Alderra in brightness. Ce stopped on the ninth step, as if unsure.

Then, ce spoke.

"If you wish to follow me where I am going, you might as well leave all your desires behind."

Cer voice rang deep in my soul. Then, ce turned around to look at me. Cer face was like a smooth, ceramic mask of beauty and wonder and cruelty.

I ascended the steps and stood face-to-face with the Champion.

"I have left everything behind," I said.

Ce took my hand, and we rose high, high up in the sky, leaving the copper bowl, the city square, the roads, Alderra below.

★　　★　　★

How many people can claim to be taught by a Florral and a Champion? Two of the most powerful entities in the realm, upending their knowledge into me. I became like water, shaped by anything and everything.

Varunnai flew with breathtaking speed, as sharp, cold winds buffeted around me. At no point did it feel that I would lose cer grip. It felt like I was flying with a god. It felt like I was indeed a god.

We soon arrived.

Varunnai spent most of cer days inside cer hut, meditating. I was tasked with bringing water for daily tasks from atop a hill where stood an eternal fountain. I would tend to cer animals, wash their piss and shit away, milk them, rear them, comfort them when they made noises in the night.

One day I spilled water in front of Varunnai's hut. I was weak from the constant trudge up and down the hill, and my knees had started to feel like matchsticks. I simply couldn't carry the weight of the pail, and stumbled, right as Varunnai was about to step out of cer hut.

Ce looked at the spilled water in anguish. Then ce slapped me hard across my face.

"I was weak," I said. "You could just wave your hand and put it back into the pail."

"It's the Eternal Fountain, whose water isn't supposed to be desecrated like this, you fool. Once the water touches the ground, it loses its essence. Why would I return something that has lost its true essence back inside the pail?"

Ce was right. I fell on cer feet and touched them in reverence and in apology, like my master had taught me. To this, there was no reaction from Varunnai. Ce went inside cer hut, back to cer meditation.

CHAPTER TWENTY-THREE

Iyena Mastafar

This is just the Hour of the Futures prolonged into one unending, cold, watery miasma. If she pinches herself, she'll get out of it. She'll be back inside the rose-colored chamber. She'll be outside the temple. She just has to pinch herself. Or better yet, scream the name of the priestess. But she has no name. She is just a priestess of the temple of Eborsen, just one among many.

Inside the cold depths of the sea, Iyena's body slowly starts going numb. Can she change the nature of her lungs to gills? The thought is at the edge of her brain but she can't bring herself to channel her ability. The utter cold doesn't let her. Maybe this is the water vision, the first one, with the unending lake and the goddess, with the crouching figure who muttered in the shadows.

The seabed comes up to meet her fast. But above her, something else speeds toward her. A dark, lithe figure. A joltfish.... Iyena screams but bubbles come out of her mouth. She mustn't scream or else....

The figure grabs her hand and pulls her. It's not a vision. She closes her eyes.

★　★　★

"Wake up, girl."

A face hovers into focus. Scar on right cheek, wet hair, jet-black, pulled back. A smile revealing white teeth. Then it goes blurry again. Waking up is like wading through honey.

"Wake up."

Iyena opens her eyes. She feels warm and dry. She is wrapped in two blankets. Light filters through a small, circular window with tattered blinds and splashes on hard stone ground. A smell of apples, bread, and cinnamon greets her. She rubs her eyes and her face. Much of the room she is in comes into focus. Beneath the window, a large ceramic pot stands, brimming with grain-like things. More such pots accompany the main pot, similarly filled, albeit with differently colored grains. There's a door to Iyena's left, but it is ajar, and not much is visible beyond.

There's a knock. A woman with gray hair and gaunt cheeks enters the room, carrying a plate full of something warm. The smell of apples intensifies, and Iyena's stomach grumbles. She realizes how famished she feels; her last meal was the measly breakfast before coming to the docks with the father.

What happened on the docks?

The woman places the tray in front of her. Apple pie, except it's divided into small, crescent-moon-shaped dumplings, equally crumbly and flaky, golden brown. Iyena can't decide if she needs information or food.

She settles on food. Everything else can wait.

The first bite is so good it almost brings tears to her eyes. Not even Maani-Ba's cooking could match the assault of flavors on her tongue. A hint of sourness mixed with apple-sweet and caramel, the rough texture of dates and almonds, and a hint of creaminess, all enveloped with fall-apart flakiness. She swallows the bite and downs it with some water. The woman simply watches her eat.

"It was mayhem when the ship exploded," the woman starts. "You have Sonir to thank, who selflessly jumped and pulled you out."

When the food settles in her stomach, and the cloudiness in her brain subsides, Iyena looks at the woman carefully. Her face exists at the cusp of Iyena's memory. Yet the memory is fogged. The shape of the woman's face reminds Iyena of home, yet she can't place why.

Iyena decides on the more urgent, present question.

"Where's my father?"

"I don't even know who *you* are, much less your father, dear. What were you doing on the ship?"

Iyena tells her. The woman listens keenly, fingers interlaced together, tapping alternately on the back of her wrist. Her eyes widen curiously at the mention of her father's involvement with the Alderran Ministry and friendship with Minister Yayati. A dark shadow hovers on her face when Iyena finishes.

"Iyena Mastafar...am I pronouncing it right?"

"Aa-i-yena, right," she says.

"You remind me of someone I knew once," says the woman.

And there's the resemblance again. All the more striking this time. Iyena still can't quite place it. The hard, angular lines on the woman's face. She opens her mouth to speak, but then decides against it.

"Well, Iyena, you look like a bright child. And take it from me, you have a bright future ahead of you. Don't get involved in your father's politics. I can't say why he brought you to the docks, but being a respected ambassador, he must have had some inkling of the attack on the ship today."

"Attack?"

"Rumors are that a group of renegades rigged the ship with explosives. I don't know what their end goal was but it seems they were at least partially successful, destroying a good chunk of the cargo."

"I want to go home," says Iyena. She is conscious of the shiver in her voice. She tries to be brave, but at this moment, in a place she can't call her own, she feels alone.

"It's deep in the night, and you're ten kilometers away from Sirvassa, in a village called Apshebdi. I've business in Sirvassa tomorrow. I'll take you home."

Iyena nods, chewing her food in silence. That's the only thing she can do now. Gone is her curiosity about her abilities, vanished in the recesses of her mind, driven there by the cold crash of falling in the sea. Gone is the curiosity about the city of Sirvassa, its old gods, its people, its culture, its seasons, its magic, the Garden. She seeks home now, a warm bed, a warmer drink, prepared by Maani-Ba. Her gaze shifts to her left, where, if she were in her room, she'd have found her mother's photo. Here she finds only an empty wall.

The woman gathers the crumbs from the bed and brushes them back onto the plate. "I'm sorry," says Iyena. "I've been sloppy in eating."

"You're sick, it's fine," says the woman, smiling.

"What's your name?"

"Yavani," she says.

"What is your business in the city, if I may ask?"

Yavani places the tray on a table and points a crooked finger at the pot beneath the window, the pot full of grain-like things. "I am a Seedmaster."

And with just one word, Iyena's eyes turn bright, and that old curiosity comes rushing back. She doesn't know what the word means, but she knows it means something important.

"What does a Seedmaster do?"

"I will show you tomorrow."

★　★　★

Morning rushes in through the small window without warning and splashes on the old, stone floor, dust motes curling around each other in one neat stream of light. Iyena gets up, washes herself, and puts on the clothes the woman named Yavani kept for her. She packs her old, wet, tattered clothes from last night in a bundle and carries it to the spacious living area, where Yavani waits for her with a steaming drink and fried flatbread.

"Have some pento, and Condeshar tea. Slept fine?"

"I did, but I also had dreams of drowning," Iyena says but realizes that sharing dream details with strangers is perhaps a little bit too intimate. She stands idly, rubbing her thumb with her index finger, unsure of what to say next. Yavani points her to a seat, which she takes immediately. The smell of the food is warm and inviting. Iyena's stomach groans, and the blur in her eyes and in her mind tells her that a full belly might bring much clarity.

She tears off some pento and plops it in her mouth. It's savory and sweet, with a hint of red chilli, and reminds her of home. But which home, she can't immediately recall, for even in Alderra, such delicacies would plunge her deep into memories of yet another place, of riverside, grass growing in golden knots, morning hymn-singing mosh-flies and beasts whose feet wouldn't fall on earth.

She drinks the tea, and finishes off the plate, without giving much thought to dining etiquettes.

"Come, now, else you'll doze on the way," says Yavani.

★   ★   ★

Yavani's footsteps are slow but assured, and Iyena follows the woman as she makes her way through a grassy trail, surrounded by ivy and vines. It's all green, all dark, like moss given a vapor form. The smell is of grapes and must and wetness and winter. The ground mulches beneath their feet, never quite solid enough to find proper footing.

"Alderra, nice that it is, is full of people who believe in rationality. Form, cohesion, logic are supreme, and anything remotely whimsical is scorned. I was in that city, once. Wasn't too fond of it. But of course, you must know all about it, child."

The woman's words stir up Iyena's insides. Her chest is hollow, her legs jelly. They are ugly words, but also true, and hearing someone say what she's felt feels like betrayal, but also relief. Inadvertently, Iyena finds herself nodding silently.

Ahead, green turns to foamy white. Vines turn to golden ribbons and curl inward, revealing a meadow, which stretches far into the distance. Trees upon trees, their barks coppery, their tentacle roots floating midair, are spread across the landscape, as far as Iyena's eyes can see. Overhead, the sky is a pristine blue. The hollow inside Iyena's chest bursts, and she's filled with an intense joy of discovery.

"What is this place?"

"This is the Burrowing. It's an in-between place."

"In between?"

"It allows us to travel a distance of a hundred kilometers in mere minutes. But that's just one of its many qualities."

The woman stands beneath a tree, which hovers in the air ten feet above them. The jellyfish-like roots, black, solid, reach for them. Iyena staggers back, her heart thumping, as a root brushes against her skin.

Then, from far above ground, a shower begins. Soon, the ground is littered with seeds, brown, mustard-yellow, and pale green. The woman bends and gathers the seeds like she's done it a thousand times before. She presses a brown seed between her thumb and index finger and it bursts open, revealing a black, vapory nothingness inside.

"The rot is still present," says Yavani.

"Does it have anything to do with the Garden?"

Yavani's face contorts, and is immediately filled with age lines, hard, unforgiving. She casts an accusing glance at Iyena. Then she softens, as if a realization has hit her.

"Of course, you've been there. Everyone new to the city goes there first."

"The Caretaker gave me a potion."

The air stills between them. The woman who had introduced herself to Iyena as Seedmaster wrings her hands free of the seeds.

"Well, hopefully you got the potion before the seeds started showing rot."

Iyena's eyes catch something moving. In the distance, near the base of another tree, a shape burrows out from the ground, spewing flaky dirt bits everywhere, like a nightmare pushing through the gossamer of sleep, entering reality.

"Is that normal?" Iyena points toward the oddity in the midst of the meadow. Yavani lets out a sharp breath. The movement ceases and becomes a pool of blackness. Yavani walks toward it and Iyena follows, her heart thumping through the fabric of her clothes, pulse coursing through her sleeve.

It's a body, or rather an idea, an imprint of what a body should be. It's only mangled shadows, half corporeal, half fantasy. Yavani examines the shape. Her hands touch the blackness and ash flows freely from her palm, not gray, but colorful.

"Something is happening. First, the rot sets in, then this." Yavani lets out a pained sigh. Then she gathers the ashes and looks at Iyena. "I'm sorry you had to witness something like this."

"Maybe I can help."

Yavani pats Iyena's cheek affectionately.

"We'll see about that. Follow me."

They walk along the lonely meadow, meeting no other surprises. The trees keep floating, and the seeds keep falling. Some show the rot Yavani kept talking about, some are fine, baby-new. Soon, the vast expanse peters out. Before Iyena can make sense of the transition, she is standing in front of a glass door. Yavani pushes against it and they enter, leaving the strange world behind.

★　　★　　★

Iyena follows the Seedmaster to a room full of earthen pots. It faintly smells of petrichor and flowers in fresh bloom. Iyena notices rows upon rows of pots, big and small. The pots are abrim with seeds. Seeds that will make magical flowers, someday.

The Seedmaster fills the pot closest to her with the seeds she has gathered from the meadow. Her hand inadvertently reaches for the other, smaller bag she's holding, the one full of colorful ash. She flinches.

"How does it all work?" Iyena asks.

Yavani looks at her, and her lips curl upward into a playful smile. "Child, just an hour ago you wanted to be with your father. Decide!"

"It was you who decided to take the shortcut," says Iyena, even more playfully, enjoying the little banter with the old woman. "Naturally, I have questions."

"These seeds contain the true essence of one particular type of Shaping. You can Shape anything in this world. When the seeds grow into a flower, and that flower is crushed to form a potion, it dilutes the essence to something more manageable, something that people like you can safely enjoy. That process is called Florrachemy."

"If one were to pop the seed right away?" Iyena mimes throwing a small pod in the air and catching it in her mouth, like one does with a peanut. "I'm assuming that would be bad?"

"The repercussions, oh, that's too horrifying a thought. If someone were to eat a seed like you just described, they would never have existed," says Yavani without flinching. Iyena imagines what it would look like. A person never having existed at all. Not being, not having been born. All deeds, all memories of a person vanishing in an instant, forgotten like a spark. The images her mind makes are fleeting, and are blown away soon. It's too vast a thought to grasp, too piercing, too haunting.

The moment is shattered by a sound. Iyena turns around and sees a man walking briskly toward them. Behind the man, the revolving door, through which the man must have entered, makes groaning sounds. The man is tall, with wavy black hair, which moves in all directions with reckless abandon. His eyes are deep, his jaw is square. One lone silver earring on his right earlobe glints in the darkness of the room. He looks questioningly at Iyena, before turning his attention toward Yavani.

"The Caretaker has asked if it would be possible to reconstruct seeds of the Tulip from...." The man stops and looks at Iyena again. Then he lets out a slow gasp. "Girl, your face...it's all over the city. They are looking for you."

"Who are they?"

"I don't know. But you seem to be important. What is your name?"

"Iyena Mastafar."

"You are related to Anaris Mastafar?"

"I am his daughter."

The man purses his lips. A vein throbs near his temple. He stops himself from saying something vile. Iyena can sense it in his demeanor. The hatred for her father.

"If I deliver you to him right now, I'll be a rich man. But I don't want to see his face. Sorry, kid, you will have to walk your way home."

"I can find my way home, thank you very much."

Silence settles around them like a stone sinking at the bottom of the river. Yavani breaks it with a cough.

"Trulio, please tell the Caretaker that what he has asked won't be possible now. There have been new developments."

"That's what you told him last time too."

The man called Trulio moves closer to Yavani. Iyena feels she shouldn't be a part of the conversation. But she finds herself unwilling to move. There's too much that is unknown all around her and she wants to know about all things.

But before Iyena can say a word, Yavani points a finger at her. "Girl, I think it's time for you to leave."

"I have seen much more than you intended to show me," says Iyena. She doesn't know where these words are coming from, but they bring with them a sudden, raw power. She feels in total command of who she is at that moment. She feels good.

Yavani looks at her, then back at Trulio, who stands expressionless.

"Fair enough. But not a word of it outside."

"How can we trust her? She'll rat on everything she has heard to her father. You know what happened in Alderra!"

"She won't," says Yavani with confidence. Iyena can't help but smile.

★   ★   ★

Iyena is four years old when she first rebels against her father. Sern Mirnya's second lesson in basic mathematics has finished and Iyena knows the numbers both by heart and on her fingertips. She knows the eighth root of seventeen, and the number of times the planet Gorner rotates on its axis. She knows the exact number of times the mythical bird Hansa flutters its wings in order to pull a chariot off the ground and into the skies.

She doesn't know what to do with the information.

"It's for your own good," says Anaris. "Knowledge rests safely inside you, ready to jump at a moment's notice. And isn't it nice to know all these details?"

Iyena nods at her father, but it's a lie of a nod.

Later, under the canopy of the palm tree in her father's orchard, she meets her friend Pulna, who had not attended her morning classes for five days in a row, and who brings with her a device, a magical construction that allows Iyena to look at picturetales. A boy moving with grace. A girl shooting arrows. An old woman performing levitation. And much more.

"Where did you get this from?"

"From the city of dreams, where else?"

It's the first time Iyena hears the name of the city of Sirvassa.

"I will bring this to morning class tomorrow."

"Sern Mirnya won't allow it," says Iyena firmly. "She will throw it away."

"I'll do it secretly."

Iyena nods, but doesn't believe in the clandestine abilities of her friend. At that moment, Iyena's gaze lingers for a second too long on the device. It holds wonders long withheld from her.

"Can I have it, if you don't mind?"

"Umm, no you can't."

"Just for one night, please? I will help you memorize the Five Incantations."

"*You* can't even memorize one."

Iyena then proceeds to recite the incantations without catching a breath. Pulna blankly stares at her, silently clutching the hem of her dress.

"Your mouth is hanging," says Iyena.

"How did you manage to learn them so fast?"

"I am brilliant. Now, do we have a deal?"

Pulna considers, then hands over the device to Iyena. "For one day only. And you return it to me in one piece."

"I am not Suminar. I don't break things." Pulna makes a face at the mention of Suminar. Iyena knows why her friend is skeptical. Pulna once gave one such fancy item made of wood and gold to another friend, named Suminar, a black-haired boy with mismatched eyes. Suminar played with it, and, as per his version of events, forgot to place it safely inside a cupboard. His pet Carunthian beast thought it was a treat, tried to eat it, chewed it and spit it out in pieces. Pulna knew Suminar was lying because Carunthian beasts wouldn't come within a mile of gold. It was the first thing Sern Mirnya had taught them about the beast.

"You'll teach me tomorrow?"

"I will," says Iyena with a smile.

Later that evening, Iyena sits in her room, watching picturetales to her heart's content. A woman sitting by a lakeside, smelling flowers, a child swinging merrily off a branch, a couple celebrating their wedding, a man walking in a garden. Independent images with no narrative to them, but still telling vast stories.

"What's that, Iyena?"

Anaris stands, his face stern, his voice a gentle whisper. He is wearing his evening kurta, white with golden borders. His eyes look tired from the day's work, but there's enough energy in him to check upon his daughter's apparent follies.

"It shows me picturetales. My friend gave me this."

Anaris takes a deep breath. "These are not things you should be spending your time with, Iyena."

"But these are just pictures. What is wrong with them?"

Anaris sits down beside Iyena and takes the device from her hands. The woman by the lakeside appears again. "If you look closely enough, you will see the woman's eyes are full of treachery.

The flowers she holds in her hands are stolen and she has come to the lakeside, running from the people who originally had the flowers. People like us."

Anaris then proceeds to tell Iyena about the child, the couple, and the man in the garden, and how they weren't the sort of people she would want to mingle with, and how their stories don't deserve any attention. When he stops, Iyena slides gently away from him. She feels too cold in her father's presence, and his words don't comfort her. It escapes her how simple pictures could elicit such a poisonous response from her father. She's too young in her mind to make deeper connections.

"Which friend gave you this?"

"Pulna."

"Pulna Abarsad." Anaris stresses Pulna's naturename. Abarsad means 'of the earth', in old Alderran. "Her father, Tedare Abarsad, is a friend. I will have a word with him."

Saying this, Anaris takes the device from Iyena.

"I'll tell Mother about this," says Iyena weakly.

"Mother will tell you the same thing I just told you."

Anaris leaves.

Later that night, convinced of her father's deep snores, Iyena tiptoes inside his room and grabs the picturetale device off his desk. She watches the remaining picturetales all through the night, gets up early in the morning and puts the device back on Anaris's desk. At school, when Pulna asks Iyena about the device, she tells her to wait.

Three days later Pulna Abarsad doesn't come to the school for her Incantation lessons. Five days later, Tedare Abarsad is transferred to a remote village at the outskirts of Unnara, a fishing town two hundred kilometers from Alderra.

Iyena is too young to understand the consequences of her actions but not too young to ascertain that her father is capable of snatching a man's shadow from underneath him.

★   ★   ★

Now, at fifteen, Iyena knows the hatred her father harbors deep in his heart for people who are not like them. And this has caused hatred in people for her father. She has seen people's faces squirm at the mention of Anaris Mastafar, from Tevair Dines, to her classmates, to the Seedmaster, to the random person she just met.

When she steps out of the Seedmaster's place, her eyes fall on a carriage. Two women sit on it, wearing elaborate dresses with simple, yet intricate embroidery patterns on them. The carriage is pulled by a Rhisuan beast toward the main market square. Above her, the sky is the pale blue of midmorning, and through the shimmering jalan she can see a shy sun in the distance. There's nothing that suggests anything untoward happened on the docks just a day before.

But then, on a pole, she sees a fluttering flag, with her face plastered on it. In both Alderran tongue and Sirvassan, the words say, *Iyena Mastafar, Girl. Fifteen years of age. Pale, lithe, a mole on her cheek — Lost. Finders would be suitably rewarded.*

Iyena's heart thunders inside her chest. She takes a couple of steps back, and almost goes back inside the door she came out of. She tears some cloth from the dress she's wearing and wraps it around her face like a mask. She ruffles her hair, making it shaggy, falling over her forehead. Then she takes a deep breath, and walks back out into the sun, toward her home.

CHAPTER TWENTY-FOUR

Iyena Mastafar

When she finally reaches home after dodging traffic, beasts, and men, Iyena notices a crowd huddled in front of her door. A strong murmur, some raised words. An antiseptic tinge in the air. Undetected, she becomes part of the crowd, her small, lithe figure allowing her to snake through gaps between bulky torsos and spindly legs. After a small struggle, she's finally in front of her door.

"Here, here's your daughter, Anaris Mastafar. Where's my money now?"

A stocky man pushes forward a small girl, hardly taller than Iyena. Her cheeks are chubbier.

"No, no, he's a liar. *This* is your real daughter."

A different woman, pushing ahead a different girl. This one is shorter, and almost looks like Iyena. The same eyes, the same pointed nose, the same mole on the cheek. Iyena holds back a gasp upon looking at her doppelganger. But before she can say anything, she hears heavy footsteps approaching the gate.

"Pests, leave me alone! None of these are my daughter."

It's her father. His hand is in a cast, and his head is wrapped in bandages. A shudder courses through Iyena. She feels bad for her father. He doesn't notice her amid the crowd. She doesn't shout. Instead, like a wraith, she slithers forward and enters her house. But even wounded, Anaris is sharp as a hawk.

"Get out this moment, thief, before I—"

"Father, it's me."

Iyena removes her mask. Anaris steadies himself. He comes closer to Iyena, as if inspecting her. It takes a long time for him to get convinced. He closes the door behind him. The voices outside grow muffled, and slowly drown out. Then, he comes closer to Iyena and hugs her tightly.

"I thought I had lost you," says Anaris, his voice barely a whisper. "I thought you were dead."

"I thought so too," says Iyena.

"Where were you? Who found you?"

Iyena tells him about a kind, old lady, blind in one eye, and her young son who had jumped selflessly and brought her ashore. Iyena tells him about a warm, comforting meal, and the perilous ride atop a Rhisuan beast back home. Iyena tells him about a harp and music. Iyena doesn't tell her father the truth.

"Where are these people? I need to thank them."

"They left, Father, the way they came. They were nomads. Kind and gentle."

Anaris takes a deep breath. "Promise me, you won't leave my side ever."

"I promise, Father."

⋆　⋆　⋆

Five days later, Iyena goes to the school despite her father's requests to stay at home and rest. In Anaris's earnest parental pleading, Iyena senses a quiet desperation to control and subdue, even if it comes from a place of deep love. Maani-Ba, too, has lately, aggressively, started taking Iyena's side in matters of her independence. How much of the city she is allowed to see, how many friends she is allowed to make – this is no longer dictated by Anaris's whims, at least not directly.

But the cold ripples of the attack at the dock reach the school as well. At the gates, burly, armed men, with both Sirvassan and Alderran insignia emblazoned on their blue cloaks, stand sentinel, unspeaking, their hard, emotionless eyes staring at ghosts that don't exist. Students flock around these men and indulge in chatter with abandon, checking if they elicit a response from them. Their bare, gaunt faces, however, don't grimace at the students.

Iyena's eyes search for Trehan, but can't find him. Inside the school premises she meets Nadya, a girl her junior, who has nervous, downcast eyes, and isn't too eager to join her classmates. When she sees Iyena, she averts her gaze and starts walking toward the opposite side, where a stony path leads to an orchard. Iyena follows her instead of going to her class.

Catching up to her, Iyena tugs at Nadya's sleeve. Nadya stops and stares at Iyena in fear.

"What happened, Nadya? What are you afraid of?"

"I don't want to go inside," she says. Her voice is shaking. "You please go. I shouldn't be talking to you too."

"What have I done?"

"Nothing, please go."

"I am not leaving until you answer at least one of my questions."

"They have changed everything," she says with much effort, and then she starts sobbing. "I am not so good. I can't...I can't keep up."

Iyena had heard about the changes in her school curriculum the last time she was in school. But Nadya's words seemed to suggest something else. She drops down on the ground and buries her head in her knees. Iyena sits beside her.

"First, they took our books."

"Who are they?"

"Tevair Dines came with two other men. They looked important. They said we were not supposed to learn from books any longer. They said something about the way of the breath and the way of the word."

The Way of the Breath is a technique Sern Aradha taught Iyena to deeply remember whatever was taught. The Way of the Word is incantations – lessons of the world woven as poems and rhythmic chants to make it easier for the learners to grasp. But if Iyena has learned one thing it is this: there is no one true way.

"I'll teach you," says Iyena. "Both the ways."

"What about the books?"

Iyena doesn't know how to respond to that. It is a terrible injustice. She knows in her heart that it's Minister Yayati's doing. When her father had said she would be helping him be better at his job, he had meant this. Minister Yayati had chosen Anaris Mastafar to change Sirvassa from its roots. And Anaris had chosen Iyena. She has become the unwitting accomplice in her father's plans. She truly knows that she is on the side of the oppressor. And so her words of solace ring hollow. Today, their books are being taken away. Who knows what tomorrow might bring?

Iyena doesn't know what this change will accomplish. She knows the history of the lands. She knows the origin of Alderra and Sirvassa, but the feud between the Inishtis and the Abhadis escapes her. She remembers her mother's words – "In the end, hate accomplishes very little" – and finds herself holding on to those words. But she can't bring herself to console Nadya and tell her that it's going to be fine. She doesn't even know how deep the rot runs.

"We'll do something about the books," says Iyena. "Now get up. Let's get you to class."

Nadya grabs Iyena's shoulder and heaves herself up. Her eyes still downcast, searching for a random mote in the dust below, she says, "Thank you, Iyena bi."

Bi, short for bini, the Sirvassan word for elder sister. Iyena holds Nadya firmly, certain that if she loosened her grip, she would crumble to the ground. Iyena holds Nadya like she is her younger sister.

★　★　★

When Tevair Amaram, a teacher of numbers and analysis, tries to teach algebra using the Way of the Word, he falters. A cold sense of failure and desperation settles in the class. In the front row of logs sits Iyena, along with Trehan and Sidhi, who look at Amaram, trying to grasp this new method and failing.

"You can't just *learn* that the third side is equal to the other two sides squared," says Trehan. "There are other applications of that rule. How will this Way...whatever this is...teach us that?"

The answer to that would be the Way of the Breath, thinks Iyena. She keeps her thoughts to herself.

"Iyena, you are from Alderra. You would know how this works, right?"

Sidhi looks at Iyena. It's almost an accusatory glare. Like Iyena is hiding something. Like there is a secret she isn't telling her friends.

"Curious, isn't it? The five days she goes missing, the school gets overturned."

This time, it's another girl who has spoken.

"What do you mean by that?"

"You were conveniently *not here* when these changes were happening. We were the ones who faced all the shock. You are from Alderra. It's clear you came here with all these plans. You know all this. Your father is in the ministry, after all."

"Yes, I do know all this," says Iyena. "The Way of the Word. The Way of the Breath. The Way of the Trees. It's difficult, and it took me the better part of my growing years to learn. I came here to unlearn that and learn a newer way of teaching. *Your* way. And I was not conveniently away. I was on a ship, and my ship was attacked. I almost *died*."

Iyena desperately wants Trehan to say something. To show an inkling that he is on her side in this conversation. But Trehan remains quiet and his silence is grating.

"First they change the *what*. Now they change the *how*."

The rest of the lesson goes by without a word from Trehan or Sidhi. Tevair Amaram struggles with the Ways. Iyena tries to insist on taking a session herself but Amaram has too much teacher-pride in him. Much of the rest of the day is drowned in a sullen quiet. Downcast eyes, curled toes making shapes on the ground, barely ten words exchanged.

At the end of the day, the Sirvassan sun twinkles against the jalan fabric, casting strange shadows on the ground. Outside the school, the Rhisuan beasts grunt as they pull their daily quota of children. The hustle and bustle of a normal end of school day isn't heard nor seen. Iyena wishes to see a magical sprinkle of petals; that would be a welcome change, but the next arrival isn't due for at least four months. She tries to talk to Trehan, but as soon as she approaches him, he hops on the nearest Rhisuan-pulled carriage, feigning a strange busy-ness.

Iyena takes a carriage that isn't her usual, but takes the same path to her home. The faces she sees sitting around her aren't her friends. A couple of them are senior to her, and others two classes her junior.

She catches some activity out of the corner of her eye. The previously stoic guard at the gates of the school marches up to her carriage. His eyes are fixed on a boy who is sitting deep inside Iyena's carriage, chatting with another girl.

"Yolan Dimar, son of Arnesh Dimar?" asks the guard in a stern, loud voice.

Yolan looks at the guard and raises his eyebrows quizzically.

"Yes, I am Yolan."

"Please accompany me."

"What is the matter?"

"I cannot answer that. My orders are my orders. Please accompany me. I won't ask again. Your father is waiting for you at the Merit Chamber."

The guard is resolute. There's a hardness to him, hammered into place by years of servitude. He can't say no, he can't *think* no. He is a yes-man out of choice and circumstance. All his words are yesses. The nature of his being is a yes.

But Iyena senses the nature of his words, his thoughts, his upcoming actions. His brain working under orders of someone much higher in social standing than him. Much like before, during that afternoon near the river, where Iyena changed the nature of a poison coursing through Trehan's veins, Iyena reaches out to the guard, his mind now hers, his thoughts now hers, the lines of his face, the quiver of his lip, the freckle on his cheek, the words on his tongue, all hers.

The nature of his being, all hers.

And she twists it, changes it.

"Excuse me?" the boy asks, befuddled. And the guard doesn't respond immediately. He stands staring, his jaw gaping, stilled, dulled, into inaction by Iyena. He looks around, unsure of himself, unsure of the ground he stands on, unsure of the air he breathes.

"I'm sorry, I misspoke. Have a good rest of the day, Yolan Dimar."

Iyena releases her control over him, but she knows that his nature has been irrevocably changed. He won't make the decisions he had made till the moment he stood on the ground in front of the carriage. He won't say the same words. He won't follow the same orders. He won't live the same life. For Iyena, the feeling is like painting over a gray canvas with streaks of violet. The grayness is still there, but it's been shadowed by a vibrancy much harder to remove.

But then, a coldness grips Iyena from head to toe and she starts to shiver. Her own mind stops talking to her. Her words come out slurred as she screams for help. On the carriage floor, a wet and warm liquid, bile and rice, green and yellow.

CHAPTER TWENTY-FIVE

Iyena Mastafar

She wakes from a bad dream to dull whispers. In the dream, she was soaring in the skies, perched on the hands of purple giants, a vision she had before in the Temple of the Half-Formed God. This time though the skies were dark and the giants had a million bulging eyes for a face.

There's darkness around her, but a single stream of light pools on the wooden floor. It's comforting to know that she is back in her room. Her memories of the day come rushing back. She changed *something*. Something big. Something that wasn't supposed to change.

She gets up. Her entire body feels sore. Her feet tingle. The overall sensation isn't something she wants to get used to.

Outside, the whispers turn loud. She takes a deep breath and walks toward the door, feeling her way through the darkness, the outside light her only beacon. She finds the door handle and pulls it. The door opens noiselessly, but she is immediately smacked by the loudness of an argument happening outside.

"…it's about teaching them a lesson and making an example out of them. Diplomacy doesn't cut it anymore."

They are her father's words. After an ugly pause, another person speaks. She has heard that person before. The crassly confident sound of the minister. But this late in the evening?

"Anaris Mastafar, what do you have in mind, then?"

"We question the Dimar family thoroughly. Their roots, their beliefs, everything. The colors they like, the food they eat. Then, we project them as enemies of Sirvassa, and anyone who thinks like them."

"You know who you remind me of, Anaris?"

"Who?"

"Me, when I was young," says the minister. "Your tactic has shades of brilliance. Where do you see Turain-One fitting in, then?"

"My words won't make as much of an impact. You will have to see with your own eyes."

Before further words can get exchanged, the light pooling on the ground flickers and gets shrouded. Iyena hears a scraping sound. She closes the door and turns around to see the source of the noise. A face at her window. Sandy, reckless hair. Impish smile.

Iyena goes to the window and opens it. Trehan's face is sweaty and slick.

"I am sorry," he says.

"What are you doing here at this time?"

"I came to apologize. And ask how you have been. I heard that you passed out in the carriage."

"I did. Why do you care though?"

"C'mon, I said I'm sorry! You have to understand...everyone is going through a difficult time. You know what happened to the Dimars?"

Trehan tells her. The Dimars, as she heard from her father's whispers, were taken to the Merit Chamber. Arnesh Dimar was stripped and beaten. His son and wife were kept separate, without food or water or clothing. All this because they were merely suspected of being behind the attack on the docks. All this because Arnesh Dimar was loosely related to Kardhan Dimar, an infamous criminal who no one knew the whereabouts of. Kardhan Dimar, an Inishti, who once stole six ships from the shores of Alderra, ships which contained gold and spices.

Despite her efforts? Despite what she did to the guard? Another guard might have taken his place. There's no shortage of people who merely follow orders, after all.

"At this moment, Iyena, your father is someone no one wants to associate with. He is feared, and so you are feared."

"But you know I am just...I am not my father. You could have said something," says Iyena. "Your silence was something that bothered me."

"I know. How can I make it up to you?"

Silence falls between them like a thunderclap.

"Look, Trehan, there are things I have to take care of right now. Things that are not right. Things that I have been experiencing."

"Tell me then. Tell me how I can be of help and I will do it."

Iyena takes a deep breath. She can trust this boy. He has an earnestness about him, and he always comes from a place of truth. Malice hasn't touched him yet, and scheming isn't a part of his nature. Yes, Iyena deeply sensed his true nature all the times they had met before.

"It's about the Garden."

"I was the one who told you about it."

"Now listen. The Delights the Caretaker gives to the people of Sirvassa, the magic...it's all temporary, right? It doesn't last long."

"What are you getting at?"

"Answer me, please."

"It's all temporary. Depending on how you use it, and the dosage you ask for, the effects could last for moments to days. That was the first thing the Caretaker told me."

"I went to the Garden after you told me. I tried the Delight."

"You also healed me with it. And that was more than four months ago."

Despite the weakness in her bones, Iyena presses her hands on the windowsill. Smoke wafts from between her fingers. A smell of burning metal and flesh tinges her nostrils. Trehan squinches his face. Iyena removes her hand from the windowsill. Instead of metal, the sill has now taken the characteristic of dark honey.

"Is this a trick? How can you do it?"

"I am not fooling you," says Iyena. "Today, I did something I hadn't tried before."

And then she tells him about the guard, and the Dimar boy. Trehan's grip almost falters at this shock, but Iyena grabs him. Trehan steadies himself, balancing his hip against the windowsill, getting a more comfortable seating position. His face is inches away from Iyena's. She could feel his shaky breath upon her cheek.

"The Caretaker," says Trehan. "You have to inform him."

"But what does it mean? Has anyone in this city experienced something like this before?"

"It could only mean that your abilities are permanent."

Iyena knew this was coming. She knew in her soul that something inside her had changed irrevocably.

"I have to meet him. But my father won't allow it. I already lied once, and he caught me."

"Who are you, Iyena Mastafar?"

Trehan's voice is a flat monotone. There's no concern in his words, but Iyena knows he is masking it behind a whisper of a voice. He genuinely wants to know.

"I am just a girl, trying to do what's right."

"What you did to the guard...would you do it to me, too?"

"Only if you have it coming," says Iyena.

Trehan smiles weakly. She can hear his heartbeats. The rush of blood she made pure once. The air in his lungs. She can hear it all. She knows if she tried hard enough, like she did with the guard, she might be privy to his thoughts. But she won't go there.

"Tomorrow afternoon. Meet me near the square. I will take you to the Garden. I just have to convince my mother. Which should be easy enough."

Before she can reply, Iyena hears footsteps from behind her. Hard, resolute, purposeful.

"You have to go now," she whispers to Trehan. He lets go of the ledge, swinging toward the pipe noiselessly. His feet find holds on the wall as he makes his way down twenty feet, like a spider. Stone and cement crumble and fall on the ground in a shower.

Iyena edges back inside, closing the window. However, the window refuses to shut completely, now that a part of the metal has changed into something else, a vile, sticky liquid. She lets go of the window and goes back to her bed. That's when Anaris Mastafar walks in her room.

"Iyena, dear, you woke up. I heard noises."

"I was cold. I was trying to close this window. It seems to be jammed."

Her father walks over to the window, and gives it yet another try. His eyes fall on the rotten metal, Iyena's handiwork, and stay on it for a long while. He grazes his hand over it. The rot sticks to his index finger like a pesky, repugnant leech.

"What's this?"

"I don't know."

"Sleep in Maani-Ba's room today," says Anaris. "Iyena, you need adequate rest, my child. After the incident in the school today, I am concerned for you. I think the attack on the ship has left you rattled."

"Who brought me in?"

"I was coming to that," says Anaris. His voice takes on a gentle, fatherly quality. Iyena knows this shift in tone all too well. Her father wants something from her. He wants her subservience. Iyena tries to do to her father what she tried on the guard, but she doesn't have enough energy left in her.

"I want you to meet someone tomorrow."

"Who?"

"Patience, child. You will come to know tomorrow. Remember, whatever I am doing, it's for your safety and goodwill, Iyena."

"Really?"

"Excuse me?"

"What is happening at the school, Father?"

"What do you mean?"

"Why is Minister Yayati here every second day? What are the changes...the changes you are making all over Sirvassa, especially in the school? Is that why you wanted me to spy on them? Is that why we are *here*?" says Iyena, stressing the last word. "The students are forced to learn the Ways. And their syllabus...their history... everything has just changed." Iyena can't bring herself to fight her father on this. Her voice shakes. Her words come out mingled, one syllable coalescing with the other, carrying neither weight nor meaning. But she has to do it.

"This place, the children...they need to learn of Alderran ways, that's all."

"Okay, then teach them about Alderran ways. Why erase what they already know about *their* history? Why erase Sirvassa from the syllabus altogether? What is going on, Father? Why *exactly* have you brought me to this city?"

"You won't understand," says Anaris. Gone is the fatherly tone. It's instead replaced by something sinister.

"Make me understand," says Iyena firmly.

"Go sleep in Maani-Ba's room. Now. That's an order."

"Or what?"

"Iyena, dear, don't make it harder for me, please."

Iyena moves closer to her father and whispers again, "Or what? You'll abandon me like you did my mother?"

Anaris raises his open hand as a vein pulsates on his head. For a small moment, which stretches to an infinite moment, Anaris cuts an old, pathetic figure. His eyes bulge in rage. There's sweat on his forehead. Whatever wheels of hate are turning inside him, it reflects on his face. But then he closes his hand into a fist, restraining himself.

"I did not abandon Sumena," he says simply, and lets both his hands fall by his sides. His cane falls too, with a soft thud on the carpet. He staggers, but balances himself. "She left on her own."

"I can see why," says Iyena.

There's a short silence, punctuated by the song of a fell-bird outside. Then, Iyena's father picks up his cane and limps out of the room, without glancing in Iyena's direction.

Iyena stands looking for a long time at the empty space where her father stood.

CHAPTER TWENTY-SIX

Iyena Mastafar

Iyena recalls a memory of her mother. It's a picture that refuses to leave her mind. An incident that has been retold to her so many times, by so many people, that a single definite version doesn't exist. Whenever Iyena tells the story to anyone, she leaves out some details, misremembering some others, forming an entirely different version of the memory altogether, cobbled together from bits and pieces.

She is four and hasn't yet learned to walk properly, despite the best efforts of her father and mother. Her father is adamant that she carries a birth defect and must be taken to Sern Healer Mithavir Mithrin, who will bring out the rot from inside her body and she will walk like everybody else.

Iyena's mother doesn't believe in it. She has heard of children who learned to walk when they were ten and then went on to become long-distance runners. She has heard of children who only learned to speak properly when they were teenagers and went on to become the best orators and diplomats.

Her father just isn't patient enough.

It's a family lunch. Relatives from both sides of the family are present. Aunt Hirdya from Timbur, Uncle Vaishoo from Old-Alderra, Grandma Irma and Grandma Surmi. Also present, surprisingly, is Sern Healer Mithavir, who Iyena's father claims invited himself, but her mother thinks otherwise. Iyena is sucking her thumb, and is being cradled in her mother's lap, as Grandma Surmi helps herself to another spoon of kheer.

It's here that Sern Healer Mithavir, a straight-shouldered, bony old man, ambles toward Iyena's mother and extends his frail brown hand, almost touching Iyena's index finger.

"Come, Iyena, I have something to show you."

Iyena's mother is slightly taken aback as this direct address to Iyena, without acknowledging her presence.

"She's fine where she is, Sern Mithavir."

Sern Mithavir purses his lips in embarrassment and retreats promptly, not uttering another word. His shoulders sink. His manner changes.

Much later, Iyena slides off her mother's lap, does a slow walk around the table, and stands near her Grandma Irma, tugging at the fabric of her suit. Grandma Irma gives Iyena a bite of cake from her plate, and that's when everyone at the table realizes that Iyena has walked for the first time.

Anaris is quick to thank Sern Mithavir for his presence. Later, Iyena's mother will accuse Anaris of being a lapdog for Mithavir first before being happy for his own daughter, an accusation Anaris will vehemently deny.

But, in that moment, even as Sern Mithavir is lapping up the praise for a deed he didn't do, Iyena's mother makes it very clear, verbally, that it was not the case. The events that lead to her mother's next decision are hazy in Iyena's mind, but the image is imprinted like stubborn ink.

Her mother standing resolutely in front of the old Healer after slapping him, hard, right across his smug face. Her father staring helplessly, a vein throbbing on his temple.

Whenever Iyena feels she is behaving too impulsively, she replays the scene of her mother in her mind and reminds herself that it's all in her blood.

★   ★   ★

The woman is wearing a white sari with gold borders. Her black hair is straight and falls on her shoulders, with streaks of blue and snowflakes of silver. Her manner is calm and her smile is arresting. She holds Anaris's hands and looks at him with a fondness of a long-time lover.

All of this, Iyena notices in one glance as she makes her way to the dining room. The table is set for a feast, despite the hour of the day. The food looks characteristically prepared by Maani-Ba's hands, but her absence is both curious and jarring. Iyena gives the woman a grim stare.

Anaris breaks the silence. "Iyena, I want you to meet Senthrina. Senthrina, this is Iyena, my daughter."

"Pleasure to meet you, Iyena dear. You are as pretty as your father says you are, if not more."

Iyena takes the seat to the left of her father, not taking her eyes away from Senthrina, whose attention has now been grabbed by her teacup.

Are you my mother now? Iyena wants to ask this strange woman she has never seen before but is now forced to talk to, to socialize with. There is no other reason for her presence in their dining room this early in the day. There is no other reason for the woman to look at her father the way she does.

"How's school, Iyena?" Senthrina asks, after taking a loud sip of the tea. Her eyes are ocean-blue and her gaze is striking. The question itself carries a certain expectation, a heft. It commands an answer.

"The usual," says Iyena, breaking a piece of the bread in front of her and buttering it. She doesn't want to maintain eye contact, because that would encourage more conversation. Her mind is somewhere else. A meeting with Trehan. Then a meeting with the Caretaker of the Garden of Delights.

"What is your favorite subject?" Senthrina asks. There's an eagerness to her question. Like she wants to get to know everything about Iyena in as short a time as possible. She is also leaning forward, her shoulders bunched, her elbows slightly touching the table.

"She likes all of them, don't you Iyena?" Anaris interjects.

"I like history the most," says Iyena. "The richness of it. The diversity of it. Especially the diversity of it."

"Interesting," says Senthrina. "We would find much to talk about, then."

"Like what?" Iyena asks flatly. She knows she is doing everything in her power to make the conversation, and herself, as unlikeable as possible. That's the only way she can be out of this misery. Whatever her father is playing at, she doesn't want to be a part of it.

"For example, have you heard of the marriage customs of Sirvassans?"

"The Room of Opposites, the snipped petal," says Iyena. "Most fascinating."

"Do you know there's a duel inside the Room of Opposites? The bride and groom are each given a weapon of a different kind and are forced to make a choice. To fight, or not."

"I find that hard to believe," says Iyena. "I am pretty sure that doesn't happen inside the Room of Opposites."

"There's a lot of fighting in marriages. What happens inside is just a manifestation. A test."

"Why are we talking about marriage customs for breakfast?"

"We could talk about trade."

"Or we could eat our food in silence."

Anaris and Senthrina exchange glances. It's a retort neither of them had expected, and Iyena knows it. Anaris looks like he's embarrassed to even have Iyena present at the table. He kneads his forehead with his fingers, while Senthrina chews her lips. Iyena doesn't wait for them to speak, and continues eating her food. But her mind is elsewhere. The food tastes bland, and she feels this entire charade is meant to put her in her place. The place doesn't even feel like home anymore.

Iyena drags her chair back, a bit too loudly, leaving a respectable amount of food on her plate, just enough that it doesn't look like she didn't eat much.

"Where are you going, Iyena?" asks Anaris.

"I'm meeting a school friend of mine," she says. "You have a problem with that?"

Anaris clenches his jaw. The woman looks at him, then back at Iyena, opens her mouth to say something but apparently decides against it. Iyena walks out of the house.

*　　*　　*

She finds Trehan near the market square, munching on a candy. His shoulders are slouched, and he is wearing an oversized bright red shirt, which gives even more of an impression that his posture is not correct. His hair is neat and slick, for a change. Iyena can imagine his mother combing his hair, struggling with those sandy wisps, which refuse to stay in one place. Trehan is too carefree to comb his hair. Iyena could tell he used his hands to shape it.

"You took your time," says Trehan. "I don't even know if the Caretaker will be in today."

"Didn't you once say that he is *always* in?"

"I don't remember."

Trehan offers her a candy, which she refuses. He opens the wrapper and eats it himself, enjoying the sugar rush.

"I did some thinking of my own," he begins. "About what you told me. About what you can do."

"Really? And what conclusion did you arrive at?"

"You might just be from another planet," says Trehan earnestly.

Iyena bursts into laughter. Trehan looks befuddled.

"I'm sorry," says Iyena, between fits of laughter. "Another... planet...?"

"Don't believe me? My mother, apart from having a huge collection of locks and keys, also has a huge collection of books. Ancient texts and whatnot. I was reading one book last night. It mentioned old magic. Of gods and goddesses, of people who don't rely on any gardens or flowers or potions for their magic. Of people who just think and things happen."

"Trehan, your research is flattering, but I think let's leave the conclusion to the man who actually knows a thing or two about it."

Trehan shrugs. "Whatever. Don't believe me. I'm sure the Caretaker will have something similar to say."

Iyena brushes the tips of her fingers against Trehan's. Trehan does the same, and then holds her hand, interlacing his fingers with hers. An electric tingle runs through Iyena. A carriage stops near them. The Rhisuan beast pulling it grunts and shakes his body, his many eyes seeking prospective passengers. Iyena approaches the beast and whispers their destination in its ear, in the grunt-language it understands. The beast shakes again, telling her to hop on.

★   ★   ★

The carriage drops them right in front of the pole with the ribbon. Iyena ties a knot in the ribbon and the path to the Garden reveals itself. The first time she came here, the road looked dusty and well-trodden with eager, hurried footsteps. Now, after all these months, the trail looks cold and lonely.

"Will we find him?" Trehan asks, but his question is not aimed at Iyena. He just says it out loud, as if expecting to find the answer from the air around him. "The place looks very quiet."

"It's not exactly a fish market, now, is it?"

Trehan seems to have gotten his answer because he doesn't reply. The trail turns to the left and opens into a wide compound. Right ahead of them is a two-storied building. Iyena remembers it as the laboratory, where the Caretaker had taken her after their first meeting. To their left is the door to the Garden, made entirely of stone.

"Normally either he or his assistant is seen roaming around this area," says Trehan.

"You know I can open the door of the Garden," says Iyena.

"You can do *what*?"

"I saw the pattern the old man drew on the door. I think I can replicate it."

"Now you're just being too full of yourself. I shouldn't have mentioned about that planet. It's gone to your head."

"Do you want to see me give it a try? I can—" Iyena stops, her face contorted in a frown, ears straining to catch a hint of something. A low rumble, a moan. Some murmurs. "Did you hear that?"

"No."

"Listen carefully."

Trehan steps closer to Iyena. His feet fall on solid, dry ground full of pebbles, making an echoing cracking noise. Iyena shifts her feet, too, and notices a well-trodden trail of pebbles and moss disappearing in the distance, toward their right. It's where the sound is coming from. Before Trehan can reply, Iyena starts walking toward the sound.

"Where are you going?"

"Following the sound," says Iyena, stopping in her tracks.

"We could be in danger!"

Iyena rolls her eyes. "Trehan, this is a safe and magical place. It's just home for the Caretaker. You should know that. We will be all right. Come, now."

"I have a bad feeling about this," says Trehan. His voice comes out shaky, his legs jittery.

"Trehan, it was your idea, remember?"

Iyena wishes he were braver. Because deep inside, Iyena is scared too. Her heart beats like a drum, ringing in her ears as she tiptoes toward the sound. Her palms sweat and the tips of her fingers feel like they're plunged into a furnace. The hairs on her neck prickle. She didn't feel like this when she was walking through that vast, glittery nothingness with the woman called Seedmaster. This place is a safe haven. There is no reason to feel like this. And yet, that incessant sound makes everything worse.

The moans intensify. Iyena and Trehan keep walking. The trail leads to a hut, surrounded by two large trees. The tree on the left looks untouched by age, pristine. The one to the right, however, has withered, its roots clawing out of the ground, its body hunched like an old man. But that's not the most disturbing thing about it.

From its gnarled and weak branches ten feet above the ground, a man hangs upside down. He is flailing his arms pathetically. The moans belong to him. The sounds of helplessness belong to him.

Iyena gasps. Trehan holds her arm. Before they can react further, the door of the hut flies open and a tall, dark man comes out. He is wearing a blue coat, and his hair is slick with oil, parted in the middle. He wears a silver earring on one of his ears, which glints in the harsh sunlight. He looks at the hanging man and lets out a snarl.

"Have you decided yet, or should I—" Then his attention falls on Iyena. His manner changes immediately. Gone is the brash disposition of a moment ago, the dark confidence. His face bursts into a welcoming smile.

"Master, this Stigmar isn't cooperating, and it looks like we have guests."

Saying this, he moves closer to Iyena, narrowing his gaze. "We have met before."

Iyena recognizes him as the man she met at Yavani's place. A man who hated her father and made it very evident. "Yes," says Iyena simply.

"Are you here for—"

Before the man can say any more, the Caretaker comes out of the hut, wiping his hands on a cloth, bearing the same kind smile he had when Iyena first saw him. He almost looks apologetic.

"Trulio, did you forget to remove the ribbon today?" says the Caretaker.

"I am sorry, Master. The matter at hand was too pressing."

The man hanging from the branch lets out a guttural scream.

"Please, please, for the sake of Yatin, and Indhrin, and the Goddess of Mercy, let me go. I will tell you everything."

There is a pause. The Caretaker considers the situation. He takes a deep breath and says, "Let's take things one at a time. Children, I hope you have your papers for the Delights you want. Let's quickly arrange for that. Trulio, it won't take me much time—"

"Actually," Iyena begins. Her heart has steadied by now. "We are not here for any Delights. We are here to tell you something."

The Caretaker looks at Iyena attentively. His gaze is gentle, but piercing. Iyena avoids looking at the man hanging from the tree, focusing solely on the Caretaker. But it's impossible not to steal a glance at the wretched, morbid sight. It's the way the man is hanging, his legs making a figure of four, and his arms flailing impossibly. His skin has gone white from fear and his voice has the quality of curdled milk.

Trehan walks up and stands beside Iyena. Even as the Caretaker seems to make up his mind to speak, Iyena feels Trehan's hands in hers, his shallow breath, and the pulse through his skin. He is more nervous than her.

"Come inside," says the Caretaker. "Trulio, bring water for our young guests and something good to eat."

"What about him?"

"We will deal with him later."

"But Master, he is ready to tell us."

"Our guests have come far. This traitor of Sirvassa can wait a little while longer."

The Caretaker nods at Iyena and beckons them both into the hut.

★   ★   ★

The Caretaker's hut is built minimally. There's a wooden staircase that leads to a floor upstairs. On the landing of the staircase there rests a bust of a woman. It seems to be fashioned out of stone and air and rivulets of honey. Iyena tries to steal her gaze from the bust, but finds herself unable to. When she eventually does, she feels the eyes of the woman on her, burning holes in her body.

There's ample room for four people to sit easily. A fire crackles near a hearth, flames sprinkling embers into the air. A small window overlooks the Llar mountain range in the distance. Beneath the window hangs an earthen pot. Beneath the pot, there rest four brass tumblers. Trulio pours water into three of them, carefully tilting the earthen pot, while whistling an old song. Neither of the men gives any impression that there's a man getting magically tortured just outside.

Perhaps it's better this way.

The Caretaker claps his hands and says, "So, what do you want to discuss?"

Iyena has thought about this moment before, yet she's hesitant now. It's like the power that resides inside her is whispering, *It's okay to not know everything.* But then she looks at Trehan, and he doesn't look back, and she feels if she doesn't make a decision right now, it will be too late. She looks down at her feet, gathers up her courage, and begins.

"About five months ago, I came to your Garden for a Delight. You gave me a bottle of a potion and told me to use it at a specific time only. I did exactly as I was told."

Iyena stops and scans the room. The Caretaker is listening to her intently. She takes a deep breath and continues. "I can...I can still do it."

The Caretaker frowns. "What do you mean?"

"I can change the nature of things."

Saying those words, she grabs the brass tumbler from Trehan's hands. The Caretaker takes a nervous step toward Iyena, his expression still inscrutable, but his manner tense. Iyena focuses on the metal of the tumbler and wills it to become actual, transparent glass.

And it does.

CHAPTER TWENTY-SEVEN

The Caretaker

For a long time, the only sound in the room is the slow crackle of fire. If one listens closely, one might hear the labored breaths of the Caretaker, as he grapples with the information just thrust on him. They might also hear the scratching of Trulio's toenails against the floor, but it's a low sound, consumed by a larger absence of sound altogether. Even the song of the fell-birds has stilled. The man outside is moaning no longer, and the branches of the trees sway no longer, and the windows do their dull rattle no longer. This all-consuming silence is punctured first by the sandy-haired boy's cough, and the Caretaker's measured words.

"When did you last consume the potion?" he asks slowly, keeping his voice as gentle as possible.

The girl looks at the Caretaker, then at Trulio, then at the Caretaker again. "Five months ago. It was a small quantity. The red liquid."

It was just a Priming potion. The Bacillus Rose, the one that gets you ready for other Delights. It shouldn't have acted on its own. Unless….

The Caretaker kneads a spot on his forehead.

"How did your abilities become evident to you first?"

"I saved his life," says the girl. "He ate a poisonous fruit when we went on a school trip in the jungle. I…I saw the poison in his blood and converted it back to…uh…blood."

The Caretaker scratches his chin. Then, suddenly, lines appear on his forehead, and he uses his thumb to press at them, as if a hard enough press would make them disappear. After a thoughtful silence, he says, "Your Delight couldn't have done something like that."

"I also made a man change his mind without speaking to him, among other things."

As if he'd caught smoke from thin air, the Caretaker gets up and announces, "Come with me to the Garden."

The children glance at each other cluelessly. Trulio claps his hands in uncharacteristic glee, like he's caught on to a secret but is unwilling to share the details.

★   ★   ★

The Bacillus Rose looks pristine from a distance. Untouched, graceful, a flower of divinity. The same Rose held by the Half-Formed God when he went into his eternal slumber. The Caretaker kneels on the soft, almost wet ground and looks at the flower. On the surface, nothing looks wrong with it. It's the same flower it has always been. In retrospect, though, it isn't a flower that has been used much. A very giving flower, its Delights range from the quiet, mystical magic of old times, to more flamboyant abilities.

"What are you looking for?" the girl, who introduced herself as Iyena Mastafar, asks.

"If there's one thing this Garden is known for, it's this – imparting temporary Delights, which enchant and entertain, and then revert the user back to normal. It's what I do. It's what I have always wanted to do, because I don't believe in exclusion. I believe that everyone should have a taste of the many wonders this world has to impart. That is my sole mission. I make my potions with care and precision. This has never happened before."

The Caretaker stops speaking and turns to Trehan. His gaze is questioning, but his manner is kind.

Trehan fidgets, but responds.

"Yes, yes, you're right."

The Caretaker turns his attention to the girl whom the Bacillus Rose had changed. "Iyena, the fact that you can change the nature of things, a Delight that has the quality of old, and very powerful magic, both intrigues me and terrifies me."

"Can I ask you a question?" the girl says confidently.

"Please do."

"Are *you* permanent? As in…do *you* carry any permanent abilities? Are you a Florral?"

The Caretaker knew that sooner or later he would have to answer such a question. He looks at the ground evasively, then meets the questioning gaze of the girl.

"I am a Florral," says the Caretaker, sighing. "I can channel my Delights to last longer. I can also do more, much more than any other individual. But age has gotten the better of me and now I am a mere shadow of what I once was. You, on the other hand…are a mystery."

Trulio gasps, placing the back of his hand over his mouth. The Caretaker lets the word linger in the air. He hasn't even spoken that word aloud in normal conversation. It feels utterly absurd, alien, now to speak of it.

"Master, what about the rot?" Trulio says simply, putting in words the Caretaker's worst fears.

"We can't be certain, Trulio. At present, there are just too many equations."

"I have also seen this rot you are talking about," says Iyena. "I saw it with my own eyes. At the place where the seeds grow. The place with the hanging trees and the beasts who run up and down those trees hungrily."

"You met the Seedmaster? You met Yavani?" asks the Caretaker.

"Yes," says Iyena. "It happened after…. She was very kind to me. I was lost…. When there was a blast at the ship my father and I were on. She…actually, her son saved my life. I spent a night at her place and the next day, she showed me the place with the trees and the place where she works."

The girl speaks as if cobbling together broken details from her memory and giving it shape and form that would make sense.

"I saw her at the Seedmaster's place when I went to get the Tulip's seeds, Master. I think this was just the next day of the attack."

"You were *on* the ship? *On* the *Kkirinth*?" asks the Caretaker.

"Yes. My father had taken me along. To show me how he conducts his trade. To show what was being brought in from Alderra to Sirvassa. Food, spices...especially whatever pleases Minister Yayati."

The lines are back on the Caretaker's forehead. He uses the back of his thumb to rub his temple. Then he looks at Trulio and says, "Trulio, I think it's time for all of us to know a little bit more about the whole truth."

★   ★   ★

The Stigmar sits cross-legged on the grass, slowly humming, bobbing to and fro. His right hand twitches and shakes, and he uses his left to stop it from doing so. His skin is the color of mud after water has been poured on it. His hair is thin, and he has two scars on his cheek.

"My name is Urnam Tysnedi. I am from the Kalendi group, a sub-faction of Corrilean. We are...uh...we are famous for our dislike of the mayor and his policies. During the General Sirvassan Assembly every year, our leader brings forth a fresh set of policies that will be beneficial for Sirvassa in the long run, and in turn for its people. Those are vehemently denied every time. The turning point was when Mayor Illyasi triggered that stupid housing policy. None of the houses were made as they were promised."

The man stops speaking. The Caretaker offers him water. He grabs the tumbler with shaking hands, and brings the water to his lips. Not much of it makes it down his throat because he is shaking too much.

"So when we found out High Minister Yayati was visiting Sirvassa, we would place our demands in front of him. We have been silently forming a bigger faction, a political opponent to stand opposite to Mayor Illyasi."

"Don't bore us with politics," says Trulio. "And I am sure these students skip history lessons in school. So get to the point."

"Actually," says Iyena, "what he is saying is most fascinating."

Urnam Tysnedi gulps down the remainder of the water and continues.

"But the minister has new plans for Sirvassa. I don't know what exactly...but four months ago I was visited by official dignitaries from Alderra and made to sign a confidentiality agreement. And then, my group was given some orders."

"What orders?" Trulio barks.

"Trulio, gently, please," says the Caretaker. Urnam's face looks like a porcelain mask of fear. Rivulets of sweat course down his body, dampening his already soiled shirt.

"I swear on the pristine body of Eborsen, I didn't know it would involve...what it involved. I thought we were just helping transfer goods in exchange for valuable consideration. Then one thing led to another and we were making explosives. And then, one day...."

"Say it," says the Caretaker.

"We ended up attacking the ship. The attack on the *Kkirinth* and the docks. My group was behind it."

"On orders from these official dignitaries. Who were they, exactly?"

"I...I don't remember names, exactly. One man, though, who was in charge...he walks with a cane."

Iyena's world swirls around her. Urnam's face becomes a blur. His mouth moves but there are no words. The rhythm of her heart becomes erratic, then loud. But something else takes form inside her. An ugly black shape, rising upward inexorably like a wave, consuming her. Her palms feel aflame. Her breathing becomes heavy.

"What did you say?" she asks, red-hot with rage.

The man stops, his jaw hanging, a nervous tic on his face, which has aged a decade in the last few hours.

"A man with a cane was in charge. He gave the orders."

"What was his name?"

The man hesitates. But then the name comes out of his mouth, just like that.

"Anaris Mastafar."

There is silence again. But it's a short one, interrupted by the cooing of a fell-bird in the distance. Urnam shifts nervously as Trulio snatches the tumbler of water away from him. The Caretaker crosses his hands across his chest and looks at Iyena.

Iyena, however, isn't interested in looking anyone in the eye, except her father.

She clenches both her fists, grabbing innocent grass and yanking it out by its roots in anger. She gets up, takes a long, lingering look at the man who told the truth, and then walks out of the Garden.

CHAPTER TWENTY-EIGHT

Iyena Mastafar

Iyena storms out of the Garden. She's numb, yet her heart is pacing.. An ice-cold pit forms in her stomach. Everything feels heavy, yet the rage drives her on. If it had been news of a tragedy, even a distant one, she'd probably be blinking away tears. But betrayal, from family, is an emotion she isn't used to. The tips of her fingers burn. A dark cloud of uncertainty fogs her brain. Who can she trust? What is this world she was thrust into?

She hasn't felt like this before. Things spiraling away from her, while she stands clutching empty air. Sern Aradha said to her once, ushering her outside the class of Albuchemy, while Sern Mirnya was busy teaching the students to control the temperature of fire in forging a metal, "Iyena, no loss cuts deeper than losing control of our own circumstances. Helplessness is the greatest anguish of all." Her advice felt useless at that time. A lesson in between lessons. Unrelated.

Much later, Iyena understood that Sern Aradha was talking about playing with fire. It was easiest to lose control of fire, and things quickly went wrong in Albuchemy. Sern Mirnya was ill-equipped to teach students about the salient, metaphorical aspects of understanding the subject. And hence, Sern Aradha had taken it upon herself.

Now Iyena thinks Sern Aradha was talking about something else entirely. She was talking about life, perhaps preparing her for this betrayal. Because Iyena feels an incredible loss of control, a helplessness so vast, which no Delight, no magical ability could fulfil.

What would she say to her father? *How dare you take your daughter to the same ship you were planning on attacking? What was the endgame?* A torrent of questions rages in her mind, leaving her breathless.

She sits down on the dusty road, hugging her knees. The white-harsh afternoon sun beats on the road, bringing with it a senseless, stupid heat. Sweat trickles down Iyena's forehead and drops with a sharp sizzle on the road.

Then a shadow engulfs her. The heat dissipates momentarily. She looks up and sees the dark face of Trehan looking down upon her.

"Iyena, I am so sorry you had to listen to that," he says.

"Why are you sorry?"

"I…. It's…it's just the right thing to say." He stutters at first, then calms himself, sitting down on the road beside Iyena. "What will you do now?"

"Have a long talk with my father, I suppose. I don't know…. What do you think I should do?"

"Turn him into a singing puppet. Then—"

Iyena gives him a dark look before he can complete his sentence. He purses his lips, and finds a spot on the ground to fix his eyes on. An uncomfortable silence builds between the two.

Then Iyena scoffs.

"He's still my father," she says. "I'll probably just go home and keep quiet around him. Just…keep deathly quiet, making my silence do all the talking."

They sit in the same spot for a long while. Soon, activity on the road increases. Sweet sellers yell their prices at no one in particular, ringing small bells to attract young customers. Carriages groan to destinations unknown, as strangers on the street cast them empty, disapproving glances. No one hazards a cursory glance in the direction of the Garden.

Trehan gets up first, and pulls Iyena to her feet.

"You want a salousse?"

"Are you buying?"

"No," says Trehan. "The seller turned out to be an old friend of my mother's. I have a year's supply of free salousse promised to me."

"Then I'll find ways to cling to your side for at least another year," says Iyena.

Trehan beams at her.

"Iyena, whatever you decide, I'll be by your side."

"I know," says Iyena. "I know."

★   ★   ★

Iyena steps inside her house late in the afternoon. Spending time with Trehan has given her enough confidence to face her father. The sweetness and slightly tangy aftertaste of the salousse lingers in her mouth, still. Trehan has eaten four complete packets, smearing his chin in the process. His mother will give him an earful for that. Iyena had two packets, and even now her senses are heightened and her body tingles with a sugar rush.

For a brief moment, when Iyena was with Trehan, she forgot about her father's abject betrayal. She completely forgot that she could be – what the Caretaker termed – a Florral. Somehow, her mind blocked that part of her experience, her entire being, that she could be something so much more than an ordinary Alderran girl.

That she could be one of the most powerful Florrachemists in ages.

But it all comes rushing back to her as soon as she steps inside her house. The coldness of the house is a stark counterpoint to the warmth of the city. The house feels cold and empty. Like an invisible force has snuffed out all life from it.

"Father...? Maani-Ba..." she calls out, in vain. No one answers her calls as she tiptoes farther inside. It's a place that looks suspended in time. She would immediately run out of the place, terrified, if it weren't for the simple fact that she left it just a couple of hours ago.

As she crosses to the staircase, she notices light pooling on the dark marble. Dirty, yellow light coming from inside her father's study. Feeble, the illumination gives the rest of the house a lost, eerie quality. A flickering lamp of a researcher in ruins, about to stumble on a secret.

The door to the study is completely open. The light is coming from the yellowed and dusty sun lamp suspended high up near the ceiling. The moon lamp, too, gives out a silvery shine. But the lamps are not what catch Iyena's attention. It's a figure standing hunched near her father's desk.

The figure has no hair on its head. It wears a bright red cloak wrapped around its body, tied with a shimmering pin on its broad, muscular shoulders. The muscles on its sinewy arms bulge outward and its body looks painted in gold. It stands unmoving, but from the rise and fall of its back, Iyena can tell the figure is breathing slowly, but surely.

Iyena steps inside, but there's a sharp crack. A gasp leaves her mouth, as she notices she has stepped on the cap of a pen. The sound is like a thunderclap against the utter silence of the room. The figure turns around to face Iyena.

It's the automaton. Except it's not anymore, at least in the strictest sense of the word. Something about it has changed. It's more humanlike than ever, and it looks even taller, more imposing, more threatening. Its eyes are dark hollows, as if waiting to be populated with irises and pupils and eye fluid.

The automaton stands straight, and leans stylishly against the desk. Its lips curve upward into a smile. And it speaks. "Iyena Mastafar, good afternoon."

It's the voice of her father. But then, Anaris Mastafar steps out of the shadows, into the light, and enters the room. Iyena's heart thunders inside her chest, making a mad, unstoppable sound.

"Iyena, you're back."

"What is that?"

"That is Turain-One," he says simply, as if pointing at a vegetable. Turain-One nods at Anaris as he makes his way toward the automaton. "I have created him."

"What's...what's it for?"

"Many things, as you will soon see," says Anaris matter-of-factly. "You left in the morning very rudely. I am still waiting for your apology."

The hatred is all back, but her heart steadies a bit.

"Maybe you should be apologizing to me, instead of the other way round."

"Excuse me?"

"I know about the ship. I know about the attack on the *Kkirinth*. You made it happen. It was *you!*"

Anaris walks toward Iyena, wearing a derisive, almost mocking expression on his face.

"What in Alderran's depths are you talking about?"

"The attack on the ship in which I…in which you…almost died. Remember? Or should I refresh your memory?" Her voice swells in anger, as the room itself seems to thrum around her.

"That's silly and absurd, coming from you, Iyena." Anaris is so calm, it's almost offensive. "You know how much raw material and import was wasted because of that attack? That was all Alderran… meant for the usage of poor Sirvassans here. Sent by the Alderran Ministry, signed by the esteemed Minister Yayati. Why would I do something stupid like that?"

Then he turns and beckons Turain-One over. The creature walks slowly toward father and daughter and looms over them menacingly. Anaris looks at it proudly, then turns his attention back to Iyena.

"What do you think of my creation?"

Iyena knows her father is evading her questions. She knows, deep in her heart, that he can't be trusted anymore.

"It's scary," says Iyena. "Where's Maani-Ba?"

"I asked her to take a vacation. She needed it, desperately."

"But this is Maani-Ba's place, isn't it?"

Anaris stays silent.

"You still haven't answered my question, Father. Was it you behind the attack on the ship or not? Just answer yes or no. If you can't be honest with your own daughter, what's even the point?"

Anaris waves dismissively at Turain-One, who dutifully turns around and walks back to the study. There, it stands in attention, as if waiting for further orders from its master.

"Just the fact that you even dare to ask me this.... How could you? Who is putting these poisonous thoughts in your mind, Iyena? Is it that boy? Is it that Caretaker? You have been to the Garden, I know it. You have been meeting with all the wrong sorts of people behind my back. I asked you to do one thing for me, and you couldn't do that. And instead, you're mingling with them. *They* are filling you with their vileness, and you are just gobbling up all of it, no questions asked."

"Yes," she says. "Yes to all of that. And they are good people, with noble intentions. Spending time inside the Garden and spending time with these people has brought me more joy than I could ever hope from living with you."

"That's it," says Iyena's father, thrumming with rage. "We are leaving for Alderra after dinner at Mayor Illyasi's bungalow. You will be disciplined under Sern Aradha, and I'll see to it, personally."

"You don't own me! I am not your slave."

"You are my daughter and you'll do as I say!" Anaris whispers, and grabs Iyena's arm, his fingers digging into her flesh, hurting her. But then, Iyena grabs Anaris's wrists, meeting his rage with hers. She can feel his skin pulsating, his heart beating with a mad rhythm. The temperature of his body, texture of his skin, the nature of his being, all hers to control in that instant.

An ugliness is born inside her and she lets go....

Smoke curls upward from where she grabbed Anaris's wrists. His skin first goes red, glowing amber, then black, and a sizzling sound comes. The smell of burning flesh singes her nostrils as Anaris's whole body recoils in horror. He howls in pain, clutching his wrists. "What did you do?" he says, with a tremor in his voice.

And then Turain-One jumps to action, coming toward Iyena at a dizzying speed. It raises both its hands, and brings them down on Iyena, grabbing her shoulders, threatening to pick her up. Its grip, hard, metallic, is ten times stronger than Anaris's, than any human's, and Iyena squirms in pain.

"*No!* Stop! Turain-One, I command you to stop."

It stops. Iyena's shoulders sting. She meets her father's raw gaze, his face going through an entire gamut of emotions, while she goes through only one – disgust. As the automaton retreats, she wonders if she could have melted it into a golden puddle. She could have, if she had the energy. But performing Florrachemy on her father, singeing his skin, changing its nature, had taken a toll on her.

She can feel her insides squirm, things upending, changing.

"Iyena," her father says, his voice broken. "Iyena, my dear, I am sorry. I didn't mean to hurt you."

"But I did," says Iyena and walks out of the study.

★   ★   ★

Iyena packs her belongings, hastily throwing her clothes into a small bag she could carry easily over her shoulders. There is only one right course of action at this point, and it is to immediately move out of this house. She doesn't yet entertain the idea that she won't have a roof over her head, nor will she have any Sirvassan Kerron to spend. Her rage-clouded mind hasn't yet planned that far ahead into the future.

Her gaze falls on the photo Maani-Ba showed her of her mother. It sits on the mantelpiece, among other paraphernalia. She grabs it, and wraps a skirt around it, so the frame sits snugly between padded layers of clothing. Then, she places the skirt between two other items of clothing.

She looks around the room. There is not much here she could call her own. In the five months she has been in Sirvassa, she has only used this room for sleeping. It's a placeholder of a place, temporary. She has invited no friends over, ever. Maybe she should have, instead of heading over to their homes, their places. Then, there would be a part of her in this room, a wisp of a memory which latches on and refuses to go. But the only memory she has attached to this place is of the windowsill. A window through which she often spoke to Trehan, a window she often climbed in and out of, a window she hurt and made rotten. The blackness is still there on the windowsill. She looks at it for a moment too long before tearing her gaze away.

She slings the bag on her shoulders and walks out of her room for the last time.

Downstairs, her father is applying balm on the burns as he stands near the door of his study.

"Iyena..." he starts, but then stops himself. He's struggling with words, it's evident. And he knows no matter what he says, he can't get his daughter back. But still, he tries, and the only thing which comes out of his mouth is another question. "Where will you go?"

"I'll figure it out," says Iyena. "Take care, Father."

★ ★ ★

Outside, it's still late afternoon. The sun obstinately clings to the sky, refusing to go down dutifully behind the Llar Mountains. The roads are relatively empty for the time of the day, but there's a smattering of people near a shop that sells footwear. The seller is yelling at the top of his lungs the price of this new material he has gotten imported from Alvassa, and how it protects from moisture. A group of women is bargaining with the seller, urging him to bring the price down because they have been to Alvassa and the material had become old news last year.

Iyena looks at her own pair of shoes. They would still last her long, and she has a couple more in her bag. She won't need another pair for a long time.

But now the possibility of homelessness grips her. And food? She hasn't given a thought to food. A fraction of her wants to go back and set things right with her father. But a better part of her wants to hold on to the decision and see what comes of it.

A carriage stops near her. A familiar face beams at her. It's Ujita, from her school, the studious girl with the bulbous glasses.

"Iyena, what are you doing out in this heat? You want to get sunstroke?"

"I, uh...." Iyena has no words to respond. "I wanted to...."

"Hop on first, explain later," says Ujita. Iyena is hesitant. But she is on her own, and there's no one to grant permission except herself now. She climbs in the carriage, clutching the string of her bag tightly. Once she is inside the carriage, she puts the bag on her lap, feeling its familiar weight, especially the bump where her mother's photo is kept.

"Where are you off to?" asks Ujita, straining to carry her own bag. Bright red apples peek out from her overflowing bag. Beneath the apples, there's some green and some orange. Iyena can't make out what else she is carrying.

"I wanted to explore the city," says Iyena evasively. Ujita narrows her gaze at Iyena. Iyena doesn't meet her eye, instead finds a spot on the carriage floor to look at. The Rhisuan beast gives a familiar grunt and ambles on the dusty, afternoon road.

"You'll get lost," says Ujita. "You know how big this city is?"

Iyena opens her mouth to say something, but decides against it. In truth, she is hoping Ujita will say something comforting. Something that won't make Iyena feel so lonely. But for that, she would have to share her predicament with her. Could Iyena just tell her that she has left her home, her family for good? Could she unload on her, without her permission?

"Listen, Iyena, it's our post-afternoon snack time. Why don't you stop at my place for a while? My mother prepares a sumptuous ghevlan. We will have that with tea, and then you can be on your way. I can give you tips on where you could go. That is, if you are adamant on traveling solo."

Ujita's words come as a relief. Iyena can only nod at her. Ujita gives her a broad smile, and her eyes become even rounder behind those odd, convex glasses.

★　　★　　★

Ujita's home has an openness to it that Iyena has rarely seen in households. It reminds her of Sern Mirnya's place back in Alderra. There's a cozy veranda surrounded by small pillars, with steps leading toward a seating area. The veranda is lit naturally by sunlight, which filters through a mesh on the ceiling. The walls are naturally cooler.

"How come this is the first time you are coming to my place?" says Ujita. Her tone, today, is unnaturally chirpy for some reason.

Iyena looks at her and smiles. "You never invited me, Ujita."

"Neither did you. And now, you have to invite me. I also want to see how you Alderrans live."

"We live normally," says Iyena.

Ujita's mother, a portly woman, who looks like she is well in the fifth decade of her life, steps out from the darkness of a room, into the light of the veranda, carrying a basket. Her face is wrinkled, but her eyes are young. Looking at Iyena, she smiles. Then, she rests the basket on the steps of the veranda.

"Ujita, will you help me, dear? And who is your friend?"

"Iyena Mastafar. She is a friend from school, Ama."

"The one from the capital."

"That's right."

Ujita goes by her mother's side and helps her unload vegetables from the basket onto a stone pedestal. Then, one by one, mother and daughter wash the grime off the vegetables underneath a thin stream of water. Iyena walks over to their side to help them, but Ujita's mother waves a hand, kindly, but dismissively. The gesture is not rude, but it's clear she wouldn't want a first-time guest to immediately start helping in household chores. As Iyena watches, Ujita and her mother slice and cut the vegetables and neatly arrange the pieces on a stone slab. Ujita keeps the slab directly under the sunlight.

"Kukarn pieces, to dry off in the sun. We will gather them tomorrow and make a pickle out of them."

Afternoon blinks into evening. A cruelly hot day makes way for an evening that comes as a solace. Iyena sits cross-legged on a stone pedestal, Ujita and her mother to Iyena's right. Ujita's mother serves Iyena a hot plateful of ghevlan, with a side of mint chutney. Iyena takes a bite of the lightly toasted roll, which contains chickpeas and lentils simmered together in a spice mix, with a healthy dose of coriander. The taste is warmth and comfort rolled into one. She wishes she could say it tastes of home, but it doesn't. Neither Sirvassa nor Alderra was her true home, nor the various other small cities she lived in because of constant travel. Still, she eats, and smiles at Ujita and her mother, because it's good food, better than she has had in a long while.

"Ama, what did Cousin Shabdi say?"

"Their coppergram arrived today," says her mother, silently chewing her food. "They have a vacant lot now. She says we can take the next ship and go there whenever we want to."

"Where are you going, if you don't mind me asking?" Iyena asks.

"We are leaving Sirvassa," says Ujita simply, like it is the most normal thing to say.

"But why?"

Ujita looks at her mother, who doesn't say anything.

Ujita continues.

"This is not the place it was before. And this will soon devolve into a mere shadow of its past glory. The changes in the school aren't helping. Sidhi left the school as soon as the new syllabus was introduced. Some of the things being taught were just too vile. I spoke to Varsha just the other day, and for some reason she actually loved the new syllabus. She had the choicest words to say about the Inishtis."

"I used to like Varsha," says Iyena in a disappointed tone.

"We were supposed to get cheap houses," Ujita's mother begins, her eyes downcast. "But nothing came of that. We pay two thousand Kerron for this place and it's becoming a financial burden. Mayors come and mayors go, yet our lives hardly improve." Iyena wants to respond, wants to provide a salve, but she knows it wouldn't help them. She feels it's partly her fault. She is hesitant to even look Ujita in the eye.

But it's Ujita who speaks next, her voice calm, assured.

"Iyena, I know I shouldn't be saying this directly to you. I felt bad when the students at the school started distancing themselves from you. I only heard about what happened to that boy and his family. Some people said it was pretty bad. He hasn't come to school since being taken away. One can't just take students away from a school. They are saying his family...his father is part of a group that's involved in terrorist activities. I don't believe that. Things like that have never ever happened before."

"Next thing you know," Ujita's mother says, "they'll come after us, with some made-up facts." There's barely a hint of emotion in her voice. She has accepted the fate of the place without even trying. Iyena doesn't blame her.

"And you know what's the worst? There are many people in Sirvassa who are welcoming this change with open arms. What's the Protector of Sirvassa doing in a time like this? What is he the Caretaker of? Who gave him the title?"

Silence falls around the table like a cruel whisper. Despite knowing some part of the truth, Iyena can't bring herself to say it. She can't convince these people to stay, or offer them words of hope. What can she do to change any of it? She's not a hero.

She can't defeat these monsters, when these monsters look a lot like her.

After they're finished eating, Iyena helps Ujita and her mother in clearing up the plates, washing them, and stacking them neatly atop a wooden shelf. Iyena notices that Ujita's family lives minimally, with little to no furniture, only the bare necessities for survival. As a result, all their belongings – mostly clothes – end up in two neat bundles, one that Ujita would carry and the other her mother would. The bundles are hardly bigger than the one Iyena is carrying herself.

"Where are you headed to, then, Iyena? And aren't you carrying a lot for a simple Sirvassa exploration?"

Iyena purses her lips, unsure of what to say. Ujita's gaze lingers a bit longer on Iyena's bag. An uncomfortable pause swells between them. Then, Iyena blurts out the truth.

"I have left my home," she says. "I currently have nowhere to go."

Ujita's jaw hangs in surprise, as she tries to make sense of the incredible information thrust upon her.

"But what happened?"

"It's a long story. But I can tell you it has a lot to do with whatever's happening in Sirvassa currently."

"Iyena, I'm concerned. Do you have family in Alderra? Anywhere beyond the shores of Sirvassa?"

She has. She has a mother who is living somewhere in Troika, a land so far off that it doesn't even show properly in a map of the Three Realms. A land that time has forgotten about. Maybe if she was brave enough, and old enough, she wouldn't hesitate to take a ship first to Alderra, then across the barren stretch of land between Alderra's outskirts and Hoshwana, brave the icy winds of Juvinter, take another voyage to Irkhutsk, and fall off the edge of the world right into the valley of Troika. She has repeated this entire journey countless times in her head before. She has seen the maps. If done properly, with her wits at her disposal, she could make this journey. Does she even want to?

Ujita is still waiting for her answer. Reaching inside her bag, Iyena takes out the framed photo of her mother and shows it to Ujita. In the photo are three women: Maani-Ba, her mother, and another short, stocky woman she doesn't know the name of. The photograph has faded even more than the last time she properly saw it.

"You take a lot after your mother," says Ujita. "What's her name?"

"Sumena," says Iyena. It's been so long since she's said the name of her mother, it feels foreign on her tongue. But the name has power, and she feels an intense sense of yearning for the love of a parent. "I miss her."

"Iyena, the vessel we are scheduled to be on must have room for another person. I can arrange it for you. If you want to come with us, that is."

"I wouldn't want to be a burden on you and your mother."

"Nonsense. To be honest, the journey is long and I could use a friend."

Iyena considers the request. Her shoulders tense up, as she bites her lips. She would have to bid a bittersweet goodbye to Trehan. She hasn't even spoken to Maani-Ba. Iyena respects her opinion and it would be unfair to leave without talking to her first.

Is it worth staying in a city where she has found kindness and brutality both? Is it worth saying goodbye when she hasn't even given herself enough of a chance to heal from her father's betrayal? The brutality she has faced is something she carried from Alderra. It is something Sirvassa has only made her recognize. By that logic, the place has only given her love and wonder.

"You don't have to decide at this very moment," Ujita says. "We leave tomorrow. You can stay here with us till then. Whatever decision you make, I'll respect it."

It's a small relief. Iyena allows herself to be calm and eases her shoulders. "Thank you for your generosity, Ujita," says Iyena. "I will never forget it."

Ujita smiles at her and gives her back the photo . Before she puts it inside her bag, Iyena's eyes linger for a while longer on the other woman in the photograph. A faint resemblance sticks out. It's in the posture of the woman, and the way she leans against Maani-Ba, one of her hands clutching her mother's. A fleeting thought, quick like the wingbeat of a fell-bird, crosses her mind, but then evaporates in the mists of memory. She puts the photo inside the bag.

CHAPTER TWENTY-NINE

Iyena Mastafar

Next morning, there's nothing much to do. The morning sun floods through the ceiling mesh, bright light pooling near the veranda floor. Iyena feels her skin tingle with excitement, but also a pang of regret.

She might leave Sirvassa.

What would Trehan think of her if she left? He would be heartbroken, but eventually get over it, wouldn't he? He looks like the sort of young guy who wouldn't dwell much on heartbreaks.

But what would it do to her?

Ujita and her mother, already packed, sit in the living area, crushing the dried kukarn pieces and wrapping them in a muslin cloth. Ujita grabs a pinch and gives the powdered kukarn to Iyena. She tastes it. The powder is tangy and spicy, with an herby aftertaste.

"Magical, isn't it?"

"Ahh…. Where can we use it?" asks Iyena, blowing air out of her mouth, trying to cool it down. The spicy taste lingers on her taste buds, giving off heat.

"Sprinkle it atop soups. Make a paste of it. Its uses are far and wide."

"Lovely," says Iyena. "And hot."

Ujita offers her some water. Iyena gulps down an entire glass.

Later, Iyena helps Ujita and her mother stuff in some last-minute belongings. While Ujita's mother moves with efficiency at breakneck speed, Ujita displays uncharacteristic callousness while packing. In her defense, there's only so much to take, so why be picky. But her mother stays adamant. The need for order and consistency, especially if packing for a long journey over the sea, is paramount to her.

A familiar grunt comes from outside their house. Through the small rectangular crack of a door, the Rhisuan beast pulling their carriage looks at them with its multiple, bulbous eyes, as if beckoning them. Ujita goes over to the beast and gives it a scratch under its ear. Then, she whispers to it where it needs to take them. Another grunt, and the beast is ready.

And just like that, it's time to leave.

It doesn't take much time for Ujita to say goodbye to the small place she grew up in. The farewell isn't dramatic and there are no moist eyes, nor are there any fond memories, or words spoken. A broken toenail because of the stairs of the veranda. Or perhaps a game played on the cold marble floor, a game of dice and gambling. All these details, Iyena recalls in her mind. Ujita must have her own, but she chooses not to share them.

Ujita's mother locks the wooden door, once and for all. Then she turns around and climbs into the carriage without as much as a word shared. Ujita and Iyena follow her.

Ujita sits with Iyena, while her mother sits opposite them. The carriage takes off. A bright, albeit nippy, morning slowly blinks into another warm afternoon.

★   ★   ★

The journey to the docks is mostly uneventful. When Iyena climbs out of the carriage, she finds the place changed since the last time she was here. Steel railings have been constructed to separate the land from the sea, where there were only short wooden ledges before. Uniformed men in blue and red, resembling the ones Iyena saw in front of her school, patrol the road, their eyes constantly in search of something, ill at ease.

An old, rusted Hansa ship stands docked about half a kilometer away, its bird-prow containing spiderwebbed markings of age and smeared with bird droppings. Its slender neck threatens to give, but it still stands proudly, a silent spectator to beginnings and endings of a thousand journeys.

The Rhisuan beast turns around and crosses the road, as another group of people climb aboard the carriage. A few of them are tourists, from far-off lands, wearing odd-colored hats and shiny clothes, unaware of what wonders Sirvassa holds for them. Ujita looks at the beast and a tear trickles out of her eye. This is the first time Iyena has seen Ujita display any emotion.

"It may not be the same animal, but I will miss telling them every morning the twisty way to our school," she says. "Sometimes, it's the small wonders like these that are the greatest magic of all. Beasts who carry you around and automatically know where to go. We don't even speak their language. They just understand."

Iyena catches a glimpse of someone out of the corner of her eye. A movement, slow, but measured. She turns. Across the road stands a portly woman, carrying a bag full of fruits. She is wearing a red shawl, and her eyes scan the docks. It's Yavani, the Seedmaster, the woman who had saved her life.

Yavani sees Iyena. She waves to her. Iyena waves back. There's something in that old, wrinkly, kind face, something about her body's slight bend toward the right. She has seen it before. No, she didn't notice it when she spent almost an entire day with her. Then Yavani was full of activity, and there was a manic energy to her. A magical purpose. But she looks different today.

It hits Iyena as clear as day. Her heart picks up pace. She retrieves the old photo from inside her bag and looks at it again. There she is, kneeling against Maani-Ba, holding her mother's hand. And here she is, across the road, a bit older. The ground threatens to give way beneath her feet, as Iyena's world swirls around her.

"Iyena, are you coming? It's time."

Ujita calls her. But Iyena is too shocked to notice, her heart racing. Her eyes flit between the photo and the woman, the Seedmaster. Her hand trembles. Yavani might not have recognized Iyena, but why had Maani-Ba hidden this detail from her?

Ujita grips Iyena. She turns to face her friend. She has a questioning gaze behind those bulbous glasses. Iyena hesitates. Ujita releases her grip as understanding dawns on her.

"I understand," says Ujita.

"I am sorry," says Iyena. "I have some business to finish here."

"If this lifetime permits, maybe I will see you again, Iyena Mastafar," says her friend, tears streaming down her cheeks freely now.

"The world is small," says Iyena. She clasps Ujita's hands in hers, warmly. Both friends stay like that for a long while, before Ujita lets go.

"May Eborsen shine his everlight on you," says Ujita. Then she wipes her tears and starts walking toward the pier that leads to the wooden stairs of the ship. Iyena feels her own eyes moisten as her friend departs.

When Ujita takes the stairs to the ship, Iyena turns around and starts walking toward Yavani, the Seedmaster.

"Iyena Mastafar, what are you doing here?"

Without speaking another word, Iyena shows Yavani the photograph. The Seedmaster looks at the photo, and repressed emotion swells inside her like a wave, crashing, finally, on her aged face. Her lips quiver, and her eyes well up. Her furrows tighten into a knot, then release themselves.

She looks at Iyena, then at the photo again. "You...you are Sumena's daughter."

"I am," says Iyena, her voice shaky and raspy. "And I need some answers."

CHAPTER THIRTY

Iyena Mastafar

They take the main road back to Sirvassa, cross the busy market square, take a detour through the Moernig Road, and arrive right in front of a door nestled between a cloth shop and a flea market. The same door through which Iyena had left in disguise. It's late in the afternoon and the ever-familiar sound of Eborsen's temple bells rings through the air. As usual, all the Rhisuan beasts stop and turn in the direction of the temple. Iyena hadn't noticed it before, but a flock of fell-birds, too, hover in the air, as if suspended, enchanted by the bells. Shopkeepers stop their selling and place their hands over their hearts, their eyes closed, their lips moving in constant murmur, thanking the Half-Formed God.

This place, too, looks markedly different than the last time. The biggest change, however, is the blue-and-red uniformed patrolmen, the same ones she had seen near the docks. The patrolmen don't turn to the east when the bells toll, and are the odd ones out. Neither did Iyena, when she arrived in Sirvassa, but now she too looks to the skies in the east, out of respect.

When the bells stop ringing, it's back to business. A fruit seller hurls abuse at a patrolman who is blocking his cart's colorful display of fruits.

"Move over, you bresna," he yells, a vein bulging on his forehead. "Don't you see I am trying to do some business here?"

The patrolman is unperturbed. Instead, he picks up a fruit from the cart and mockingly takes a bite. This makes the seller even angrier, but he can't do anything about it. Instead, he grumbles silently under his breath, about an upcoming rebellion. As this goes on, Yavani silently ushers Iyena through a thinning crowd, inside the door.

"Things are changing extremely fast around here," says Yavani in a whisper. Her shoulders are hunched, and she now looks older than her years.

"Why are you whispering?" says Iyena. "We are inside."

Yavani sighs. Inadvertently, her fingers touch a lock of Iyena's hair. Then, with a motherly gesture, she presses her palm on her head, as if giving her a blessing. Her voice chokes up when she speaks.

"Eborsen bless you, child, your manner of speaking reminds me so much of your mother. I knew there was something about you when I first met you, but couldn't place it. Come with me. Come inside."

The Seedmaster takes Iyena deep inside her home, first through the seed-chamber, where earthen pots lie filled with seeds yet to be picked up, then to another, more open room where all sorts of Delights await Iyena. A spacious room, domed at the top, it's filled with glittering vines, some hanging from the ceiling, some merely hovering in the air. Then, there are statues that move and speak, reminding Iyena oddly of the monstrosity her father created. These, though, look harmless. Kind, even.

Yavani points Iyena toward an empty chair near the corner of the room. The walls here are covered in murals. A robed figure of a man, his skin pale golden, sits atop a log, carrying a Rose. While half of him is the form of a man, the other half is shaped out of the elements surrounding him. Trees, vines, animals, grass, birds, reptiles, stones, water, sky, fire. A true rendition of the Half-Formed God.

As Iyena looks at the mural, Yavani comes and sits in front of her with a cup of tea in her hands. A moving statue arrives with a plate of cookies. Iyena is hit with a strong whiff of cinnamon and nutmeg. She takes a cookie, nervously looking at the white ceramic statue, who smiles at her and leaves.

"When I first met you, I couldn't shake off the resemblance," says Yavani. "But I didn't mention it. I had to be sure."

"How did you know my mother?"

"Your mother, her sister, Mansa, and I grew up in a small Inishti fishing village," she says. "This was way before the Abhadis decided to wage an out-and-out war against the Inishtis. Most Inishtis have a calling for Florrachemy, which is the ability to channel Delights. Many are also born without that ability and it's fine. No one ostracizes them, or judges them for it. But your mother was special. She was a Florral, someone who could harness all Delights without needing to ingest any potion. And not just any Florral. She was the most powerful Florral in Inishti history, second only to Alvos Midranil."

"Alvos?"

"You have met him," says Yavani with a smile. Iyena gets it. The Caretaker has a name. For some reason, she cannot associate the name with the figure. He will always remain the Caretaker for her.

"We grew up. Your mother fell in love with your father, a devout and true Abhadi. For a brief moment of time, until you were born, it looked like Abhadis and Inishtis were truly at a truce. Your father and your mother's love could really transcend all barriers. But then, the political turmoil between the Abhadis and Inishtis ripped our realm apart. Battle lines were drawn, and your father had to choose sides. And you know what he chose." Yavani stops, as if scrambling for words, her mouth twitching with grief.

"It broke your mother's heart and she left."

"Why didn't my mother take me with her?" Iyena's voice is now down to a whisper. A torrent of complex emotions courses through her.

"Abhadi Laws of Marriage and Custody," says Yavani, her voice laced with deep anguish. "The place you were born was, and still is, an Abhadi stronghold and upholds its customs and values."

Iyena takes a bite of the cookie, but it gives her no taste. The bitterness of her own past has overwhelmed all her senses.

"We kept in touch, your mother and I, until last year, when her coppergrams stopped coming."

Then, keeping the teacup on a side table, Yavani leans over to

Iyena and clasps her hands in hers. "You should have been aware of all this," she says.

"I was ready to leave Sirvassa today. To go in search of my mother."

"I'm glad you didn't," says Yavani. "You are among your people. Sirvassa is an Inishti haven, and you have Inishti blood running through you."

She is also half–Abhadi but she doesn't say as much. Yavani is right. Iyena has felt a closeness to Sirvassans since the day she stepped foot on the pier. The city is in her blood.

"But Sirvassa might not be the same for long. I have heard murmurs around here," says Yavani. "People who are consuming Delights are becoming sick. And it's all working in favor of the Abhadis, who, among hating Inishtis, also don't hold Florrachemy in the highest regard. The rot in the seeds isn't helping either."

"The patrolmen outside...."

"They are all Alderran soldiers. They are ultimately doing the bidding of Minister Yayati."

"My father...he has been involved in this since we arrived. It's probably the reason we arrived here. There's a dinner at the mayor's bungalow in two days. I fear something terrible is going to happen there."

"The Caretaker has been invited to the dinner at the mayor's place," says Yavani. "He has been trying his best to contain the rot, but age, unfortunately, is not on his side. Seeds of distrust against the Caretaker were sown long ago. The minor Abhadi population of Sirvassa has been vocal about their dislike of the Garden and the Caretaker. If this goes on, and Sirvassa goes into the hands of the Abhadis, the Garden will be the first to take the hit. The Delights are already corrupting people. And soon, no one will be able to channel Delights anymore."

Iyena looks at the Seedmaster and sighs. Then she inhales the room around her. The Seedmaster's room is a testament to the ingenuity of Florrachemy, to all those Delights present in the flowers of the Garden, present in the seeds outside, where the trees hover high above the ground, their roots flailing like old, withered tentacles.

This is a beauty that deserves to be saved.

The statue comes over, gently picks up the cup and the saucer from the table and takes them away. There's an ease to the statue's motion, as it's bewitched with a Delight. It's not crude, like Turain-One. It's almost human, but ever so slightly different. The statue nods at Iyena from a distance, and the gesture is warm and welcoming.

This too is a beauty that deserves to be saved.

The fell-birds and the Rhisuan beasts of the city, all a part of the magic that runs through the heart of Sirvassa. The people, their homes, their struggles, their history, their culture.

It deserves to stay, prosper, and flourish.

"Can you show me the rot?" says Iyena. Her voice is strong, determined. She has made up her mind. Yavani's previously anguished expression changes. Now, she looks at Iyena with curiosity.

"Why do you want to see the rot? It's just glittery darkness, which you already—" Yavani stops, as realization dawns on her. Then she taps hard on the handle of her chair, and gets up, suddenly consumed with the energy of youth. "Light of Eborsen, I did not realize. Come...."

Iyena follows Yavani out of the spacious room, into a smaller, more intimate space. This room smells of roses and apples, and there's a wall made entirely of glass, overlooking a grassy expanse. Yavani moves closer to the glass, and it immediately vanishes, as if following orders. Iyena walks through the gap in the wall, and her feet land on soft grass.

The hanging trees have become darker, their vines frayed, as vapors ooze out of them. The tailed creatures that resided somewhere deep inside the branches of the trees are nowhere to be seen now. Instead, there's a constant ash shower from above, littering the grass like gray snowflakes of death. There are no seeds to be collected today.

Yavani walks toward a gaping hole in the ground beneath a tree, where before they had seen a glittering shadow of a man. The shadow is no longer there. In its place, a collection of bone-white hands sprouts from the black hole, reaching upward, eager to grab the roots of the hanging tree. Iyena shudders at the grotesque sight.

"My research has come to a dead end, but this much is sure. Someone entered this place under my nose and caused this rot. This is a desecration of the works of Eborsen. A calamity."

Iyena kneels beside one of the hands. It protrudes from the blackness, and an entire arm goes deep inside, disappearing. But there's a slow, subtle motion to it, barely discernible, but there.

"Aunt Yavani..." she says, and stops. "Can I call you Aunt?"

"Yes, yes, of course," says the Seedmaster.

"Aunt Yavani, you said that my mother is a Florral. Not just any Florral, but possibly one of the most powerful ever. What does that make me?" says Iyena.

Then she grabs the wrist of one of the hands and closes her eyes. She feels the hand's utter vapid lifelessness, the cancer of its evil courses through her. She feels the other hands jerk and shiver in rebellion. Bloodless, they feel like a blot on the land around her. A sentience threatening to consume the spirit of Eborsen. A powerful mind throbbing somewhere deep inside the earth. Another godlike presence slowly waking from its slumber, eager to destroy everything once it rises. An unnatural presence.

Iyena's mind reaches to the depths of the earth from where the veins of the hands sprout. From where they take their un-life force. She feels the nature of that force. Malevolent. Unkind. Full of hate. Numbness threatens to consume her as the godlike force fights back.

But Iyena can fight too. She is here to fight monsters.

She lets herself get filled by the blackness of the force and then... ...she changes it.

Her insides go aflame. The hands tremble with spasms. Their white veins, white as snow, detangle from the depths, their connection with the entity severed, unmade, and remade in a different image, their nature forever changed. Color returns to those hands, like blood flowing into a lifeless body. Then, Iyena pulls with all the might remaining in her body, and the hands collectively sprout from the depths of the ground. She's jerked violently back by the horrific dying push of a life force.

She lets go and slumps on the grass, motionless.

Yavani looks up. The tailed beasts come out of the branches, crawling, slithering, across the tree bark. One, two, three...then ten, twenty, they come, relentlessly, out of their hiding places, in fear no more, because the rot is now gone. The roots of the hanging trees flow with renewed vigor. Ash no longer falls from above.

Instead, seeds do.

CHAPTER THIRTY-ONE

A Melancholy Bargain –
A Journal of Travel, Trauma, and Teachings

Varunnai was disappointed in me. But cer face expressed neither resentment, nor anguish. It all came out in cer voice. After the incident with the water pail, Varunnai started giving me curt instructions. Like one would give an automaton, or a beast.

Go. Fetch. Eat. Sit. Stand. Run.

If ce was teaching me obedience, then ce wasn't doing a very good job of it. For all intents and purposes, Master Alvos was a better teacher. Yet, I felt myself drawn toward Varunnai. Ce was a walking god among mortals. For that matter, even Master Alvos was one. But Varunnai could shape an element to cer liking, something Master could never do. No Delight had the ability to shape the basic elements, as far as I knew. Florrachemy didn't work that way.

One day, as I sat outside Varunnai's hut, picking at overgrown reeds, two villagers arrived at cer doorstep, one man, one woman. Their skin had spiderwebbed creases, and their hands were calloused. Their faces were contorted with a deep, lingering sadness. It was not grief they carried. Grief brings about a different expression, a hollowness that is not all too evident. This was a sadness brought about by poverty.

The woman carried a small child at her hip, while the man carried a jute bag overflowing with green vegetables. They both wore dry and tattered clothes that looked like they hadn't been washed in ages. And yet, the vegetables – spinach, brinjal, kale and cauliflower – seemed fresh.

"Peace of Geversen be upon you, friend," said the man.

"May Eborsen shower his petals upon you," I said, responding with blessings of a god I prayed to. At my greeting, the farmer frowned.

"You are not from these parts?" he asked.

"I am a servant of the world, but I pray to only one god," I said.

"We are here to offer our harvest to Varunnai, and ask for cer help," said the woman, as her toddler clenched her blouse.

"Ce is occupied at this moment," I said. "May I ask you to come after sunset?"

"Our villages are in trouble," said the man. "Much of our sustenance has been in jeopardy ever since the flow of the River Ashra was diverted by the Alderran City Council. We're left with measly trickles while the city enjoys an uninterrupted supply."

"But why?"

"They're building a giant rail system for the city folk. This happens to us every time. While in the past we made do with fewer resources, we are left with nothing now."

"And how do you think Varunnai will be able to help you?"

I knew the answer to the question, but I wanted to hear it from their mouths.

"Ce is a god," said the man. "Ce has helped many villages and cities in the past."

I felt cold on the nape of my neck. I turned around and saw Varunnai standing beside me. Both the villagers sat on the ground immediately, and refused to look cer in the eye. The woman pushed the basket of vegetables toward Varunnai.

"Fetch the spinach," said Varunnai, and I knew it was an order for me. I crawled over to the farmers, grabbed a bunch of leaves from the basket, and came back. Varunnai's eyes were affixed on the child the woman carried as ce took the spinach from me.

Ce took a bite of the big leaf and began chewing. For a long time, I sat cross-legged on the ground while the god beside me chewed the spinach like a cow. Green spittle formed near cer chin, but ce ate the vegetable unbothered, until the entire chunk was finished.

"It's fresh," said Varunnai. The green stain vanished from cer chin as soon as it had appeared. "How can I help?"

The farmers told cer. At the end of their tale of anguish, Varunnai looked at me and said, "You will come with me and observe. You'll take notes and narrate them back to me once we return. Is that clear?"

"As you say, Master," I said.

There was little preparation. While Varunnai carried no belongings with cer, ce told me it was a two-day operation, and so I carried a change of clothes. Our food and lodging were to be taken care of by the generous couple. I couldn't fathom – they didn't have water to drink, and yet they offered us hospitality.

The village was a haphazard smattering of huts and blocky cement houses by a narrow stream. It wasn't a river by any stretch of the imagination. I could have urinated more in a single day than the thin, embarrassing stretch of water the villagers lived by. River stones looked drier than sand, and whatever water splashed over them soon got dried by the sun. Stone slabs by the riverbank lay unadorned. They would have been used to beat and wash clothes on a normal day.

The village had its own drainage and plumbing system, not as advanced as the city it was bordering, but functional enough to serve its population.

"Look toward the west and strain your ears," ce said, as we stood near the edge of the stream. "Can you hear a rush?"

I tried. I couldn't. I shook my head.

Ce grabbed me by my collar and hoisted me up in the air. The world fell below me with a shock, and I could see clearly beyond for miles. I felt I was kissing the clouds, yet Varunnai was only holding me at cer arm's length.

I looked toward the west. I could see the river. And I could see the stream too, twisting, easing between trees, becoming a mire, a puddle, and then another stream, until it came to the village. I could see where it was cut off. A construction that diverted water to the city.

"What will you do?" ce asked.

"I will break the device," I said. It was the only way to restore the flow to what the village had before.

"You hear but you don't listen, you see but don't observe," said Varunnai. "The construction is there for a reason. The fault is with the land."

"So it isn't illegal, what the city is doing?"

"Their reasons are malicious, but because of a geographical oddity, they might come across as benevolent. If you remove the device, this stream gets flooded, and the village sinks in a matter of minutes."

"What options do we have?"

Varunnai exhaled sharply. Then, ce put a gentle hand on my shoulder. "Whose life is worthless?"

"I don't understand."

"How do you measure the value of a life? The needs of the many as opposed to the needs of a few. The construction in the city requires a continuous supply of water, and it would benefit thousands. The same supply would provide livelihood to a population of mere hundreds."

"It's sustenance versus privilege. It's not hard to understand, Master."

"And who are you to decide?"

I wasn't anyone to decide. But this altruistic thinking was drilled in me by Master Alvos, who was, of course, a different kind of teacher. But Varunnai didn't have benevolence or altruism in mind.

Master Alvos would have approached this problem differently. He was a man of words, and he could have convinced the city not to divert the water in the first place. But Varunnai was a brute-force god, a cruel all-powerful entity whose rationale of doing anything bordered on madness. Despite cer decisions, Varunnai exuded an uncanny calm, something I was vicariously drawn toward.

"It's what I think is right," I said. But even as the words were out of my mouth, I found their shape changing. Indifference was written on Varunnai's face. I knew my answer wasn't the answer ce wanted, nor cared for.

"Find me a person in this village who has nothing to live for," ce said.

Cer requests were certainly more mysterious than Master Alvos's. And so, I went door to door, as the villagers offered me meager food, a cold ground to sit on and listen to their stories. The first home was of an old man who was waiting for his son to arrive. His son had gone to the cold city of Mitrone to learn the forgotten art of Derrachemy, a magic derived from food. The man offered me some daal he had made himself. He was so old and his hands were so thin that I could see the color of his bones through his skin. At one point, and my eyes weren't playing tricks, I swear I could have seen his frail pocket of a stomach slowly digesting the food he ate.

"When my son comes, I will make a special daal for him. And with Derrachemy, he will give me the magic of living forever, and the magic of youth. All it would require, he says, is a bowlful of daal."

And so, he had something to live for. I thanked the man profusely and visited another home.

Two women welcomed me. While one prepared a delicious, rustic vegetable stew, the other prepared fragrant rice. While one put a jute mat on the floor for me, the other washed my feet, because they were dirty and had grown sharp, painful-to-touch calluses. Both the women did those things out of the pureness of their hearts, and would have done the same for any guest. A guest, they said in unison, was a reflection of a god.

I was no reflection, and the god I served was a cruel one, who wanted impossible answers.

These women lived with one another, for one another, and in servitude of the society they lived in. They were happy doing what they did. No one forced them to perform this service, nor was the service performative. They claimed that their hearts swelled when they saw full bellies and fuller faces.

They had something to live for.

I thanked the women and stepped out of their hut into the blazing sun. But the heat did not bother me. I scoured the neighborhood homes, uttered my greetings, savored my goodbyes, had good food and better conversations with village folk who were all looking forward to something in their lives, even when the specter of a certain death loomed upon them.

When I went back to Varunnai, ce was meditating on the stone-speckled, bone-dry riverbank. I sat down beside cer noiselessly. Varunnai was so motionless, that a small bird perched upon cer knees, digging its claws in cer skin, rotating its bean-sized head in all directions. For a moment the bird stayed there, and I didn't swat it away. If my Master didn't feel any pain, who was I to take action?

I remained there for an hour, gazing at Varunnai and cer shallow breaths, the shore without water, the trees that stood unswaying in the sweltering heat. When Varunnai ended cer meditation, ce looked at me with red eyes.

"What did you find out?" ce asked.

"Everyone in the village has something to live for. Everyone celebrates life in their own way."

"And what about you?"

"What about me?"

"What are you living for?"

I didn't have an answer to the question. Half of my waking moments were spent in the apprenticeship of Master Alvos. Before that, I was a runaway boy. I had no past, and I was barely wading through the present. The future, I took as it came.

"Your silence is your answer," said Varunnai. "Now we begin."

Immediately, I felt my cheeks getting sunken. My hands, which had the barest hint of sweat, looked leathery, devoid of any moisture. And progressively, I saw cracks appearing all over my limbs, my body, a spiderweb crawling across the barrenness that was my skin. My lips were dry, and I licked them, but even my tongue had no saliva. My throat felt clogged with sand, and my voice came out raspy, rubbery.

"What are you doing?" I croaked.

"I am using you as a source of water," ce said. And then it dawned on me. Ce had deemed me unworthy of a life. That was what the charade was all about, sacrificing one life for the needs of the many.

Ce knew ce wouldn't get it from the village, and ce was testing me. How far would I go following cer orders, on a useless quest?

Cer twisted mind had surmised that I had nothing to give to this world. I was unworthy to live. And so, I must be sacrificed.

But one body wasn't enough to provide the villagers with what they needed. That meant Varunnai was just harnessing me to channel cer vast powers. If ce wanted, ce could have used a part of the stream beyond the mire, beyond the trees, but ce didn't.

And soon, I saw a blob of water dance in front of cer, as ce molded it into a stream. Through blurry eyes, I saw all my body's water exploited in front of me. Weakness engulfed me like a wet blanket, and my body fell heavily on the stones with an iron finality.

CHAPTER THIRTY-TWO
The Caretaker

Dawn arrives swiftly, without warning.

The Caretaker turns the invitation over and over, his aged fingers looking like dried prunes, a dull ache settling in his joints, moving aggressively toward his temples. The activity of the past days has caught up to him, finally. Now, standing in front of Mayor Illyasi's bungalow, at the cusp of change, alertness eludes him. The Caretaker straightens a crease on his kurta, his palm moving over the smooth, white fabric, feeling the patterned roughness of the embroidered Inishti letters on the button seam. Trulio, dressed in a sharp black sherwani, a slight smear of kohl on his eyes, a single silver earring glinting against the moon, thrusts out his chest in pride, eager to charm and please, and if needed, kill. There's an impatience in Trulio's manner, something the Caretaker wishes wasn't there, tonight of all nights.

Behind them, a smattering of caravans, empty, their inhabitants already flocking inside, with their glitter-dresses and mascaras, their wavy hair and sharp-cut beards, gathered deep in facile conversation about the three great inevitabilities – death, taxes, and the rain of petals.

"Master, how long do we wait before someone attends to us? Are we not guests of importance?"

Ahead, three security guards pore over documents, exchanging them, letting out sharp laughs intermittently, idly tapping their batons against their knees, their eyebrows arching at appropriate intervals at the rude surprises and the maudlin mere-presence of the gentry inside. The guards are not the regular ones, who were friendly with the Caretaker, and hence the delay.

"There has been a change of command," says the Caretaker. "Hold-ups are inevitable."

As if hearing their voices, a man dressed in black approaches them, balancing a fat ledger on both his arms, the pages swaying silently against the wind. His hair is slick with oil, parted in the middle, and his face bears an expression of incompetence crossed with befuddlement.

"The Caretaker of the Garden of Delights and his apprentice, Trulio Gathvani. Am I correct in the pronunciation?"

"There's a sound of '*th*' you're missing. Not from around these parts, are you?" Trulio remarks sharply.

"I am sorry," says the man, then fumbles. "This is a big event, and I have taken over from someone else. Please, please, come inside. May I double-check your invitation card?"

"Is there an irregularity?" asks the Caretaker.

"No, I merely want to check the veracity of the invitation."

"The stamp and signature are the mayor's and the mayor is a friend," says the Caretaker.

"I know, I know. We have seen many a counterfeit in recent times, so we have to be extra cautious."

"Who is 'we'?" asks Trulio, with barely disguised contempt.

"My team and I," says the man, wriggling his fingers to his right, where there's only empty air. The security guards, too, have disappeared inside. Behind the man, the bungalow of Mayor Jaywardna Illyasi looms large against a violet sky, and a white smear of the moon. Light spills out from the first floor through a large window overlooking an orchard. Three gables face north, and three more toward the west where Sirvassa's main road meets three others.

"You mean the birds?" Trulio cocks his head to his right, sneering. The man with the ledger looks around, hoping to find someone who is no longer there.

"Ramada, for heaven's sake," he whispers under his breath. "The dinner hasn't even started yet." He recomposes himself, as if suddenly reminded of the duty he is here for. "I am sorry, dear guests, my subordinates have decided to leave me deserted. This promises to be a long night and it seems I am the only one in charge."

"It's okay. If you would just hurry."

The man checks the invitation, nods, then hands it back to the Caretaker. He places the register on the window ledge of the guard cabin to his right and sighs heavily.

"You may go," he says, his face red with sheer embarrassment.

★   ★   ★

A mammoth door made of many woods flies open as if anticipating their arrival. Light floods out onto the pavement and the Caretaker is almost careful not to step on it, for stepping on it would mean desecration, so powerful is its presence on the white marble floor. It comes from chandeliers suspended on the ceiling, of course, made from everlamps enchanted by none other than the Tulip of the Seven, a favor the Caretaker did for the mayor, who wanted the light of his mansion to automatically adjust to the light of the universe outside.

It's a bungalow of many, many rooms, some dotted along a large corridor emanating from the main ballroom, some above, their doors lining the wall that runs parallel to the railing of the staircase. A crowd is gathered in the main ballroom, as a dozen fell-birds sing enchanting, welcoming arias, some perched on the staircase, some on the shoulders of the guests, their faces unbothered, their smiles warm. Concentric rings of green and violet light fall on an empty stage right in the middle of the room.

The magic in the room is old magic, potent and charming.

A tall, graceful man approaches the Caretaker with a measured gait, as if one wrong step would offend his senses. He is wearing a crisp suit, neatly tailored to fit his bony, angular shoulders and negligible waist.

The Caretaker smiles at him, the smile he reserves for his customers. "The Moon of Alderra and the Sun of Sirvassa, ever lighting a sky so dark," the man says.

"Secretary Anuv, a pleasure to meet you," says the Caretaker, not bothering to reply to a puzzling greeting with an equally poetic response.

Secretary Anuv nods.

"What is the fruit of all labor, Caretaker?"

"There's no fruit," says the Caretaker, after a moment of thought.

"Pardon my curt question," says Anuv, interlacing his fingers, standing in a much more formal position. "I am now employed under the minister. And so, I have to keep speaking in riddles, gauging interest, accepting only answers the minister would like."

"And what kind of answers is he expecting today?"

"The profitable kind," says Secretary Anuv, in a tired manner.

"I've been hearing things about you." His eyes dart toward the Caretaker's hands. The Caretaker doesn't miss it, and drapes his right arm with his brown shawl. "What is it with your Delights going wrong suddenly? I myself was expecting an enchantment today. A little something to impress my wife across the shores."

"That was an unfortunate turn of events, but it's something that has since been taken care of."

"Regardless," says Anuv, "the minister hasn't taken lightly to that development. He wanted the Garden for the population of Alderra, but now he is of two minds."

The Caretaker glances at Trulio, sensing his apprentice's tense shoulders. It wasn't for nothing that Trulio was suggesting an expansion of the Garden.

"I merely run a business, Secretary, a nonprofitable one," says the Caretaker. "All my customers come to me of their own volition. All my customers are happy customers."

"I think the twins are about to begin their song," says Trulio, one bony finger pointing toward the stage. The Caretaker is almost grateful for the interruption.

On the stage, concentric rings of light give form to two individuals, wearing skin-hugging, vibrant blue tunics that shimmer and create myriad shapes on their chests. The shapes change as they move on stage, a dance in sync, their bellies gyrating, their chests heaving, their legs moving like jelly one moment, but in sharp, angular motions the next.

Ira Garbansa holds the bulge in his throat and pinches it. A sharp crack follows and Ani Garbansa does the same. A hush falls over the crowd like a blanket. Then the twins begin to sing.

The Caretaker's gaze falls on a short figure, black hair falling on his shoulders in tufts, wearing a white-and-gold sherwani. He has a pale brown face covered entirely in a thick beard and a thicker mustache. His cane rests lightly against his knees, and his fingers tap on the shiny, metallic handle as he listens to Garbansa's singing. Minister Yayati.

To his right stands the tall, imposing, thin-mustached Mayor Jaywardna Illyasi, who favors his right leg more than the left. Despite his height, the shift in power dynamic is palpable in the air. His frame seems to tilt to the side, almost as if seeking approval from the short minister. *How's the show I have put on for you, Minister Yayati? If it pleases you, might we discuss urgent matters of state interest? Perhaps the long-overdue sovereignty treaty?*

"He looks harmless," whispers Trulio.

"Wait till he starts speaking."

The song the Garbansa twins have chosen is a different rendition of a famous folk song, telling the tale of a traveler from an ancient land bearing news both good and bad. The song then becomes a ballad of a power struggle between two races, one the oppressed, and the other the colonizer, told from the point of view of an aging tree that saw everything. Their rendition, however, delves more into propaganda, the lyrics obviously chosen to please Minister Yayati, who listens to them with the attention of a hawk, betraying neither his pleasure nor scorn.

Ira Garbansa goes to a higher pitch as he hits a difficult note. Ani Garbansa follows with a lower pitch as they both crescendo, hitting a high point in the ballad. Then Ira's voice breaks. And so does Ani's. Together, they unfold a shroud of melancholy that rushes through the crowd, silencing even the peskiest of the audience. Sniffles emanate from deeper in the room, and soon eyes get moist all around. Even propaganda has the ability to move.

The light rings on the stage begin to dim. Minister Yayati's impassive face turns to look at the mayor. Yayati smiles, placing a hand on Illyasi's tense shoulders.

The Caretaker observes the proceedings as his black, aged right hand shivers. A coldness travels through his spine, and with that, a cruel unease. The twins consumed his potion for the purpose of this performance. For better or for worse, he indirectly played a hand in elevating Yayati's propaganda this night.

★   ★   ★

The dinner hall is silent. The air is taut with discomfort, stretched to the point of snapping. The Caretaker stands unperturbed, holding a plate full of fragrant rice topped with fried almonds, raisins, and pistachios. His spoon is poised above the dish he hasn't taken a bite from, his eyes on the table where Minister Yayati is having a private conversation with the mayor.

"I like what they've done with dinner," Trulio says, playing with a particularly large chunk of fried potato. "Doesn't make me miss what I make at all! This potato consistency, for example. Sublime. And dipped in that curry, with brinjal, tempered with mustard seeds. I might ask Illyasi who he employs as the cook."

"You seem to be enjoying yourself, Trulio," says the Caretaker, taking a measly bite of his rice.

"It's an enjoyable evening, Master, but not necessarily for us. And so, I'm taking whatever I can," says Trulio. "The center of control is shifting. Power is changing hands. The look on Illyasi's face says everything. He has no say in what happens tonight."

"He's a coward," says the Caretaker. "I expected better of him. Alderra wants a share of the water from the River Inigee. Which he agreed to, but it was a smokescreen. He has now signed papers that will allow engineers from Alderra to experiment and see if they can manufacture petal-rain in their skies."

"But I thought that matter got buried in the ground with Minister Ravi's demise?"

"Changes of government always bring about a change of policies, even if it means digging up old graves," says the Caretaker. "*Especially* if it means digging up old graves."

The Caretaker takes another bite of the rice. The texture brings rushing back a wisp of a memory, a time of youth, a time of frolic, of roads that made blisters on his feet, of seas crossed in voyages on ships run by ghosts and skeletons. Then, he swallows the rice and the memory vanishes.

The mayor raises his hand, beckoning the Caretaker. The gesture feels almost like how he would call a servant over. But keeping up appearances is far more important in such a setting, and the Caretaker doesn't quite mind.

When he reaches the table, he sees a spoon levitating in the air beside Minister Yayati. The spoon bends and then bends more, before twisting impossibly into such a shape that it could no longer be called a spoon anymore. It could no longer be called anything, for that matter, so grotesque is the shape of the metal.

Then the metal becomes a face, and the face speaks. It's the voice of a thousand gods and a thousand demons, snip of a feather, shard of a bone, both rubbed against a watery shore.

"Nice trick," says the Caretaker. The blue Chrysanthemum in the Third Sector would allow someone to reanimate an object and do their bidding in any way they want. Easy Delight to consume and use for a small trick, but toughest to master. But the minister couldn't have gotten hold of the flower from anywhere and he definitely hadn't visited the Garden. This is something that troubles the Caretaker.

"I have heard great things about you," says the metal. The Caretaker shifts his gaze toward Minister Yayati, who is busy having his soup.

"So have I," says the Caretaker. "Can we speak face-to-face, like proper gentlemen, if the tricks are over?"

The minister wipes his chin with a cloth. The metal goes back to being a spoon, uncoiling upon itself, in the blink of an eye.

"I was talking to my friend Jaywardna," says the minister. "Sirvassa needs Champions and even more so...the world needs Champions. But not everyone can be one."

The word 'Champion' isn't thrown around in casual conversation, and the Caretaker knows the reason. Champions, who could move mountains with thought, bend air with a fingersnap, and see through time at a whim. Drawing their powers from a new and potentially more powerful source of magic – the secrets of which are known only to the highest echelons of the Alderran Ministry – the Champions are known to be bashful, arrogant, and reckless. The Caretaker knows this intimately, in his bones, because he defeated a Champion once.

"The minister says we need to be looking out for dangers we can't comprehend," says Mayor Jaywardna Illyasi. "He offers us the protection of three Champions in exchange for a more reasonable share of the water from the Iniga."

"Inigee, Jaywardna. It's a holy river, where are your manners?"

"I apologize," says the mayor. The Caretaker scratches his chin, waiting for the inevitable.

"The incident that took place at the docks," says the minister. "That kind of attack on the wellbeing of Sirvassa isn't desirable. A Champion would never have let that happen."

"I am not sure what you're implying here, Minister."

"I am no one to judge from my plush seat in the Alderran Office, but I am skeptical of these *Delights* of yours. As I said earlier, it's not in everyone to be a Champion, and by giving freebies to the populace of this beautiful city, you're only doing harm."

The Caretaker narrows his gaze, regarding the minister as he finishes the last of his rice. He can feel Trulio's eyes drilling holes in the side of his head, and hear his heart hammer twenty feet away.

"They're not freebies, Minister. The effects of my Delights are temporary. Also, I am not in the business of making Champions. I want people to have some joy in their lives."

"Even I want some joy for my people," says the minister. "But I've heard so many dark tales about the Garden, I'm now thinking otherwise. Since arriving in the city, I've changed my opinion. Now, I think the continued existence of the Garden is a blight, and it must be closed down."

"If I may intervene, Al—" The mayor stops, reconsiders, and then starts again. "The Caretaker has healed me and I am forever indebted to him."

"Debts accrue interest over time," says the minister, playing with his spoon, holding the gaze of the Caretaker. The Caretaker pinches the bridge of his nose, then exhales sharply.

"Minister Yayati, with all due respect, half knowledge is a dangerous thing. You know nothing about the Garden and my intentions with it, to impart judgment. As for the attack on the docks, I am hearing different things. The group that was responsible claims that the orders came from someone who was working inside the ministry." The Caretaker moves closer to the minister, leaning to whisper in his ear. "So, be careful what your words imply, Minister."

Minister Yayati staggers back, as his nostrils flare. He gazes at the mayor, whose jaw has hit the floor at the Caretaker's biting words. Minister Yayati stands, laboriously, scratching his scraggly beard, his eyes fixated on the Caretaker. But when he speaks, his words are directed at the mayor.

"These threats are empty, laced with half knowledge. But I am a forgiving man. Here's my final offer, Mayor Jaywardna Illyasi. I will give Sirvassa four Champions, with control over four tenets that run this world – water, wind, land, and fire. Alderra gets the main tributary of the Inigee, namely the Uvindhya. I don't even want an increased share of the petals. My only condition – the Garden of Delights has to close down. Forever."

★ ★ ★

"What were you hoping to achieve?" Mayor Illyasi says, massaging his right thigh aggressively with one hand, while balancing a glass of mead in the other. He cuts a sorry figure, a man caught between two giants, helpless in his position. He would have more political leverage if he had heeded the Caretaker's warning earlier. But the man is now a mere shadow of what he once was. Age has brought about a certain gullibility to Mayor Illyasi, one that his political opponents are far too eager to exploit.

"I was telling him the truth, and now you know too," says the Caretaker. "I have the testimony of the leader of the Corrillean. I could get the Red Guards here right now, and they would name the man who actually gave them the order to move. I was *there*, Illyasi. We fought those men. We captured the Stigmar who told us everything."

The mayor shifts uneasily. He places the mead glass on the table, as his hands are too shaky to hold it. His eyes keep darting toward the door, toward the main hall, where the minister has gone to have a word with Secretary Anuv. Illyasi pleaded with the minister to try the new house mead, prepared especially to please his palate, but he shrugged off his request, choosing to attend to urgent political matters, which was mostly code for, *I have no use for you now, leave me alone.*

"Even if you reveal what you have learned, he would shame you in front of everyone, my friend," says the mayor. "No one will believe you. I know his tactics."

"So you are admitting that you *knew* about the attack and didn't do anything about it? That's political suicide."

The mayor sighs. "I *didn't* know about the attack. I gave the orders because I thought I was helping him. He is here for a treaty. Naturally, I thought he had shipments coming in from across the Three Realms. One day he told me to ease the security around the docks because the Red Guards were creating unnecessary hindrance. Who was I to deny him?"

The Caretaker kneads his eyebrows with his index finger.

"There's one more thing you should know," says the mayor. "The Restoration Pact. Yayati has found loopholes in it, and is using it to his advantage, and to further the Abhadi agenda."

"When were you planning on telling me this?" the Caretaker says. The Restoration Pact has been a bone of contention for the Abhadi ever since the Second Abhadi-Inishti War. The Caretaker has lived in exile in numerous cities, traveling, carrying the curse with him, while the realm around him changed for the better, because of the war he helped bring to an end. Inishti don't live in hiding anymore, and thrive in pockets around the Three Realms. The Vaishwam Chair soon announced a Restoration Pact, a document that runs for five hundred pages, signed by the representatives of both Abhadi and Inishti states. The pact imagines an equal world for everyone, imparting equal say in all matters to all races of the realms.

"I came to know about this from Secretary Anuv himself," says Mayor Illyasi, before taking a big gulp of his mead, then scrunching his face. He reaches for the mead bottle, but the Caretaker taps lightly on his hand, stopping him.

"If you want to drink yourself to political oblivion, that's fine by me," says the Caretaker. "But don't do it on my account. I want out of this."

Mayor Illyasi's face falls. He cups his hands over his eyes and blurts out his next words in anguish. "I don't know what to do! I am helpless! If it were up to me, I would go out there and announce that the minister is playing games with everyone. But the rich gentry out there are so buttered up by the minister's charms that my words would just slide right off them. And in the end, we all have to comply with the pact! If he exploits the loophole, then it's his brilliance, not my incompetence!"

"Then, we change the pact! We ask the Vaishwam Chair to reconsider the clauses."

"Oh really, that's your solution? You know one change takes years of deliberation! They spent half their lifetime thinking Florrals were aliens descended from the skies before realizing they are normal true-born Inishtis. The Vaishwam Chair are just mere mortals who are close to dying each raspy breath they take. And I have been hearing troubling reports of Yayati himself eyeing the Chair. If you had just listened to me and taken my place."

"That wouldn't have changed things if Yayati had already made up his mind. But you know what troubles me the most?"

Mayor Illyasi arches his eyebrows. "What?"

"Champions never showed any political aspirations. They went into their own self-imposed exiles, just like Florrals. They don't offer allyship lightly, and so, their return is completely odd. I would like to meet these Champions of his."

"And what would you do? Swat them like flies?"

"If it comes to that, yes," says the Caretaker, his voice thrumming with barely disguised rage.

"I just think if one is offered the protection of gods, one should take it," says Mayor Illyasi, exasperated. Desperation oozes out of the man's voice like honey from a honeycomb. The Caretaker, though, can't find it in himself to empathize with him. Illyasi could have done things differently if he had wanted. He just didn't want to. It is a hole the mayor has dug for himself. Now, Illyasi will have to sign an agreement that he has been deliberating on with the minister for the past seven months, or else the Three Realms will see him in a less than favorable light.

The Caretaker catches sight of the minister's stout frame entering the dining room. Mayor Illyasi lets go of the tired, helpless facade, and dons a new one, bearing a smile to please. The minister smiles back and says, "Gentlemen, have you made your decision?"

CHAPTER THIRTY-THREE

The Caretaker

The Garbansa twins soothe their throats with spiced mead and rum, as Trulio darts them poisonous glances from afar. The Caretaker notices this with only mild amusement, as he finishes his plate of fragrant jasmine rice topped with mutton. At this moment, far more important things trouble him than Trulio's disdain for the twins.

The twins are soon joined by a tall, gaunt man with a cane. After an animated greeting, Ira Garbansa gestures toward the man's leg, to which he responds with casual indifference, like the leg itself is an afterthought for him. Ani Garbansa points a crooked finger at the Caretaker. The man looks at the Caretaker but soon averts his gaze, shrugging at the twins, then leaving them.

"Master, is that...is that the person...?"

Before the Caretaker can answer, Secretary Anuv joins them with his own plate full of roasted chunks of chicken with a side of mint chutney and rings of onions. He has a wistful air about him, but his eyes twinkle with glee with each bite of food he takes. He seems like he is perennially on the verge of saying something, but the food is not letting him. Finally, he swallows much of the chicken, and speaks.

"If I have to stay in the company of that fool much longer, I'll jump out of the first-floor window."

It's clear the jibe is directed at the most hateful person in the room, Minister Yayati. The Caretaker puts his plate on a side table, and wipes his mouth with a napkin. "Who, may I ask, is that man over there?"

The Caretaker gestures with his eyebrows toward the man with the cane, who is now speaking in hushed tones to Minister Yayati. Secretary Anuv casts a quick glance, then exhales sharply.

"The second most annoying person in the ministry," says Anuv. "Anaris Mastafar. Kedhran. Heads Culture and Miscellany. The greatest expert in Albuchemy the Three Realms has seen. His devices and machines run half of Alderra." He stops and sighs, as if it pains him just to speak out loud the bitter reality of his next words. "Just wish he could construct something that would take care of his family. He is a broken man. I heard recently his lovely daughter left him. He has been quite morbid since then."

Anaris Mastafar. The man who the Stigmar claimed had given him the orders. Father of Iyena Mastafar, the girl who had come to the Garden only two days ago, claiming she could change the nature of things.

"He sure is bringing a lot of culture to this place," says Trulio, spite lacing his words. "Eborsen's aged balls, what's that bell-shaped trouser bottom he is wearing? And what's that half-sleeved jacket? Who even wears that anymore? That style went out of fashion when Master was born."

"Trulio, will you keep it down with the swearing?" remarks the Caretaker sternly. Trulio bows his head, only slightly, in apology.

"He is tasked by the minister to do many things," says Secretary Anuv. "I can't talk about any of them."

A tall server ambles up to the three of them, carrying a tray full of wines and mead, and a decanter of aged whiskey. The Caretaker remembers the smoky, peaty whiff of the whiskey sourced from the Isles of Avram. The last time he had that drink was when Mayor Jaywardna Illyasi was in his prime, eager to make Sirvassa the greatest city in the Three Realms. Now his mousy frame looks eager to grovel in front of the minister.

The Caretaker goes for the wine, instead. "Why are you here, then, Anuv, fraternizing with the enemy?" he says, taking a sip of the wine. It's sweet, but will have to do.

"Just keeping up appearances," says Anuv. "In my position, I have to seem like a good person. To make *you* seem like good, reasonable people, who will comply with any demand. It's nothing personal, just politics."

The Caretaker doesn't reply. There is no proper response to a statement like that. When people loan their humanity in exchange for petty politics, there is no depth to which they won't descend.

Anuv notices Minister Yayati, who beckons him with a pudgy finger.

"Now, if you gentlemen will excuse me," says Anuv. The Caretaker nods, finishing his wine. Trulio reaches for some caramel-coated walnuts kept on a nearby table full of candied fruits and dry fruits and other desserts, and grabs a bunch, pocketing them. In his hurry, he drops some on the floor. A couple of smooth, round caramel-coated walnuts roll on the ash-colored marble and move toward an oblivious dinner-eating, wine-drinking crowd.

Trulio watches this with a detached amusement as he takes a bite. One walnut, however, stops its inevitable roll and comes to rest near the shoes of Secretary Anuv, who continues eating his chicken, blissfully unaware, walking toward the minister. The other walnut keeps on rolling, and meets a crunchy end beneath the boots of the Caretaker. The Caretaker stops, looks at the sole of his shoe, and removes the crumbs.

"Sorry for the mess, Master," says Trulio.

"It's fine," says the Caretaker, scratching his forehead with his thumb. "Trulio, I have to tell you something important." Then he tells Trulio in a sharp and quick, ancient tongue what went on inside the mayor's dining room, the uneasy conversation between him and the minister, the spinelessness of Jaywardna Illyasi. Trulio darts his eyes toward Secretary Anuv even as he listens to the Caretaker. Secretary Anuv makes a movement, his shoes fall over the innocent walnut, and he slips, falling on the ground with a resounding bone-crunch. Anuv squeaks, not even a proper scream of pain, rather the puny sound of a man approaching the latter decades of his life.

"That didn't sound so good," says Trulio. The Caretaker looks at Anuv struggling on the floor. He moves swiftly toward the fallen man, his boots crunching against the fallen walnuts. When he reaches him, he sees the secretary's eyes scrunched, his face a visage of utter agony. Minister Yayati and Anaris Mastafar look down upon him as if he were some bothersome child, not bothering to offer a helpful hand.

"I...ahhh...I can't feel my legs," says Secretary Anuv, his words tumbling out. He looks up at the Caretaker, and his hands reach toward him, like a baby reaching for its mother, eager for comfort. The Caretaker moves with unmatched grace and hoists the secretary up with the vigor of a much younger man.

"Trulio!" the Caretaker shouts. He looks at Secretary Anuv. "Do you feel pain?"

"He will be fine," says the minister. "Anuv, join me in the mayor's study after you have applied something cold to your hip. We have to go over some final clauses in the treaty and your sharp eyes will be needed."

Casting a look of casual indifference at the Caretaker, the minister leaves with Anaris.

"Ants...I feel ants and numbness," says the secretary. "What was that bloody...ahh...thing?" Trulio arrives to their left, taking the secretary's arm over his shoulder. Secretary Anuv huffs and pants as the Caretaker carries him toward a high-backed, cushioned chair.

"I don't think I'll be able to enjoy the pleasures of a good seat anymore," says Anuv, as the Caretaker plops him in the chair like a wet rag. He lets out a pained sigh.

"We'll get you fixed in no time, Secretary," says Trulio.

"Or, maybe, a Champion could fix you instead," says the Caretaker. "We are, after all, closing down for good."

The secretary fixes a stare at the Caretaker. "Did he finally pull that trick? Champion? Really? I wasn't expecting he would go that far for Sirvassa, not this soon at least. That's certainly interesting."

"You fell down, but it seems Jaywardna Illyasi lost a spine instead," says the Caretaker, with barely disguised snark.

"He wasn't born with one in the first place," says Secretary Anuv. "But I can't blame him. The next treaty is in Akhmer. I have to accompany the minister to the frigid peaks of Ameria to oversee that. He wants to give them the protection of two Champions in exchange for a chunky percentage of land in the valley."

"The way it looks, the minister will have to drag you across the valley," says Trulio.

Secretary Anuv gives an exasperated sigh. "Have you ever seen a Champion?" he asks, and then his eyes glaze over. Silence ensues. The Caretaker is intimately familiar with such silences. They gnaw slowly at your bones, an ugly disquiet that comes from knowing enough of a truth that causes discomfort, but not enough to hurt. Champions were spoken about in hushed tones even in the Caretaker's youth, a time long gone by. But now they are out in the open, heralded by a man who claimed he would save the world.

"I've heard they have bright, golden eyes, without pupils," says Trulio. "Master, I have dedicated a good chapter to them in my travelogue."

"They are basically gods," says Anuv. "Yayati was supposed to be escorted by one here today. It was supposed to be a show of strength. An intimidation tactic, if you will."

"It doesn't take much to intimidate Illyasi," says the Caretaker. "A cutlery trick was enough."

"The Champion is referred to as Thavelir. One who shapes air and water, *both*."

"All this talk about Champions is making me dizzy," says Trulio.

"And making my old bones hurt," adds the Caretaker. "Secretary Anuv, why don't we get to the meat of the matter. Why don't you tell us how to get out of this pickle and maybe I can heal your damaged lower half."

"Five years of acquaintance and it has come to this? Why wouldn't you just heal me? Why do you have to resort to these tricks?"

"Consider it a bribe."

"If the minister came to know about it, I can kiss my trip to Akhmer, and my subsequent promotion, goodbye."

"You just laid out the reason why you need us more than we need you," says the Caretaker. "Trulio, how fast can you run?"

"Very fast, Master," says Trulio, positively buzzing with energy.

"I have two potions made out of Dark Lily and the Night Hibiscus. Different concentrations. Fourth Sector flowers, if you remember. The vials are in my cupboard."

Trulio disappears before Secretary Anuv can say 'Alderra'.

★　★　★

The apprentice arrives carrying two bottles, one filled with a liquid so dark it could shroud the night sky, and the other with a water-like liquid so clear it gives the impression that the bottle is empty.

"One restores, and the other strengthens," says the Caretaker, taking the bottles from Trulio.

"Wouldn't a petal–Healer do it faster? I mean, Sirvassa did have quite a torrential outpour this season."

"This hour, all Healers of Sirvassa are asleep," says the Caretaker, chuckling. "The petals need careful peeling, and I don't want to get into the mechanics of that. Now, do you want my help or not?"

"As long as I can walk again."

The Caretaker removes the cork from the bottle that holds the clear liquid. A sharp hiss follows, and the neck of the bottle becomes cloudy. A thick plume rises out of the bottle and disappears in the air.

"Two gulps, no more, no less."

Secretary Anuv does as he is told. He squirms on the first gulp, and his face crinkles, as if the liquid is causing him pain. On the second gulp blood rushes to his face for the span of an eyeblink, then leaves entirely. His body shivers and then goes still.

"What was that?"

"It's just starting."

The next second, Anuv jerks and his body is thrown out of the seat. Breath is knocked out of his lungs and he gasps. The Caretaker opens the second bottle, the one with the dark liquid.

"This is terrible," Anuv says, his words coming out in a whisper.

The Caretaker grabs the secretary's head and pulls it toward him.

"Open your mouth," says the Caretaker. Secretary Anuv does so, and with a surgical, Healer-like precision, the Caretaker tilts the bottle so only three drops fall on Anuv's tongue.

Anuv's hands grip the edges of the cushioned seat, muscles bulging with effort as he hoists himself back.

"I feel warm inside," he says. Trulio kicks him on the shin and he winces in pain.

"Why would you do that?" Anuv says, rubbing his legs. Then he stops, immediately realizing the obvious.

"See, now you feel something in your legs instead of just numbness," says Trulio. "You have a rather strange way of expressing gratitude."

"You can try to walk now," says the Caretaker. "There will be some residual back pain, which will abate in a day or two."

Secretary Anuv nods. Then, he takes a deep breath. "Look, I know how that man thinks. I told you – Champions are an intimidation measure. They have already proven to Sirvassa that it needs help from 'forces beyond its control'. But, there's something larger at play here."

The Caretaker moves closer to Secretary Anuv.

"Promise me, not a word of this to anyone. I am only telling you because I am grateful for your help."

"I promise on Eborsen's ashes," says the Caretaker.

"Alderra is getting impatient. Much of it has to do with your Garden, my friend. Travelers, vacationers…anyone who has had a taste of your Delights, now wants something like that in Alderra. The pressure from the public, just to *feel* good, to feel something, is immense. The ministry can't just keep sitting on their asses. And the Champions can't offer something like that. Yes, the way they shape water and air and earth has protected Alderra from earthquakes and tsunamis and whatnot. But the Champions can't give away their abilities for charity. Like whatever you are running here."

Secretary Anuv waves his hands animatedly.

"The first logical step was to put pressure on the mayor, to convince you to expand the Garden."

"That was a while ago," says the Caretaker. "I know. I refused, vehemently."

"Yeah, let's just say your refusal wasn't met with acclaim. So what does an egotistical man with power in his hands do next? He plays games. If he can't have the Garden, then nobody should have the Garden. It's that simple. This way, he can convince his public that the Garden is a fickle thing. The loopholes in the Restoration Pact...that's just Yayati's way of accomplishing his end."

A heaviness descends upon the Caretaker. He can see all the pieces finally fit into place, except one.

"But why would the Champions agree to side with him in his political chess? It doesn't make sense."

"That's something I have been struggling to make sense of myself, but can't. The minister, I feel, has been sidelining me ever since he started visiting Anaris Mastafar."

"What if we just slit both their throats in their sleep?" says Trulio. "That will take care of the situation once and for all."

"As much as I would like to do that myself, you don't want a civil war with the Abhadis, trust me," says Secretary Anuv. "There's only one way you can get out of this situation," he says heavily. "The Champions arrive the day after tomorrow. Declare yourself worthy."

"What does that mean?" asks the Caretaker.

"Defeat the Champion and you get to keep the Garden."

"What's this nonsense? Are these your words or the minister's?" says the Caretaker. Secretary Anuv's words seemed to suggest a duel, which was the First Age way of solving problems, about five hundred years before the First Abhadi-Inishti War. That was when the most powerful representatives of two factions would just sweat it out, and the duel would end either in the death of one opponent, or in a stalemate, when both participants would just get tired.

"He is old and so are his politics. He operates on ancient codes, and believe me, if he got his way, the Three Realms would *also* be taken back hundreds of years. All that progress you see around these parts, gone, like a petal in a storm." Secretary Anuv blows air at his fingertips, to make his point even more dramatically. Trulio's teeth are bared in a snarl. The Caretaker looks at his apprentice, and sighs. Secretary Anuv continues.

"Make a show of strength and he might just concede. Intimidate him back, and he might not have anywhere else to go. But first, declare that you are willing to do so."

"Declare what?"

"You have to understand what the minister is doing. He is offering protection against an unknown, uncertain, invisible enemy. But really...Champions are a controlling strategy." Secretary Anuv pauses, and his eyes stay on the Caretaker. The Caretaker nods, appreciating the silence, knowing the sentence that comes next, almost verbatim. "Declare that you, my friend, are just enough. That Sirvassa needs the Garden, beyond anything else at this point. That the people of Sirvassa are dependent on the Garden. That Sirvassa is safe and you are its Protector."

CHAPTER THIRTY-FOUR

The Caretaker

A pungent whiff of alcohol mixed with the wet-sandal-like stench of the Daisy of Uhad greets the Caretaker when he enters his laboratory deep in the night. He instantly knows there's a leak somewhere. The Daisy of Uhad is a Fifth Sector flower and he hasn't visited that part of the Garden in months, much less extracted anything, except for his nightly ritual.

The heavily embroidered kurta has started to dig into his shoulders and his back. He removes it, feeling thin gashes made by the sharp, frayed fabric on his arms. The cold night air prickles against his skin as he moves toward the leak.

"Trulio," he barks. The cupboard where he must have taken the two bottles from looks slightly askew. The smell of alcohol is much sharper in this part of the laboratory. And sure enough, he finds a bottle lying on the stone floor, its contents meeting with water. The Caretaker's eyes follow the water. It moves through crevices in the stone, through other cracks, until it reaches a valve connected to a pipe. The Caretaker bends down to examine it.

He notices a rot — clear as day, and ugly as a two-beaked parrot — eating away at the metal of the pipe, a green mold that clings to the already rusting exterior.

"Master." Trulio arrives, his hands folded over each other.

"You didn't notice this when you came to collect the bottles?" says the Caretaker, pointing toward the damaged pipe.

"No, Master. I had one and only one task in mind."

"What about that spilled bottle of alcohol?"

"I might have kicked the cupboard in a hurry," says Trulio, his eyes downcast.

"And you didn't bother to clean up?"

"I thought there were much more pressing matters at hand, Master, than some spillage. I am sorry."

"Well, there's not much point to anything anyway. I will lock the Garden with the thousandfold charm at the first crack of dawn."

"No, no, no Master..." says Trulio, pleading. "You can't let go so easily. We must rebel."

"And do what exactly? How do you plan on defeating a Champion?"

"Master, I can't believe you are saying this. You can make those Champions taste dust with the clap of your hands."

"That life is behind me and I don't plan on returning to that. I am much too old for that sort of thing, and I have taken a vow not to meddle in the larger affairs of this city."

"No one is asking you to do it alone," says Trulio. "What am I for?"

"What will you do? Smack the Champion on the head?"

"Maybe that could work if their head is soft. But...you've forgotten I have written about them in my travelogue."

"Show me..." the Caretaker says. But then his voice catches in his throat, barely a croak. He winces, turns, and leans heavily against the wall behind the pipe. His chest rises and falls, slowly, even as the wrinkles on his skin turn back, over on themselves, revealing a hidden, smoother skin, the skin of youth. The blackness on his right arm is still there, but looks less ugly on a younger hand. His face becomes bright, square, yet tired.

Trulio's mouth hangs open, as he staggers, his feet desperate to find purchase. This is not the first time the Caretaker has turned before him, but the apprentice behaves like it is.

"Master, I—"

"You know this is what I struggle with each night," says the

Caretaker. "You see how weak I already have become. I can't fight anymore."

"But Master, don't you see? This is your true self!" says Trulio. "If age is what is stopping you from challenging the Champions, we can set the duel at a time of our choosing. This hour of the day to be precise."

"No, Trulio, that won't happen."

"But what of the Garden?"

"Even before the events of tonight, I was thinking of closing the Garden down. I have to investigate the rot in the seeds before I can plant more. Maybe it's for the best. Maybe the people of Sirvassa truly can live without the Garden, like everyone else in the realm. It will be difficult to accept at first, the absence of Delight, but they will get used to it."

Trulio sits in front of him, and takes the Caretaker's hands in his.

"Master, even in doing this, you have Sirvassa's best interests in mind," he says. "I will leave you to decide what path to take."

The Caretaker opens his mouth to speak, but remains silent, choosing to let Trulio's words linger in the air for a moment longer. The apprentice picks up a cloth from the long table and goes to work on the spillage, whistling a tune of a song he might have heard on his travels.

★ ★ ★

Sunrays splash on the entrance of the Garden of Delights in a misshapen oval, slowly diminishing, withering at the edges, giving way to a dull gray on the cobblestone as the clouds overtake the sun, then a final darkness, a last light before the door is forever closed. The stone door, cold and unmarked, in the perennial embrace of the flame vine, blood jasmine, and the ivy, waits for its user, its shaper, assured footsteps slowly approaching, eager to bring forth to the world the numerous Delights it hides behind.

★   ★   ★

It's afternoon, a time the Caretaker usually spends in the Garden, tending to his flowers, speaking to customers who arrive at his doorstep with a twinkle in their eyes, their eagerness to ingest Delights a delight of its own. Today, the Caretaker stays in his room, after cleaning his laboratory thoroughly in the morning. He sits in a chair, deep in thought, his eyes constantly finding something to look at, a nail on the wall, the distant temple spire visible through the window, the rectangular niche in his wall where the coppergram strings are housed, the deep blue silhouette of the mountains against the bright afternoon sky.

He gets up and reaches for Trulio's journal, something he hasn't even touched until now. He flips through the pages, his eyes glazing over at Trulio's neat, cursive, almost hypnotic handwriting. Trulio took his task to heart, and it shows on the pages. He began with the chapter of him leaving the Garden one year ago. The Caretaker finds a mention of himself on the first page, twice on the second, and four times on the third page. He flips past the initial chapters and arrives at the section where he finds the ship to the Riadhim, sees flying chariots being pulled by bird-humans, steals the Eternal Spear from the vaults of a small-time king, pays the price for it, falls in love with a woman named Shahina, visits the town of Bacille, and in a moment of foolhardy bravado, loses her to a demon. All this in the span of a year, a year that made him older, and at least a sliver wiser, if not more.

He doesn't find the mention of Champions until much later in the journal.

This one walks like water and talks like fire. As he talks, houses move around, crumble to dust, rebuild themselves in better images of themselves. This one is known as Mithyan.

I met with one who showed me this moment in time when I am sitting in front of the window, gazing out at the beautiful Sirvassan peaks, and penning my memoir. For what purpose, I know not, but I have seen it in the eyes of the one they call Ananthasamaya.

All of them wear robes that are pure light. All of them have eyes that are pure light. But perhaps their weakness is their selves — when they speak, it's like blades on stone. Their words are often cruel and might cause harm. They do not see anyone as their equal, even fellow Champions. There is discord between them and their ambitions are ambiguous.

The Caretaker turns another page. It starts with Trulio reaching the shores of Alderra, and meeting a Champion who stopped a tsunami. It continues detailing Trulio's tutelage under cer, as the Caretaker's eyes glaze over at the fine print. His apprentice, someone who was learning Florrachemy, was also the apprentice of a Champion? A coldness settles deep inside the Caretaker's stomach.

Then, his vision swims. He reads the part where the cruelty of the Champion named Varunnai is described in painstaking detail by Trulio. Pain drips from his words, and the Caretaker can feel Trulio's anguish through the cursive of his handwriting.

His mentee has described his own death.

And yet, Trulio is still very much alive, and he's not a concoction, a smokescreen, a doppelganger. The person who is now his apprentice has always been his apprentice. The child he picked up crying from the streets. He is no lie. Perhaps, he should have been a better mentor. He should have been more present for him.

The Caretaker is aware of what a Champion is capable of. He was fighting an unending war during the time of their genesis. He saw a Champion slaughter half an army with a word and a breath and a half. Their existence was immoral, an affront. No one should be allowed to have so much power.

He almost calls Trulio. He wants to cradle his head and tell him that everything will be all right. Trulio must not face that affront once again, or it would ruin him. No, this battle, the Caretaker must fight alone.

But then, another thought rankles him.

Trulio would deny his request. He has far too much pride in him, and he would want to face the Champion once again.

The Caretaker goes back to bed, weary from too much thought, but with a decision half made in his head. But as soon as his head touches the pillow, he hears a melodious twang of an incoming coppergram.

He opens the small wooden door of the coppergram device. Seven strings gleam with a dull, metallic shine, with numerous pointed golden slivers tipped with ink hanging from their length, making shapes of a language long-lost on a board underneath, language made only of music. The music continues, as the first, the fourth and the seventh string cause the slivers to paint an urgent message.

It's from Yavani, the Seedmaster. She is coming to visit him, and she has something important to discuss. The Caretaker turns a dial on the wooden door and the strings cease their melody. The golden slivers get replaced, and the board beneath is wiped anew, waiting for a fresh incoming message. The Caretaker could string a response back, but he knows Yavani will be on her way. He decides to wait, instead.

★   ★   ★

She is waiting for him near the door of the Garden. Her small frame is illuminated by the passing afternoon light, her face bearing an expression of extreme grief. When the Caretaker approaches her, she hugs him, nestling her face in his shoulder. The Caretaker can feel the thin fabric of his kurta getting wet with her tears.

"She is gone," she says amid sobs. "The girl. She is gone."

The Caretaker grips Yavani's shoulders gently. "Tell me what happened?"

Yavani chokes and gasps and sobs, as more tears stream down her cheeks. "Iyena Mastafar. She is...she was...Sumena's daughter. She's the daughter of a Florral, Alvos. She is a true-born Florral. She came to me...Eborsen curse me, I should have known earlier. Now she is gone."

"How do you know she is a Florral?"

Yavani stops sobbing, then wipes her tears with her sleeves.

"Open the Garden, please," says Yavani.

"I can't do that," says the Caretaker. "I have decided to close it down now. I am taking responsibility for all that has gone down in Sirvassa since the rot came in the seeds. Those disfigured Sirvassans who consumed my Delights are my responsibility to heal. I will talk to the Healers and we will come up with a plan of action to use the next petal-rain harvest."

"Alvos, you aren't *listening* to me," says the Seedmaster. "Iyena Mastafar healed the rot."

"What?"

"She just…did it. She consumed and became one with it. And the rot took her. The ground swallowed her. But then, the seeds started coming afresh."

The ground gives way beneath the Caretaker's feet. The coldness that was present deep inside him subsides, but only momentarily. Then it's compounded, made worse by an onslaught of more complicated emotions. For a moment, he stands rooted on the spot, undecided, unsure. He crosses and uncrosses his fingers, rubs his thumbs against each other. He curls his toes inside his slippers, his soles now sweaty. This hasn't happened to him before, this feeling of utter helplessness. Not knowing, not being in control. The rot had come without warning, and he couldn't do anything to contain it. And now, it is gone, too, without so much as a preamble, and that by the heroic efforts of a girl. Where does that put him in the large scale of things? He is not a Protector of any kind anymore. He is just a withering old man, grappling with a curse, failing at everything.

"Alvos, please…."

He looks at the Seedmaster and her pleading eyes. Her tears have dried now but the anguish is still there, like a stubborn ghost that lingers for far too long despite all efforts of exorcism to vanquish it.

"Come," he says and moves toward the door of the Garden. He taps twice on the stone and moves his fingers in a gentle arc. The door complies soundlessly, as the blood jasmine uncurls and the ivy shifts aside. The Caretaker steps inside and the Seedmaster follows him.

Immediately, he is welcomed with a smell of fresh bloom. The Bacillus Rose and the Tulip of the Seven stand majestically as superior flowers carrying Delights both majestic and harrowing, beauty and cruelty. The Rose is back to its usual deep crimson color, while the Tulip complements the Rose's beauty with its own dual hues of yellow and pink.

Yavani kneels beside the Bacillus Rose. The Caretaker can sense her fingers itching to reach for its petals. He sits beside her. The grass beneath the Tulip isn't a lifeless gray anymore, and the stem doesn't ooze out the tar-like blackness.

"The rot is truly gone," he says with a heavy sigh. Then he pulls out a couple of blades of grass and eats them and his eyes get moist. "I should have known when she first came to the Garden. I should have known when she told me she could change the nature of things. But I didn't act. And now she is taken by the very earth she healed."

Yavani puts her hand on the Caretaker's shoulders, and gently caresses him. The Caretaker buries his head in his palms in grief.

"She told me she felt one with this city, Alvos," says Yavani. "Her love for this place trumped her love for the place where she was born. She was shaken by her father's betrayal, by his abjectly opposite ideals. I could tell it from her face. She held in her heart such innocence, and yet, she was stronger than most of us."

There's a long silence between them, vast as a glacier and just as cold.

"What will you do now?" says Yavani after a while.

"Iyena Mastafar once told me she wanted to kill monsters," says the Caretaker. "She has done her part. Now it's my turn."

★   ★   ★

Sirvassa's market square, a conjunction of three city roads and a mostly dirt path that leads to a creek with water of impossible colors, thrums with a kind of manic activity not seen in the city. On most days, it's a lazy spectacle, slow-moving fruit carts, cloth merchants on elaborate carriages eager to stop women to sell their newest fabrics, and an occasional trickster who promises a never-seen-before magic, a magic Sirvassa is intimately aware of because of the Garden of Delights. On most days, the trickster would be tricked in return, by someone who has just ingested a Delight potion and is still experiencing its many effects.

This day is unlike most days.

The Caretaker shields himself from the bulbous Sirvassan sun, wrapping his head with a scarf so only his eyes are visible, slit-like. As more people trickle into the square, he shuffles his feet, avoiding contact – eye or otherwise – with any citizen, yet becoming a part of the crowd. He darts a quick glance at a salon rooftop, where Trulio hides in plain sight, an onlooker of proceedings to the casual eye, but serving a different purpose in actuality.

The Caretaker reaches the square. A colorful podium has been set up, and a great cloth banner is held in the air by fell-birds, four corners clutched in four respective beaks. The banner announces the arrival of Minister Yayati to the general populace. It's in the same garish color of the pamphlets he saw earlier. The Caretaker has seen better propaganda art before, and in worse times. The banner carries a caricature of Minister Yayati, where even his smile is etched in a ghastly ink, with blots at the edges of his lips. Written in an ancient, cursive script are the words: *He brings sustenance and glory. Yayati of the one, Yayati for all.*

A hastily constructed slogan, if ever there was one. The Caretaker muses to himself, as his gaze settles on an innocent bystander. The bystander has wisps of gray hair falling over his eyes, as he looks at the podium. His manner is uneasy. He clenches his fist.

The Caretaker can't tell where his rage is directed. He doesn't want to find out.

He stays quiet like an autumn leaf, waiting for winter to arrive.

A murmur runs through the crowd, and then a hush falls over it like a giant blanket. Mayor Jaywardna Illyasi takes the podium. He looks uncharacteristically pale, and weaker than two days before, as if the signing of the treaty has done something to his appetite and appearance both.

"Sirvassan, I welcome you to a new beginning in the history of our proud city-state."

His voice holds distress, but his regal composure doesn't show it. The Caretaker, however, can glean it, as if the air around him is bloated with grief of a loss that has not yet taken place.

"Two days ago, I had the pleasure of holding a dinner for our esteemed guest, Minister Yayati, Chief Spokesperson and Minister of the Department of Miscellany. In the words of the late Emperor Kinshuka, change is often inevitable and necessary, beautiful and merciful. We Sirvassans are being heralded into a new beginning, and it gives me immense satisfaction to be a part of this beginning."

"What is he talking about?" a woman, carrying a child on her shoulders, asks the Caretaker, who leans casually against a pole.

"Just platitudes," says the Caretaker. "He doesn't mean any of it."

The mayor clears his throat and announces, in a pitch much higher than before, "I welcome Minister Yayati to the stage."

Yayati takes the mayor's hand and climbs onto the stage. He looks mousier than two nights before, his stout frame trembling with effort. His hawklike eyes, though, look more alive as they scan the crowd.

"Three years ago, when I joined the Alderran Ministry, I wouldn't have envisioned that such a moment would come. That I would visit a state as beautiful as Sirvassa and be fortunate enough to speak to as graceful and attentive an audience. This union of our two states will prove to be mutually beneficial."

Minister Yayati pauses, almost reveling in the silence. The Caretaker hears a distant din, as if a long-dormant beast is awakening from the depths of the Inigee. The air is suddenly sharp, electric, and the ground beneath him groans with agony. It's no earthquake, though.

"I must say, I have been troubled since I arrived in your beautiful city. It's haunted by its past, a past it's too eager to clutch closer to its chest. A past that could take the form of cancer in your bones. I am here to remove that cancer and make sure it has no business coming back."

For the Caretaker, it's obvious what Yayati is getting at. To innocent Sirvassans, not so much. The words are directed at him, only him.

"The Garden you so blissfully cling to has betrayed you, after all, hasn't it? Oh, I have heard of grave mishaps."

It feels like a slap. The Caretaker feels his insides harden, and hot bile rising in his throat.

Someone from the crowd raises his hand. "I lost my tongue. It took me six weeks to gain back my voice."

"My son lost his feet."

"I could not see for a week straight after ingesting that vile potion of his. When I gained my eyesight, I could only see in blues and greens."

And soon, many such testimonies ring in the air around him. Some are somber, words spoken in quiet agony, of true pain. Some are harsher, louder, and crass. But all of them are lies. Actors hired to make a point.

"I'm sure many of you feel that way. And what about that monster that keeps coming back, but never seems to disappear altogether? Oh, I am sure it's part of a plot to keep you guys subservient. A plot by none other than the person you so lovingly call the Caretaker."

Silence. Minister Yayati chews on what he has just said. He seems to enjoy the silence that has fallen on the crowd. The Caretaker feels numb, but he knows the moment is close now.

"But you must not live in fear any longer. To protect us from enemies we know not yet, but anticipate in the near future. To keep our people safe and help them prosper and live a life of dignity. I provide Sirvassa with the protection of a Champion."

"Who's a Champion?" a tall man asks, his teeth stained from eating the bledwan fruit raw. The Caretaker looks at him. Then he turns his gaze toward Trulio, who points to the sky. Foam-white clouds part to reveal a deep crimson smear against a bluer sky. The shape descends, and takes a form – a large, impossible, androgynous form. A shaved head, body covered in one single red cloth, naked feet, a thin streak of gold, which runs from forehead to jaw.

The Champion descends to the podium, slowly, gracefully. A collective gasp travels through the Sirvassan crowd. Minister Yayati stands in awe of the magical, superpowerful being. Mayor Illyasi stands still, fingers of his hands interlaced, his eyes affixed on the Champion.

The Caretaker moves through gaps in the crowd, occasionally looking toward the rooftop, where Trulio is sitting, scanning the proceedings. He makes his way to the front of the crowd, a few feet away from the podium, where the minister can clearly see him.

He can see the person he is about to battle. He is standing at the edge of the podium. The Caretaker can sense a deep yearning inside him.

A gray, desolate battlefield. A placid lake. A curse. All of it, in the past.

The present needs him more.

"Sirvassan, I present to you your First Protector," says Minister Yayati.

"Why does Sirvassa need protection?" the Caretaker says, in as loud a voice as he can muster. "What does it need protection from?"

Minister Yayati looks at the mayor and frowns. The mayor shrugs and gestures to him to answer.

"I have seen other states being overrun by blights and monsters and shadows, deep and ancient and unforgiving," says the minister confidently.

"Blights are things of the past. The jalan I have constructed atop the city is enough to stop the monster and keep it in its tracks. And I'm sure Sirvassans don't fear shadows."

Some laughs follow. The Caretaker looks at the Champion, who, thus far, hasn't moved from his spot, hasn't spoken a word, hasn't batted an eyebrow. The Champion is silent as a rock, calm like the middle of a sea.

"You don't know what you're talking about," says the minister.

"I do," says the Caretaker. "Sirvassans don't need protection. They're more than capable of handling their business themselves. And if ever anything untoward happens to this place...." The Caretaker pauses. He lets his words linger in the air and wash over the minister. "I'm here." The Caretaker removes his headcloth, revealing himself.

Minister Yayati scoffs, then lets out a chuckle. "I should have known," he says.

"I'm the Protector of Sirvassa," the Caretaker continues, and darts a glance at Mayor Illyasi, who looks like he has just swallowed ice.

The minister shifts his weight from one leg to another. "Prove it," he says nonchalantly.

As if on cue, the Champion moves, ever so slightly. He takes two steps toward the Caretaker. The Caretaker retrieves the Bacillus Rose from inside his robes. He holds it high in the air, letting sunlight splash on its crimson petals. The Champion glides over to the Caretaker, now standing a hair's breadth away from him.

The Caretaker bites down on the Rose.

★   ★   ★

His veins surge with madness as his life blood swirls and mixes with the flower's concentrate. His skin aflame, and his eyes bloodshot, he perceives the world as it is, as it will be, and as it once was. Time slows down. The hairs on his arm answer to him. The wind around him speaks to him. The space between his heartbeats seems like an eternity.

He sees the Champion's arm before it comes. He doesn't allow it to hit him where it would have hit him. He holds out his palm, surging with sun-bright Delight, and pushes it against the Champion's chest. The Champion is thrown back by the impact, and he flies thirty feet into the air, making a cruel arc before his body hits the cobblestones in a sickening crunch.

The Caretaker's vision splits. Another shadow grows large in the sky and descends upon the crowd. Stronger, more muscular, more gold upon his skin than the earlier Champion, the second Champion has a red band on his temple that looks like a bloodied insignia. His thick, large robes flutter as he walks toward the Caretaker, his gait godlike, yet mechanical, almost as if they weren't the motions of his mind.

But it isn't time to dwell on the anatomy of Champions. The Caretaker clenches his fist, and closes his eyes. The Delight of the Rose surges inside him once again. With one swift motion, the Caretaker fashions a chain out of the shattered stones and beckons it toward himself. Then, he sets the chain on fire with a thought, and sends it speeding toward the second Champion. The fiery stone-chain coils around his body, wrapping his torso and his legs, singeing them, burning them.

But the Champion breaks the chains. The stones hurl toward the crowd. Mayhem ensues around the Caretaker as innocent Sirvassans find cover.

"Kill him!" announces Minister Yayati from the podium.

The second Champion is upon the Caretaker swifter than thought. He grabs the Caretaker's throat with his bare hands and starts to dig in his fingers, throttling any sound he could make, choking him. The Caretaker grabs the Champion's arm. It doesn't feel fleshlike, but rather steely, almost metallic. He calls upon another, final death-surge of the Delight, the power of the Rose, and *thinks* the arm to melt.

Under the Caretaker's palm, the Delight begins its work. The arm of the Champion singes, melts, reshapes and becomes fluid.

But then the Caretaker's hands go limp. The last surge vanishes as quickly as it came to him. His knees crumble beneath him. He had anticipated this, but not so quickly. He glances at the rooftop to his right.

Now is the time.

Trulio appears from behind a ledge. The Caretaker's eyes meet the eyes of his apprentice, as a dark shape materializes in Trulio's hands, long and sleek. The Caretaker's bow. Even as the Champion continues strangling the Caretaker, Trulio nocks a sharp arrow and aims for the Champion's eye.

The moment becomes two moments, and the Caretaker sees two visions simultaneously, residual surge from the Delight of the Rose allowing him sights both beautiful and terrible.

In the first, the arrow speeds toward the Champion and pierces his left eye, leaving his skull through the other side, showering the podium with red-gold blood, ending the duel once and for all.

In the second, the Champion speeds toward Trulio, whipping through the air, grabs his throat and hurls him toward the cold, hard ground. Trulio's back hits the pavement with a sickening bone-crunch, blood pooling around, traveling through cracks on the crusty Sirvassan road. The Champion waves a hand and the crows shred into black ash, falling all around the Caretaker as he lies on the ground, breathing, the Delight leaving his body one pulse at a time.

The second vision is the one that comes to pass.

★　　★　　★

First, screams. Sirvassa, a quiet city, has never seen violence, nor heard guttural screams, of pain and fear and desolation. But as Trulio's limp body lies shattered on the cobblestones, the air is rankled with cries of shock and agony, thrumming with an impossible notion – that the average life of a Sirvassan is about to change.

The minister's voice booms. He urges the Sirvassans to stay calm and let the authorities do their job. Let the Champion guard them, and safely take them to their homes. Let the mayor's police hold the culprit accountable.

The Caretaker brushes past harried and panicked Sirvassans, his heart a steel drum inside his ribs, but his steps measured, careful. He has repaired broken bodies before; he has almost brought people to life before. *Trulio will be fine.* The Caretaker says this to himself as the world swims in front of his eyes, the aftereffects of the Bacillus hit waning.

He sees Trulio, his legs mangled, his arm twisted at an impossible angle. His eyes are bloodshot and the ground around him bleeds with him. It's all his blood. The Caretaker's feet stumble and he falls, the sight of Trulio's distorted frame sucking all energy out of him. He scrambles toward his apprentice, breathless.

"Trulio." His own raspy, curdled voice surprises him. "Trulio, wake...." Trulio's hair is matted with red. Blood pools in the hollow between his eye and sharp cheekbone. He struggles to turn his head to his left, to see his Master approaching him.

"Master, I failed you," he says, his voice slowly approaching death. "Master, I am sorry for what I did."

"No, no, no, Trulio, you will be fine," says the Caretaker, not believing his own words. "Get up, we can still reach the Garden... we have to stop this madness, please get up...."

"No Master, you have to go. Don't wait for me." Trulio lets out a cry of pain so bloodcurdling that it pierces the Caretaker's skin and reaches in his bones, settling there, finding a home. That cry will haunt the Caretaker later, in moments of solitude, in moments of grief, as many such cries of the past still do.

"It's not fair, Trulio."

"You're the Protector of Sirvassa, Master. Finish what you started, but without me. It was always meant to be that way."

"Don't say that, Trulio," says the Caretaker and takes the apprentice's head in his lap, cradling it like a child. Behind him the crowd begins to disperse. Harsh tapping sound of boots on gravel.

"I am sorry for what I did, Master," says Trulio in a half breath. "I am sorry for bringing the rot."

"What are you talking about, Trulio?" says the Caretaker, sternly, gently, cruelly, as his apprentice's dying words wash over him, the lie Trulio held in his heart to this day. Trulio's final act is handing the Caretaker a folded piece of parchment, shadows of ink visible through the back, and the rest smeared in his blood.

The Caretaker pockets the parchment as his own body thrums with shivers of grief. His breath comes out shallow and he moves, holding Trulio's shoulders, dragging his body across the cobblestones, trying to keep it safe so he can spend a little more time with his apprentice.

The Caretaker has to tell his apprentice that it will be all right. Even if he won't listen anymore.

But it is too late. Mayor Illyasi's police, the Sirvassan Blue Guard, flank him from all sides. One of them has a birdlike face, but speaks with the authority of a lion.

"You're the one they call the Caretaker."

The Caretaker looks at the police. His left arm rests beneath the left shoulder of Trulio, and he can feel his skin going cold, his heartbeat slowing down, until it stops completely. At that moment, the Caretaker gathers whatever is left of the Bacillus in him. He raises his hand, his left hand, black and emaciated already with the failed de-aging potion he had consumed.

The hand twitches, then falls limp by his side.

★   ★   ★

When he wakes, the first thing he feels is a slight shiver in his bones. His clothes cling to him, clammy from sweat, but air sieves in through a gap in the cold, stone wall. With air comes a hint of suffused sunlight, which splashes on the cell floor and the bars. His right temple throbs. He brings his hand to touch the area – no feeling at first, but then a stabbing pain. He tries to recall if it was the baton that hit him or the hard cobblestone when he fell.

To his right, jail bars shine against the dim sunlight. He recognizes the place. An abandoned underground prison near the base of the Llar Mountains, a stone's throw away from the Temple of Eborsen. This is the infamous torture cell constructed by King Trimani, back when Sirvassa wasn't a sovereign state. But that was so long ago it isn't even a memory.

The Caretaker gets up and investigates the bars. They're old and not rusted, sturdy, made to take the weight of the ground above. A brass lock the size of his hand shines to his left. The cell in front of him holds no prisoners. It's clear he is the only inmate here.

More sounds of boots crunching soft, muddy ground, from above. Then, hard tapping from his left. Stairs, perhaps. The Caretaker sits, and breathes in deep the musty, acidic air of the cell, which almost singes his nostrils. It reminds him of a pungent wine he consumed in Ursi, which gave him a two-day hangover. He waits.

The sounds grow closer. A face is illuminated by the light falling on the cell bars. Mayor Jaywardna Illyasi looks wrinkled, like an overripe jackfruit, his eyes sunken pools. Behind him, two other men stand erect, robed in blue.

"Time passes fast down here, doesn't it?" says the mayor.

"I wouldn't know," says the Caretaker.

"I think we'll find out together."

The cell door opposite to the Caretaker groans as it opens. The mayor is ushered unceremoniously inside by the same men who followed orders from him only a week ago.

"You Inishti are all the same. Stubborn." Mayor Illyasi looks almost apologetic even as he makes the remark. One of the men locks the cell door.

"Is this all about me being an Inishti?"

"No," says the mayor. His voice is broken. "If you had only avoided your show of strength out there, I might have done something to help your cause. But you gave me nothing and now here we are."

"If you really wanted you would have done something at the dinner, Illyasi."

Silence descends. Ugly and oppressive.

"You!" the mayor barks at the man who locked his cell. "Dilmar is your name, isn't it? I was present at the naming of your firstborn, remember? Where's your sense of loyalty?"

Dilmar says nothing as he pockets the keys. He glances at the Caretaker, as if searching for answers. Finding none, he walks away, the other man following in his wake.

"I should have known. It was never about the river. Or the petal-rain. Or the Garden, for that matter." Mayor Illyasi grips the bars tight, desperation and anguish doing an ugly dance on his face.. Then he starts banging his head on the bars. "I should have known, I should have known!"

"Stop!" the Caretaker yells.

Jaywardna stops. "Sirvassa has always been a thorn in the realm's side. They just couldn't stomach its success, its sovereignty." Saying these words, Mayor Jaywardna Illyasi, once a man who held great promise to do great things for Sirvassa, now a husk, disappears into the shadows of his cell.

The Caretaker leans back against his cell wall, wishing he held more power to change things, wishing he was young, wishing that he was the same Florral he was twenty years ago.

★   ★   ★

He is woken up by the bells of the Temple of Eborsen. Mayor Illyasi murmurs to the god, his wishes striking against the bare walls and not going beyond. The Caretaker smacks his lips as he scratches absently at the wall, thinking. His gaze falls on his blackened right hand, but he chooses to ignore it. Weariness fills his bones; the Bacillus tends to be unforgiving if taken in a dose unsuitable for age, and now he feels every sweet ounce of that flower he ate turn to bitterness inside his body.

He has been in jail cells before, but all of his previous captors showed some amount of mercy. He doesn't know how much time has passed; from the suffused light and the temple bells he can tell it's evening. But evening of which day? A sense of time escapes him.

"Illyasi," he calls out to the mayor. There's no response for quite a while. He closes his eyes and replays the incident of the previous days in his head. What happened after he was captured by the Blue Guard? He had seen a lifeless body on the shattered road, its limbs twisted at an awkward angle. He remembers raising his arm to touch the body, before he was taken away by the guards.

He hears a shuffle from the other cell. Then a pained groan.

"What? What did you want?"

The memory of the body shrinks inward in his brain, where it finds a permanent home. He turns his head to face Mayor Illyasi.

"If I remember correctly, there's a passage outside this jailhouse that leads straight to a pass in the Llar?"

"If you don't die here, you'll surely die on the cold slopes of Llar, my friend. Your fancies escape me sometimes."

"Don't tell me you aren't thinking of escaping."

"I am thinking of talking," said Illyasi. There is a pause, only punctured by the bells outside. A fell-bird chirps, a lonely sound, and then stops. "I still believe an effective dialogue is the key to—"

The Caretaker scoffs. His ribs ache, and his skin tingles from sweat and cold. "Your fancies escape me, friend," he says, in a consciously derisive tone. It's meant to hurt and mock. And the mayor replies predictably.

"You...you have never sat on a seat of power. It's easy for you to ridicule me."

"I want you to hold a truth in your heart, Illyasi, and take it to your burning pyre," says the Caretaker. "You never negotiate with power-hungry despots like Yayati."

Silence, again. The Caretaker can sense Illyasi mulling over his words. A crass sound of nails on rusty iron emanates from his cell. "Do you have a plan?" he asks.

"I do not," says the Caretaker.

The clang of the bells recedes. Silence descends on the jailhouse like a fever, slow, sure, burning. The Caretaker waits for the night to come, and for his bones to be new again, if only for a short while. If only to keep the pain at bay. A young body would have been more equipped to handle the excruciating withdrawal of the Bacillus. A young body would have handled the fight with a Champion and defeated it.

He closes his eyes and begins a chant, slow, full of cracked, throaty whispers, but still melodious. A prayer for Eborsen, a song to please the gods, to garner their mercy, a song that has all but lost its meaning in recent times, because all gods are in their century-long slumber, leaving the Three Realms to the races of humans. Soon, Mayor Illyasi joins the Caretaker, and the prison is filled with the prayer-song of two broken men.

CHAPTER THIRTY-FIVE

A Melancholy Bargain –
A Journal of Travel, Trauma, and Teachings

This is the part I find myself slowly remembering, and penning the last.

This is the part of my story I am ashamed of. I can't bring myself to tell Master what I have done, and so I put it down on paper, so Master, in his quiet moments, may find it in himself to forgive me for my deeds. This is the part Master might not read, because it's not a part of the punishment he gave me.

This part I write for myself.

After I was killed by Varunnai, I was resurrected by another, kind-eyed god.

I lay buried beneath river-smooth stones where Varunnai had done cer deed. I lay unmoving for two days, as slugs and spiders and sea animals crawled inside my nose and my open mouth, and found new homes in the cracks on my skin. For two days, frothy but clean water from the newly alive stream washed over me, drenching my body. But my insides were scrubbed clean of water, as my blood became progressively thicker and slowed down to barely a crawl, my heart almost giving up its will to go on. If there's a level beyond dehydration, and before death, I found myself there. At the end of it all, if anyone would have stepped on me, they'd have found a crackle of an autumn leaf.

That's how dry I was.

Until I felt my body being lifted from my tomb of stone. That sudden, light and airy feeling was the only thing I felt.

I opened my eyes three days later to a beautiful face staring down at me. I blinked several times and the face came into focus. Hair pulled back, pale skin, sharp eyebrows, and ocean-blue eyes. Another Champion.

"Who are you?" ce asked.

"Trulio," I said. My voice was a hoarse whisper, the words scraping against my throat.

"Strange name," ce said. "My name is Tyi."

Tyi. The name existed on the slopes of my memory, ever tumbling down, and I couldn't catch it. But later, much later, when Master revealed his true self to me, I realized I had met his mortal enemy. The Champion whom he had defeated on that battleground, all those years ago, before the curse of eternal old age was placed upon him.

Tyi helped me get up. The room swam into view, as my bones cracked and ached. The place was far removed from Varunnai's thatched hut I had been spending my days in. This had tiled floors and an actual ceiling. The walls were painted a soothing yellow, and the windows had curtains. I was on a bed that felt soft as feathers, although feeling still hadn't quite returned to my body. My insides were still healing.

"How am I alive?"

"Because of me," said Tyi. "That mad god took away all your body's water. You were more or less dead. But I have ways."

Cer voice was gentle, and cer eyes moved as ce spoke.

"Did I look like a raisin?"

Ce laughed. "It's way more complicated than that, but if your simple brain wants to accept it, then yes, you were a raisin. But you are a grape now."

This Champion had a sense of humor. I found myself strangely attracted to cer.

"You need to eat to thrive, Trulio," ce said, and then clapped. I heard a hard tapping sound. Ahead, some curtains fluttered and separated, and through a gap in the wall entered two bronze men. They weren't wearing anything, but that didn't matter, because they didn't possess what could be termed bodies. Light danced off their skin, which looked like it was assembled from parts. Their walking was more like marching.

They were carrying plates of food. Toast, marmalade, butter, apples and bananas, and a big jug of water.

On a closer look, I could see their joints were soldered. Tiny pinpricks of nails had been hammered, keeping the bronze skin in place. But what was inside them?

"Trulio, meet Narkal and Vehman," ce said. I greeted both of them, and they nodded at me. Their greetings were genuine, lifelike, and would have fooled anyone from a distance. When Tyi waved at them, they retraced their steps and walked back.

"The newest marvels of Albuchemy," ce said, like it was the plainest thing to say. "But I have given them something extra. It's because of me that these automatons can dream."

It was evident that I was in the presence of the most powerful Champion to ever exist. Master Alvos's abilities would pale in front of what this gentle being in front of me was capable of doing.

"What do they dream of?"

"They don't tell me," ce said. "Maybe sheep, maybe horses. Fell-birds, Amaran beasts. Fruits and wine and delights."

"Delights, like the ones we get from flowers?"

Tyi's face contorted. A fly buzzed near cer, but immediately lost all control, disintegrated, and fell down like black dust. There was a long silence between us, but when ce spoke next, cer voice was flaming iron.

"What do you know about Florrachemy?"

I told cer whatever I had learned from Master. I told cer all my truths. Ce deserved to know, because ce had saved my life. And I found myself divulging everything to cer, despite my best intentions. The words spilled out from my mouth like water from a jug. In hindsight, I realize I shouldn't have been so gullible. But how couldn't I be?

I was alive because of Tyi.

★　　★　　★

Tyi lived in a place called the Sectarium, to the east of Alderra, where the city ended and patchy wilderness began. The Sectarium, simply put, was a town of Champions, a self-sustaining abode for the gods. While Tyi lived inside a small palace of cer own, which rested on a platform of jade and marble, the other Champions had relatively humble housing units.

Tyi told me that Varunnai was an outcast, and ce shouldn't have been my mentor in the first place. It was because of Varunnai's reckless, irresponsible practices that ce was shunned from the Sectarium, and so ce lived atop a mountain, spending the rest of cer days in solitude. While Varunnai was old-fashioned and wanted the townsfolk to pamper cer before ce deemed it necessary to help them, the Sectarium had rules of engagement strictly set. The Champions in the Sectarium only meddled in affairs that had a long-lasting impact on the prosperity of the Three Realms.

And so, they immediately knew that Varunnai had been called upon to do a service for the villagers.

"You are fortunate," Tyi said, as we walked in the glades to the east of the Sectarium, with mammoth oaks kissing the skies and overlooking our brief stroll. Here, the wind was crisp, and the world looked baby-new, prim green all around. Tyi had been continuously reminding me of my good luck, and cer own benevolence. And yet again, I wondered if I was in the company of the right god. I wondered if cer words contained a hidden meaning.

"I know," I said. "I carry my luck on my sleeve."

"I want to show you something," ce said, and took me deeper inside the woods. The oaks became taller, the grass thinner, and the light dimmed. Soon, we arrived at a clearing. Here, the grass was of three colors, purple, bone-white, and black of the night. Amid the grass, I noticed nettles, poison ivy, and night jasmine.

My words died in my throat when the truth hit me. Tyi looked at me and smiled.

"This is my Garden," ce said. "The Garden of Sorrows."

My heart became a pebble scuttling on cobblestones. I was witnessing a dark miracle in front of me. A miracle I knew not the meaning of.

Tyi kneeled beside a purple-black flower, whose petals were blade-sharp. When ce touched it, blood spurted out of cer delicate fingers and dripped on the grass like honey. Then the wound healed of its own, and cer flesh became one again, earthy-pink. She plucked out a petal, and nibbled on it.

"What are you doing?"

"Ingesting a Sorrow," ce said.

"For what?"

"To do something I couldn't do as a Champion," ce said. "To help you, Trulio."

Ce got up. My mind went blank. And all I saw in that moment was the Champion, and a darkness swirling around cer. Soon, even that evaporated, and all I could see were eyes. Two white pools, in a mist of purple. And then a voice. Bones rubbing against bones, feather-like softness. A crash of salty sea against a rock. Silence.

Ce spoke, and I saw visions of a love I had long lost. I saw her. I saw Shahina.

Shahina was walking on polished marble, in a room full of bronze pillars. Her figure cast no shadow on the ground, despite the room being bathed in ample light. My fingers itched to feel her hair once more, to trace her soft skin. My lips against a memory of hers, a forgotten breath expelled, saying her name, wishing for her to return. My feet moved, but my body was still.

"She is trapped," said Tyi. "But still alive."

"What are you talking about?" I said. "I saw her die."

"There are many deaths other than death. I have died one such death. But rest assured, I can bring back your love, Trulio."

"Anything," I said, and my words weren't mine anymore. They felt compelled out of me, by a different force. Was it love? I don't know. But I know I said those words, and now I wish I hadn't. "I'll do anything to get her back."

"Trulio, you are gentle and kind. But what I'm asking you to do is cruel, but necessary."

Cer voice spoke to me. Cer voice commanded me. Cer voice controlled me. I could have shrugged cer off, but ce had promised me Shahina.

Ce showed me three Sorrows – Thorn, Juniper, and Night Jasmine. My task was simple.

Before entering the Garden that night, I paid a visit to the Seedmaster. I told her a lie that you needed urgent seeds for the sowing of an important Delight that couldn't wait. I faked urgency, and she relented. While she gathered the seeds, I sneaked into the Burrowing, and just beneath the white trees, I planted the Thorn, deep in the ground. The Sorrow the Thorn carried was extremely potent, and its rot had the power to pervade through the Burrowing, killing whatever seeds sprouted next. Yavani didn't suspect a thing.

That taken care of, I proceeded to plant the Juniper in the Garden. Another potent sorrow, Juniper could kill the Tulip and the Daisy immediately. And it would have, killing half the best Delights of the Garden. But at the last moment, the grief of Shahina's passing wrecked me, suddenly, and I realized my true folly. Her words came back to me, instead of Tyi's, telling me to stop. Her soft voice compelled me to end this useless charade. And I ceased, cradling myself, that night, before I could ruin the Garden. I was clutching the grass, desperately, because I needed to touch something rooted and real and alive.

And then you came.

I would have done the deed eventually, but you held me through the night. You took care of me, again, like you'd done so long ago. You healed me, like a child.

Master, when you read this, inevitably, I hope you find it in your heart to forgive me. If you don't then I'll muster courage to tell this to you myself. And then, my fate rests in your hands alone. Then I'll be ready for my final departure.

CHAPTER THIRTY-SIX

Iyena Mastafar

Her body sinks deep inside the earth where the roots of everything disappear into a swath of dirt and worms and darkness. Here, there's only a rumble of the magma below. A river of fire, ever bubbling. Smoke and blackness and metals and minerals, binding the earth together.

Nothing grows here. Not even nothing.

She sinks, she sinks.

Out of her toe, a green twig sprouts, and digs into the earth around her. More twigs appear, out of another toe, her ankles, her shin, her hip, her torso, her shoulders, her palms, her neck, her face. Her hair becomes wraith-like, white, and then olive-green, digging similarly underground like the twigs. These tendrils ensconce her body in a sarcophagus of soil and leaf and wood. Then the sarcophagus sinks farther.

From the depths of the earth, a sound. Not human, nor beast, something ancient. The soundwaves travel through rocks and tectonic plates, shifting, coursing between cracks of earth, moving like sludge sometimes, racing like thunder at others. The sound, inevitably, makes its way toward the sarcophagus of Iyena Mastafar, curls around the green tendrils, seeps inside her slowly decaying corpse with only one intention.

Undo. Unmake. Remake.

Iyena. The sound takes the form of a recognizable whisper, a frequency understood by a human.

Inside the sarcophagus, inside Iyena's cortex, a pinprick of activity.

Iyena. The whisper again. Coarser. Harsher. Like rubbing sand on bones.

Like a tap on an everlamp allows the Delight inside the dead copper lamp to surge into brightness, the coarse whisper allows Iyena's cortex to respond. A feeble sentience. No words. Response of frequency with frequency.

The whisper understands because it has always understood. The sound of a seedling sprouting. The sound of the sky in the morning. The sound of dead things waking. The sound of nothing to everything.

Iyena Mastafar. Your name means mirror. It also means change. Two ancient tongues giving two meanings to your being. You held in your body such immense power to change things, that it ended up changing you. I'm here to help with your molding. Accept it. It's a boon.

"Ma."

Iyena's lips don't move, but it's a sound her heart makes first when it begins to beat. Her heart has swelled in size, feeding blood to organs and limbs that didn't exist before.

Sumena Mastafar. Your mother is safe but on another continent.

Slowly, a surge of life. Feelings return. Blood and oxygen and minerals. And deep in the nature of her being, something else, the seed of a Delight. She has changed, irrevocably.

"Who is inside my head?"

She shifts. But finds a new response to her discomfort. A flap, a flutter. She can sense a scaly protrusion on her torso, her elongated limbs, and like two blades working in tandem, something slicing her back.

The pain will be short.

The blades cut through her back and the pain wrenches out breath from her lungs. She screams. But it's not a scream. Rather, a bestial sound. A screech. Something she has heard before. On the Sirvassan streets. In the sky. A beast soaring. Eager to land on the streets, but defeated by a magical meshwork.

"Who are you?"

I am the one who gave life to the Earth, who made everything possible. Remember the Hour of the Futures, Iyena. You flew in the palms of giants. That was a mirror, an iyenam to your true nature. The Hour of the Futures just pushed it to your subconscious.

"Eborsen?"

The world calls me that, among other things. My true name can't be pronounced by anyone because it's not a name, it's just a sound. A frequency. A sliver of the original sound that made the world, then me. A broken shadow of that now resides inside you.

Life surges inside her.

She opens her eyes, and she sees rocks around her. Stalagmites reaching toward her like claws. Worms crawling on walls, disappearing into black crevices. A smell of earth and rain. But everything is bathed in red. She blinks, blinks again, but the bloody aura remains.

Your nature has changed, Iyena. But you hold in yourself immense power to change it back, too. Be wise when you go out into the world. Because it's your world.

She feels her engorged insides. She brings her hands in front of her face. They aren't merely hands, but sharp talons, black and white. She looks down. Where there were supposed to be feet are now claws, digging into the earth. Her torso is scaly. She feels strong from inside, stronger than ever before.

When she blinks, she blinks differently. When she thinks, she thinks differently. When she moves, she moves differently. A bestial urge to rip apart a small animal takes root inside her. Is it hunger? Or just a violent urge to break things?

What has she become?

She takes in her rocky surroundings. Every passing second they close in on her. But claustrophobia is a sensation that is reserved for her human form. Now these walls seem like long-lost friends. Protectors. They're not encaging, they're almost liberating. They feel like home.

But she must also look toward the skies. She has friends and family and people she could call her own in the city. Their names float in the vicinity of her swelled-up beast of a brain. A sharp mixture of vowels and consonants. Hard sounds. Names. They go by names. Her kind, no, they only go by a guttural sound and smell.

She notices a gap through which light trickles in and makes wells on the hard, rocky ground. Whistle of air, whiff of salt. Dew on grass-blades. A steep slope, giving way to a muddy plain, leading to the city. All outside. All where the light is coming from.

When she goes out, she has to be wise. When she goes out, she has to change. She can always come back.

The mouth of the cave opens to a short slope. She turns her head to look to her right and her left. Far to the left, waves brush against the tapered edges of the Sirvassan land. To her right, the plains stretch, rolling up and down, first in grassy meadows, then giving way to rocky terrain, a road looking like a small crack on an overly baked, hard bread loaf, leading all the way to a different sister-city. A river breaks this continuous landscape neatly into two, coming from the east, a tributary of a much larger river far beyond. The river snakes around Sirvassa and then eventually meets the sea, as all rivers do.

Her claws dig against the slope as she finds a precarious balance. She is still used to her human feet. Her nose is now an oddly toothed beak. What sort of a hybrid monster is she? Can she turn herself back? The voice in her head made it sound like she could.

She reaches for the Delight that had taken up permanent residence inside her heart. She imagines her claws becoming feet, her talons turning back into her hands, her wings snapping, closing, folding back inside her back and becoming a part of her spine, and her snout retracting into her face. Most of all, she imagines the scales on her monster-head becoming her once-lustrous hair again.

The transformation comes, but at the cost of immense pain, once again. She feels like she is being carved out alive, bones reshaping, reforming, fitting into a smaller frame. Her organs restructuring against the new skeleton, the bestial organs becoming vestigial in her human form.

She lies on the slope of the mountain, breathing heavily. She looks at the mud and the scars on her body. She tries to sew together memories. Trees. Seeds. A woman. A place that wasn't a place. Before that, two women. A fight. Family. Her father.

Like knitting together a patchy fabric, she mends her memories, coming up with a cohesive whole. But she soon gets distracted by the cold. She realizes she has no clothes. Her hard, leather hide in the previous form was keeping her warm. But this form is frail. She can't keep switching back and forth at such regular intervals. The pain is too much.

But she can change the nature of things. She scrambles back inside the cave to find an object.

Inside the cave, though, is another story altogether. What once seemed like a friend, now looks like a desolation. The stalagmites encroaching on her like so many knives, and the rocks and boulders sitting like so many beasts. There is no warmth here, despite the smallness of the space. She looks around, bracing herself for something to pounce on her. But nothing lives here, in the deep recesses of the mountain, except her, except the beast that she becomes.

She finds a flat rock, the size of a kitchen slab on which dough is molded into rotis and other flatbreads. She reaches for the Delight inside her and tries to mold the stone into something flatter, changing its hard nature into the softness of a fabric. She succeeds, partly. The rock relents, but the fabric that comes out is frayed and torn and of the same ash-gray color.

It will have to do.

She wears it, no, rather wraps it around her bare torso, like the cavewomen of the past she has read about in so many books. Sern Aradha was the one who had first told her about the pre-settlers, the Amhumen, who roamed naked around the Three Realms. This was supposed to be even before the gods existed. Perhaps the Amhumen were the true gods. But if the gods, the Eborsens of the world, created what she knows as the world today, who were the pre-settlers?

She shrugs off the thought. There's no mirror to check her appearance or straighten her frizzled hair. All those luxuries seem like they belong to the past.

But she doesn't know why these morbid thoughts plague her. Perhaps because of a hard brush with death. She actually died. The thought sends shudders down her spine. But then, she calms herself, holding a piece of rock jutting out of the cave wall. She died, but she came back, changed. Whatever she had seen inside the Temple of Eborsen, in the Hour of the Futures, is coming true.

She was riding in the palms of giants. Now she can turn herself into a giant beast whenever she wants and soar the skies.

She moves out of the cave. The sky is tinged with a pinch of orange in the distance, while the rest of it is a swath of clear blue. Time has passed languidly since she healed the rot. It's only midafternoon in Sirvassa, and evening is further yet. Is it the midmorning of the same day, or a day later? She really can't tell. She misses the comfort of her home, which she left in a rage. Now she wonders if she should head back and mend ties with her father.

No, she thinks. She should go back to Yavani, and together, they must search for Maani-Ba and bring her back. Then they can go in search of her mother. But she feels like she owes something to the people of Sirvassa, whose lives she touched, and whose lives were upturned because of her arrival on their shores. Trehan, most of all, who promised to be by her side whatever decision she took.

The climb down the hill is steep, but with rough outcroppings and stray but solid rocks littered along the way providing friction, Iyena manages to slide down while keeping momentum. She uses the jutting stones as ledges and fixes her legs in alcoves, making her way across and down, down and across, until she finds solid, plain footing. On the downward climb, she never looked up or down, lest she lose balance. But when she stands on solid ground, with the city's borders a stone's throw away, she hazards a glance up. The cave she has left looks impossible to reach from her vantage point. She looks at her hands, all calloused and coarse and muddy.

She washes her hands and her feet in a stream nearby. The clear, sweet water slithers down the mountain and pools into a clear pond, surrounded by a wooden railing. The area is indeed touched by human hands, and is not as remote as she thought. After quenching her thirst, she takes the dusty road back to the city.

★　★　★

It's only by walking by herself that she realizes how big the city actually is. She remembers the water tank atop which she once sat with Trehan as being on the opposite side of the city. The tank is hardly visible behind the rooftops of Sirvassa. Here, buildings of all sizes are closely packed together, like haphazard clay blocks tossed by a child. This area, sparsely populated, is a far cry from where she lived, where there was a more cohesive design to the living quarters.

As she walks deeper into the city, keeping away from the main roads to avoid unnecessary eyes, she notices the buildings straighten, their materials improving, the people looking bright and healthier, used to a certain standard of living. The gullies and the alleys become much less narrow, and cleaner. The smells go from dirt to defecation to must to roses. But she also notices the ever-increasing presence of the policemen, the Sirvassan Blue Guard.

She reaches a turn she recognizes and a house she has been to before. But there's activity near the house. The Sirvassan Blue Guard is here too. She notices Trehan, standing cluelessly, arguing with the three men with batons and a wooden device that doesn't look like it would do any good. Trehan's mother is also there. She nods alongside the guards, aggressively, while wringing her hands. Iyena takes a side step, and hides behind a wall, to listen closely to what is being discussed.

"...close association with the Caretaker. I won't repeat myself but we will have to confiscate the vials. They have been deemed undesirable properties." The Blue Guard standing closest to the mother-son pair speaks with authority. He has brown hair, parted in the middle, and a mole on his chin.

"But we don't have any of those vials," says Trehan.

"We never had," says Trehan's mother.

"Then we'll have to search your house. We have reason to believe that you are hiding them. All over Sirvassa, people have co-operated with us, and returned their half-finished bottles of Delights. The Garden has been clamped down forever. So I will ask one last time – if you have the vials, please bring them to us."

"We don't have any," says Trehan. "I drank and used all of those Delights."

This annoys the Blue Guard even further. He discusses the matter with his two colleagues, whispering near their ears, while aggressively scratching at his mole. Iyena considers the situation. Could she risk revealing herself? Using the Delight to change the nature of one person's thought had taken a toll on her. She couldn't do that on three people, all together. She is weakened, and hasn't eaten in a long while. Could she try a different tactic?

A thought so unhinged occurs to her that she shudders to even entertain it. It would require a willful suspension of all her ideals, and it would be painful. She would still be exposing herself, but that's a risk she will have to take.

She clenches her fist. She breathes deep the warm, ever flowery-smelling Sirvassan air. Then she walks out of the corner she has been hiding in, into the open.

"Let them be, men," she says, with as much unabashed – even bordering on rude – confidence as she can muster. She doesn't like it, but at that moment, she sounds exactly like her father.

The men turn to look at Iyena. The Blue Guard who spoke to Trehan puckers his face. Iyena steals a glance at Trehan, who is standing confounded at the turn of events. Trehan's mother stifles a gasp. It's probably a mixture of how Iyena looks and the suddenness of her appearance. Iyena wagers on the former.

"And who might you be?" the man asks, then laughs, looking at the other men. "Last time I checked, no street vermin gave orders to us."

"Oh, if you are confused about the chain of command, let me refresh your memory," says Iyena. "I am Iyena Mastafar, the daughter of your boss, Anaris Mastafar."

The men exchange glances. The guard with the mole laughs.

"Why would I take orders from a little girl?" he says, narrowing his eyes at Iyena.

She tilts her head to the side and smirks at the man.

"Because that little girl will tell her father that you harassed his daughter in broad daylight. Are you sure you want to take that risk?"

The three men shift their weights. An uneasy pause swells between them. The guard with the mole takes a step back and whispers something in the ear of his colleague. Iyena grabs this opportunity, not giving them an upper hand.

"And you, boy," she continues. "You still have to prepare the assignment I asked you for in school. The Homegoing Pact and its Consequences on the Culture Wars. Remember, or should I refresh your memory?"

Then, Trehan does something both incredibly stupid, and astonishingly clever. He drops on his knees and crawls to Iyena's feet, grabbing them, making an expression of anguish.

"I am deeply sorry, Bini Iyena," he says. "Please don't tell Tevair Talavi about this. I...." He turns to face his mother. "Ma, please tell Bini I have been a good student. The assignment is just difficult and is taking more time than usual."

"H-he has been a fine student." Trehan's mother stutters at first, but then regains her composure.

The Blue Guard with the mole on his chin takes a deep breath. "Okay, we are done here," he says, eyeing Iyena with an inscrutable expression. "It's clear you have much more important things to discuss. We won't interfere. But we will still give a full report to Kedhran Anaris Mastafar."

"Please do, with haste," says Iyena. "Father loves his reports."

The guard chews his lip and clenches his fist. Then, without another word, he marches away, followed by the two other men.

Trehan gets to his feet, dusting his knees, shaking his fist at the men. Then he looks at Iyena.

"Where were you?"

"Iyena dear," says Trehan's mother. "Please come inside. It looks like you need a shower and a fresh set of clothes."

★ ★ ★

It feels strange to be inside a normal home. The beast inside her craves the jagged and rocky interior of the cave, or the open skies. But Iyena's true nature wants to grab a soft blanket and wrap it around herself, sipping Enjing tea all day long. It's a struggle to balance the two urges. She doesn't know what would happen if the beast ever took over.

But then she remembers. That's precisely what her boon was. To be the beast *and* the human whenever she wanted. However long she wanted.

Trehan sits cross-legged on a sofa, stirring his tea loudly with a metal spoon. His mother sits on a carpet on the floor. Trehan begins by telling Iyena about the events that transpired in her absence. About the Caretaker's capture, and the Garden's closure. About Sirvassa's new Civil Code under a new mayor. Iyena listens to his story intently. He tells her about the two Champions, tall, bronze entities who roam the city at any time they want, though they prefer early mornings.

"Champions?" Iyena asks, staring at Trehan over the rim of her cup.

"*Legends and Lore of the Three Realms*. Chapter Six. 'The Way of the Champion'."

"I remember the lessons," says Iyena curtly. "But why are they here? Aren't they famously averse to politics? Didn't they go into their own exile after the Second Inishti-Abhadi War, vowing never to meddle in political affairs?"

"That's what's written in the books. I have been thinking the same thing, and I am sure many others are too," says Trehan. "It seems like the minister has made some sort of pact with at least two Champions, convincing them to do his bidding."

"Can't be," says Iyena. "The minister can't really offer the Champions anything in return."

"I saw it," begins Trehan's mother, her haunted eyes downcast. "My own eyes. One of them, the one who came first, grabbed a man who was on the rooftop, swung him around like a rag doll and threw him on the road, shattering the cobblestones. The Caretaker tried to fight the Champion, but ce did not relent. I believe it. They are the new gods of our city."

"There's something else," says Trehan in a shaky voice. "I have seen men and women with haunted eyes, roaming alongside the Blue Guard. Like something has been snatched out of them, like they don't belong to the living realm anymore. At the square, when the Caretaker was captured, the loyal Red Guard came to protect the mayor. They even fought the Blue Guard. But most of them were brutally culled down by three of those *things* with black, vapor-like eyes."

"Where is the Caretaker now?"

"They put him in a prison," says Trehan. "Along with the mayor. Next, they plan to destroy the Garden."

"How do you know all this?" says Iyena.

"They told us, with their big speeches. Just the next day."

Iyena takes a breath, which becomes a shudder. It is clear that more than a few days have passed since she took care of the rot. Days in which the entire canvas of the city was repainted in hatred. She looks at her own hands, which are mildly shaking from the news she has heard. Her insides feel cold, but her skin feels clammy.

"Ujita left the city," she says. "With her mother. I bade them goodbye. She knew what was coming. She just knew."

"The winds of hate come not as winds, but a soft wisp scented with a promise of better times," says Trehan's mother. "*Legends and Lore of the Three Realms.*"

"The winds of rebellion are often sharp and brutal, like a gale traveling at the speed of thunder," says Iyena. "The same book, different chapter."

Trehan's mother shakes her head, then closes her eyes. She rubs her knees vigorously with her hands; all her actions say what she can't say. Lines of grief appear on her forehead, as if her own skin is battling against what is raging in her mind. All thoughts of a comfortable life, now locked behind a door that has no key.

She gets up, gathers the cups and the saucers and the spoons, and walks out of the living room, leaving the two teenagers to their own devices. Trehan's eyes follow his mother.

He looks at Iyena and exhales sharply. "Where were you all this time? What happened after we visited the Garden?"

"I left my father," Iyena says, putting into words the action that led to her state. If she had stayed at home that day, she wouldn't have met Ujita, and she wouldn't have met Yavani, she wouldn't have known the truth about her mother, and herself, and she wouldn't have died, unmaking the rot. She wouldn't be here.

Perhaps her father would have convinced her that he wasn't all that bad. That whatever he was doing was better for Sirvassa and the realms.

Perhaps she would be by his side, had she listened to his reasons patiently. But her father's actions had told her more than his words would ever say.

She continues, her voice fiery, yet calm. Brutal, yet gentle. Rage and roses.

"Trehan, I found out that I might not be what I had always thought I was."

She tells him her story.

CHAPTER THIRTY-SEVEN

Iyena Mastafar

"No," says Trehan. "Eborsen's hair, you can't be serious!"

Iyena looks at him, and is yet again reminded of that moment in school when Trehan refused to take her side. It's all written on his face. Doubt, mixed with revulsion. A sliver of rage. But most of all, fear.

"I can show you," says Iyena. She stretches out her arm, and reaches for that dark pit inside her, which has been simmering all this time. Scales form on her skin, sharp as blades, black as tar, with flecks of white. Trehan stifles a sharp scream with the back of his hand. Iyena controls herself, and the scales go back inside her skin.

Trehan staggers back, afraid. Iyena approaches him and takes his hands in hers, pressing them gently, expecting him to shirk them off with anger. But she knows he is capable of more than that. And Trehan, surprisingly, doesn't disappoint. He lets her hold his hand.

"You promised me outside the Garden you would be there, whatever decision I take," she says softly. "Now is the time to honor that promise."

Trehan tries to speak, but can't, fear snatching away his ability to speak coherently.

"Trehan, I am the same Iyena you saw on the first day. A girl who wasn't sure of the ground she stood on. A girl alien to this city. I am an alien still and I am still not sure, but I know one thing. I can't let this city's history get into the hands of the men adamant on unmaking it."

Trehan looks around, as if waiting to ask permission from someone. Then, scratching the bridge of his nose, he takes a deep breath. "Okay, what are we going to do? What *can* we do?"

"We rescue the Caretaker first. And then we stop the Garden from getting destroyed. We tell the truth to the people of Sirvassa."

"But we don't even know *where* they're keeping him prisoner."

"Where else would they keep him? It's the Kalpanin Prison, the jail with no locks. It's in your history books, if only you had read them carefully."

Trehan's mother steps out of another room, carrying a duffel bag and two linen shirts. She drops the bag on the floor and raises the shirts to eye level for Trehan to see.

"Which one do you like better? The red one or the pale yellow one?"

"I.... The pale yellow one..." Trehan says, suddenly scrambling for words. "What's going on?"

"I think the red one would look better on him, though," adds Iyena. "And I have the same question – what's going on?"

"We are leaving, Trehan. Going to Alhassa, to Aunty Sheema."

"When did we decide that?"

"When it became obvious that we can't continue living in this city anymore. We can't keep opening our gates to Sirvassan Blue Guards every second day, when we are just trying to live our lives in peace. Today it's one of those vials of Delights, tomorrow it might be our clothes, our food."

"But that's exactly why you should remain and fight for the city!" says Iyena. But something tells her that her plea falls on deaf ears. "And what makes you think they won't come to Alhassa next?"

"Then we move to some other city that will take us, because that's what Inishti do. Always the refugees."

Trehan's mother's voice is a pained whisper. She jerks both the linen shirts, folds them neatly, and sets them aside.

"Maybe it's just in our destiny to be colonized," she murmurs. "Maybe we are too delusional, or too happy with our own devices. Or maybe we are just too weak to do anything about it."

"Happiness is not our weakness," says Iyena.

"*Our*, you say. You are not even from this city. You are an Abhadi girl." There is no contempt in the older woman's voice, and it's not even personal. But the words come out tinged with red-hot rage, and clench Iyena's heart. This is a woman who has been kind to her. This is what hate does to people.

"Half-Abhadi," says Iyena after a brief pause. "Inishti blood also runs through me. When I came into this city, I only knew so much. But it's astonishing how much one can learn in a span of seven months. Being a half-Abhadi, my own history was kept hidden from me, because it's so full of blood and hate. But now I truly know. I know about all the wars that have been fought in the past, and something tells me there's another one coming. And I am willing to fight to keep safe what is right."

"Fight, really? Look at you. What makes you think *you* can stop anything? That one time you healed my son and you think you are some—"

"Florral," says Iyena. "I am a Florral. My mother was – is – a Florral, the best one, they say."

An uneasy pause stretches between them.

"I won't come between you and your decision," says Iyena, mustering as much courage as she can. A needle prick of anguish pierces her heart. She doesn't want to lock gazes with Trehan at this moment, because this truly looks like goodbye. How many goodbyes will she have to make?

But then she feels the tips of Trehan's fingers brush against her.

"Ma, we must do the right thing," says Trehan. "If we don't try, what will we say to our families who live in other lands? You once told me about our Uncle Yvnar, who led a battalion of four hundred men against ten thousand. He wasn't even a Florral, yet he mustered enough courage to fight a Champion!"

"Uncle Yvnar was also a fool," says Trehan's mother sharply. A vein bulges on her forehead and her hands tremble. She grips the edge of the sofa, closing her eyes, and takes five deep breaths, as if making up her mind. To Iyena, the gap between each of those breaths feels like an eternity.

"Eborsen help me," the old woman says finally, opening her eyes. "If you have decided what you are going to do, then I'll do what all mothers do."

"And what's that?" asks Iyena.

"Help," says Trehan's mother.

★   ★   ★

Trehan's mother gives Iyena the key to open all locks. It's not gold, or silver, or copper, as Iyena expected it would be. It's not even shaped like a key. It's a mere stick, seemingly forged out of grain and stone and sand. Along the length of the stick are five sharp points, which, according to Trehan's mother, hold the true map of every lock's insides.

"How did you make this?" asks Iyena, admiring the key that's not a key.

"This is a copy, but it works as well as the original," says Trehan's mother. "The original was gifted to me." Then she lowers her voice, flits her eyes around, as if afraid the walls will listen to her. "Everyone in Sirvassa knew that I was in possession of this key. That's why the last time someone was imprisoned in that jail, the Red Guard came and confiscated the key. But I had already made a copy. I thought the Blue Guard had come to take this, the copy, away from me. Thankfully it wasn't the case."

"So you knew such a time would come," says Iyena, her voice a cracked whisper, a torrent of emotions running through her mind.

"There's an old Inishti saying," says Trehan's mother. "The debt of an Abhadi's hatred incurs interest with blood. When I first heard it, I didn't pay much heed to it. I was new to Sirvassa, and enamored by the kindness of its people. Even the minor Abhadi population here soon became like our brothers and sisters. Empathy, gentleness, these were the words people lived by. But of course all of that was too good to be true."

"Don't we owe it to ourselves, then, to put a stop to this? To let kindness prevail again?"

"I'm tired now, and I don't want any part in this," the old woman sighs. "Ideally, I would want Trehan to stay away from it as well. But it looks to me like he has made up his mind."

Trehan's mouth opens and then closes. He scratches at the ground with his toe, absently. He looks at Iyena, then back at his mother, like a dove caught in a hunter's trap. Iyena knows what he will say, so she says it for him.

"Your son is with me," says Iyena. "He will be safe."

★ ★ ★

Iyena and Trehan take the narrow road that snakes toward the mountains. To their right, the city opens up in a sprawl of shanties and awnings, the evening market ready to get its bearings on. To their left, close-knit buildings of unruly shapes. A smattering of people on the roads, perhaps trying to pretend everything is normal. It's still a Sirvassan day, and in the large scheme of things, nothing has changed.

They avoid the curious stares of evening shoppers and stray beggars. A group of Sirvassan Blue Guards stand where the road peters off toward a rougher area and leads toward a hilly terrain. It has only been a couple of hours since Iyena took that route to enter the city, and now it is manned by the guards. She takes a dozen side steps, very quickly, almost pulling Trehan toward her.

"Will you go easy?" says Trehan, balancing on his heels, almost teetering on the sidewalk. Iyena is standing at the opening of a alley, her eyes focused on the Sirvassan Blue Guards.

"Come inside," she says, completely ignoring Trehan's plea. Trehan shrugs and follows Iyena inside the alley. Iyena exhales sharply as she rethinks the plan.

"The Kalpanin Prison is not easy to find," she says, as if reminding herself. "Firstly, it has no walls. It's basically burrowed deep into the ground. As such, the cells have no windows. *That* way is not the best way...."

"Are you talking to yourself?" Trehan asks incredulously.

Iyena stops, frowning at Trehan. She sits down on the concrete, leans against the wall, and sighs.

"I am sorry," she says.

"It's okay," says Trehan. "I'm sure there's another way. We just need to find it."

Iyena crosses her arms on her knees and buries her head in them. There is a way. She could simply turn back into the beast and soar across the ocean toward an unknown country. Turn her gaze away from the atrocities and pretend they never happened. Who would blame her? Besides, the more time she spends in the body of the beast, the more her morals will get reshaped. The beast only thinks of its next meal, and the wind that rips through its scales as it flies. The righteous words she spoke just a moment ago come back to haunt her. Is it too late to turn back? Who would ask her?

Trehan snaps his fingers, once, twice. Iyena looks up.

"Iyena, that man has been looking at us since we entered this alley," he whispers, pointing a shaky finger toward the road. A tall man with gaunt cheeks, wearing a faded blazer and cotton pants, stands across the road, at the edge of the sidewalk.

Iyena grips Trehan's finger and forces it down.

"Don't point," she whispers back. She looks around. There's a dead end to their right, where the alley ends in a high wall, topped by iron spikes. To their left, the open road, where it would be easy for them to be spotted.

"Come with me," says Iyena, making up her mind. She gets up and starts walking toward the dead end. Trehan's uncertain footsteps echo in the quiet alley.

"He's following us, where are we going?" Trehan's voice is at the edge of panic. Iyena places her hand against the hard, concrete wall. The surface is cold, and slightly wet to the touch. She feels a sticky residue of slime on her hands, but can't see it. A musty odor persists in the air.

"Are you going to climb the wall?"

"No," says Iyena. She closes her eyes and senses the nature of the wall. Its depth, its flaky concrete slowly dying inside, the bricks crumbling under the weight of age. Behind the wall, there's an absence. It's not a true dead end.

She imagines a gap, just enough for them to get through. A door. Then she reshapes the wall, the brick, the concrete, into nothingness. Vapors curl out of the brick wall and rise. Bricks crumble and fold upon themselves. Stones rub against stones and then vanish.

Trehan gasps, as a path appears. Another gully, wider, opening toward another road, on the opposite side.

"Hurry," says Iyena, and walks inside the gap. Trehan follows her.

When they cross, Iyena turns around. The man quickens his pace and enters the alley. Iyena places her hand on the bricks that had folded, and reimagines the absence into a solid presence. The bricks respond, unfold, refold, the stones rise up, the vapors condense, and soon the gap is sealed. It's not perfect, but enough to stop whoever was approaching them.

She looks at Trehan, who is standing with his mouth agape.

"What did you just do?"

Iyena's heart clenches and she feels a sudden cold at the end of her fingertips. She grabs the wall and takes a breath. She feels drained, unable to continue.

"Are you all right, Iyena?" says Trehan, concerned.

"I am fine," says Iyena. "This happens, nothing to worry about."

But then, behind her, motes of dust begin to fall from the wall she sealed. A spray of concrete, a fall of bricks. Trehan pales.

"We have to keep moving," says Iyena.

The alley opens to a wider road, filled with even more crowds. Iyena had not realized it earlier, but they are now in the main Sirvassan market, the north end of which peters away toward the small road that leads toward the Garden of Delights. This is a road she knows. Confidently, she steps out from the alley, onto the cobblestoned sidewalk, as the wall she repaired continues to crumble under the effects of age and magic.

As Iyena scurries along the sidewalk, Trehan matches her step, teetering close to where the road begins but still keeping away from the bangle sellers and the fruit sellers and the cloth merchants, who eye them with curiosity. A woman reaches out to Trehan, offering a packet of sweets, yelling her discounted price in a shrill voice. Trehan shrugs her off, and catches up with Iyena, who is walking with a single-minded devotion.

Iyena has her gaze fixed on the upcoming market square, where the city truly opens up. She remembers the busy East Road that winds down toward the Temple of Eborsen. Flanked on both sides by tall marble pillars with handcrafted shapes of flowers atop them, the road is a symbol of true Sirvassan majesty. Today, the road is empty, as most of the population seems concentrated in the north and the west. Perhaps no one is in the mood to offer anything to the Temple of Eborsen. Perhaps they have all stopped believing in their gods.

Iyena and quickens her pace, as Trehan struggles to keep up with her. She takes a sharp left turn, leaving the sidewalk, crossing the street, excusing herself, rubbing shoulders with a busy, stinking crowd. She reaches for a pole and grabs it, jumping onto a different sidewalk.

She looks around. Trehan catches up to her, heaving, panting.

"Where are we going?" he asks, bent, grabbing his knees, catching his breath.

"The Temple of Eborsen," she says. "If there's one person in this city who is incorruptible, who might just be able to help us, it would be the Priestess of the Temple."

"I have only ever spoken to the junior priests, there," says Trehan. "When did you…? Uh, leave it. Never mind."

She starts walking in the direction of the temple, as Trehan follows her. But then, out of the corner of her eye, she senses a movement. She turns around to look, and immediately regrets her decision. There's a smattering of Sirvassan Blue Guards to their right, some standing idly beneath awnings, chatting with vegetable sellers, inspecting their wares, some walking casually down the road. The civilians mingle with them with a jittery ease.

One tall Sirvassan Blue Guard catches Iyena's gaze. He whispers something to his partner, and points toward both of them.

"Oye, stop!" the guard screams. The onlookers turn their heads. More guards join the one who had pointed, and soon a wave of blue begins to descend upon them.

CHAPTER THIRTY-EIGHT

Iyena Mastafar

For a fleeting moment, Iyena considers letting go, letting the beast take over, and soaring into the sky, taking Trehan with her. But that would be a mistake. They have attracted enough attention already. To convert now would be futile and counterproductive.

So they run. As fast as their young legs can carry them.

Walking stealthily, wriggling between gaps, comes easily to Iyena. In Alderra, where the crowd took the shape of a mammoth wave, she would venture into the market to get pineapples and soltan fruit for Sern Aradha, whose myriad tasks for her often took her to the four corners of the city. Later, when Iyena complained, Sern Aradha simply said, "Don't you know the city in your heart by now?" And Iyena responded with a blank stare, because all those water runs, those haggles with tailors, those fights with the blacksmith, were for a reason. Her feet knew each stone on the road and the direction they came from.

But due to the sheer size of Alderra, and the population, she never had enough space to run freely. Now, as Trehan's feet catch wind alongside her, she is forced to run, and the sensation is liberating.

Even if the run is not for joy, but for her life.

For every stride they cover, the guards cover two. The road narrows, and the shops grow sparse. Iyena can feel their breath on her neck. She wants to just stop. Her legs feel like blocks of lead, and her thighs cramp up. Her stomach is ready to heave whatever she had to eat at Trehan's home.

And then she bumps into someone and comes to a harsh, jarring stop. Trehan slides, tries to balance himself, but falls on the road. A sickening scrape of skin against concrete, and then a pained gasp from Trehan. Iyena feels strong arms grabbing her and pushing her aside. Before she can understand what's going on, Iyena is behind the figure she bumped into.

The figure is wearing a shawl. It's the same figure who had followed them in the alley.

"What's the hurry, men?"

The voice is gentle, almost caring. Iyena recognizes it, too intimately. Because it's a part of her. Frail and pudgy hands come out of the shawl, carrying a vial of amber liquid each. The Blue Guards stagger back, fear writ on their faces. One guard, though, steps gingerly forward, and raises his arm.

"Hand us those," he says. "Those items are deemed undesirable now."

"Who said so?" asks Maani-Ba, removing the shawl, revealing her kind, ever-familiar face. Iyena's heart leaps inside her ribcage. "I find them very desirable, in circumstances such as these."

"Batons at the ready, men!" says the guard at the front. Immediately, with refined, precise motions, the Blue Guards bring out their weapons. Hard, metallic, gleaming.

"We don't want to hurt you," says the guard, raising one hand. "Please give us those."

"Cowards, all of you, fighting an old woman and two children with batons," says Maani-Ba with barely a hint of rage. But Iyena knows it's simmering inside her. It has been simmering for a long while.

She removes the stoppers from both vials and drinks both the Delights.

"Stand back," she says. "*I* don't want to hurt *you*."

But the men charge at her. And Maani-Ba claps, ever so gently. A wave emanates from the point of impact of her palms and rages toward the men, swirling around them, carrying them up, up, and away. At first it looks like the men will smash on the concrete, landing in a mangled, bloody heap of bones and muscles. But the wind carries them and places them softly in front of a shop, still in a heap, but mostly of entangled limbs and confused faces.

Maani-Ba turns around and gathers Iyena in a hug. Warmth gushes through Iyena like it has never before. She thought she had no family left in the world anymore. And now, Maani-Ba is here, and for a moment it looks like everything will be all right again. Tears stream down Iyena's cheeks, and Maani-Ba wipes them away with her shawl.

"Are...are you...are you a Florral?" asks Iyena, her voice shaking between sobs.

"I am," says Maani-Ba. "And I know that you are too."

★   ★   ★

In the end, they hail a carriage. Maani-Ba's instructions to the Rhisuan beast consist of whispers and clicks, a complicated jargon of directions, to which the beast responds with an assuring grunt. Iyena could never manage that level of accuracy, despite enjoying giving directions to the beasts. The last time Iyena was inside the carriage, she made up her mind to leave Sirvassa. Instead, she ended up saying goodbye to Ujita.

The tarped, musty interior of the carriage feels comforting to Iyena as the carriage ambles along the rocky Sirvassan road. Maani-Ba looks at the wound on Trehan's leg, which is now a patchy brown. There isn't a lot of blood, but the gash is long, running from his knee to his ankle. Iyena tries to do what she did to him before, reimagining the scrapes and the wound to become whole skin once again. But she is feeble, and the Delight flows out of her in a weak manner, sewing the wound in places, opening it in some others. Trehan winces as he motions for Iyena to stop.

"I am sorry," says Iyena.

"It's okay, it's okay," says Trehan. "The sound of the scrape was worse than it actually is."

"Boy, you don't have to come with us if you don't want to," says Maani-Ba. "We have a dangerous task ahead of us."

"No, I'll come," says Trehan, with whatever pride he can muster in that moment.

Maani-Ba shakes her head, then looks at Iyena.

"I know you have a lot of questions," she says. "Yavani must have answered some of them."

"You never told me about Yavani. You held the truth from me all this time, why?"

Maani-Ba's lips pucker. Her shoulders tighten, and sharp lines appear on her forehead. "I always wanted to tell you. But with your father around, I didn't want to broach the topic. Any topic concerning your mother would put him on edge, *especially* her dabbling in Florrachemy. But when things started to go bad in the city, I began to find ways of giving the information to you. You think I didn't notice when you casually turned things into other things? I had my eye upon you since the day you visited the Garden. I *wanted* you to visit the Garden, and if *I* were your guardian, you wouldn't have to forge any signatures."

Iyena breathes heavily. "Father said he had to let you go on a vacation. It didn't add up."

"Anaris's mountain of lies becomes ever taller," Maani-Ba says. "I always believed he would turn over a new leaf. I expected grief, shame, at least something to catch up to him, to show him the error of his ways. When he coppergrammed me from Alderra that he was visiting with you, I couldn't have been happier! But I soon came to know his intentions. Especially when I had a glimpse of that monstrosity. Things took a darker turn when Minister Yayati kept visiting. He spent countless nights holed up inside his study and would only appear in the morning, his eyes sunken."

"He.... He orchestrated the attack on the ship. I was almost killed. He is no father to me."

Maani-Ba frowns. She clearly hadn't known that. The information hits her like an ocean wave. Rage storms to her face.

"One day, I confronted him," says Maani-Ba. "That was the day I left. I had to warn Yavani about the developments in the city. I had to warn the Caretaker."

"What happened? Why didn't you?"

"First, I lost my way. Then I stumbled into a group of Stigmars."

"Those zombies," says Trehan. "Their eyes…Eborsen bless me… their eyes."

"Rotten users of Florrachemy. We drink Delights, they smoke it. I injured myself heavily while warding them off. I spent more than a week at a Healer's place. She was thankful that the petal-rain had arrived in droves just last week, and was able to heal me. Then, when you…." Maani-Ba seems to gather strength to utter her next word.

Iyena squeezes her hands.

"I died. But now I am here."

"Yavani came to me. We both saw your body sink to the ground, and we both couldn't do anything about it. I wept in Yavani's arms like a little child, but I knew in my heart that Eborsen would make you come back. You wouldn't just *die*. You cured a rot that threatened Eborsen's best creation, and the Half-Formed God is always gracious with boons."

Iyena wouldn't call it that. If there were an impossible definition that toed the line between a boon and a curse, then that would be it.

"I think we've taken a smoother road now," says Trehan. Iyena can feel it. The carriage hasn't bumped in quite a while. She glances outside. Gone are the cramped spaces of the city, the awnings and small doors, the blocky buildings. The smooth, tar road is surrounded by stooped ferns, grass, and nettles. One side curves slightly upward in a gentle slope of a rocky hill, not too dissimilar from the one Iyena had descended.

"This is Hnirama, a lost district," says Maani-Ba. "Early Sirvassan settlers used to live here. Later it was named as a heritage area. Not many people from the city visit this place, though. Even later, an angry old mayor had the bright idea of converting a performance area into a prison. It was her idea of poetic irony, imprisoning the singers and dancers who raised a voice against her, in the same place where they created their best works. Sirvassa, and other Inishti strongholds, have had their fair share of populist autocrats."

"There's so much stuff I recently got to know against my will," says Trehan.

The carriage shudders to a stop. Maani–Ba yanks the tarp off to look outside. Iyena leans toward her and follows her gaze. They are still in the same area, albeit with more dense shrubbery around them. To their left is a sheer fall to a curving road; Iyena realizes that the carriage has taken them up a hilly road. But why the sudden stop?

Maani–Ba steps out, and Iyena follows her. Trehan's face is half hidden inside, half out, and his face contorts in bewilderment, as he seems to consider joining the women.

In front of the carriage, the road curves and is blocked by a mammoth garland of nettles, brambles, vine, and thorn. An impossibility in the middle of nowhere, a nightmare in green, in broad daylight. The vines curl and rise, wrapping the brambles in a dark embrace. The nettles hiss and slither, making the thorns partners in their monstrosity. It looks like an entrance to a dark orchard. The Rhisuan beast grunts in pain, then simply sits on its haunches, refusing to go any farther.

"What's this?" says Iyena, walking slowly toward the oddity in the middle of the road. "Did we lose our way?"

Black smoke oozes out of the garland, its tendrils reaching toward Iyena. She doesn't stagger back; instead, she walks toward the smoke, inexorably pulled. It draws her ever nearer, playing tricks in her mind.

"Iyena, don't."

Maani–Ba's cry is feeble. Trehan's scream is a mere whisper. The smoke curls around Iyena and pulls her toward the garland, toward the door of the dark garden. Blackness soon engulfs her.

Inside, the road continues as it would have even if the garland of nettles and brambles weren't there. But the sky has stooped to dusk, here, and the road tapers off farther ahead. On the road, blackened petals are strewn haphazardly, some broken, some torn. Lilies, and roses, and tulips, all the same monochrome shade, spring out of the wall of the dark hill that slopes upward on her left. She keeps moving ahead. The road snakes to her left, and then disappears into a swath of more algal green. Here, moss lies suspended a few inches from the ground, along with stones and dirt.

A few paces ahead, a stone outcropping, then gray stairs, then an entrance, a gash in the rocks like a festering wound, with blackness oozing out of numerous cracks. She knows it's the prison, but it's also something else.

A hunchbacked figure comes out of the shadows from her left, as if detaching from the grassy slope of the hill. It offers a frail, pockmarked hand to her. But then the hand becomes pale, then creamy white, devoid of any age marks, young. The figure straightens itself and reveals its face to Iyena.

Alvos Midranil. Are you Alvos Midranil?

Iyena stifles a gasp. The face is eyeless, mouthless, a mask of cracked porcelain. Frazzled nothings jut out of its bare head, nail-thin shadows of what was once hair.

"I am not Alvos Midranil," says Iyena.

Shame. Alvos would have loved this Garden of Sorrows. I sense his presence around these parts, and I grow weary of the things I have to do for him to listen to me.

Then the figure grabs Iyena by her neck, and brings its mouthless face ever closer to her.

You. You look like someone willing to listen to reason. You see I was once not like this. I was so much more. I was a Champion. I could move the earth with a mere afterthought. I could reshape entire continents. Change the shape of roads that travelers took.

Iyena shrugs off the wraith-hands and staggers back.

"Don't touch me," she says aggressively.

I have to touch you to see you. To sense you. Are you a Florral? Only a true Florral can help me. Someone like Alvos Midranil.

"What are you?"

I told you. I was a Champion, once. My name once rhymed with death and the thing you use to color a fabric. But then I took a Delight, which corrupted me from the inside. I took the Delight to fight with Alvos, but he bested me. The Delight itself took my nature and twisted it. I realized one can't be a Champion and a Florral both. It's like oil and water. They don't mix. I have spent years trying to find Alvos, but to no end. I prayed to the Goddess of Form and Shape, the Goddess of Passage, the God of Love, and above all the Half-Formed God. But they are all in their slumber. In my vengeance and my rage, I created a blackness that took root deep underground. A rot. From that rot, I formed this Garden.

"You...*you* created the rot. You were behind all those—"

I created the rot, yes. But I found I couldn't bring it here myself. And so, I used someone. A pawn. A pawn closer to the king. A person closest to Alvos. And oh, how gullible he was. He followed what I said like a baby. But things didn't exactly go as I had wanted them to. So I came back to finish what I started. And now, I am trapped. Free me! Free me!!

The figure attacks Iyena, lunging at her, clawing at her throat and face. At the figure's touch, Iyena is plunged deep into a sorrow of her own. Nothing exists in the world, no Delight. Only an unending morass of anguish. Iyena falls, falls further into the deep pits of despair, as the figure digs its sharp fingers into her skin, its being becoming her being, tendrils of darkness slowly pulling at her insides, gouging out her soul, looking to end it.

Until they meet another soul, the soul of the beast inside Iyena.

Iyena's insides harden. Rage simmers inside her belly. The rage swells, taking her organs, reshaping them, her skeleton making room, expanding, her spine reshaping, her hands and her feet becoming claws and sharp wings and talons, and her face metamorphosing into the monster she doesn't want to be.

And with her talons, she grabs the figure, and rips apart its face. Then, bit by bit, she takes away every shred of what the figure once was, a living, breathing entity, and unmakes it, eating it, pulling away all viscera, bone, sinew, and blood, until nothing remains of it except a dark blob on the ground.

Then she claws at the nettles and the dark flowers and eats them too, as their darkness becomes her, but dissipates inside her. She takes the Sorrows of the Garden, all the hate, and turns it back into Delights. The dusk of the skies becomes a bright afternoon again, and the curving road joins the road she had left behind, the black garland of thorns disappearing in smoke and ash, and a bitter fragrance of burning flowers.

Ahead of her, the Kalpanin Prison, a gash in the mountainside. Guarding it, two Blue Guards, and two Stigmars, the black-hollow-eyed consumers of the Delight. The beast in her takes over completely. She shrieks at them, then swoops down upon them, a winged black death. The guards she makes short work of, swiping at them with her talons, and they stumble over the edge of the hills, falling to their inevitable deaths. The Stigmars she shreds, bone by bone, their dark Delight no match for her sheer power.

She shifts her gaze to the two figures that accompanied her, standing a few paces behind, and the beast that carried them. They are family. But they are also food.

The smaller figure, the boy, runs in fear, his face aghast at the sight of the monster that she has become. She reaches out to him, to stop him. No, she can change back, this isn't who she is, not completely. She is still Iyena Mastafar of Alderra and Sirvassa.

The smaller beast, too, hunkers to its feet, and backs away in panic, the tarp and the wood of the carriage hitting the side of the hill and getting half dismantled, barely holding shape. She tries to stop the figure too. *No, you are not food. But you are. But you are not! Stop!*

The stout figure of the woman stands her ground. She would understand. She reaches for Iyena with a caring hand. She would always understand.

No, she won't. She will leave you, too, like your mother left you.

It's the dark Delight speaking, the Sorrow, a part of which hung around, latching on to her heart, the part that she didn't change, the Nettle, the Thorn.

She grabs the woman in her talons, threatening to tear apart that old skin, hoping to find a good morsel of meat inside that ancient cage of bones and muscle. But the woman touches her claws with a gentle hand, the kindest smile never leaving her face.

She could just rip her heart out and eat it.

But in the tussle of Delight and Sorrow, Delight wins in the end.

★   ★   ★

Iyena lies panting on the stone ground, near a dense outcropping. The Garden of Sorrows is no more. The path is clear. The road still tapers off, but bends to the east, dips, and finishes in a black gap nestled in the mountains. The Kalpanin Prison.

Maani-Ba holds Iyena's hand. Iyena sobs, burying her head into Maani-Ba's chest. The slow rise and fall, rise and fall, reminds her of the times she slept in her mother's arms. This is similar, but not that similar. Maani-Ba is cradling her, the young girl. But she is also cradling a monster, she thinks.

Maani-Ba is giving her love despite the murderer she has become.

She doesn't deserve Maani-Ba. Iyena doesn't deserve them.

She gives the key to Maani-Ba. "Use this to open the door with no locks. You will recognize it when you see it," she says. Then she shifts out of Maani-Ba's warm embrace, and stands to her feet.

"What are you doing, Iyena? Where are you going?"

"I can't be with you," she says, her eyes red, her throat struggling to make words. "I will...I will always try to kill the people I love."

"Iyena, child, you can't be alone," says Maani-Ba.

"I can," says Iyena. "I have always been alone."

Saying this, Iyena runs away from Maani-Ba, toward the ledge, toward the looming drop to the edges of the city below. Maani-Ba screams her name, but Iyena doesn't hear. With a single-minded purpose, Iyena jumps over the ledge, and falls to the depths below. She lets the air whip past her face, her hair, and lets gravity do its job. Then, midair, she completely lets go of her true nature, and the monster takes over.

Inches before hitting the ground, her wings come back out. She glides over grass, rocks, and the stony, rough-hewn edges of the road that leads to the city. She takes full flight and soars over the rooftops of Sirvassa.

CHAPTER THIRTY-NINE

The Caretaker

Sounds.

Hard tapping on the floor, but not measured, assured, like the soldiers before. The steps are hurried, uncertain, like a rat scurrying across broken cement. The steps come closer. A hiss, then a flame flickers to life. The Caretaker narrows his eyes, allowing the sudden brightness to diffuse so he can see.

"Alvos Midranil? The Caretaker of the Garden of Delights?"

The lantern illuminates the small, round face of an old woman. She is almost exactly like Yavani, but a bit smaller in height, and with a more confident gait.

"Who are you? How did you get here? What do you want?" Mayor Illyasi barks from the other cell. The woman ignores him, and instead, moves to the cell occupied by the Caretaker.

The Caretaker shuffles to his feet and reaches for the bars.

"The mayor has lost his sense of hospitality," he says, managing humor in misery. "Yes, I am Alvos Midranil, although I don't go by that name any longer. It's for reasons I would rather not go into, for now."

"My name is Marina Alsafar," she says. "I am a dear old friend of the woman you know as the Seedmaster, and the dear aunt of a girl you might know as Iyena Mastafar."

"The girl who stopped the rot," sighs the Caretaker. "I will forever be indebted to her. I will never find peace when I finally go into the halls of Eborsen to rest, knowing that I caused her demise."

"She is alive," says the woman. "So you can stop pitying yourself. Now, let's hurry. We have to stop them from destroying the Garden of Delights. The minister has already given orders to the Blue Guards to march toward the Garden at midnight."

Saying this, Marina Alsafar jangles a bundle of keys in front of the Caretaker. A wild bunch, silver and bronze and gold, they shimmer against the low light.

Mayor Illyasi laughs, then laughs some more, before going on another patronizing spree. "These cells were made to keep in the worst criminals the realm had ever seen, woman. Thought of by a king who was madder than all the madness in this land combined. These cells aren't *locked* by ordinary locks. They're fused."

"He's being unnecessarily rude, but also right," says the Caretaker. "There are no locks here."

"That's why they can't just be opened by a normal key," says Marina Alsafar. She takes out a bronze, multi-patterned stick. A scratching of metal against metal tells the Caretaker that the woman has some sort of a plan in mind. Another metallic groan purrs through the cell bars and then a harsh click. Marina grabs a cell bar and pulls it toward her with all her might. The Caretaker pushes it, using his legs. Rusting iron groans and scrapes against a cement ground as the cell door slides open. The Caretaker walks out of the cell.

"Illyasi, you have to promise us to be more mature and polite if you want to come with us. Trulio, come, let's go—"

He pauses, his eyes tearing away from Illyasi, darting inside his own cell, finding only the absence of his apprentice and friend clawing at his heart. The image that had haunted him whenever he closed his eyes was of his dear apprentice lying mangled on the broken road, killed by the hand of a Champion. Trulio, whom he had let in, all those years ago when he was just a small, hungry child. Trulio, whose young and nimble fingers he had held and traced the exact arc for opening the stone door of the Garden. Trulio, who was quick to judge people, but was gentle at heart. Trulio, who learned quickly, and failed harder, and fell harder, but rose stronger, always.

Trulio, whose quips, laced with his trademark wit and charm, would never fail to bring a smile to the face of the Caretaker. Trulio, who did as he was told, without complaining. Trulio, who is no more.

He clenches his fist, his nails digging into his palm, and closes his eyes. His knees crumble beneath him. He hugs himself, and for the first time in many years, wails like a little child. His body shakes from grief, as he sinks lower onto the ground. A gentle touch on his left shoulder, and his wail descends into a soft sob. He turns to look at Marina Alsafar, the woman who has just freed him.

"Alvos Midranil, I am sorry for your loss," she says. Illyasi stumbles out of his own cell and gazes mournfully at him, his face losing all the madness and all the snark after witnessing the Caretaker's grief. "May Eborsen shower his petals on him," says the mayor. "He was always a gentle and amusing presence, your apprentice."

"Thank you, Mayor," says the Caretaker. Then he turns toward Marina Alsafar. "I can't express in enough words my gratitude, Marina."

"You can express it by saving *your* Garden with me," says Marina with a twinkle in her eyes. She wheels around and starts walking toward the door of the prison.

★　　★　　★

A thin passage that leads from the darkness of the cells rises sharply into the light. Stone steps are etched into the walls, leading up to a broader area where the main guards of the prison once sat. Now, as they climb out of the narrow, breathless space, which smells of mold and must, and arrive at the foyer, they see mere bodies, lying prone on the cold floor, their eyes dreamy, glassy, their mouths whispering nothings.

The Caretaker straightens his faded kurta and looks at Marina. "Is this your doing?"

She nods dismissively, as they step around the fallen soldiers. The Caretaker doesn't pay heed to Mayor Illyasi's oddly specific complaints about the color of mold on the prison walls, and the cold draft of air from the outside, even the size of the shoes Marina is wearing. A man who is a hair's breadth from losing his mind completely would talk about such facile things.

Outside, the world looks blasted and born anew. More and more bodies are strewn, some on the grassy slope where the prison is housed, some on the narrow road that leads outward. Black things grow in the grass, and it looks like their incessant growth has been cut short by a magical hand. Remnants of broken flowers and broken bodies lie on the cold cement. As they skirt the slope, the Caretaker's gaze falls on a group of torn nettles, blackened at their edges, as if a rot has taken hold of their stem and grown upward. He recognizes the blackness, but not the flower. He picks up a nettle and examines it. The Garden of Delights never grows nettles because it isn't a plant that ever gives a suitable Delight. It is stubborn, sharp-edged, and often poisonous. But the slope around him looks like it has become a playground of such rejected flowers and plants that couldn't find a home inside the Garden of Delights.

"Iyena fought a vile thing here," says the woman. "It took a lot from her. I couldn't help, because she won't have it any other way."

The Caretaker pockets the nettle, making a mental note of examining it further.

"I will write a stern note to the Vaishwam Chair," says Mayor Illyasi. "My coppergram will sing the bloody stubbornness out of them. How can they—"

Marina places a finger on Illyasi's neck, and his next words are throttled in his throat. When he tries to speak, only wind comes out, nothing else. The Caretaker can't help but be amused. If Marina hadn't done that, he would have done the same, but perhaps he is far too accepting of Illyasi's quirks, having known him so long. Perhaps, he would have hesitated.

"Daffodil," says the Caretaker. "A potent potion imparting such a Delight. I don't remember giving it out to anyone in recent times."

"I am a Florral, Alvos," says Marina simply. "Let's hurry now. Minister Yayati will be gathering the entire Blue Guard."

"I won't be surprised if he calls one of the Champions to do the job of destroying the Garden," says the Caretaker. "Why send the Blue Guard when one person could do the job with a swipe of their hands? It would send a message. It sounds like something Yayati would do."

A moment passes between the two, as Marina considers this. Her eyes swell, a faint sliver of fear crosses her face, and lines appear on her forehead. But then her expression softens.

"I trust your judgment," says Marina. "I am here to help."

"How powerful are you?" asks the Caretaker, after a minute of consideration.

"Look, I can't open portals and walk through them like the Florrals of the past, like my sister. But I have the essence of many Delights, and can hold my own."

"That's both specific and vague enough," says the Caretaker. "I myself find much of my abilities waning, owing to old age."

"What do we do about *him*, though?" She points toward the mayor, who looks like he has been choking to death on his own unsaid words.

"We put him to sleep in my room, once we reach it," says the Caretaker, touching the mayor's shoulders reassuringly, but sternly. "My friend needs a good rest."

Mayor Illyasi winces at the Caretaker's words, but then helplessly falls in line.

Afternoon fades into late evening by the time they skirt around the hilly road and enter the city. The Caretaker leads them through dirty, well-trodden alleys between densely packed homes, where cracks in roads are filled with muddy water and curdled milk, and the air smells of Rhisuan shit and vomit. The mayor tries to show his dissatisfaction by occasional grunts but can't complain with words. Instead, he keeps tugging at the Caretaker's shawl like a little child. Marina walks along with the Caretaker, nary an expression on her face.

By the time the streets of Sirvassa are splashed with a pale moonlight, they reach the dusty road that leads to the Garden.

They wait near a corner, to act as soon as there's a sign of activity. But the area is morbidly quiet and deserted. Not even a chirp of a fell-bird rings through the air, no footsteps, no whispers, no sound. It's so quiet that the Caretaker can hear the rhythm of his own pulse. His eyes go toward the ribbon on the pole, frayed, dull green now with years of exposure to wind and dust and grimy hands.

"Something doesn't feel right," says the Caretaker.

"He declared in so many words that he was going to destroy the Garden today."

"There's one more thing, though," says the Caretaker. "One could enter the compound by twisting a knot on that ribbon. One could destroy my laboratory, and my living quarters. But no one knows the pattern to the door of the Garden, except me."

"What are you implying?" says Marina.

The Caretaker replays in his head the events that have transpired before. Minister Yayati is clever, but also fond of a spectacle. If he wanted to destroy the Garden, he would also want to see it with his own eyes, show it to the world, as his bidders uprooted the flowers and desecrated the grass. It is clear to the Caretaker by now that the rot wasn't his doing, but it came just at the right time for him to take advantage. So, even if he sent the Champion to destroy the Garden, that wouldn't be enough of an event for him. No, he would want something bigger.

Then, it hits him, plain as daylight.

"He wants me inside," says the Caretaker with a heavy sigh. "He wants me to open the Garden."

Marina looks at the Caretaker with a pained expression. She shakes her head, even as Mayor Illyasi struggles and chokes with pleading eyes.

"Did we fall into his trap?"

"No," says the Caretaker. "This time, he falls into ours."

★　　★　　★

They enter the Garden's compound when it's still ten minutes to midnight. The moon hangs low in the sky, and numerous stars litter the blackness like fine ash. Marina looks at the sky, her pupils glinting, red tendrils of fatigue streaking the whites of her eyes. But soon, a thin smile crosses her face. "Tonight is ominous," she says. "It's the Night of the Unending Stars."

The Caretaker looks at the sky, and truly, the stars are too many to count, sparkling from their genesis-light from eons ago, some dying, many living, their shine thriving, soon making the dark night sky bright as day. And the words spoken by a goddess ring in his ears once again.

Watch out for the Night of the Unending Stars and you will know.

The Caretaker's heart speeds up as he remembers his tryst with Goddess Ina, the curse that had spilled out from her lips and latched on to his soul. The curse he had been trying to get rid of all these years, waiting for the Night of the Unending Stars, waiting for *someone*, waiting for a boon.

And now the night is here.

The Caretaker turns toward the Garden and makes the opening pattern on the stone. The door opens, and the Caretaker is met with an ever-familiar, friendly whiff of the Bacillus Rose, and the Tulip of the Seven, the flowers of the First Sector.

Then, a rush of footsteps. Loud. Brash. Confident. Across the narrow path that leads to the Garden, the Caretaker sees three figures, two tall and imposing, one short. The two Champions, and the minister. And by a cold command, both Champions glide toward the Caretaker. The minister follows in their wake, walking with a dignified gait.

"I knew you would come here," says the minister. "Didn't you wonder *why* there are no guards around this area? In fact, I removed *most* of the Blue Guard from around your prison too. Because the dead hands of fate are powerless to keep the Caretaker away from his precious Garden."

"I'll be here, always, to protect the Garden," says the Caretaker. "From pests and vermin and rot. From people like you."

The air rings with the midnight chime of the Temple of Eborsen. For a moment, the minister looks in the direction of the sound, and so do the two Champions, but not in respect, rather in annoyance. When the ringing stops, they turn their attention back to the Caretaker.

The minister gasps in shock.

The Caretaker feels a renewed surge of blood in his veins as his muscles tighten around his rapidly changing skeleton, the gray of his hair becomes jet-black, the marrow in his bones gushing with a vigor he had decades ago. He crosses his hands, and then immediately spreads them apart. Dust rises from the ground and coils around the two Champions, taking the minister in its cold embrace. The three figures rise in the air as the Caretaker brings out another Delight from his blood. Holding the three bodies, he fixes his eyes on the minister and enters his mind, just like he did to the Champion Tyi, all those years ago. He finds all the elements of sanity and hate inside Yayati and twists them. His head hangs to the side, as his eyes glaze over.

He tries the same with the Champions. But inside their heads he finds not blood and veins, but a network of metal and wires, running with a different Delight, perhaps not even Delight, but another fuel source. Something he can't change, because he can't map his mind with theirs.

They aren't Champions at all.

And suddenly, he loses all his focus as his hands go limp. The three figures crash on the ground. The minister scrambles to his feet and finds refuge beneath a marble pillar, terrified out of his senses. But then the two un-Champions move inexorably toward the Caretaker. One picks him up like a rag doll. The Caretaker knows they can't channel what the Champions have, but they still contain brute force and the machinations of Albuchemy inside them. They can still hurt.

And hurt they do. One un-Champion picks up the terrified mayor and hurls him across the compound. He hits the base of a tree with a sickening thud and limply falls to the ground. The Caretaker screams and channels the purest, angriest Delight inside him. But before he can do anything, the other Champion throttles him. With one hand he picks up the Caretaker by his neck, and with the other, he picks up Marina. The un-Champion's dead eyes, a bulge of copper, a glint of silver, look at the Caretaker without mercy, without judgment, operating under the orders of a different entity, programmed only to kill.

The other un-Champion races inside the Garden and begins the handiwork of uprooting the flowers. First, he grabs the Tulip and yanks the flower mercilessly out of the ground. Then, like a child given free rein, he jumps around, destroying everything, stomping the flowers to mulch.

The second un-Champion's metal hands tighten around the Caretaker's throat, crushing it, about to find the jugular to finally squeeze the life out of it.

"Turain-Two, cease."

Its grip becomes limp. The Caretaker falls to the ground, and as does Marina. She chokes and sputters, and crawls toward the Caretaker, who massages his throat as bile sputters out of his mouth.

"Turain-One, cease."

The first Champion stops inside the Garden, mid-activity, one hand in the air, holding a flower, his torso bent, his legs splayed wide apart. The voice that stopped them was the voice of a man, a cold command.

"Anaris?" Marina whispers, and looks toward the entrance.

But the figure that stands near the entrance of the Garden is a girl. Petals fly around her in a helix, as she glides toward the Caretaker. Her face radiates, and the tips of her fingers shimmer brilliantly. Marina's words are caught in her throat, as the Caretaker helps her to her feet, his eyes rooted to the spot where the girl is standing.

It's the girl who ingested the true Delight of the Bacillus Rose. It's the girl with the power to change the nature of things, who had just changed her own voice to stop the automaton. It's the girl who was the most powerful Florral he had seen in living memory.

It's the girl who had said she would defeat monsters.

Iyena Mastafar.

"Maani-Ba," says Iyena as she comes and kneels near Marina.

"Iyena, you…uh…came back," says Marina, pained whispers coming out of her mouth instead of cohesive words.

"I couldn't do it," says Iyena, tears streaming down her cheek. "I couldn't just go, leaving everyone behind."

"But how…. How did you do this?" the Caretaker asks the girl, too many questions plaguing his mind.

"I…who are you? Where's the Caretaker?" the girl casts a questioning glance, holding Marina's hands. The Caretaker scoffs. Of course, she wouldn't recognize him, because she has never seen him in his true form, the form of youth.

"*I* am the Caretaker of the Garden of Delights. My name is Alvos Midranil. This is my true form. But I won't be in this form for too long. As the night turns into day, I'll go back to how I looked to you previously. That's my curse."

"I am also carrying a curse," she says. "Except, I feel it's more of a blessing. I contain two forms in me. One a girl, one a monster. But I am learning to defeat that monster, keep it inside, so it comes out only when needed, to defeat others far worse. I can't do anything about what I am, but I think I can still help you. Because you once helped me. For better or for worse, I am like this because of you. Because of the Delight of the Bacillus Rose you gave me."

Watch out for the one with two souls in one body, one young, one old, with a heart as kind as you….

The words of the Goddess Ina rush back to him in a moment of absolute clarity. The Caretaker braces himself. If it is truly the will of the gods, who is he to deny it?

"I don't know if I should apologize or thank you," says the Caretaker. His eyes go moist, and his words come out slow. He can't believe what he's going to say next. "My apprenticeship position is empty, Iyena Mastafar." His voice shakes from the grief of acknowledging the absence of Trulio. His knees crumble under him, and he falls on the ground. His head bows inadvertently in front of Iyena, as if she were a goddess, giving him a boon. "Would you consider taking it up?"

"I will give it a thought," she says. "But first, something else needs to be addressed."

Saying those words, the girl comes closer to the Caretaker, kneels in front of him, her deep brown eyes fixed on his ocean-blue ones. The Caretaker knows what she is about to do, but he doesn't have the courage to accept it. The Caretaker hesitates, and for a moment, he's an old man again, his mind shrouded with a cold blanket of uncertainty.

"It won't hurt, I promise," says Iyena, softly. The Caretaker closes his eyes and nods.

Iyena places her palm on his heart.

CHAPTER FORTY

The Caretaker

It takes six weeks for the Caretaker to plant the seeds of the Bacillus Rose and see a bud in full bloom. The damage done by the automaton was restricted to the First Sector, but trampled flowers and grass still take their own time to heal. In the six weeks, as he gave the Garden the nourishment it needed, the Caretaker would often look toward the skies, see the blue-white dawn turn to day, the day into night, and wait for the ghost of youth to cover him again, often forgetting that he need not wait now, for his curse was lifted at the Night of the Unending Stars by the girl known as Iyena Mastafar, who holds in her hands the power of both gods and Florrals. He is reminded of this fact whenever he gazes at himself in the mirror. Gone are the hard lines of age, the shriveled, prune-like skin, the rickety bones and the frail paper-thin hands. He looks at the face of youth, of a man who is still in his third decade, but has experienced a lifetime.

In the first week, after planting the seeds of the Rose, the Caretaker pays a visit to the Mritkhana, the dome-shaped building where the dead are housed, where their bodies undergo a triple cleanse, before being shrouded in petals and vines and leaves and drowned in the sea. It is believed that the petals latch on to the seabed, sand and oysters swirling around the body, forming deep-sea graves. Except the body finds its purpose inside the earth, feeding the ground. But this is a privilege, even in death, for the bodies to become one with the earth. Many become a flowery mulch, glittering in their watery squalor, becoming fodder for beasts without shape or form. It depends on the lives they lived and the souls they touched.

Not wanting that fate for Trulio, the Caretaker oversees his triple cleansing. First, his body is remade anew, not the misshapen husk it was when Trulio died. Trulio's eyes are taken out, and the sockets are stuffed with thumb-size lilies. Next, they cleave out his heart, which is cleansed of all its life blood, and inside the chest cavity go a bouquet of roses. The third cleansing is superficial, where his skin is made glassy, transparent, almost like a deep-sea organism whose insides are visible.

After the three cleansings, the insides of the deceased become a Garden too.

Finally, Trulio's transparent shell of a body, surrounded by its flowery coils, is taken to the sea in a vessel that houses other such bodies. That day, though, the vessel is reserved only for two. As the vessel reaches the point where the land slopes inexorably downward and the sea rumbles with an earth-deep sound, the Caretaker pushes Trulio's body over the edge, with an aching hollow in his heart. The body hits the water with a dull sound, made so light by the cleanse. Soon, the sea envelops the body. As the vessel keeps bobbing up and down with the low tide, the Caretaker wipes tears off his cheeks with quivering hands.

★　　★　　★

The three cleanses and the final goodbye in the sea are meant to provide ample grieving time. But it's not enough for the Caretaker. During sleepless nights he often finds himself calling out his apprentice's name, wanting him to brew a potion for his knees, then swiftly realizing the utter uselessness of his words. In the morning, he looks around his lab for a footstep, for a quip, a hush, a remark, a joke, but none come. In the afternoon, he sits idly, flipping through the pages of Trulio's memoir, sipping his Enjing tea, his mind at unease, still.

In the fourth week, he pays a visit to the Fifth Sector and sits beside the pink Lotus, and casts a pondering gaze at the time-flower.

In these weeks, another obsession has gripped him, a dark thing that pushes him, again and again, toward the last sector of the Garden, toward the sharp, unforgiving specter of time itself. The absence of his apprentice gnaws at his soul, and he finds in himself a yearning to go back in time, and undo the death of Trulio. To hug him, to forgive him.

He is young again, and powerful. He is a Florral. He could do it. He could channel enough of the Lotus's Delight not only to stop Trulio's death, but undo many more events. He finds his hands moving, reaching toward the pink petals of the Lotus in its prime, the murk below it ready for a plunge back in time.

He touches the flower.

"Alvos."

He stops, the tips of his fingers still feeling an electric spark of possibility. He looks up and finds Yavani standing at the entrance of the Fifth Sector.

"How did you find me?" says the Caretaker absently.

"You left the door to the Garden open," she says. "Why are you here?"

The Caretaker wants to say so much but his words are clasped by the cold hands of grief. He takes a long, deep breath. He smells a mild stench of the algae beneath the Lotus, mixed with the fragrance of the shrubbery around it, and is suddenly reminded of the magic, the possibility of the future that lies ahead, instead of the sludgy, murky depths of the past. He touches the Lotus in reverence and gets up.

"I was merely here to check on the Lotus," he says. "Let's go. My customers are waiting."

★　★　★

Survan, the boy, stands eagerly at the door, accompanied by his mother, his legs now fully healed. The boy rubs his hands in anticipation as the Caretaker approaches him, wrapping his brown shawl around his shoulders. Yavani, the Seedmaster, stands a distance away, overlooking the proceedings.

"Survan Amhansa," says the Caretaker. "How is your leg?"

"Losing all my toes was odd at first, but the Healers did a good job restoring all of them."

"I would like you to meet my friend and business partner, Yavani. She helps me in gathering the seeds for the flowers in the Garden."

Yavani smiles at the mother-son pair, then briskly walks away, nodding a goodbye to the Caretaker. The mother's gaze lingers on Yavani for a moment too long, then switches back to the Caretaker.

"Do you have anyone else to help you in the Garden?" the woman asks. The words hang in the space between them, then abruptly, sting the Caretaker's heart, like an arrow meant specifically for him, laced with the dual poison of grief and longing. The Caretaker takes a moment to reply.

"Not at present."

Her face is a mask of skepticism, the edges of her thin eyebrows curled upward. The Caretaker shifts his gaze toward the boy. "Survan, how may I help you today?"

"Mister...Mister Caretaker," says the boy. "It's not me who wants a Delight today. It's my mother."

Survan's mother clears her throat. "I figured since the boy has already experienced it, I must also try. But because of the events that transpired in the city over the last few months, I was horrified. I was hearing some bad things."

"Months of a bad experience doesn't wipe out years' worth of good ones," says the Caretaker with a wistful air. "What Delight can I help you with?"

"I merely want something that allows me to be quick around the house. With Survan's new school and my husband's business of assorted spice mixes picking up, I find myself with too much on my plate and too little time."

"It curiously seems like you don't need a Delight, rather an assistant. And probably an extra-large mug of Enjing tea in the morning."

The lady, whose name is Ravina, looks at her son, then back at the Caretaker, then at her son again. Then she lets out a chuckle full of mirth.

"I have heard about your humor," she says. "But no. Another person around the house would be far too much."

"But my Delight would only give you a temporary burst," says the Caretaker. "You would still have to solve the problem of efficiency yourself."

"Do you always have so many reservations?" the woman asks, but her question is seemingly meant for her son, who has suddenly found something else to look at on the ground beneath his feet.

"Survan will tell you," says the Caretaker. "I don't give away Delights casually."

The woman sighs. "Yes, yes, I'll solve my problem of efficiency. But for the time being, may I please have something?"

The Caretaker's face cracks into a beaming smile. "I think the Dahlia would work perfectly for you," he says. "If you would join me inside the Garden, I will also give you a tour."

⋆　　⋆　　⋆

When the Caretaker visits Mayor Jaywardna Illyasi three months after the events at the Garden, the mayor is composing a furious coppergram, the air in his study ringing with the angry twang of the metal wires, the ink nib straining to catch up with his rage. While the Caretaker waits for his friend to finish, the Waystrewer comes up to him and wraps its tentacles around his leg, like everything is all right.

When the mayor finishes, he leans back on his seat with a heavy sigh. The Caretaker clears his throat. The mayor looks at him with tired, bloodshot eyes.

"You must rest," says the Caretaker.

"You know what I was doing? The message I just sent?"

The Caretaker shakes his head.

"You were right, Alvos. I should have acted earlier. I just sent the Vaishwam Chair a stern-worded letter, urging them to reconsider the troublesome clauses of the Restoration Pact, the one that favors the Abhadis. I also suggested changes, so asses like Yayati can't...."

The mayor stops. The Caretaker can't stop smiling, amused at another one of Mayor Illyasi's self-explanatory tirades.

"I have to stop doing this," he says. "I am the mayor. I don't owe anyone an explanation for my decisions. Good *or* bad!"

"That's like the Illyasi I know from ten years ago," says the Caretaker.

"You should have seen the face of Yayati when I confronted him in front of the Sirvassan public, Alvos," says the mayor, getting up from his chair like an excited child, clapping his hands together. "The Vaishwam Chair didn't take kindly to what he tried to pull off. Seriously, Albuchemy-enhanced automatons masquerading as Champions! Who thinks of that?"

"Psychopaths," says the Caretaker.

Mayor Illyasi lets out a hearty laugh, his eyes almost watering.

"But it's not over yet," he says. "The real Champions are still in Alderra. The discontent among the Abhadi remains. Yayati just lit a match. I don't know what the future brings, Alvos. I don't know if I'll be ready for it."

"I'll be here to protect your future, and mine, both," says Alvos Midranil.

The mayor smiles. "It's good to see you," he says. "I still haven't really come to terms with your new appearance though. All this time you were hiding that curse. It must have been so painful."

"Oh, Jaywardna," says the Caretaker. "You don't know the half of it."

"Will you play chaupar with me? For old times' sake?"

"If we are talking of old times, then why not chess? Are you scared I will beat you?"

The mayor shrugs. "Okay, then we play the chess of Kinshuk, not of Avhram."

"That works for me," says the Caretaker. "You know what, I will play without my two Hansa chariots. I'll give you a head start."

"Don't patronize me, now. We play as equals. On the chessboard, I'm more than a Florral could ever be on a battlefield."

The mayor gives a hearty laugh at his own remark. The Caretaker grins at him. As if to capture a moment between friends, the Waystrewer comes and wraps its tentacles around both their legs, a warm embrace by proxy. And when the chirpy beast actually lets go, the men hug each other regardless.

CHAPTER FORTY-ONE

Iyena Mastafar

Iyena is ten years old when her mother tells her that she will be going on a long vacation.

Iyena has been expecting this news for a while. Children who look at a simmering unrest between their parents learn to grow up fast, and for Iyena that is most of her waking moments, and sometimes, even sleeping ones. All those late-night arguments that keep her awake, detached from the warm embrace of slumber. She would look at the moon hanging low in the bronze-dark Alderran sky and imagine herself soaring atop a Hansa ship, talking to birds in the sky, going so high that the cotton-ball-shaped clouds are now below her, and the only thing between her and the zenith is the moon itself, her imagination being her only refuge.

"Will I be seeing you often, Mother?" asks Iyena at the doorstep. Sumena Mastafar's hands strain from holding the luggage, but Iyena can tell they are yearning to hold her close. Iyena offers to take one of her bags, but Sumena refuses.

"As often as I can manage," says Sumena. She finally places one of her bags on the floor and takes out a crumpled piece of papery nothing from inside a pocket of her kameez. She unfolds it, straightens it. It's a flower made mostly of paper and twigs and waste. Sumena presses her palm against the rough, unhewn petals of the un-flower and waits. When she removes her palm, she is holding an actual flower. A lily. Iyena's eyes swell in surprise. Sumena tucks the flower inside Iyena's breast pocket.

"This is my parting gift to you," says Sumena. She cups Iyena's face in her hands and kisses her on the forehead. Her mother's kiss is dry and rough, and the lips scrape against Iyena's forehead. She doesn't mind. Her mother is holding back tears.

Sumena leaves without another word spoken. Iyena can't raise her arms to bid her goodbye.

Five years later, Iyena will realize that Sumena's casual reshaping of the flower was not just a gift. That was the first and the only time Iyena actually saw her mother channeling a Delight.

★   ★   ★

Six weeks after the incident at the Garden of Delights, Iyena steps on the pier. A clarion call of the *Arenham* booms. The vinasia, large, feathery cousins of the singing fell-birds, find a perching spot on the wooden railing of the pier leading to the vessel. The Sirvassan edge of the sea froths and roils impatiently.

Iyena's feet fall on petals, honey-amber, lemon, and the bright yellow hue of the afternoon sun. She bends and picks up a handful of them and sniffs their earthy, sweet fragrance. Behind her, Maani-Ba opens her purse with a loud click.

"Give them to me," she says. "I'll keep them safe inside. The collectors sometimes don't sweep enough, and these precious petals go to waste, flying away into the sea."

Iyena hands her the petals.

"Did you meet your father?"

Iyena frowns at Maani-Ba. She doesn't want to answer that question. After the night at the Garden, Iyena spent most of her days at the Seedmaster's place, where Yavani prepared two warm beds for her and Maani-Ba. The three women had spent many peaceful nights discussing the lore of Sirvassa and the Three Realms, the legends of the old Florrals, the Albuchemy-led industrial age of Alderra and how it made the cities flourish, including Sirvassa, to some extent. Iyena spent a lot of time at the Burrowing, collecting seeds, helping

Yavani prepare pots, separating them according to the Delights they offered. The Caretaker would visit them every week, each time asking Iyena about her intention of joining him as an apprentice with a smile, each time getting an evasive answer.

One day, Iyena snuck out of the Seedmaster's house with the intention of going back to her home, of seeing her father, perhaps for the last time. She wanted, in her heart, for him to apologize to her. But when she reached the doorstep of her familiar home, she saw Anaris standing idly by the cobblestoned path, talking to the same woman he had introduced Iyena to. The woman gave Anaris a kiss on the cheek before leaving. Anaris's gaze fell on Iyena, and his eyes brightened for a moment. Iyena, too, took a step farther, but restrained herself. This was a man who had done evil things. Iyena barely controlled the urge to storm up to her father, and change the nature of his entire being. The Delight was there, surging inside her, eager to come out.

But then she remembered the words of the Caretaker. He had told her, once, only to use the Delight in times of elation and happiness. In times of sorrow and anguish, the Delight would turn to a dark, redolent thing. In times of doubt, the Delight would go either way.

When she had saved Trehan, she was new to Sirvassa, and her heart was brimming with promise. She was successful and her body had taken it. When she had changed the mind of the Blue Guard, she had been doubtful, and she had paid the price. When she had cured the rot and fought that being in the Garden of Sorrows, her heart was in a muddled, dark place, and hence, the Delight that had come out had plunged her into a place of self-doubt.

Anaris looked like he wanted to call out to her, but he stepped inside the house instead. Seeing this as a sign, Iyena turned on her heels and returned to Yavani's place.

She looks now at Maani-Ba, her expression easing into serenity. "I didn't and I don't ever intend to."

"Spoken like the daughter of Sumena Mastafar," says Maani-Ba. "Iyena, it will be hard, at first, upon seeing your mother. She might not be ready, she might not even be expecting to see you. But that's why I am going with you."

"I know, Maani-Ba," says Iyena.

Iyena's eyes catch a figure in the distance. Wavy hair, streaked with the color of sand and ash, round face, bright eyes. Legs with wind in them. Shirt the color of roses and promise. Trehan is running toward the pier, battling the crowds at the docks, excusing himself, balancing himself, almost teetering at the edge.

"Where are you looking—" Maani-Ba turns to look at Trehan, who is flailing his hands in the air like a mad person. Iyena walks briskly toward the edge of the pier, the wooden rampart groaning under her hurried feet.

"Trehan, what are you doing here?"

Trehan struggles to catch his breath. "You..." he heaves, his words getting choked up. "You are leaving?"

"I am," says Iyena.

"I came to apologize," he says. "I wasn't myself that day. It was too much for me, seeing you that way. I am truly sorry."

"I understand, Trehan," says Iyena. "It wasn't your fault."

A silence builds between the two. Trehan finally stands erect, taking a deep breath, blushing. To his right, a fell-bird swoops in, and perches atop a wooden pole. The sudden appearance of the bird shatters a moment. A lump forms in Iyena's throat. She knows what Trehan is going to say. She hopes he won't say it.

"Iyena, can you...is there any way you can...stay?"

Iyena reaches for his hair, and plays with its sandy curls. Her fingers shake, and then she pulls herself away.

"I wish I could," she says, after a pause. "But I have to do this. I have to meet my mother. She's my only family in the world right now."

Trehan's face falls. The bird flutters away. He grabs the edge of the wooden pole. He looks small, very small, a boy who is just trying to do what's right. His shoulders sink inward. He bites a cuticle off his thumb, wincing in the process. Iyena knows Trehan's habit of making odd, foolish movements when he is feeling something he can't put into words.

Iyena gathers a bunch of petals off the cemented ground. She places one palm atop another, cupping the petals, and closes her eyes. Her heart, full at the moment, doesn't want to think of the anguish of leaving behind a city she has come to love. And so, the Delight she channels now is pure and full of love.

She opens her palms. Trehan's eyes go wide. A small, thornless rose rests gently on Iyena's palms.

"Remember me by this," says Iyena, tucking the rose in Trehan's pocket. "The world is small. We will meet again."

"Look at you, Iyena Mastafar," says Trehan, smiling. "Being so sure of the ground you stand on. No one could tell you are not from this city."

Iyena chuckles. Trehan brings out a crumpled paper from his pocket. It seems to be covering something. Its surface looks soiled and black, but the smell wafting from the package is familiar.

"I brought some fresh salousse for you. Something to remember me by."

Iyena grabs the packet of sweets. Then, she hugs Trehan. For a long time, she doesn't let go, hoping to etch the moment in her memory, because she will need it on the long voyage. She'll need all the warmth she can get.

When they separate, Trehan's eyes are moist. When he speaks, his voice comes out as a throaty crackle.

"I'll mi—" he starts. But then, the *Arenham* booms again, this time louder, the sound drowning out the chirp of birds and the rush of the sea, momentarily. If it hadn't, Iyena would have heard Trehan's parting words, instead of trying to make them out from the shape his mouth makes. The sound startles Trehan, who staggers back awkwardly, muffling his ears. Iyena is distracted too, as her gaze shifts to Maani-Ba a few feet away, beckoning her.

When the sound stills, Iyena says, "Goodbye, Trehan. Until we meet again. Till then, may Eborsen shower his petals on you."

"Goodbye, Iyena," says Trehan. "May you never be short of Delights."

Then, he turns around and disappears into the crowd. For a long time, Iyena stands there, looking at his wavy, sandy hair, hoping he will turn around, just once, for a glimpse. But he doesn't. Iyena walks toward Maani-Ba, pocketing the salousse.

"He is a good boy," says Maani-Ba. "Come, let's hurry."

Iyena follows Maani-Ba, feeling the reassuring weight of the packet of salousse in her pocket. When she steps on the deck, she feels a hollowness tug at the edges of her heart, a cold feeling that threatens to consume her. She thinks of all the cruelty of the last few days, the sorrow that ravaged parts of the city. The monster of the city is now the monster that slumbers inside her. It all would have seemed impossible a year ago, but it's now a part of her.

She feels it's partly her fault.

But then, her hands gripping the railing of the deck, she looks back at the road leading to the center of the town and thinks of all the beauty too, of both sorrow and delight. She remembers the first time she stepped foot into the city, inside the Garden, the whiff of the flowers, the gentle eyes of the Caretaker, the friends she made, the fights she fought, the stories she lived. All those are an indelible part of her now too.

As the ship breaks away from the shore of Sirvassa, Iyena mouths a silent goodbye, but also makes a promise, to come back again, and do more, and live more, and love more, and be more.

ACKNOWLEDGMENTS

How does one write a book? I'd just say, one word at a time.

But how's a book really made? How does it exist? How does it go from being a seed to a flower to a garden (pun absolutely intended)?

By careful tending.

This garden was tended by so many hands.

I'd like to thank my incredible beta-readers and friends – Prashanth Srivatsa, Kehkashan Khalid, Pritesh Patil – for reading the unwieldy mess of a first draft. I'll forever be grateful for your kindness and support, and your patience at the random plot questions I threw at you.

This book wouldn't be here without the championing of my agent, Kanishka Gupta, who acted as a counselor, a guide, and a friend throughout the submission process. I am thankful for Amish Mulmi's keen editorial eye on this and the incisive initial feedback, which only strengthened this manuscript.

To my editor, Don D'Auria, and the entire team at Flame Tree Press for trusting this book.

This book wouldn't exist without the words that have come before it. The many words on many pages I have read, written by authors I have admired. To all the editors who have taken a chance at my short fiction.

To the many cats I met and petted on my many late-evening, plot-detangling walks. To Natasha, who held my hand during those walks and often said, "It will come to you."

And finally, to my family.

To Mummy, for the constant reassurances and endless cups of tea in those early days when I was figuring out this thing called 'writing.'

To Papa, who once told me to try publishing as a career if you like reading novels so much.

To Vibhav, for everything.

FLAME TREE PRESS
FICTION WITHOUT FRONTIERS
Award-Winning Authors & Original Voices

Flame Tree Press is the trade fiction imprint of Flame Tree Publishing, focusing on excellent writing in horror and the supernatural, crime and mystery, science fiction and fantasy. Our aim is to explore beyond the boundaries of the everyday, with tales from both award-winning authors and original voices.

•

•

Join our mailing list for free short stories, new release details, news about our authors and special promotions:

flametreepress.com